OUT O

MAISIE MOSCO is a Mancunian now living in
London. A former journalist, she began writing
fiction in the sixties. Her early work was for the
theatre. She is also the author of fourteen radio
plays.

Her *Almonds and Raisins Trilogy* established her
as a novelist of worldwide status. *Out of the Ashes*
is Maisie Mosco's tenth novel.

MAISIE MOSCO

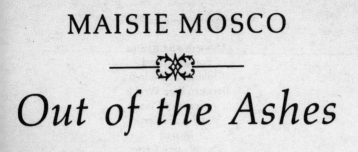

Out of the Ashes

FONTANA/Collins

First published by William Collins Sons & Co. Ltd 1989
A continental edition first issued in Fontana Paperbacks 1990
This edition first issued in Fontana Paperbacks 1990

Printed and bound in Great Britain by
William Collins Sons & Co. Ltd, Glasgow

In memory of my mother

'The evil that men do
lives after them . . .'
Julius Caesar

THE FAMILY

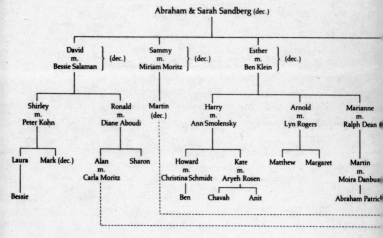

Abraham & Sarah Sandberg (dec.)

David
m.
Bessie Salaman } (dec.)

Sammy
m.
Miriam Moritz } (dec.)

Esther
m.
Ben Klein } (dec.)

Shirley
m.
Peter Kohn

Ronald
m.
Diane Aboudi

Martin
(dec.)

Harry
m.
Ann Smolensky

Arnold
m.
Lyn Rogers

Marianne
m.
Ralph Dean

Laura   Mark (dec.)

Alan
m.
Carla Moritz

Sharon

Howard
m.
Christina Schmidt

Kate
m.
Aryeh Rosen

Matthew   Margaret

Martin
m.
Moira Danbur

Bessie

Ben   Chavah   Anit

Abraham Patrick

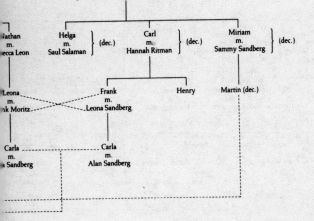

Sigmund & Rachel Moritz (dec.)

Nathan
m.
Rebecca Leon

Helga
m.
Saul Salaman
} (dec.)

Carl
m.
Hannah Ritman
} (dec.)

Miriam
m.
Sammy Sandberg
} (dec.)

Leona
m.
Frank Moritz

Frank
m.
Leona Sandberg

Henry

Martin (dec.)

Carla
m.
Sandberg

Carla
m.
Alan Sandberg

Acknowledgements

My editor, Marjory Chapman.

Stephen Mosco and Miranda Selby for assistance with research in Germany and Austria.

The Institute of Jewish Affairs Library.

PART ONE

1982 . . .

Chapter One

MARIANNE WAS BROWSING through her family album, a sentimental pastime in which she rarely indulged, but not unfitting today.

An early-morning telephone call had wakened her and she had afterwards come downstairs to make some tea. Wrapped in the cosy old dressing-gown she could not bring herself to throw away, as if doing so would denude her of a comforting bit of the past, she was now curled up on the living-room sofa, only the hissing of the gasfire impinging upon the silence.

She had known before picking up the receiver that the caller was her Uncle Nat, wanting to share with her his anxiety lest anything mar the family event due to take place this afternoon. The sole remaining elder of the clan, its one-time black sheep was incongruously proving himself capable of wearing the patriarchal mantle. But Marianne wished he would choose someone other than herself with whom to confer about family matters.

'Supposing the out-of-towners who haven't yet arrived don't get to Manchester in time?' he had said on the phone. 'They shouldn't have left their travelling until today, and that includes your son and your brother, Marianne!'

Outside Marianne's window the back lawn stretched pristine white, the poplars at the far end ghostly figures against a leaden sky. Her uncle's fear of a last minute hitch had materialized as an overnight snowfall, and she imagined him now pacing the floor in his big house, with nobody but the ageing Irishwoman who looked after him for company.

Bridie, though, is like one of the family, Marianne's thoughts meandered on while her fingers turned the pages of the album. She had been with Uncle Nat's branch of it since her teens and Marianne's childhood.

A snapshot of herself in uniform reminded Marianne that she had left home, via the Women's Services, at the age of eighteen, never to return. What a rebel I must have seemed! The more so, she reflected, when she had subsequently married out of the faith in the days when, for a Jewish family, there was no worse disgrace.

The man for whom love had caused Marianne to do so had, a few years later, elected to convert. And, she thought poignantly, was now buried in the cemetery where the in-laws who had not wanted him lay, his death the last in a series of family bereavements in the first two years of the eighties.

Marianne had still not accustomed herself to her grandmother no longer being there. To not being telephoned at least thrice daily by her mother. To Uncle David and Aunt Miriam too being gone.

But those of whom she had just been thinking were old people. Hardest of all for her to accept was her husband's being cut down in his prime.

She returned her mind to the afternoon that lay ahead. Though it would be a pleasant change for the family to get together other than for a funeral, the occasion was in its way a solemn one.

David's will had instructed that a stained glass window honouring the founders of the Sandberg-Moritz clan be consecrated in a Manchester synagogue, in the presence of every branch of the family tree that had sprung from those roots.

'Every *twig* and branch' was how David had put it, and it was, of course, his estate that had paid for the window. The carrying out of his instruction he had entrusted to his brother.

Marianne turned back the pages of the album to look again at a faded photograph of the two couples whose meeting in Manchester's old Strangeways ghetto in 1905 would, in 1982, impel their descendants to demonstrate the unity David's wish required.

Her grandmother, Sarah Sandberg, would say, 'What's with the honouring? It's enough that we are now resting in peace.' But Sigmund Moritz, whose ego had matched his intellect, would consider it his due, Marianne thought with a smile.

By noon, when she had dressed in her best for the occasion, and her son had not yet arrived from London, she found herself anxiously eyeing the weather, as Uncle Nat was probably doing. A flurry of snowflakes was scudding by the window, and a high wind hurtling around the cottage that in summer had roses around the door.

A reminiscent smile fleetingly lit Marianne's olive-skinned face, enhancing the gamine appearance lent by her short black hair, and her petite figure. It was summer when she and Ralph had moved in, and the picture of their new home, so idyllic was it, had seemed a portent for their ending their days as the proverbial Darby and Joan.

Instead, Marianne, though she was a successful author with little time to brood, was having to come to terms with a personal loneliness she had never before experienced. She had gone from under her parents' roof to the midst of a hutful of ATS girls. Marriage had followed. This was the first time Marianne had lived alone.

'Is my outfit okay?' she would now be asking Ralph, if he were here to look her over. Oh, the simple little things one missed. Since there was only the mirror to tell her, she surveyed the middle-aged woman reflected there and decided that a scarf at the neck of her dark suit would not come amiss.

She selected the blue silk square her son had bought for her at Saks, on one of his frequent trips to New York, and looking in her jewel box for a scarfpin picked up the gold filigree brooch, dented with age, that Sarah Sandberg had brought with her from Russia. Ought I to wear it for the ceremony? And Sarah's antique ring?

Marianne hesitated to do so. Her cousin Shirley, not she,

was the eldest of Sarah's three granddaughters, but Sarah had left to Marianne the pieces she had valued most.

Marianne would not forget the day when Sarah's treasure trove was opened. How Shirley, as materialistic as her father, David, had immediately put a monetary value on the pieces, scrutinizing each in turn as if she were a jeweller.

'Don't bother looking at the filigree brooch, or the garnet ring, Shirley,' David had said. 'They're for Marianne.'

'What do you mean, they're for Marianne?'

The ensuing confrontation, for such it had felt, had taken place in Marianne's mother's flat, a week after Sarah was laid to rest. With my mum lying ill, in the next room, Marianne recalled.

Uncle Nat, too, was present that afternoon, with his daughter Leona. But Leona had displayed no resentment about Marianne's being left their grandmother's most treasured jewellery. It was she who broke the silence that followed Shirley's antagonistic words.

'Marianne had a very special relationship with Grandma, and everyone in the family knows it.'

'But I've never understood why,' Shirley had replied. 'And while Grandma was growing old and frail, where was Marianne? Living it up in London. You and I, though, were right here, doing our granddaughterly duty, no matter how inconvenient it sometimes was for us.'

'Marianne had to live where her husband's business was,' Leona countered.

'And if it hadn't gone bust, she wouldn't have returned to the bosom of the family,' Shirley retorted, 'which my dad's generosity made possible.'

'My asking Ralph to run the art gallery I was thinking of opening in Manchester was a business proposition,' David interceded, and received a tight-lipped smile from his daughter.

Another silence followed, and Marianne glanced at the armchair her grandmother had occupied until she became bedfast. It was there that Sarah had sat when the family came from wherever life had scattered them, to celebrate with her on her ninety-ninth birthday.

It was the last happy occasion for which the entire clan had gathered. All had brought Sarah gifts, and the old lady had received them with the graciousness of a queen seated on her throne. Later, while the party went on around her, she had sat pensively fingering her little Russian brooch, as always pinned at her throat, and Marianne had wondered what she was thinking. If she was perhaps re-living her long years; remembering the bitter along with the sweet, which she had always referred to as the almonds and raisins of life.

Marianne's marrying a gentile had contributed to the many almonds that Sarah had been obliged to chew and swallow. I'm surprised that Shirley didn't throw that at me, too, she had thought on the day her cousin's animosity towards her was made overtly plain. Though she and Shirley had never got on well, Marianne had not felt, until they stood with Sarah's jewellery spilled on the table between them, that Shirley hated her.

'Just because you look like Grandma, you've always been her favourite!' Shirley had finally flared.

Marianne had let that pass. It was not just her looks that she had inherited from Sarah, but in some respects her character, also. Like Sarah, Marianne had found herself capable of bending with the wind of change. And she too was equipped by Nature with the strength to see a difficult situation through.

These were Marianne's thoughts and recollections as she tried to decide whether or not to wear Sarah's ring and brooch for the window-consecration ceremony. The pieces themselves were not what the confrontation was about, and Marianne had felt sorry for Shirley, a wealthy woman who, time and again, had been made to realize that there are things that money can't buy.

Two more telephone calls, both from motorway service station call boxes, cut short Marianne's rumination.

The first, from her Tory MP brother, Arnold, resulted in

19

one of their usual tiffs. 'I'm on the M1, Marianne. Something I had to sort out for my constituency manager delayed me.'

'And that's more important than what you're coming to Manchester for?'

'Look – it's snowing like hell, I've got a terrible cold, and I'm doing my best to get there in time! But I might not.'

'The one you should be letting know is your wife.'

'Lyn and I aren't on speaking terms at present.'

'What have you done to upset her now?' Marianne demanded. But her brother had rung off, and she visualized him stomping to his car, the picture of self-righteousness, his thinning hair sent awry by the wind.

The second call, from her son, was to assure her that he *would* arrive in time. Were Martin's wife and child with him? Marianne brushed that doubt aside and cast another glance at the still swirling snowflakes, thankful that Martin had got as far as the M6.

Suddenly, it was as important to her as to Uncle Nat that every member of the family be present today. Nor would her grandmother have been surprised to know it.

She slipped Sarah's ring on her finger and pinned the meaningful little brooch to her scarf.

Nathan Sandberg was blowing a speck of dust from the sideboard when Bridie entered the room.

'An' whut, Doctor surr, do ye think yere after doin'?' she inquired. 'Fussin' an' wurryin'!' An' still gettin' under me feet, like ye've bin after doin' since ye rose from yere bed, is whut!'

Bridie put down the tray of china she had brought in with her, and began laying the table for the tea-party Nathan was giving after the consecration ceremony.

'How many times am I after tellin' ye, Doctor surr, that the family won't be findin' Bridie's burnt the kuchen an' the strudel, jus' because the missus is still away.'

20

The delicious aroma of baking cakes was drifting in from the kitchen, and Nathan surveyed Bridie with affection. She was loyalty personified. And who but she had held together the everyday warp and weft of his tempestuous marriage?

Tempestuous until a few years ago, he corrected himself. But Bridie had behaved throughout as though nothing untoward was going on in the household, taking all in her stride. What would Nathan have done without her when post-natal depression caused his wife to reject her newborn child? Thankfully, Leona knew nothing of that traumatic episode, or she might have grown up believing her mother didn't really love her; in addition to realizing, all too soon, that her parents didn't love each other.

Nathan glanced at the photograph of himself and Rebecca on their wedding day, the gleaming silver frame a testament to Bridie's housekeeping, and reflected that their marriage hadn't stood a chance. Nor had this house ever been a home. Just a battleground until eventually the fight had gone from both of them. After which an indifferent peace had reigned. He had not minded in the least when Rebecca went to spend the winter in Florida, with her sister who lived there.

Nathan would not have been surprised had he known that Marianne thought of him as the one remaining elder. Little by little his wife had distanced herself from the family.

Bridie, busy folding the starched napkins that matched the damask tablecloth, gave him a long-suffering look. 'If yere after makin' sure I do me job properly, Doctor surr, why don't ye do it sittin' down?'

Rather than argue with her, Nathan did as he was bid, the vacant Queen Anne chair on the other side of the hearth serving to heighten the bitterness his present thoughts could not but evoke.

So much for the arranged marriages of his youth, when a wealthy girl was offered by her parents to a lad whom money could help on his way. Nathan's friend, who later became his partner, had thought Nathan fortunate to be offered a girl whose beauty was an unexpected bonus. Yet Lou's arranged marriage, to a girl as plain as she was good-natured, could not have been more contented.

Nathan's, however, had begun with a built-in handicap; his love for the gentile nurse he had met while a medical student. And a lifetime wasn't long enough for Nathan to forget how David had castigated him when he found out about Mary.

He could still see himself sitting in David's car, a puny youth, his brother already a married man, being told that if he wanted to kill his parents, marrying a *shiksah* was the way to do it.

The introduction to Rebecca was afterwards hastily arranged. And how mortifying it had remained for Nathan that he had been too weak to defy his big brother. A man who had himself married for money.

Raking up old coals will get you nowhere, Nathan told himself, absently watching Bridie take some cake dishes out of the sideboard and line them with paper doyleys. But how could the floodgates of remembrance not open for him today? And the memory that had just returned to him accounted for his lifelong hostility towards David . . .

In his childhood, Nathan had idolized David. When the Sandbergs still lived in the Strangeways ghetto the possibility of one of her sons becoming a doctor could not have entered Sarah's mind. How to make ends meet would have been her major preoccupation. But Nathan was then too young to have realized that. He alone of her four children had taken for granted that there would always be a meal for him on the table.

Then a day came when Nathan's childhood illusion that all was well with his world was shattered. He had called at the Moritzes' house on his way home from school, to borrow a book from Sigmund's library, and had found Sigmund parcelling some books in order to sell them.

How incongruous it now seemed that so humble a home had housed that library. Goethe and Galsworthy, Dickens and Shakespeare, Robert Louis Stevenson, among the literary giants cheek by jowl with the works of the great philosophers, Nathan recalled, in a small room lined floor to ceiling with shelves built with Sigmund Moritz's own hands.

Incongruous too was the friendship between Nathan's parents and the Moritzes, so different were the cultures from which the two immigrant couples had sprung. Sarah and Abraham Sandberg were products of the insular background that Tsarist oppression had imposed upon Russian Jews; Sigmund and Rachel Moritz, he, though a tailor by trade, an intellectual, and she with the elegant refinement that had characterized the Viennese Jewesses no less when they settled in their new country.

Half of Sigmund's library was now in Nathan's study. The other half, packed in boxes in the attic, was awaiting the building of extra bookshelves.

Sigmund had bequeathed the library to Nathan – his godson – and David. But no mention of the books was made in David's will. As if, thought Nathan now, David could not bring himself to make what would have been a conciliatory gesture to me. The books had come to Nathan only because David's daughter did not want them, and his son could not accommodate them.

It was Sigmund Moritz who had nurtured Nathan's love of literature, encouraged him to partake of that literary feast, given him *Silas Marner*, the first book Nathan had ever owned. And still imprinted upon Nathan's mind was Sigmund's explanation, that long ago day, for selling some precious first editions: You can't eat books.

Decades later, amid the trappings of affluence of which the Sandbergs and Moritzes could not then have dreamed, Nathan's journey backward in time caused his throat to ache as he saw again, like figures in a distant landscape, those who had peopled his childhood.

David helping him with his homework. His father snoozing in the rocking chair beside the kitchen hearth. His sister Esther, ironing a blouse. His middle brother Sammy, patiently carving with a penknife the ornaments he had made from bits of wood. And Sigmund and Rachel Moritz arriving with their family for Sabbath tea, their daughter Miriam, who had loved David but had married Sammy, as beautiful then as she was in old age.

As for Miriam and David dying together, in a car crash . . . What was it but another twist in the tangled history of a clan welded ever closer by time and events? Part of which was Nathan's daughter marrying Sigmund's grandson. And my granddaughter marrying David's grandson.

Bridie, whom Nathan had not noticed had left the room, returned to place a bowl of sugar on the table and surveyed his expression.

'Oy'd be surprised, Doctor surr, if the whole family wurrn't doin' a bit o' rememberin' today. It'll do sum o' the young ones gud to think on whut were sacrificed for their sake!' she added before departing.

Including my father's health, thought Nathan. But how could today's young Jews comprehend what it was like to work in a sweatshop? To live in a back street, in the shadow of Strangeways gaol, sit shivering in winter on a lavatory in the backyard. Bridie was right. With each succeeding generation, more and more was taken for granted, as the twentieth century gallops towards its end, sweeping aside religious beliefs and family values.

Now Nathan, like Bridie, was a dying breed, the familiar figures of his humble beginnings dead and gone, and he responsible for carrying out his brother's posthumous instruction.

Like hell I will! he had wanted to exclaim when David's lawyer laid upon him the task. Honouring the clan's founders was fine with Nathan, and such commemorations not uncommon in the Jewish community. What went against the grain was David's instructing Nathan to do what he himself would eventually have got around to doing.

Only, given the sort of folk his parents and the Moritzes were, Nathan would have commemorated their names in a manner of which they would surely have approved. With the endowment of a hospital bed. Or a bench in a park.

Instead — well, if there was a hereafter, David was now doubtless sitting plucking his harp strings, feeling highly pleased with himself! The well-meant, if often misguided, acts of kindness performed while he lived would have assured that he not be consigned to the other place, though many were the occasions when Nathan had told him to go there.

Nathan had nevertheless wept at David's graveside, and had thought then, as he was thinking now, that if ever there were a love-hate relationship it was his own with David.

Meanwhile, snow was still falling outside the window. The way things were looking, Marianne would need a sledge to get to Manchester from Cheshire. And the planes bringing those of the family due to arrive shortly from far afield might be unable to land.

Though David would have employed emotional blackmail to ensure the show of family unity he had desired for this special occasion, that wasn't, and never had been, Nathan's way. What was the use of unity if it had to be imposed? If the loyalty instilled by Sarah Sandberg had, with her going, gone too, so be it.

Which wasn't to say that Nathan wasn't hoping that it was still there. Today would be the first test.

Chapter Two

IN THE EVENT, Nathan had cause to be a proud and happy man. Though one or two twigs were missing, every branch of the clan was represented at the ceremony. Even Henry Moritz was there, which surprised no one more than it did his sister-in-law, Leona.

Since in an orthodox synagogue men and women are seated separately, Leona did not notice Henry slip into the seat beside her husband, and said, when her daughter nudged her and pointed, 'But wouldn't you know it, Carla, he arrived late.'

'Uncle Henry still can't do anything right for you, can he, Mum?' Carla whispered.

Leona allowed herself to glance at her brother-in-law, who caught her eye and smiled. The same old handsome charming Henry! But unlike his twin, Frank, the sort who let people down. Leona hadn't seen him since Sarah's final birthday party, the last time he did the family the favour of showing up. Frank, on the other hand, had a strong sense of family. But they were not identical twins in any way. Nor would Leona be amazed if, when Henry left Manchester after this visit, he would leave with yet another handout from Frank.

Shirley was thinking that Marianne had a nerve to flaunt *that* jewellery this afternoon. But Shirley had one satisfaction that Marianne would never have – a Jewish grandchild. Though it would have been better if little Bessie hadn't appeared as if from nowhere, as unfortunately she had. The six-year-old sandwiched between Shirley and her daughter, Laura, was a real doll, if an overweight one. But who her father was, only Laura knew!

Shirley would never forget the Sabbath tea-party, at Sarah's house, when Laura announced that though marriage was of no interest to her, she had decided to have a child.

Laura's resembling her mum was limited to her physical appearance, Shirley thought, re-living the ignominy she had publicly suffered via Laura. And she would far rather Laura had settled down to conventional domesticity than be the successful photographer she had become, roving the world camera in hand, her fatherless child left in the care of a housekeeper.

Shirley felt little Bessie's hand creep into hers and gave the child a warm smile, wondering what her own mother's reaction might have been to having an illegitimate grand-daughter named after her. One who also looked like her, dark haired and sallow. Who hopefully wouldn't when she grew up still be the pudge her namesake was!

Marianne, whose grandchild was seated beside his father, noted that the boy seemed fascinated by the service and by his surroundings. Like his mother, he was a Catholic, and this the first time he had set foot inside a synagogue. But Judaism as well as Catholicism was his heritage, as his name, Abraham Patrick, implied.

Though Marianne would not have wished him to be raised in the religious vacuum that was the lot of many children of mixed marriages, to later be faced with the adult dilemma of which, if either, religion to espouse, it seemed to her unfair that her daughter-in-law's devoutness had kept him from enjoying the age old traditional aspects of his father's back-ground.

It was not unknown for gentiles to accept an invitation to a Passover Seder, or a Chanukah party. But when Martin came north to be with his family for a Jewish festival, Moira would not allow their son to accompany him.

Martin's expression as he glanced at Abraham Patrick left Marianne in no doubt that this was a doubly emotional occasion for him. Though his own father was born a Christian, the strength of Martin's Jewishness had never faltered, raised as he was in an atmosphere that had not pulled him two ways.

Marianne watched Martin straighten the threadbare *yamulke* on his son's unruly red hair, both the little cap and the fiery colouring passed down by Marianne's grandfather, Abraham Sandberg.

When Martin arrived in the world shortly after Abraham Sandberg departed it, Sarah had given Marianne the *yamulke* and told her to keep it for him. Martin, shabby though it was, had insisted upon wearing it for his Bar Mitzvah – a day on which Martin, still only thirteen, had indicated that family mattered to him.

That had to be why he had wanted *his* son to wear Abraham Sandberg's *yamulke* today, as if doing so would bring home to the boy that the blood of the immigrant Jew Abraham flowed in his veins no less than that of his Catholic grandfather, Lord Kyverdale.

A title that Abraham Patrick would one day inherit. To which Sarah Sandberg had never accustomed herself, Marianne thought with a smile, and how would she have? A descendant who was one of England's aristocracy still seemed to Marianne herself a far cry from the story Sarah had told of sailing to England on a herring boat.

Equally difficult, if in a different way, it must have been for Sarah to believe that one of her descendants had German blood in his veins. When Marianne's nephew, Howard Klein, married the fräulein he had met on a ski-ing holiday, it was as if a thunderbolt had hit the family.

It would take more than the years that had since passed for the Holocaust to recede from the Jewish memory. Marianne could not bring herself to set foot in Germany, to rub shoulders with the nation which had perpetrated that barbarity, innocent though its post-war generations were.

Her brother, Harry, whose son Howard was, had felt unable to show his face among the Jewish community, and his wife, Ann, had initially refused to meet her daughter-in-law. But before Howard returned from Munich with his bride, Sarah Sandberg, the arch-peacekeeper, had called the family together, counselling them to make the best of it since what was done could not be undone.

We didn't yet know that Christina was pregnant, Marianne recalled, but my grandmother's words to the family were probably those she used when Laura did what *she* did. Making the best of the unarguable and the inevitable was how Sarah had succeeded in holding the family together. How many such family conferences had Marianne, over the years, attended? And in her youth, there would have been some at which this or that of her numerous rebellious acts were discussed, and her parents advised how to deal with her.

Despite everything, the rifts and resentments and disagreements, the family had in Sarah's time shared their troubles, major and minor, as though what affected any one of them affected all. But would they continue to stand by each other now Sarah was gone?

Marianne shared a glance with her Uncle Nat across the synagogue aisle as the stained glass window, through which wintry sunlight was now filtering, was finally unveiled.

Neither could have known how uncannily Marianne's thoughts at that moment echoed Nathan's hopes.

Chapter Three

LIZZIE, ONCE THE DOMESTIC PILLAR of David's household, had emerged from retirement for the afternoon to help Bridie serve tea to the family and stood with her in Nathan's spacious hall, greeting each of them as they stepped in from the cold, mindful to wipe the snow off their feet before doing so lest they receive a scolding from the two elderly women who were to them institutions.

Hearing the congratulatory *Mazeltov* trip from their tongues as they shook hands with everyone seemed as natural as Lizzie's taking Shirley's mink, to hang it up for her; and Bridie's allowing Leona to hang up her own coat – tweed, not fur, since Leona and Frank were conservationists. Nor would their income from the neighbourhood law practice they ran together have allowed fur to feature in Leona's wardrobe.

Leona, whom Bridie had not spoiled as Lizzie had Shirley, would not have let the kindly Irishwoman wait upon her and reflected, as she went to warm her hands by the log fire, that childhood sets the pattern for the rest of one's life.

Here in this house she had spent her own young years. The adored only child of a still handsome man and a beautiful woman. Unaware, until they began using her as a go-between, of the emotional undercurrents which as she grew older had become unbearable.

Would she have married Frank, had it not been an acceptable way of escape? I could have done worse, she thought eyeing her brother-in-law. Lucky that Henry didn't want me!

How many women had Henry lived with and scrounged

from, since the days when Leona had thought herself madly in love with him, but had not let him know it? And many were the scrapes he had since got himself into, and Leona and Frank got him out of. Including, she recalled, the time he got involved in Danny the Red's student uprising in Paris, in '68, though he was by then years older than its participants.

Leona had on that occasion gone with Frank to get Henry out of gaol. What a source of anxiety he had been to his grandfather, and still was to Frank.

Everything from nuclear disarmament demonstrations to the Polish Solidarity movement had been actively supported by Henry. Nobody could say he wasn't fearless. He had fought in the streets alongside Chilean dissidents, and that wasn't all. But Leona had always suspected that the excitement, not the cause itself, accounted for Henry's putting himself at risk as he so often had.

She could hear him now telling her son-in-law, Alan, who was studying for the rabbinate, that neo-Nazism was on the rise in Europe. As if that was inside information that he, the now middle-aged crusader who had made espousing political causes his way of life, was in a position to dispense.

'But those orchestrating it haven't a chance of getting anywhere,' Alan replied, 'which isn't to say that Jews shouldn't be vigilant. The signs are there all right that the evil we're talking about wasn't entirely stamped out by the war.'

A brief pause followed, and Leona remembered other such awkward moments when Germany and Nazism were mentioned in Howard Klein's presence. On this occasion, though Germany *wasn't* mentioned, the implication remained. And the family's feeling about Howard having a German wife, delightful though the girl was, had not gone away.

Christina, however, was not among them, but visiting her parents in Munich, with her little boy, Ben, a child as Semitic-looking as his mother's appearance was Aryan, and now three years old.

It was Laura who ended the silence with a remark no less

embarrassing for Howard. 'I seem to recall hearing that Germany went through a denazification programme, but I wouldn't say it extended to those born after the war being made to face up to what their elders let happen.'

'Since when were you an expert on the subject?' Howard flashed at her.

'I'm not claiming to be,' Laura replied, 'but I'm entitled to my opinion. I was in Berlin on an assignment recently and – you know *me*! – I deliberately raised the subject of the Holocaust at a party I was invited to. Those there were my age and younger, but nobody wanted to talk about it. What I'm saying is, though they were no more than the proverbial twinkle in their parents' eyes when it happened, it seemed none of them could bear to look that bit of the German past in the face.'

'So they're ashamed of it. What's wrong with that?' Alan inquired.

'Shame isn't enough,' said Laura. 'And you could've heard a pin drop when I told them I'm Jewish. There was an immediate change in the atmosphere. Make what you will of that. And now I have an announcement to make. I'm getting married.'

Shirley stopped wiping little Bessie's nose and sat down with a thump. Nor was it any wonder that the kind of silence Laura had just described preceded the family's crowding around her to say *Mazeltov*.

When the excitement had subsided, little Bessie, always quick on the uptake, said happily, 'I'll be getting a daddy then, won't I? And I've always wanted one.'

'But your mummy hasn't yet told us who he is,' said Shirley.

Laura picked up the child and hugged her. 'Can you guess, Bessie?'

'I think so, Mummy, and if I'm right, that means I'm getting a big brother and sister, too. Isn't that lovely?'

'*How* big?' Shirley inquired.

'Well, they won't need you to wipe their noses,' Laura

answered with a laugh, 'and Marianne thinks they're nice kids.'

Shirley sprang from her chair. 'Marianne has already met them? Their father as well, I suppose!'

Marianne tried to salve Shirley's hurt feelings, and with the truth. 'Last time I was in London to see my publisher, I dropped in at Laura's and this man and his children just happened to be there.'

'Come off it! You've always been Laura's confidante,' was Shirley's cold response. 'Who is he?' she asked Laura.

An expression Marianne had never before seen in Laura's blue eyes entered them now. But then, Laura had never before been in love and it was of her beloved she was thinking as she replied to her mother.

'His name is Jake Bornstein – '

'A nice *Jewish* name,' Shirley cut in with relief. 'But what does he do?'

'He's what you might call an entrepreneur.'

'Which could mean anything,' said Marianne's business-man brother, Harry.

'What he does isn't important,' Laura answered. 'I love him.'

Harry addressed Shirley. 'All the proposals your daughter must've had and turned down, he has to be something extraordinary.'

'As a matter of fact, he isn't,' Laura informed them. 'And will you two please stop behaving as if I'm still a girl and in need of family guidance? I'll soon be thirty-seven.'

'A good reason for your making the decision you finally have,' said Harry.

'But not *the* reason,' Laura countered. 'And by the way, Jake is South African. We met when I was there last year, taking pictures of Winnie Mandela – '

'And little Bessie left at home with the chicken pox,' Shirley interrupted.

'She didn't go down with it until after I'd gone.'

'And who got the call from your worried housekeeper?

33

When she told me the blisters had spread to my poor darling's throat, well – I couldn't get to London fast enough, I drove all the way down the M1 in the fast lane. And may I say, Laura, that I wish you luck finding a housekeeper able and willing to take care of *three* kids. Have you told Jake what I don't need telling? That you don't intend giving up your career and staying home?'

'Anything I want is fine with him, Mum.'

'What sort of man can that be?' said Harry.

'The only sort likely to stay married to my daughter,' Shirley declared. 'I just hope all the household help she'll need won't bankrupt him.'

'Oh didn't I mention it?' said Laura. 'Jake is a millionaire. But I'd rather you left that out of the conversation when you meet him,' she added when her mother's eyes lit up.

'And when is that likely to be?'

'It's hard to say, Mum. Like me, he travels a lot. At the moment he's in Amsterdam doing a diamond deal.'

'In that case, your mum can get hers cheaper from now on,' Shirley's brother, Ronald, joked from his armchair by the window, and Marianne exchanged a smile with him. His opinion of Shirley was the same as hers.

The arrival in the room of Bridie and Lizzie, each carrying a teapot, diverted everyone's attention to the spread on the table.

Marianne watched Laura seat little Bessie on her lap and tuck a table napkin under the child's double chin. Laura was a devoted mother. But could she, given her many absences from home, cope with raising two older schoolchildren in addition to Bessie? There was a good deal more to bringing up a family than attending to the creature comforts a housekeeper could deal with as efficiently as a mum.

Marianne brushed aside her doubt, helped herself to strudel, and went to chat with her sister-in-law, Lyn, the coolness between Lyn and her husband emphasized by Arnold's having stationed himself on the other side of the room.

'What's up with you and Arnold this time, Lyn?' Marianne asked, sitting down beside her. They were not just sisters-in-law but friends, and had never been less than direct with each other.

'Arnold hasn't seen Matthew for weeks, and he promised me he would,' Lyn replied.

Matthew again, thought Marianne. Their actor son's homosexuality had served to erode their marriage.

'Why can't Arnold be like me?' Lyn said angrily. 'Be thankful that Matthew is well and happy.'

Though Matthew had lived for years with his friend, Pete, their relationship more stable than many marriages, Arnold could still not accept it.

Some of Marianne's generation of the family, she reflected, preferred to pretend they didn't know Matthew was gay. Uncle Nat, though, had taken it in his stride. But he had always been a good deal more tolerant than some of his younger relatives.

Sarah, bemused by the experimental production Matthew had persuaded her to see, when a tour took him to Manchester, would certainly not have guessed why he had remained a bachelor. Moving with the times as she had wisely done with respect to the family, her mind could not have encompassed the possibility of one of its number being homosexual.

Mercifully, Sarah had not lived to know that Matthew's sister, Margaret, a nurse at a church hospital in India, was thinking of entering a Holy Order that would cut her off from the outside world.

While she and Lyn sipped their tea in thoughtful silence, remembrance of two little girls playing on the rug in Sarah's parlour returned to Marianne. Margaret and Harry's daughter, Kate, dressing their dolls. Marianne glanced at Kate, who had flown in from Tel Aviv last week and was now deep in conversation with her mother, on her head the kerchief that singled her out as an ultra-orthodox Jewess. How more different could the lives of Marianne's two nieces have been?

Thanks to Kate, there was now an Israeli branch of the family. And visiting Kate and her children was a source of joy for Harry and Ann, compensation in some measure for the blow that Howard's marriage was to them.

Marianne was noting that Kate was not partaking of the spread, lest it was not truly kosher, when Lyn interrupted her musing.

'How do you suppose I feel about neither of my children being at the ceremony?'

'My grandmother wouldn't have considered it more important than the sick babies Margaret is nursing,' Marianne replied, 'and I seem to recall her having a lot of respect for Matthew's always honouring his professional code that the show must go on. He couldn't have got here from Australia and back there in time for curtain up tomorrow night, could he?'

'That alters nothing for me.'

Lyn's forlorn expression said more than words. She and Arnold had had no luck with their children and Marianne was filled with compassion for her. Though theirs too was a mixed marriage, they had not subjected Matthew and Margaret to an emotional tug-o'war. Instead, they had agreed to follow their own religions, allowing their children to participate fully in both.

Nevertheless, on a personal level that was for Matthew and Margaret the religious vacuum on which Marianne had mused a few hours ago. She could remember, when Chanukah and Christmas coincided, seeing the candles lit in the *menorah* on Lyn and Arnold's mantelpiece and a Christmas tree ablaze with coloured lights in a corner of the room. Each represented an exciting festival for children, and Matthew and Margaret had enjoyed both. But Marianne recalled thinking that the day would come when it seeped through to them that one was their mum's festival and the other their dad's. That they themselves were not part of what either stood for.

Though Margaret had seemed a self-contained child, even

36

her parents could not have suspected that beneath her quiet exterior was an intensity of feeling which must eventually find expression. When finally she had opted for her mother's religion, the family was not surprised. Arnold's parliamentary obligations had led to his renting a pied-à-terre in Westminster, largely removing him from his children's lives. From Lyn's too, and that was still the case. He had never yet failed to be returned to Parliament.

Matthew was now the family atheist, and Marianne had thought that decision an act of cynicism that included paying his parents back for leaving it to him to decide. Nor had she blamed him. Wasn't it hard enough, sometimes, not to doubt the Faith that was unquestionably your own?

Margaret, though, had moved on from Lyn's Protestant beliefs to Catholicism. It had begun with her deepening friendship with Marianne's daughter-in-law. Had Moira felt she needed an ally in the family? Whether or not, there had to be more to it than that. Perhaps the mystique Catholicism offered. Marianne visualized Margaret's madonna-like face framed in a nun's wimple, and thought that even Sarah Sandberg's wisdom could not have come to terms with a great-granddaughter becoming a Bride of Christ.

'The mistake you made, Lyn,' she said bluntly, 'was not making your home in London, when your kids were still young.'

'Do you really think that would have changed anything?'

'Well, at least it would have given Matthew the chance to have a real relationship with his dad, like Martin had with Ralph despite their disagreements.'

Lyn gazed for a moment at the tea leaves in her empty cup. 'At the time, Marianne, not uprooting the kids from their schools seemed right.'

She looked up and put down the cup and saucer. 'A bigger mistake I made, and my children have paid for it, was I should never have married Arnold. Or he me, come to that. Whenever I have to make a public appearance with him there's a row before he gets me to do it. When the Queen

37

visited his constituency and I had to play hostess at the luncheon that was part of it – well, I don't know how I got through it!'

'But the Queen comes over on TV as being absolutely charming,' said Marianne.

'Of course she is,' said Lyn. 'It's me, Marianne. No different now than how I've always been.'

Marianne did not agree with the latter. Well, not when it came to looks. But the lovely fair-haired girl Arnold had brought into the family, distinguishing himself by being the first of its members to marry out, was long gone. In her place was a faded English rose. Unlike Marianne, who looked younger than her years, Lyn's face bespoke the ravages of time. And her figure was evidence that she had turned to food for comfort.

But that's preferable to turning to drink, thought Marianne, as Leona's mother had years ago. Or to the tranquillizers Harry's wife was prescribed to help her accept her German daughter-in-law. Was Ann still taking them?

Marianne was thankful that work had always served as her own therapy. Had she not had to meet the deadline on her next novel, she might after Ralph's death have found herself resorting to all three of the comforts upon which she had just mused, such was her sorrow.

'Arnold should've married someone like Shirley,' Lyn went on. 'A woman who wouldn't have to dress specially for the part, and look all wrong when she does, like I do.'

'You've never looked less than presentable to me,' Marianne replied, 'and I like the dress you have on today.'

'Arnold doesn't. The first thing he said, after he'd pecked my cheek, was that I hadn't made much effort for the occasion and how does that look for him!'

At least they were on speaking terms again. 'Well, my brother's the family bigwig, isn't he?' she said with a laugh.

Lyn managed to smile. 'That's certainly how he sees himself, though we have names more well known than his to boast about. You and Laura, and Matthew haven't done

38

too badly. And now Shirley's getting a millionaire for a son-in-law the whole town will know it, she'll make sure of that!'

'But,' said Marianne, 'she'll have a fit when she finds out that Jake is her generation, not Laura's, and I have to say I myself am wondering if it will work. Laura's going to have to put her liking for discos and all that behind her.'

'But she's starting out with a big advantage,' said Lyn. 'What I mean is – well, how could I have known that the boy I fell in love with when I was a Wren would turn into the man Arnold became?'

Arnold was then an officer on a minesweeper, one of the war's unsung heroes, and Marianne remembered how proud of him she was. And how handsome he had looked in his uniform. But the war had lent a glamorous aura to all who served in it. Even Harry, missing in action for so long the family had believed him dead, had not looked his nondescript self when clad in khaki.

Harry's son returned Marianne to the present, raising his voice above the hubbub of conversation. 'Would everyone mind being quiet for a minute? I've got something to tell you.'

And from the expression on Howard's face, it wasn't good, thought Marianne.

'If it weren't for one aspect of it, I'm sure you'd be pleased,' he said when he had his relatives' attention. 'Christina hasn't gone to Munich to visit her parents. She's left me.'

A moment of silence followed and Marianne saw Howard's mother pale. Then Harry bellowed, as only he could, 'I'm not having my grandchild brought up in Germany!'

'Then perhaps you'd like to go with me to try to get Ben back,' said Howard.

'What do you mean *try*? Ben is your son as well as Christina's!'

'And she's as entitled to have him as I am, isn't she, Dad?'

Harry's reply was, 'Look what you've done to your mother!'

Ann had begun weeping hysterically. 'Why did you let her take him?' she sobbed to Howard.

'As a matter of fact I didn't,' he revealed. 'I believed it was just going to be her usual Christmas trip. That, like always, she'd be back in January – '

'And I might as well tell you now,' Harry interrupted, 'which I refrained from doing before, that for people who were in the Hitler Youth Movement, for whom *Mein Kampf* was their bible and their Führer their god, to celebrate Christmas – well, it makes me want to throw up!'

'Only my father-in-law was in the Hitler Youth Movement,' said Howard. 'My mother-in-law was too young. But leave it to you to exaggerate, Dad!'

'What's to exaggerate?' Harry retorted. 'And while we're at it, why don't we mention Christina's great-uncles? The ones who were in the SS?'

'One of them is dead now,' Howard answered.

'And that happening to the other one can't come soon enough for me,' Harry said. 'But meanwhile he's still alive and kicking, and before I know it I'll have a half-Jewish grandson telling me there wasn't a Holocaust, accusing me of exaggeration, like you just did. Like Henry was saying before, the neo-Nazis are spreading their poison in Europe. And who do you think is putting them up to it – ?'

'They don't need putting up to it,' Henry cut him short.

'But what's left of the old lot must be rubbing their hands with glee,' Harry declared.

Howard thumped his fist on the table, causing the cake dishes and crockery to reverberate. 'Let's not turn my personal problem into a political discussion! This is harder for me than for any of you. But fool that I am, I waited to discuss it with the family before making a move. I've had a letter from Christina telling me she wants a divorce – '

'The sooner the better,' said Harry.

Kate, who was trying to comfort her mother, interceded. 'If Dad wouldn't mind my saying so, his desire to get rid of his German daughter-in-law is irrelevant right now.'

'I agree,' Nathan asserted his seniority. 'What matters is getting little Ben back.' He turned to Leona and Frank. 'What is the legal situation from Howard's point of view?'

Before the lawyers of the family had time to utter, Marianne said quietly, 'Oughtn't the first consideration to be the possibility of a reconciliation? I was always under the impression that Howard loved his wife.'

'Trust my sister the novelist to take a romantic attitude when commonsense is called for!' Harry snorted.

Again Howard banged on the table. 'Of course I'm still in love with Christina. And if it weren't for the bloody past we could've been happy ever after.' He managed to calm down. 'But there's little chance of us getting together again. When I called Munich to speak to Christina – the day I received her letter – she refused to come to the phone and her father hung up on me,' he said miserably. 'I've tried several times since and the same thing happened.'

'But don't let it get you down,' said Frank. 'Leona and I are accustomed to encountering that sort of thing in the early stages of a marital separation, including the parental interference that sometimes goes with it – '

'But none of us, thank God, is accustomed to dealing with Nazis!' said Harry.

'The Schmidts are not Nazis!' Howard yelled at him. 'Would I have married their daughter if that's how they'd come over when I met them?'

'But with Germans one can never be quite sure, and that's the trouble,' said Henry, unhelpfully.

Arnold then had his say, pompous as usual. 'Nonsense, Henry. Utter nonsense, if I may say so. And if Britain had taken that attitude since the war, refused to trust Germany and Germans, we would now be the laughing stock of Europe.'

'But that isn't to say that there aren't elements in Germany, as elsewhere, biding their time and laughing behind their hands,' Henry countered. 'If you'd like some evidence of that, Arnold, I'll be pleased to ask one of my contacts to send it to you.'

'I'm standing here with a broken heart and they're discussing neo-Nazis!' Howard exclaimed.

'You do want Christina back then, no matter what?' Marianne asked him.

His reply was brief and crisp. 'It wouldn't work, Marianne. She said in her letter she couldn't live feeling herself an enemy in the camp.'

Poor Christina, thought Marianne. Try though the family had – even Harry and Ann – to be warm and natural towards her, an invisible barrier had remained. Would it have been any different with *any* Jewish family? Yet Howard had loved her enough to take that chance. And she had borne him a child.

'I suppose my son is blaming us for this,' Ann said while drying her eyes.

Howard went to kiss her. 'No, Mum. I brought it on myself.'

'On all of us,' Harry said roughly, 'and as if how you disgraced us wasn't enough, your mother and I now have to worry about our only grandson being where he is. You've got to get him back, Howard.'

'Try offering Christina money,' Shirley suggested.

'Coming from you, that idea doesn't surprise me!' Howard snapped. 'Would you have taken cash in exchange for Laura?'

'Probably not,' Laura chimed in, 'though there must've been times when she'd have paid it to get rid of me. If my wedding wasn't looming up, Howard, I'd offer to go with you to Munich – '

'Thanks, but all I need with me is a hothead like you. I guess that cuts my father out, too – '

'Well, I couldn't guarantee it wouldn't end up with fisti-cuffs,' said Harry. 'You should have someone with you, though.'

Nathan exchanged a glance with Marianne.

'All right, Uncle Nat,' she said. 'I agree that it had better be me.'

Chapter Four

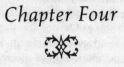

ON THE PLANE to Munich, Marianne surveyed her nephew's set profile. How old would Howard be, now? Thirty-five, she reckoned. A year older than Martin, to whom he bore no physical resemblance though they were first cousins.

Marianne's son was the image of his father and now Ralph was gone, Martin's smile, the way it crinkled his face, and his lively hazel eyes, brought back for her Ralph at Martin's age and how happy they were together.

Later all had not gone smoothly. Her own success and Ralph's failure had not been the recipe for a perfect relationship. Marianne's belief in herself as a writer had never flagged and eventually she had made it. Ralph, on the other hand . . . Though his paintings were good they had, to the end, lacked that certain something that could make an artist's name.

Though Marianne had long known it, she had kept her doubts to herself, and worked steadily at her typewriter as her own career escalated. Ralph, coming home each evening from the ad agency where commercial art served to provide him with a living, had resumed work on one of the canvases this gallery owner or that would try to sell.

When a sale was made Marianne was happy for him. His spirits would briefly soar. But afterwards depression would set in. Then the day came when he told her he would never paint another picture. That it was time he stopped fooling himself and had decided to set up his own ad agency, in partnership with a man he knew.

Marianne had afterwards watched her husband's new

affluence, his allowing himself to go with the tide of a commercialism he privately despised, change him into a different man from the one she had married.

By then their son was at Oxford and they had moved from their small flat to a spacious home in Hampstead, which Ralph had thought more suitable for entertaining the business friends he had rapidly accumulated.

Marianne could remember having to swallow her distaste for some of those whom he had brought home – men for whom money was their god, their wives seeming no more than the decorative appendages necessary to enhance their image. And Ralph's expecting me to dress for the part, she recalled. In order not to let him down, she had gone out and bought herself some suitable outfits. And if Lyn were here now, Marianne would have said to her, 'What makes you think you're the only woman whose husband expects her to play a role?' Wasn't that, give or take the details, what being a wife meant? And if you loved your husband you did it even if it went against the grain.

As for Lyn's saying that she couldn't have known what Arnold would turn into – who did, when they and the object of their affection were young? You couldn't know then what life would turn you yourself into, for it was life that did the changing: the opportunities of whatever kind that came your way, or didn't, the lifts and the let-downs, the chance meetings that could dictate a twist in your path, with happy or catastrophic results.

Marianne glanced at Howard, who had not spoken a word since they boarded the plane. His chance meeting with a German girl on a ski-slope had, despite the opposition of both their families, led first to happiness and later to the catastrophe neither could have envisaged.

Had they lived on a desert island . . . Instead they had been prey to the outside influences love was not necessarily able to withstand. Marriages were not unknown to fall foul of in-law trouble. But this was different.

Marianne was aware that her own daughter-in-law felt an

outsider in the family. But not in the way Christina did. As if she represented to her husband's family the nation that had sent six million Jews to the gas chambers and crematoriums.

Marianne's compassion for Christina had not, however, lessened her mixed feelings about going to Germany. Her efforts to apply logic to her repugnance had not succeeded.

Howard emerged from his thoughts and turned to smile at her. 'I'm grateful to you for lending me moral support, Auntie Marianne.'

'There's no need to be. And I can't remember when you last called me "Auntie".'

'Well, you've always been more like one of *us*, haven't you?'

'And what does that mean?'

Howard paused before replying, and Marianne noticed some grey amid the unruly red hair that he, like her grandson, had inherited from Abraham Sandberg. It seemed the private torment he and Christina had endured together had prematurely aged him.

'I suppose what I mean,' he said eventually, 'is you're easy to talk to and never censorious. I'm never conscious of the age gap when I'm with you, and I wasn't surprised when Matthew once mentioned you being the first one he told about him and Pete.'

Howard managed to laugh. 'But how I feel now is like I did the time when I was still a kid and you went with me to the dentist. You'd come to Manchester for some family emergency – I was too young to know what it was, but I recall my mum not having time to go with me – and the dentist letting you hold my hand while he filled my tooth.'

Over the years there had been no shortage of such emergencies, Marianne reflected. Now, along with the rest, it was just part of the family tapestry woven by time and events, and another strand was about to be added.

The arrival of the drinks trolley interrupted their conversation and she was not surprised when Howard ordered a brandy, though he was not a drinker.

'Tomato juice for me, please,' she said. 'One of us had better keep a clear head!'

'Munich is an interesting city,' Howard said when they had been served and were sipping their drinks, 'steeped in history.'

'Some of which we could have done without.'

Howard put down his glass. 'That's the sort of remark I'd expect from my dad, not from you.'

'Then I'm sorry to disappoint you, Howard, and I may as well tell you that only for you would I be on my way to where we're going.'

'Believe it or not there are plenty of good Germans, Marianne – '

'I have never believed otherwise.'

'My mother-in-law for instance,' Howard went on. 'If you met her and she weren't German – '

'The fact remains that she is,' Marianne cut in, 'and I can't help my feelings. What sort of man is your father-in-law?'

'Well, let's just say that I'm now prepared to admit I've never felt comfortable with him – which helps me to understand how it's been for Christina with our family.'

Klaus Schmidt watched Christina cut up the food on her child's plate. As was his habit, he had closed his print shop for the lunch hour and was eating at home. But how could he enjoy the *Bratwurst mit Sauerkraut* his wife had put before him with his only child's unhappiness before his eyes?

Christina had not heeded Klaus's warning that for a German girl to marry a Jew, go to live with him in his country, among his family, would not be easy for her.

Klaus would not have wanted the marriage even if Howard were a German Jew, but even so, that would be different. They would have lived in Germany and here, he reflected, we are host to the Jews who returned, as we always were. Who would try to make their host feel uncomfortable? A

46

word not strong enough to describe how Klaus's daughter had been made to feel by her husband's relatives in England. He had not seen Christina smile since she came home. This time to stay.

'Must we now eat all our meals in silence!' he exclaimed. He quaffed some beer to wash down the food his sudden surge of anger had caused to stick in his throat. How dare those people do this to his beloved daughter!

'Is my grandson to grow up in a house where nobody laughs?' He unwedged his belly from where it rested against the table and went to fondle the cheek of the alien-looking child whom he nevertheless adored.

Eventually, he told himself, Christina would marry again and the man be a Bavarian, with whom she would provide her parents with a brood of happy grandchildren who looked like German children should.

'Do not be sad, little one,' he said to Ben. 'All will be well.'

Christina put down the fork with which she was toying with her meal. 'Would you please tell me how, Father? Ben is too young to understand what is wrong, but he can feel that all is *not* well.'

Though the child was bilingual the conversation was of course beyond his comprehension. But as Christina had said, he was sensitive to the atmosphere, and now glancing back and forth from his mother to his grandfather.

'One day he will perhaps blame me,' said Christina with distress when Ben dug his knuckles in his eyes and began crying.

Her father replied, 'I do not wish to hear that word spoken in this house again. What but blame is at the root of this trouble?'

'I want my daddy,' Ben said in English.

'He will forget that language when he no longer hears it spoken,' said Klaus.

'But he will not forget his father,' said Christina, 'and I would not wish for him to.'

She too began weeping and Lisl Schmidt gave her husband

47

a rebuking glance while cradling Ben against her ample bosom.

'It is not good to discuss such matters in the little one's presence,' she said to Klaus. 'And should you not now be on your way back to work? The *Apfelkuchen* you do not have time to eat I will save for you to have tonight.'

Lisl surveyed Christina, who was drying her eyes on a corner of the apron she was wearing. 'And if our daughter does not quickly recover her appetite, Klaus, we shall soon not recognize her,' she added as he departed.

Once a younger version of her buxom mother, Christina had shed weight along with the tears she had been unable to stem since returning to Munich.

'Your father is right,' Lisl said gently. 'Our life it must continue as always, despite what has now happened. You have made a painful decision, Christina, but the hurt will pass. You will not go on crying forever.'

Lisl, however, was less inclined to believe, as Klaus did, that once their daughter's initial distress was over, all would be well. This could not be like the broken marriages experienced by the sons and daughters of some of Lisl's friends. More was at stake here than the usual matters of alimony and arrangements for the children to spend time with their father.

Divorce was always painful for the children, Lisl reflected. But the reason for Christina's leaving Howard was, as Klaus had said, rooted in a matter Germans preferred not to think about. Until Howard entered their lives it had not been necessary for Lisl and Klaus to think about it.

Munich's Jewish community had a synagogue, also a centre for their activities, Lisl had heard. But their number was small, lessening the odds of encountering any of them. Lisl never had. Nor had she paused to ponder on the fate of the Jewish children with whom she had played at kindergarten, in the days when Munich, like every major German city, had many Jews among its citizenry.

It wasn't until her daughter gave her a Jewish son-in-law

that she had questioned her own indifference. Then an evening had come when she had found herself facing up to a good deal more than that.

It was Klaus's uncle's birthday and the family was helping him celebrate it in a beer hall. Many toasts were made amid the drinking and the laughter, and Uncle Ernst had stood up and raised his *Stein* to the good old days. It was possible that he had done so at his previous birthday celebrations and that Lisl had thought nothing of it. But what those good old days had included for Uncle Ernst and his cronies, some of whom were present, had suddenly come home to her and she had got up and left.

A terrible quarrel with Klaus had taken place when he followed her. He had demanded an explanation for her rudeness to the elder of the family, but she was too sickened by his requiring one to provide it. By then they were the grandparents of a half-Jewish child.

Lisl returned Ben to his chair and began feeding him his unfinished meal, affected by the docility with which he allowed her to do so, though he was by nature a spirited little boy. Destined to grow up with a built-in inner conflict passed down by his parents, she thought eyeing him compassionately.

His growing up would now be on his mother's ground, and it might perhaps have been easier for him had he remained on his father's – in a country where his appearance would not single him out as a reminder to its citizens of the sins committed in their name.

Her daughter's broken marriage had brought to Lisl's mind a passage from the bible; that the sins of the fathers shall fall upon the children. So it had proved for Christina, now listlessly clearing the table. What but the unthinkable crimes committed in the years Uncle Ernst still saw fit to drink a toast to had risen from the past to mar Christina's happiness with the man she loved?

Though the Nuremberg trials had ensured punishment for many of the war criminals, it was well known that there were those who had escaped justice to make new lives in other countries. And it was not a secret that lesser figures had gone unpunished, returning to the positions of trust they had held in Germany before the war.

'You are no less subdued than I, Mother,' Christina interrupted Lisl's thoughts while brushing some crumbs from the tablecloth, 'and for that too I am to blame.'

Lisl sliced some *Apfelkuchen* for Ben. 'Did you not hear your father tell you that word is not to be spoken in this house? But I myself will speak it one more time. Though blame is responsible for why you have come home, Christina, you yourself are responsible for none of this.'

Lisl left Ben to munch his cake and went to kiss her daughter's cheek. 'Now, *Liebchen*, instead of feeling sorry for yourself, though you're entitled to be, let's put our minds to practical matters. You cannot go on refusing to speak to Howard on the phone.'

Howard was at that moment helping Marianne into a taxi on the forecourt of Munich Airport.

'Kindly don't treat me like an old lady!' she said with a smile. 'And get that apprehensive look off your face. There's nothing to be scared about.'

Howard got in beside her. 'Except for the reception I'm likely to get.'

'Will your father-in-law be home at this time of day?'

'Normally, no. But under the circumstances – well, it wouldn't surprise me if he was there standing guard in case I arrive out of the blue and try to grab Ben.'

'Was that the impression you got when you last rang up?'

'Well, let's just say he didn't hang up on me that time, but he was the opposite of friendly.'

They fell silent and Marianne surveyed the rustic environs through which they were travelling, which matched her preconceptions of Bavaria. Pastel-pink rooftops peeping between tall trees, ahead the gleaming steeple of a little white church. The fairy-tale quality of the surroundings, though, was at odds with her feelings when they reached the city, a place of spacious squares and stone buildings mellowed by time.

The genial taxi-driver, who spoke some English, assumed they were tourists and reeled off a list of historic edifices they must not fail to visit. Was it from the balcony of one of them that Hitler had ranted at his Munich rallies?

Marianne was tempted to inquire, but thought better of it. She was in the country where Hitler was understandably unmentionable. But that hadn't stopped the evil from rising as a phoenix from the ashes. According to Henry Moritz, neo-Nazi activists like the British National Front were spreading their poison and biding their time in the States as well as in Europe.

'You haven't told me what, exactly, you're hoping to achieve from this visit?' she said to Howard, returning her mind to practical matters. 'And if it's what your dad is expecting, and your mum hoping for, let me warn you now that Ben is unlikely to be with us when we return home.'

Howard gave her an agonized glance.

'It's no use looking at me like that,' she said gently. 'Only a fool, and you're not one, would let himself think that Christina will allow you to have Ben. She loves him as much as you do – '

'There's no need to tell me that.'

'But it seems to be something that my brother Harry, who's always been a fool in some ways, hasn't paused to consider.'

'As if I didn't upset my parents enough by marrying Christina – look what I've done to them now,' was Howard's response.

Marianne patted his hand comfortingly before saying what she must. 'You're going to have to harden yourself to that and to a lot of other things, Howard. Or how shall you cope if your father-in-law won't let you over the doorstep?'

She kept her tone firm, though she could have wept for

the sadness in Howard's eyes. 'Since you're still Christina's husband, you have the right to speak with her. If I'm allowed over the doorstep with you, I shall insist that your discussion take place in private. If I'm not, I suggest that be the line you take.'

Howard would wish anyone luck to get the better of his Aunt Marianne the way she looked right now, her shoulders squared and a determined gleam in her eye.

In the event, Marianne's intervention was not required. It was Lisl Schmidt who opened the door to Howard's ring, nor did she hesitate before inviting them in.

'How nice to meet one of Howard's family,' she said when he had introduced Marianne.

As if we've dropped in for tea, Marianne thought, and one platitude calls for another. 'But it's sad that we should meet in these circumstances,' she replied.

Christina then appeared from the living-room, avoided looking at Howard and came to kiss Marianne.

'I shall not forget your many kindnesses,' she said, 'and if only things had been different . . .'

When was 'if' not the operative word? Marianne reflected. Many of the crises in her own life could be traced back to that little word with which most people's lives were liberally strewn, causing their paths to twist this way or that, for good or for ill.

The first 'if' in this case was Howard's opting to ski in Austria, instead of going to Switzerland as he usually did. And there he had met Christina.

But the 'if' Christina had just mentioned could not be related to the making of a decision. The family hadn't decided en masse not to like its new, German member and likeable she had proved to be. A girl with a lively personality and a caring nature, who had done her best to fit in. But how long was it before Christina became aware of something unspoken? From which she had finally fled.

'We have just put Ben for his afternoon rest,' Lisl said. 'This would be the good opportunity for Christina and Howard to talk with each other. I am sure that Howard's aunt will agree.'

Displaying that she was not a woman to stand on ceremony, she led Marianne into her roomy kitchen, where the German version of a Welsh dresser occupied one wall, the blue and white china reposing on it reminiscent of Marianne's willow pattern dinner service.

Dominating another wall was an Aga stove, on which stood a huge copper saucepan, its simmering contents sending forth an appetizing aroma to mingle with the scent of cinnamon and spices of which the room was redolent.

By the lace-curtained window was the sturdy table at which the Schmidts ate their meals, and Marianne's impression of Frau Schmidt was that her dinner guests too would eat in the kitchen, and eat well.

Christina had said that her parents still lived in the house where she was raised. A cosy home for a child to grow up in, Marianne reflected, and Munich was certainly a charming city. But just a few kilometres away was Dachau, the notorious concentration camp, now a public memorial to those whose lives were cut short there.

Marianne willed herself to stem the association of the past with the present that had dogged her since she stepped off the plane, but did not succeed in putting from her mind that the homely woman whose kitchen this was had once been a flaxen-haired girl in the wildly cheering crowds for whom their Führer had replaced God, and his ravings become their creed.

'Please to sit down, Mrs Dean,' Lisl said. 'May I offer you some refreshment?'

'No, thank you.' Had that sounded as brusque to Frau Schmidt as it had to Marianne?

'This is for all concerned the difficult situation,' Lisl said as if she had divined Marianne's thoughts. 'And it is possible that we shall not know the outcome today.'

With that, she changed the subject. 'I have seen in paper-back some of your books here.'

'In English, or in German?' Marianne asked politely.

'I believe in both languages.'

'And you speak mine as well as your daughter does.'

'I had, like Christina, the excellent education,' Lisl replied, while noting Marianne's black leather trousers, that would have made her own hips look like the back of a leather armchair.

'But my English speaking,' Lisl went on, 'it was how you would call rusty, and was much improved by talking with your nephew.'

They had heard Christina and Howard enter the living-room and shut the door, and Lisl was suddenly unable to hide her distress. 'My heart it is breaking for them – '

'Mine, too, Frau Schmidt.'

They abandoned their attempt to make conversation and sat listening to the tick of the grandfather clock, and Marianne thought, The hell with what her people did to mine. Right now we're just two middle-aged women wishing we could put things right for the young couple in the next room.

It had taken but one glance at the girl he loved for Howard to think it impossible that there would *not* be a reconciliation.

The moment they were alone he had taken Christina in his arms, what they felt for each other no less strong now than it had always been. How, then, could something so impersonal come between them?

'Please don't do this to us, Christina,' he pleaded.

They were seated on the sofa, the last of the day's wintry sunlight enhancing the sheen of Christina's hair. Serving too to emphasize her pallor and the weariness circling her eyes.

Not for the first time Howard silently cursed the ghost of the past, whose presence had haunted his marriage from the day he and Christina set up home in Manchester.

Once they were man and wife, the family had kept their

feelings to themselves, counselled no doubt by Sarah Sandberg, who wisely had welcomed an outsider rather than alienate one of her own.

But Christina was no ordinary outsider and her presence in a Jewish family *extra*ordinary. The first outsider, Howard's Aunt Lyn, was by now part of the family fabric and loved and respected by all. Martin's wife, though, was a different dish of tea. Moira hadn't let herself be drawn in, but that was her choice.

Christina hadn't had a choice. History had decreed the consequences of her marrying Howard. She would require the skin of a rhinoceros not to be aware of his family's reserve with her.

Howard stroked her hand. When he slipped that gold band on her finger, could either of them then have foreseen this? But hope had not quite died in him.

'Come home with me, Christina,' he said quietly. 'It's me you're married to, not my family.'

She managed a wan smile. 'I have tried many times to tell myself that, Howard. But with *your* family, it is not true. And England is not home for me. Only for you.'

'Also for Ben.'

It was the first time either had mentioned their child. As if doing so could be treading dangerous ground, and Howard refrained for the moment from stepping farther in that direction, lest doing so smash to smithereens his fragile hope.

'There's nothing I wouldn't do for you,' he told his wife.

Christina put that to the test. 'Then come to live with me in Munich.'

To Howard it sounded like an ultimatum. 'Don't be ridiculous,' he said, 'we have to live where my livelihood is.'

'My father would find for you a place in his business.'

'What do I know about printing?'

'You would not work in the print shop. His head clerk in the office is soon to retire. A replacement will be needed.'

Howard had a vision of himself kowtowing to his arrogant father-in-law and blotted it out. 'No thanks, Christina. I've worked with my own father since I left school and one day his business will be mine.'

'But you would not live in Germany on principle, would you?'

Howard thought of how seeing 'Dachaustrasse' on the street signs of the broad highway that bore that name always caused him to avert his eyes. Of the way he found it impossible to pass by the police station in the city centre without picturing what the Gestapo must have inflicted there upon their innocent victims. Of how he had not yet been able to bring himself to visit Dachau.

Since he and Christina had reached the point when total honesty was required – and possibly the point of no return – he replied, 'Leaving principle out of it, the answer to your question is no, I couldn't live in Germany. And it beats me how any Jew can.'

Christina got up and went to gaze through the window. For Howard it was as if the ghost stalking them had reached out and touched him with icy fingers.

'So you see,' Christina said, 'you are no different from your family, Howard.'

She turned to look at him and he would not forget the tragic expression on her face. Or the dignity of her stance, silhouetted against the window in her simple black dress, as she said the words that set the seal on Ben's future.

'You have given me much happiness and a child, and I thank you for that. But you will have to accept that your son will be raised where his father could never bring himself to live.'

Chapter Five

SARAH SANDBERG'S 'almonds and raisins of life' had been known to present themselves side by side, and so it was now for the family. While they feared for little Ben's future, Laura's wedding was being planned.

Shirley was compiling a guest-list on the evening Marianne and Howard returned from Munich – empty-handed, as Howard's father irately put it.

It was at Shirley's penthouse that Howard delivered his news, since his parents, together with Leona and Nathan, had been called in to help her.

'A relative is a relative!' Harry was declaiming when the doorbell chimed and Leona went to answer it. 'No matter how distant, or what they did to you years ago.'

'You sound like our late grandmother,' Shirley informed him, 'but even she might have thought me entitled not to invite a fifth cousin who sided with Peter when I got my divorce. And by the way, I'm not inviting Peter.'

Nathan said on behalf of all present, 'You can't do that to Laura.'

'It's me who's paying for the reception.'

Marianne entered in time to hear that typically Shirley statement and paused with Howard on the room's upper level, feeling as always on the rare occasions she came here that this could be a Hollywood film set and Shirley playing Bette Davis in her heyday.

Leona, who had returned to the table around which the others were seated, coughed to command their attention.

Harry turned and saw his sister and his son, took in their

57

expressions, and gave Howard a piece of his mind that caused him to pale.

'Your going to Munich was a waste of the plane fare,' Shirley capped it.

'Is there nothing', said Marianne, 'that you don't see in terms of money?'

'Who do you think you're talking to?' Shirley retorted. 'And in my own home!'

Marianne replied, 'I shan't stay a moment longer than necessary, Shirley, lest I throw up on your expensive white carpet. If you'd like that in plain English, I have never found you more sickening than I do right now. Nor would I be here if Harry and Ann had been at home when we rang them from the airport. We then rang Uncle Nat's and Bridie told us – '

'Save your boring explanation for someone who's interested!' Shirley cut in. 'I'm not.'

'When', said Marianne, 'were you ever interested in anyone but yourself?'

'Would you two mind cutting the dramatics?' Harry interceded. 'I'd like to hear what my son has to say.'

Howard, his freckled face crumpled with distress, sat down on a decorative but uncomfortable chaise longue. 'What is there to say, Dad, that you can't see for yourself?'

The finality of his tone was such that Harry was momentarily speechless and Ann rummaged in her handbag for her pill box. Harry then snatched it from her, brandished it in the air and shouted, 'See what you've done to your mother, Howard!'

'But your saying so helps nobody,' Nathan informed him. 'What's required is a cool head and the right advice. What are Howard's chances of getting custody of Ben?' he asked Leona.

'Off the top of my head, Dad, I can't answer that. I'll discuss it with Frank when I get home.'

Howard cleared his throat. 'Thanks, but it won't be necessary.'

'What does that mean?' Harry demanded.

Marianne saw a vein on his forehead throbbing with anger and told him to calm down.

'You getting yourself into a state isn't going to change anything,' said Howard.

'What is there to change! Ben is *my* grandson. Named after my father, whom he also looks like. He doesn't belong where he now is!'

'I agree.'

'Well that's something!'

'But I'm nevertheless not going to subject him to a tug-o'war between his mum and his dad.'

'Does that mean you're going to let him be brought up by Germans?'

Harry's sallow complexion was now a purplish hue and Marianne prickled with alarm when she saw him tug at his shirt collar. A moment later he had slumped to the floor and Nathan was taking command of the situation.

Her brother's having a stroke was for Marianne like family history repeating itself. A seizure had cut down their father, and in similar circumstances.

Much about Harry reminded her of her father: the acumen and the tenacity that had enabled Ben Klein to build a sizeable business from small beginnings; the integrity for which he was throughout his life respected; but most of all the devotion that made him the archetypal family man and the more vulnerable to the blows children are liable to deal their parents.

When Nathan rose from examining Harry and instructed Leona to phone for an ambulance, Marianne had looked at her brother's face and seen again her father's twisted grimace twenty-one years earlier – distress that climaxed with a family quarrel responsible then as it was now.

An hour later she was seated in a hospital waiting-room, her arm around Ann's shoulders. Leona had called Frank and

59

he too was there sharing the tension, he and Leona flanking Howard.

Shirley had put herself alone in a corner and Marianne thought with distaste that her mind was probably still busy planning an ostentatious wedding reception. Well, half of her mind.

'Uncle Nat's been gone for a long time,' Shirley said glancing at her Cartier wristwatch. 'And oughtn't we to call Kate?'

'My sister's only just returned to Israel,' said Howard, 'and I'm not bringing her back unless I have to.'

'Who are you to make such decisions!' his mother said stridently. 'If you'd listened to your parents in the first place, your father wouldn't now be lying where he is!'

Howard got up and left the room.

'He didn't need you to remind him of that,' Marianne said to Ann.

'Whose side are you on?'

'This doesn't seem to me the time to be taking sides. Or for recrimination.'

'I agree,' said Leona.

By then Ann had disengaged herself from Marianne's arm and Howard, shepherded by Nathan, was re-entering the room.

With them was the consultant called from his home to attend Harry. No, he must have been at a dinner, thought Marianne, noting his formal attire.

'The *good* news is there is no immediate danger, Mrs Klein,' he told Ann.

She rose to face him. 'And what is the *bad* news, Doctor?'

He removed his pince-nez and replaced them on his nose. 'Well let me put it this way – '

'I'd like you to tell me straight.'

'Your husband is likely to be confined to a wheelchair.'

After he had bade them goodnight and departed, Ann said to Howard, 'So you've lost a son and gained a business.'

But Marianne silently wagered that it would take more than being in a wheelchair to keep Harry from minding the store.

Chapter Six

MARTIN ARRIVED HOME from an all-night work stint with his partner, Andy Frolich, the song they still had not succeeded in getting right beating like a drum in his head.

His wife came downstairs in her dressing-gown and said, 'How nice to meet you!' passing him on her way to the kitchen.

Martin followed her, got himself some juice from the refrigerator and watched her make coffee.

'Gone are the days when we lived in a commune and everyone did their bit,' she remarked.

'If I had to make breakfast right now, Moira, there wouldn't be any,' he replied. 'I'm bushed. But you don't have to make any for me. Just coffee will do.'

'Since I'm making it for Abraham Patrick and me, I may as well include you. I don't mind doing it, Martin.'

'Then why the sarcasm? You hit me with it the minute I stepped into the house. And yearning for the days when we lived in a commune is like saying you wish we could get back our youth. Who doesn't?'

Moira began cracking eggs into a bowl. 'Instead, the years roll by and look at us now.'

Martin chose to take that literally. 'You don't look all that different to me.'

But in some ways that wasn't true. His wife was still as strikingly beautiful as the day they met in an Oxford pub. Martin remembered catching his breath when he saw her. A tall, graceful girl in a tweed suit, a string of pearls around her neck and the satiny sheen of her long black hair enhancing her creamy complexion.

'What was that scent you used to wear?' he asked, its headiness returning to him.

'Shocking de Schiaparelli.'

'It sure turned me on!'

'Perhaps I should begin wearing it again.'

A below the belt jibe if Martin had ever heard one. And one of the ways in which Moira had changed. She knew that his frequent absences from their bed were obligatory. Due to work. That he wanted her no less than he always had.

Though Andy sometimes played around on their trips to the States or wherever, Martin never had. Rhoda Frolich, though she didn't know it, had more to complain about than Moira. And coming home to this, after breaking his head writing lyrics all night, was all Martin needed.

Andy, on the other hand, would now be being fussed over by Rhoda, to whom he seemed to be husband and child rolled into one. The Frolichs had no kids and that was Martin's impression. Or, he conjectured, had Rhoda set herself up in competition with her mother-in-law? Something had to account for the attention that guy got from his wife!

A picture of a limousine arriving at the commune then returned to Martin. And of a uniformed chauffeur carrying a huge earthenware dish. 'Remember how Andy's mother used to send him a Sabbath Eve dinner, every Friday?' he said with a grin.

Moira said tartly, 'Well he married a *shiksah*, like you did. His mother didn't want him to forget he's a Jew.'

'In this world it would be impossible to forget,' Martin informed her. 'Even for those who'd like to, and Andy's never been one of them. All it takes is for someone to make a slip of the tongue. As for Andy's mum – well, I'll grant she's a fusspot. But couldn't your interpretation of why she sent him those dinners be all in your mind?'

Moira was now scrambling the eggs and kept her gaze fixed on the pan. 'It was what Rhoda and I thought at the time, and my experience with your family has done nothing to change my impression.'

Their son's entrance cut short what might otherwise have become a contentious discussion, and it struck Martin that once again religion was at the heart of it.

The stressful aftermath of his putting his foot down with Moira and taking his lad up north for the window consecration had lingered on and was not yet gone. But it seemed to him now that what ailed his marriage had begun long ago. Why else had Moira discussed with Rhoda what she had just revealed? When they were newly-wed wives. Rhoda a stringy-looking girl hoping to make her name as a sculptor, which she had since achieved. And Moira doing freelance work for the publishing house where she was now senior editor.

Though Martin and Andy had not known it, their wives had, from the off, felt threatened. Even though neither he nor Andy was religious in the formal sense of the word. But it wasn't only the religion itself. Moira could not have made more clear than she just had that it was also what went with it. That well-known caricature the Jewish mother, clucking over her children and ruling their lives even after they had flown the nest – an image that didn't fit Martin's mum, and there were plenty like her, with the wisdom to let their children go. But it was with that stereotype preconception that Moira had married Martin, he was reflecting when she put his breakfast before him.

'If you two wouldn't mind my breaking the silence,' said their precocious son, 'I have something to tell you. I've decided that from now on I'd like to be called A.P.'

'Your mother's been letting you watch too much telly,' Martin said with a laugh.

'How would you like it, Dad, if you got called Martin William?' the boy asked.

Moira brought his and her own breakfast to the table, warned him not to talk with his mouth full, and sat down opposite Martin.

The only change in her appearance is she now has lines of discontent around her mouth, he thought, though what we've achieved materially, between us, many would find enviable. Martin would be surprised if Moira didn't end up as editorial director. And though Frolich and Dean were not yet names on a par with Rodgers and Hart, that day could come. Martin and Andy were now writing the words and music for their first West End show, into which American money was being poured. If all went well, Broadway would follow. But Martin would happily trade success for what his marriage lacked.

Spring sunlight was flooding into the room from the picture window overlooking the rear lawn, where daffodils flaunted their bonnets beneath a weeping willow, reminding Martin of Wordsworth's classic poem.

'I've never told you, have I,' he said to his son, 'that the Martin I'm named after wrote poetry.' His other namesake, William, was the New Zealander grandfather he had never known. Nor, on a working trip to the country his father had come from, had he succeeded in tracing any of Ralph Dean's relatives.

Mindful of his mother's presence at the table, Abraham Patrick did not reply until he had swallowed the food in his mouth. 'All you said was he was Grandma Marianne's cousin who was killed in the war.'

'In an accident during the war,' Martin corrected the inaccuracy. 'When he was in the RAF and your granny an ATS girl.'

'So your mother said,' Moira interceded. 'And if you keep chatting to Abraham Patrick he will be late for school.'

'I've never been late yet,' the boy said.

And Moira knew he had more than enough time to catch the bus this morning.

But something comes over her when I talk to Abraham Patrick about my family, thought Martin. And the kid is right. He can't be expected to go through life addressed as the living symbol of a mixed marriage that hadn't worked.

'All right. A.P. it is from now on,' he said to his son's delight.

'You give in to his every whim!' Moira exclaimed. 'But *I*

don't intend to.' She saw them exchange a wink. 'And I am not having you and him in cahoots against me, Martin! Now if you'll excuse me, I have an editorial meeting to get to and I still have to take my shower.'

Her exit in her bright blue dressing-gown could be likened, thought Martin, to lightning streaking across the room.

'If I'd known wanting to be called by my initials would cause trouble, I wouldn't have suggested it,' the boy said eyeing his mother's unfinished breakfast. He glanced at the clock. 'And it's only half-past-seven. Mum would have to have a flat tyre to be late for her meeting.'

'Hampstead Village can be chock-a-block in the mornings,' Martin said in Moira's defence.

'Why doesn't Mum go by tube?'

'She doesn't like using public transport, A.P.'

'Thanks for remembering to call me that, Dad.'

'And don't worry, your pals and your relations will soon get used to it,' Martin assured him. 'It will probably be a welcome relief to them,' he added with a smile.

'But I'll bet you a week's pocket money that Mum will go on calling me Abraham Patrick.'

After his son had left for school, Martin recalled the day he was baptized and how unreal it had seemed. But it had been the price of Martin's marrying the girl he loved. A precondition of their marriage.

He had had to steel himself to attend the christening, but not to do so would have been letting down his wife, and her afterwards agreeing that their son be circumcised had seemed a portent for the future. As if she was telling him that she knew how he felt.

But that was eleven years ago, when Martin and Moira were still living on the commune, their undergraduate days not far enough behind them for them yet to have learned that the golden dreams of youth bore no relation to reality.

In retrospect it seemed to Martin that it hadn't been a commune in the true sense of the word. Its members had lived under one roof, eaten together, enjoyed each other's company. But there had been no common aim. Each of us, he reflected, was concerned with doing our own thing.

Under that roof was a lot of talent. Martin and Andy, and Rhoda, were not the only ones who had since become well-known names. Martin's friend Bill Dryden, with whom he had remained close, now made TV documentaries that topped the ratings, and Bill's wife, Sukey, was making a fortune with her beautiful ceramics.

What the commune did was relieve us all of individual everyday responsibilities, Martin now saw. Living there together allowed what was in each of us to flower. Even those whose talents were not the creative kind had, as though it were a breathing space, benefited from that shared interlude before blossoming into what they had later become.

When had that euphoric little world begun to disintegrate? When for each of us in turn recognition, or promotion, or whatever, had its inevitable effects. And what was there to do then but go our separate ways towards the top of whichever ladder?

Since Andy and I are climbing the same ladder, in harness, we are still together. But how long was it since I saw Bill? Along with success came demands on your time and the first thing to go was your social life. Not to mention your sleep!

Martin stifled a yawn as Moira entered wearing one of her smart city suits, pecked his cheek and left, returning him full circle to her remark while she made the coffee. Gone are the days was right! And now here he was, alone in a kitchen that looked like an illustration in a glossy magazine – if you didn't notice the dirty dishes.

He had better stack them in the dishwasher and go get some shuteye, or before he knew it Andy would be on the phone snarling, 'Where the hell are you? We decided to take a short break, not half a day!'

For Andy, composing music came easier than writing the lyrics did to Martin. Martin's experience was that *nothing* in this life came easy! Marriage included.

Chapter Seven

AFTER HIS FATHER'S DISCHARGE from hospital, the strain to which Howard was subjected was such that at times he thought he would surely break.

Though he was capable of running the business alone, Harry continued to send for him in order to issue instructions. Nor did Harry ever fail to raise the subject of little Ben.

Howard, for his part, was obliged to hide his own feelings, to accept silently the daily recrimination meted out to him, lest a heated exchange ensue and his father have another seizure.

'You're not seeing enough of your boy,' Harry would tell him repeatedly, though he must be aware that Howard's increased business responsibilities kept him from visiting Ben more often. A tirade invariably followed, its theme by now engraved upon Howard's mind: 'When Ben grows up you'll be like a stranger to him, and what he could turn into thanks to those Germans will be on your own head!'

Since his mother considered it inadvisable to reply that the Schmidts were good people – Howard had never thought otherwise – he refrained from doing so. Instead he would try to keep a smile on his face, and afterwards leave Harry's sickroom feeling as if he had been hit on the head.

Thankfully, though, his mother's attitude towards him had softened, he thought, while she served his dinner one evening. Initially, despite his now living alone in a house that echoed with emptiness, she had not invited him to eat with her at the end of his working day.

'It's a comfort to chat to you, Mum,' he said when she sat

down opposite him in the kitchen where he and his sister had eaten before they left home.

The wallpaper was different, but the simple, cream-painted units that reflected his mother's taste were still there. And the collection of Poole pottery, accumulated on trips to Bournemouth, in one of the glass-fronted cupboards. Only the atmosphere had changed, Howard thought, glancing at the chair his father had once occupied and would no more.

Though Kate was gone from here before she was twenty, Howard had stayed put until he married. It wouldn't have occurred to me to get myself a bachelor pad, as most of my friends did, he reflected. Staid was the word for me.

It struck Howard now that if his cousin Martin had fallen for a German girl, the family, though they would have liked it no less, might not have been quite so astonished. People in the arts were not expected to conform. But when suburban Howard Klein stepped out of line –

His mother interrupted his thoughts. 'I'm glad to have you here, Howard. These days I can use some comfort, myself.'

He watched her take away their soup plates and bring a platter of fried fish to the table, noting her weary demeanour. 'Are you still taking tranquillizers, Mum?'

'As a matter of fact I'm not. Uncle Nat came here and gave me a talking to. If my father were alive, he'd never have let me begin taking them, Uncle Nat said. And it's true. Your Grandfather Smolenksky was also a doctor of the old school. Help yourself to fish, Howard. And I've made you some potato salad,' she said taking a dishful of it from the refrigerator.

She had garnished it, as she always did, with gherkins and sprigs of watercress, and Howard told her that it was not necessary to go to such trouble on his account.

Ann served him an ample helping and spooned some on to her own plate, her expression bleak. 'It would be all too easy for me, right now, Howard, to go to no trouble about anything. To let myself get into slipshod ways. I can't be bothered to make up my face any more, but I force myself to. Not doing so would be the beginning of me going to pieces. I can't let myself. Your dad needs me.'

Howard nevertheless feared that she might. He'd been too busy licking his own wounds to notice what was happening to his mother. She had always been a smart dresser and had on one of her linen frocks, the brown one, with a brooch pinned to the breast pocket. But beneath the surface appearance she was determined to maintain . . .

'I also have to force myself to eat,' she went on, 'to keep up my strength. If I didn't – well, Marianne would have to stop writing her book and come here to look after both me and your dad. Not that she'd stay after one day of looking after *him*!'

'Marianne is like a real sister to you, isn't she?' Howard said after a pause.

'Since I've never had one – nor a brother – I wouldn't know. But Marianne is certainly the one in the family I know I can rely on. What I also know is that she wouldn't stand for what I'm getting from your dad.'

Ann forked some fish into her mouth and put the ketchup bottle closer to Howard. 'You forgot to drench your food with it! And about your father – well, I wouldn't say this to anyone else, but I now know what a friend of mine meant when her husband became bedfast and she remarked that an invalid could also be a tyrant. And when their condition is such that you daren't risk upsetting them . . . Need I say more, Howard?'

'Not to me you needn't.'

'I can't wait for the day your dad progresses to the wheelchair the specialist mentioned,' said Ann.

'Does he have you running up and downstairs all the time?'

'What else?'

'Then let's convert a downstairs room to a bedroom for him. I should have thought of it before. Frank will help me and we'll do it on Sunday – '

'Your father won't hear of it,' Ann cut in. 'I suggested it

70

myself, and my advice to you is, don't even mention it to him.'

'Then he isn't considering you, is he, Mum?'

'But he always did before his stroke.'

They went on with their meal in silence.

Then Ann said quietly, 'What we have to remember, Howard, is that what we're seeing now isn't him. I'd also like you to know that, though what Germany conjures up for Jews gives me the shivers, I'd rather not believe, like your father does, that they're still a nation of Jew-haters. A fixation is what Uncle Nat called it.'

And it isn't getting any better, thought Howard.

'All the same,' said his mother, 'when I think of my grandson being there, and of what Henry Moritz told us about the neo-Nazis – '

'I've heard there are less of them in Germany than elsewhere,' Howard cut in.

'But Germany is where it all began, and if your dad has to have a fixation I'm not surprised it's the one it is. It would perhaps be easier for Ben to grow up there, if he didn't look so Jewish.'

Howard hid his own qualms with a joke. 'Would you like him to have plastic surgery?'

'Let the anti-Semites have surgery on their evil tongues!' Ann flashed. 'But it's nice to hear you laugh for a change, Howard.'

'And for me to see that you haven't lost your spirit, Mum. Despite the tyrant upstairs,' Howard added as they heard from above the tinkle of the handbell with which Harry summoned his wife.

Chapter Eight

SHIRLEY'S ELABORATE ARRANGEMENTS for her daughter's wedding were deftly foiled by Laura.

'You didn't have to elope, you had my permission!' was her tart response to learning that the marriage had taken place minus her presence.

They were talking on the telephone and Laura tried to soften the blow. 'But wouldn't you say that flying to Paris to get married was romantic, Mum?'

'What I would say is it's in keeping with your harum-scarum way of life. And I didn't *see* you get married, did I? I'm having to pinch myself to believe you've actually done it.'

'I'll show you my marriage lines.'

'More to the point is when do I get to see the man who's worked this miracle? A reference from Marianne is the opposite of reassuring to me! And what is all that noise I can hear going on? It sounds like bedlam – '

'My stepdaughter has just thrown a potted plant at her brother and the housekeeper is threatening to leave. The minute Jake and I stepped through the door she began telling us what a terrible time she'd had with the kids in our absence – '

'Exactly as I predicted,' said Shirley. 'You'd better offer her a rise if you want her to stay.'

In that respect, Laura, for whom money had always been a minor consideration, was due to learn what her mother never had.

Also to suffer her first doubt that living happily ever after would be the outcome of her marrying a widower with two teenage children. Who stopped scowling at each other and scowled at her, when she entered the living-room.

Laura's own child then set herself up as the family tell-tale. 'It was Jeremy who started it, Mummy, and Janis – '

'Shut up, you little sneak!' Jeremy cut her short. 'My sister doesn't need a baby elephant to defend her.'

Bessie ran to Laura. 'I'm not a baby elephant, am I, Mummy?'

But Laura had the wisdom not to cuddle and comfort her. It would seem like taking sides. Instead she said to Jeremy and Janis, 'Who started it doesn't matter. All I saw from the hall was Janis throw the plant at Jeremy. What is it all about?'

'Who started it *does* matter,' said Janis. 'Our mum believed in justice, didn't she, Jeremy? She was anti-apartheid like our dad.'

While Laura was trying to relate that to the situation in which she now found herself, the housekeeper, standing by tight-lipped, said, 'What those two kids need is a smack on the bum but it isn't my place to give it them. I'm going upstairs to pack my things.'

'Please don't, Doris,' Laura appealed to her.

'It's as good as done.'

The forthright Yorkshirewoman marched from the room. And if someone like Doris couldn't cope . . . thought Laura. But she'd got used to there being only Bessie, whom her no-nonsense manner had scared into submission from Day One.

Laura rushed after her. 'If you'll stay, though I've already given you a rise, I'll double your salary.'

Doris paused on the stairs and turned to give her a pitying glance. 'I'm more interested in keeping my sanity.'

She went on her way, sensible shoes clomping and blue nylon overall rustling. With her went Laura's hope of a stable beginning to her married life. It was all fine for Jake! He'd escaped to a business meeting. Now he was to be based in London, not Johannesburg, he had set up an office in Mayfair. Laura, though, worked from home and had not yet had time

73

today so much as to pop her head in her darkroom. The kids had begun squabbling at breakfast and so it had continued.

Was Jake going to make a habit of working on a Sunday? But since when did Laura think twice about doing so herself?

She returned to two teenagers with contrite expressions on their faces and a jubilant six-year-old.

'Hurrah!' Bessie was shouting. 'I shan't have to keep my room tidy any more. Agnes and Astrid and Isabella were lovely,' she listed Doris's predecessors, 'but Doris was very strict. She said I'd been neglected, Mummy, and it was time someone knocked me into shape.'

'Does that mean she smacked you?'

'No, she just used to say she'd like to.'

'Jeremy and I won't let anyone smack you,' said Janis. 'You're our little sister, now.'

'I'm happy to hear you say that,' said Laura.

'But it doesn't mean we like it,' Jeremy informed her.

Laura's heart sank.

'Are you going to make Janis and me pay for the damage?' the boy inquired.

The potted plant – a mother-in-law's tongue Laura's husband might think aptly named when he met Shirley – had been hurled complete with its china jardinière, now lying shattered on the parquet floor amid a pile of soil and a clump of spiky leaves.

Janis's slender shape belies her strength! thought Laura. 'There's a window pane broken, too!' she exclaimed, suddenly noticing it. 'How did *that* happen?'

'They were fighting, Mummy, and Jeremy's elbow went through it – '

'If this were South Africa,' said Jeremy, 'that kid would be a candidate for the Secret Police. Are you going to charge us for what we've done, or aren't you, Laura?'

She thought carefully. Trivial though on the surface it seemed, this was the first crisis in her new family life. Her hope was that in time Janis and Jeremy would come to love her. But first she must win their respect.

What would your mother have done? she wanted to ask them. But Laura couldn't wear a dead woman's shoes. All she could do was tread carefully in her own. Do her best for that woman's children.

She gave them a smile. 'Who do *you* think should pay for damage? Those responsible for it, or the innocent party? Which in this case is me. If justice really matters to you, it has to be applied to everything. Now help your big brother and sister clear up the mess on the floor, Bessie.'

'That wouldn't be justice, she didn't make the mess,' said Janis.

'But I *want* to help,' Bessie piped, already on her chubby knees beside the debris.

'Be careful not to cut your hands on the broken china,' Laura warned them too late. Bessie was solemnly showing her thumb to Janis and Jeremy.

'It isn't as bad as a snakebite,' was Jeremy's way of comforting her.

'But to be sure you don't get infected from the soil, we'll give it a suck anyway,' Janis said before doing so.

'It was me, not you, who sucked the poison out of Dad's snakebite when he took us camping,' Jeremy reminded his sister. 'Let me take over – '

'Why can't I suck my own thumb?' Bessie asked as he did so.

'Because you might not suck hard enough,' Janis patiently explained. 'If you tell me where you keep your first aid box, Laura, I'll fetch it.'

'I'll fetch it for you.'

Such was the family picture the threesome made, Laura had to get out of the room, lest her emotion was written on her face.

She hadn't known that Jake had been bitten by a snake. Nor could she envisage him going camping. By no stretch of the imagination was he the outdoor type. But he was the sort of father who would do anything for his kids' sake, the more so after their mum died. Though Jake had told Laura that his wife had suffered a lengthy illness, her mind had not then encompassed the full effects of that upon him and his children.

Now, she imagined Janis and Jeremy tiptoeing into their mother's sickroom when they came home from school. And Jake's taking them to visit her during her frequent spells in hospital, afterwards returning with them to a house that no longer resounded with Julia's laughter.

The children had said that their mother had laughed a lot. And that their family was known among friends as the Four Jays, on account of their all having names beginning with that letter.

When Laura first met Jake, at a cocktail party in Johannesburg, there was about him a sadness no longer there. Would he have invited her to dine with him if she hadn't remarked that his face was the kind she wouldn't mind photographing?

Probably not, she thought now. It was as though he had needed prodding from a trough of despondency in order to return her smile. Also as if he hadn't really looked at her until she made that remark.

'I'm not chatting you up, I'm a professional photographer,' she recalled saying.

'Then I'll make a bargain with you,' he had replied. 'I'll let you take my picture if you'll let me take you to dinner.'

Their relationship had proceeded from there. Blossomed described it better. But it had not included their sleeping together and Laura would have been surprised if it had. She was aware from the first that Jake was a conventional man. Nor had she failed to see the irony of his kindling in her heart what her long list of bedmates had notably *not* kindled.

Love was the word for it. And with love's entrance her belief that marriage was something she could well do without had made its exit. She could remember pitying Marianne the necessity to defer not just to Ralph, but to marriage itself, which had then seemed to her the proverbial ball-and-chain, serving to slow down the progress of an otherwise independent woman.

Only now was Laura able to see that sharing your life with

someone who cared deeply for you, and you for him, was a good deal more fulfilling than the freedom she had valued.

She returned to the living-room with the first aid box and the dustpan and brush, warmed by her thoughts, congratulating herself on her wise handling of her first family crisis. All would be well. She was still feeling her way with two kids she barely knew.

Come to that, what did she really know about Jake, other than that he'd been happily married for twenty years? Or he about her? A romance largely conducted over the phone, with the infrequent meetings its participants' working lives had allowed, was not conducive to their boring each other with the details of a now defunct past.

But what had gone before didn't matter. Only the present and future does, Laura said to herself. Jeremy and Janis sucking Bessie's cut thumb was the nearest they would come to a blood tie, she thought with a smile. But the concern Jake's kids had shown for Bessie augured well for the tie that Fate had imposed upon all three.

Laura's great-grandmother would have told her that she was wrong in one respect: That what had gone before *did* matter. But Sarah Sandberg had learned that the hard way and so it was to be for Laura.

Chapter Nine

As spring gave way to summer, Marianne's working day extended into the evening, which she had not allowed to happen when Ralph was alive.

Now, there seemed little point in her not returning to her desk after eating a snack while she watched the *Six O'Clock News*. Or was it that she was continuing to use her work as a therapy against loneliness? And how long could she go on not bothering to cook for one?

Though her mother and grandmother too were widowed in middle-age, and neither had remarried, both were of that sensible ilk of woman whom widowhood does not cause to neglect herself.

If they saw me in front of the TV set with a sandwich and calling it my dinner, the riot act would surely be read!

These were Marianne's wry thoughts when she returned to her typewriter on a sultry July evening. The first draft of her new book was almost completed, and if she didn't call a halt to her present régime the finished manuscript would be delivered long before deadline date.

She was promising herself that she would take tomorrow afternoon off to watch the Wimbledon Ladies' Final, when the phone shrilled beside her.

'Am I interrupting the author at work?' said her cousin Ronald.

Since the family had long thought her a 'workaholic', Marianne was accustomed to such remarks. But unlike his sister, Shirley, Ronald's tone was dry, not sarcastic.

'Yes, as a matter of fact,' she replied, 'but for you I don't mind.'

'I need to talk to you, Marianne.'

'Go ahead, I'm listening.'

'Not on the phone, if you don't mind. Could you spare me an hour if I drive over after surgery?'

'I'll have the kettle on when you get here.'

After she had rung off, a memory returned to Marianne of herself in a call box dialling her grandmother's number, when something or other had gone wrong in her young life. There were buses and lorries rumbling by as she made the call, so it must have been when the Kleins still lived behind the shop near to Salford docks, before a wartime bomb destroyed both home and business at one fell swoop, precipitating the family's departure for leafy Prestwich and the midst of Manchester's north side Jewish community. An empty shop nearby had enabled Ben Klein to continue trading, but had not included living accommodation.

Back with the phone call, Marianne could still see herself with dripping wet hair – it must have been raining – a red knitted muffler around her neck, and re-lived her relief when her gran picked up the receiver. Who but Sarah did the whole family, adults and children too, turn to for advice? The old lady had retained her faculties to the end, and if she were still alive it wouldn't be Marianne to whom Ronald would come after his surgery tonight.

She had not yet returned her attention to her work when the telephone rang again.

'Got a minute to spare, Marianne?'

'Sure, Uncle Nat.'

'When did you last visit Harry?' he said without preamble.

'If you rang up to prick my conscience – '

'That isn't the reason for my call.'

He had succeeded in doing so nevertheless. Though Marianne spoke regularly on the phone to Ann, three weeks had slipped by without her visiting her brother. Harry's rudeness to everyone and anyone was becoming hard to take.

Her uncle's next words confirmed it. 'Harry has just forbidden me to cross his doorstep again, and in my opinion Ann is heading for a breakdown.'

'She seemed fine when I last called her,' Marianne replied, 'and you don't have to take what Harry said seriously – '

'You're wrong on both counts, Marianne. Ann has become very good at bottling her feelings and sooner or later the cork will blow off. As for Harry – well, he's become an expert at manipulating both her and Howard. What I'm saying is, he uses their fear that crossing him will have dire results to get his own way. Since I'm not about to let him manipulate *me*, this evening I gave him a lecture which resulted in nothing more dire than his barring me from the house.'

'What had Ann to say about that?' Marianne inquired.

'That she isn't prepared to increase her anxiety by going against him and I had better stay away. But someone has to do something, Marianne, and I suggest it be you.'

With that, her uncle rang off. Did what he had been telling her account for his strained tone? Perhaps. But Uncle Nat also had troubles of his own. He had said recently that he wasn't getting on too well with Leona nowadays. Nor had Aunt Rebecca yet returned from Florida.

It was no secret that Leona had blamed her father for her mother's once turning to the bottle, Marianne reflected. Or that her childhood was far from ideal. And it looked now as though Aunt Rebecca's staying with her widowed sister might become a permanent arrangement. Leona was at present in Fort Lauderdale visiting her – and probably trying to persuade her to come home.

Marianne did not let herself contemplate what might transpire between Leona and her father if her mother said that she would never come back. Florida was a long way off and that would be for Leona tantamount to losing her mother at her father's hand.

As for what was going on at Harry's house . . . Marianne pitied Ann. Howard, too. Wasn't the separation from his child trouble enough?

Other than listen when he called her, there was nothing

that Marianne could do to help Howard. But she could and would offer to give Ann a break. Take over nursing Harry – teeth gritted! – for a few days, while Ann enjoyed some peace and quiet here in Marianne's cottage.

She can take walks and sit in the garden, it will be like a country holiday for her –

The sound of a car door slamming interrupted Marianne's planning. She watched Ronald walk up the path, noting how handsome he still was. As much like Uncle Nat in appearance as ever, and as silver haired nowadays. Ronald, though, had gone grey at an early age, Marianne recalled, and who could wonder? Their son, Alan, was a joy to Ronald and to his wife, Diane. But Sharon, their daughter, was born brain damaged. Diane had dedicated her life to caring for her to the exclusion of all else.

Marianne opened the door and received a hug.

'I got carried away by my thoughts and forgot to put the kettle on, Ronald – '

'A frequent occurrence, no doubt,' he said following her into the kitchen, 'and especially now Ralph isn't here to prod you. How are you doing in that respect, Marianne?'

She put the kettle on and unhooked a couple of mugs from the Welsh dresser. 'I don't give myself time to think about it.'

'Then may I, as a doctor, say it might be better if you did? Eventually you're going to have to, Marianne, and the sooner the healthier. Burying yourself in work is just putting off the moment when you finally come to terms with your loss and begin adjusting.'

'I'll bear that in mind, Ronald.'

'You do. And could you manage to rustle me up a snack? I didn't have time to eat before surgery.'

Marianne went to rummage in the refrigerator. How did you come to terms with losing not just your loving companion, but the rock to lean upon you hadn't appreciated until you lost him?

When they were seated at the table, Ronald munching

bread and cheese, and Marianne nibbling a biscuit, he said hesitantly, 'You're going to be upset by what I'm about to tell you, but I must. There are signs that Uncle Nat ought no longer to be practising medicine.'

Marianne was unable to hide her distress. 'Are you saying that he's cracking up?'

'If that's how you want to put it, I'm afraid so.'

But Marianne did not want to believe it. 'Couldn't you be mistaken, Ronald?'

'Since I'm in partnership with him, no. It isn't that he's making wrong diagnoses. For that he's able to rely on his long experience. But there have been a couple of instances of his prescriptions being questioned by the pharmacists the patients have taken them to – '

'Even young people make the odd mistake,' said Marianne.

'Uncle Nat didn't when he was young, nor did he until very recently. And a doctor making a mistake can be highly dangerous, Marianne. In the two cases I've cited, the patients were lucky. The pharmacists had been supplying their drugs for years and rang the surgery to check that the higher dosages were intentional.'

Marianne refilled their mugs with tea and sipped some of hers. 'Why are you discussing this with *me*?' she said after a pause. 'Oughtn't you to be talking about it to your other senior partner?'

'Lou knows about it, Marianne, but he isn't taking it seriously. He's Uncle Nat's age, remember, also his closest friend. He wouldn't *want* to take it seriously, would he?'

Marianne fetched a solitary Eccles cake from the old-fashioned larder that led off the kitchen. 'This is all I can offer you for dessert, Ronald.'

'I didn't come for a banquet.'

'Nor could you have come expecting me to provide a solution to your problem.'

Ronald bit into the cake and said after digging a currant from between his front teeth, 'I came to tell you how *I'm* going to solve it. I'm leaving the practice.'

82

'Couldn't that be equated with leaving a sinking ship, and with two elderly men you're fond of still aboard? And how would your departure help the patients?'

'Without me Uncle Nat and Lou will retire,' Ronald answered. 'They've always said that in that event they would.' He paused and glanced away, but Marianne had seen that there were tears in his eyes.

'I remember the day I joined them,' he said collecting himself. 'How honoured I felt that they'd invited me into the practice they'd shared since they were little more than lads. It wouldn't be putting it too strongly to say that I looked up to them, Marianne. And to Uncle Nat especially. No need to tell you that I'd never got on with my dad. And if I had to say which brother was more like a father to me, I'd say it was Uncle Nat.'

Marianne hoped her Uncle David hadn't known it, though he probably had. He had been a highly perceptive man.

'That doesn't mean I didn't love my dad,' Ronald added. 'And the way he died – well, I didn't get the chance to set things right. To tell him how much I admired his achievement even though I left it to my sister to be his right hand in the business.'

Our family hasn't gone short of people who left it too late to make their peace, thought Marianne.

'Returning to the gist of the matter,' said Ronald, 'I've decided to facilitate my elderly partners' retirement by making a real change in my own life. Diane's too. I wouldn't say she's really had a life, would you?'

Marianne shook her head.

When Sharon was little, Diane used to bring her to Sarah's Sabbath tea-parties, and there the child had lain on the parlour sofa, in a private world where none could reach her. Though Ronald had continued coming to the family gathering, bringing his son, Diane's accompanying him had suddenly ceased.

From then on Ronald had had to watch his wife become a near-recluse, and it seemed to Marianne now that only for funerals did Diane emerge from the imprisonment she had imposed upon herself.

'How will your leaving the practice help Diane?' she asked Ronald. She made herself smile. 'Not thinking of retiring yourself, are you? – and keeping her company all day.'

'On the contrary. I'm all set to begin a new career,' he replied. 'In New York, as a matter of fact, and Diane is going with me.'

'What about Sharon?'

'Sharon,' said Ronald gruffly, 'is now twenty-one. Her birthday was last month and Diane broke down and cried, which she hasn't done for years. I was choking with emotion myself. Alan had sent Sharon a birthday card. He never fails to. It was propped on the sideboard with one from Diane and me, and I had to stop myself from saying, "What a bloody farce!" Sharon wouldn't know a birthday card from her big toe . . .

'Diane asked me to cut the birthday cake, she always makes one for Sharon, but I didn't get around to it. We had to blow out the candles first, and when we'd done so I heard myself say, "There go twenty-one wasted years of our married life." It was then that Diane broke down. But instead of comforting her, I told her I couldn't go on watching her martyr herself to no purpose. Either she stopped it, or I was getting out.'

Ronald paused reflectively, fingering his tie. 'I didn't know I was going to say it, Marianne. It just came pouring out of me. I expected Diane to tell me to get the hell out. Instead – well, she said she hadn't realized what she was doing to me. I believe that, though you may not. You see the way it's been – as if nobody but Sharon existed for her. And I have to say that was very hard for Alan while he was growing up. He was only seven when Sharon was born, and when I think back – '

'It doesn't seem to have harmed him,' said Marianne, 'and I don't recall his ever being other than kind and gentle with his sister. You're blessed with a son who is right for the calling he's chosen, Ronald. Alan is equipped by nature to be a pastoral rabbi and his flock will be fortunate to have him.'

'I agree, and my hope is that one day the way he's turned out will be the consolation to his mother that it is to me. When we get to New York, Sharon will live where she will be well cared for. The trust fund my father-in-law set up for her will pay for it. As for the new career I mentioned, I'll be working with two of Diane's American relations who own a clinic.'

'I'll miss you, Ronald, but I couldn't be more pleased for you.'

'Thanks. But once Uncle Nat is retired – well, I want you to promise that you won't let him go to seed.'

Why me? she silently replied.

Chapter Ten

WHILE RONALD WAS PLANNING his move to New York, Leona was experiencing a slice of life in Florida which in some respects seemed to her more like a soap opera.

Well, not exactly experiencing, but observing, she thought while surveying her mother and wishing she had inherited Rebecca's dark colouring that allowed her to bask in the sun.

They had been on the patio all morning, Rebecca in a well-cut swimsuit, her long legs as trim as when she was young, Leona feeling frumpy and frowsty beside her – who wouldn't when they had to keep their arms and legs covered lest the ultra-violet rays do their worst to the sort of skin that goes with red hair?

Nor had Leona inherited her mother's stature. Like Marianne she was petite, as their grandmother had been, and as Leona's daughter was.

'You're looking very pensive, darling,' Rebecca said.

'I was thinking of how the genes that run in a family make their mark, one way and another, in each succeeding generation,' Leona summarized her thoughts.

'But I can't say there's much of *my* family's genes in you,' her mother replied.

'If you and Dad had had some more children, you might have had that pleasure,' Leona countered.

'Is that a rebuke because you have no brothers or sisters?' Rebecca took off her dark glasses and said without waiting for a reply, 'You'd better adjust that parasol, darling, or you'll go home with a red nose.'

While doing so, Leona said, 'I could hardly rebuke you for my being an only child, Mum, when my daughter is, too.'

Rebecca said after a pause, 'I imagined that you and Frank wanted more children but it just didn't happen – '

'But you never talked to me about it, did you?' Leona cut in. Oh the things that had gone unsaid between Leona and her mother, and this was the least of them.

A recollection rose before her of being advised by her grandmother to make her mum feel part of her own life. It was the day Leona found out that Rebecca was an alcoholic, and had gone to unburden her distress to Sarah. Leona would not forget the shock of seeing a bottle of gin hidden behind a pile of sweaters in her mother's wardrobe, when she was looking for a cardigan.

Rebecca was not at home. Leona had gone to the house to pick up her child whom Bridie's taking care of allowed her to pursue her career. Bridie, not my mother, she thought now – but when was the beautiful woman I'm looking at ever a real mother to me? It was Bridie, not she, who raised me and I didn't stop resenting it until I began pitying her and asking myself why.

Leona had taken Sarah's advice, tried to make her mum feel needed, found ways of occupying her time so it would not hang so heavily on her hands, and little by little Rebecca had overcome her addiction. Leona's asking herself the whys and wherefores, though, had reflected badly upon her father . . .

'Since you didn't ask me, I didn't tell you, Mum, that Carla's being an only child was my decision and Frank went along with it. Our neighbourhood law practice seemed more important than increasing our family and it needed both of us.' Leona smiled wryly. 'Twenty years ago we were imbued with an idealism it's been hard to sustain.'

'And how you can go on working in that district – with what Moss Side now is – !' said Rebecca. 'Have there been any repetitions of Frank getting punched up?'

'That sort of thing goes with the territory and, believe it or not, makes our work the more rewarding. Our reputation is such that we're preferred to black lawyers and that's rare in the current climate. As for what Moss Side now is — well, it's just a different kind of ghetto from the one the Sandbergs sprang from.'

'Hardly, darling!'

'What do you mean, "hardly"? For those Jews prepared to admit it, it's a parallel situation, including the poverty and the humiliation. The blacks are struggling for acceptance just like we had to. Uncle David once told me he used to get stones thrown at him on his way home from school, when the family lived in Strangeways, and in a house you and I would call a hovel, may I remind you. He also said he once took Laura to see it, to take her down a peg or two. It's a pity he didn't give Shirley the same treatment!'

'Thankfully, those days are over,' said Rebecca while applying Ambre Solaire to her gleaming shoulders.

'But they're not for the blacks and Asians,' Leona replied, covering her ankles with a towel. It was far too hot to wear socks. 'Even for those who've achieved material and educational equality,' she went on, 'the real struggle is still going on. And by the way, Mum, when are you coming home?'

'I was wondering when you'd get around to asking.'

Again something had gone unsaid: *It was why you came, wasn't it?*

Since directness between herself and her mother was on a personal level no more possible now than it had ever been, Leona kept her tone light and answered, 'We've barely had a minute alone, have we? What with all the socializing!'

Only by pleading a headache had Leona escaped yet another luncheon party given by one of the wealthy widows with whom her aunt passed the time.

All of whom were on the lookout for a man, Leona reflected, casting her mind back to the party given by Auntie Ray's best friend in a poolside setting similar to that in which Leona and her mum were now lounging . . .

Exotic described it. Palm trees and luxuriant bushes, the tiles surrounding the pool, as on the patio, pastel pink, the water a mirror for the brilliant, Florida sky, and a buffet resplendent with salads as colourful as the ambience.

Leona's first impression was that she had never before encountered so youthful a gathering of elderly ladies. Was it the Florida air? No, the answer was a face lift – which her aunt had confessed to when Leona remarked that she hadn't aged since her last visit to England, years ago.

But it wasn't just their appearance, Leona had registered. It was something they exuded.

When a man entered the action – Leona could think of no more accurate way of putting it – she had realized what the 'something' was. They hadn't given up hope. And good luck to them!

A lady named Nettie had brought him along and Leona recalled his immediately casting an eye over the buffet.

'Oh my, isn't that a picture!' the tubby little chap said to the hostess. 'Nettie told me there would be a spread, Ruby, but I sure didn't expect a banquet!'

Nettie patted her blonde coiffure, before linking his arm to establish ownership. 'Ruby always uses the best caterer in town, Al. Me, I prefer to prepare the food with my own hands, even if I'm up all night – '

'Which you look like you were,' said Ruby sweetly, 'and which caterer but the best *would* I use? What is money for, like my poor husband used to say.'

'But me, I'm not extravagant,' Nettie informed Al, and Leona wondered if he was making a mental note of that, to file with a list of pros and cons attached to the women available to share his remaining years.

Listening to the exchange between Nettie and Ruby, Leona had noted the competitiveness. But how lovely for the men, so evidently in short supply, she reflected as an elderly gentleman clad in a garish shirt and white trousers, a bright blue peaked cap on his head, arrived alone and was introduced to Leona and her mother.

'If you English ladies ever get to Delaware, be sure to look up my daughter,' he said, removing his cap to mop the sweat off his bald head. 'And I have to tell you I am never going to get accustomed to the year-round heat here!'

After he had proudly displayed some snapshots of his daughter and his grandchildren, Leona said, 'If the climate doesn't suit you, Mr Pitkin, why do you live here?'

'A good question, young lady! But to retire to Florida is what I worked for all my life. And what's to go home for?' he added with a shrug.

This seemed at odds with his demeanour when he showed the snapshots. And why was Leona's mum now avoiding her eye? Had Mr Pitkin taken the words from Rebecca's mouth? No, the thought from her head, since she would never voice it.

Leona took a cocktail from the tray with which a waiter was circulating and felt like downing it instead of sipping it, such was her hurt.

'Not for me, thank you,' Rebecca said to the waiter.

'With my blood pressure, me neither,' said Mr Pitkin.

Leona saw him look her mother over and like what he saw. But why wouldn't he? Rebecca, though she alone among the women here had done nothing to disguise her age, was, with her natural elegance, the most striking female present, from which Leona did not exclude herself and she an attractive redhead still in her forties.

My mother's simple, beige outfit makes Auntie Ray and her pals look overdressed, thought Leona. And the hostess' face lift made her something of a travesty, given her dowager's hump.

'So you and me, we have something in common. Neither of us drinks,' Mr Pitkin was saying with a smile to Rebecca. 'How are you enjoying your vacation?'

'I've always been a sun-worshipper, Mr Pitkin.'

'Call me Joe.'

'My elder brother's name is Joe.'

'And I have a sister named Rebecca! How's that for coincidence?'

The rapport the two seemed to be establishing impelled

Leona to inform Mr Pitkin – and remind her mother – of her father's existence.

'My dad loves the sun, too,' she said conversationally, 'but he couldn't come with Mum to visit her sister. He's a busy doctor.'

Mr Pitkin looked as if he was thinking, Why are the ones I fancy never available? 'And I guess your dad is missing your mom,' he said, allowing himself to add, 'I sure would if I were him.'

The Mr Pitkin incident was ten days ago and while Leona was remembering it, her mother had got up to take a swim. Nor had she yet answered the question Leona had come to ask. Instead, she had let it hang in the air and it occurred to Leona that she was perhaps putting off the moment.

Rebecca had swum to the opposite side of the pool and was now seated chatting to some of the women for whom, like Leona's aunt, it was a facility that went with living in one of these expensive apartments.

How easily my mum has adjusted to this lifestyle, Leona reflected. To the daily dips in the pool, and the non-stop socializing – as if its participants were determined to enjoy every minute of the time left to them – the morning shopping before the day grew too hot, the elaborate luncheons, and in the evenings a game of bridge in someone's air-conditioned living-room.

Leona had found herself marvelling at the energy Auntie Ray and her friends managed to muster at their age. But was it perhaps the energy of desperation? As though if they let themselves wind down they'd be out of the race against time.

A conclusion that led Leona to wonder if deep inside themselves they truly enjoyed an artificial Indian summer in the autumn of their lives. If most wouldn't prefer carpet slippers and TV if they had someone with whom to *share* their lives. As for the dearth of men – well, only one conclusion could be drawn.

Leona didn't know if Mr Pitkin's wife had lived to retire here with him. But his outliving her made him a rare specimen in this setting. What the women in Auntie Ray's circle were enjoying, *if* they were, were the fruits of their dead husbands' lifelong labours. And some had seemed to Leona the sort whose acquisitiveness had spurred on their men to a too-early grave.

In retrospect, that probably included Auntie Ray, whose husband was a lovely man. The kind who did card tricks for kids and gave them sweets when their parents weren't looking.

Leona could remember too her aunt having three fur coats. And Uncle Murray arriving home from work dead beat, when Leona and her mother were staying with them. Also her being awed by their vast drawing-room and the grand piano that nobody ever played.

Leona's annual trips to London with her mum had been the highlights of the year. Not just because she was taken by Uncle Murray to see the sights. Those were the only times her mother had seemed relaxed and happy.

Not until she grew older had Leona realized that her mother had never stopped being homesick. Marriage had transplanted Rebecca when she was still a young girl from London to Manchester. Away from her own family and into the midst of a down-to-earth provincial clan, among whom she must have felt swamped, to put it mildly.

But if Dad had loved her, that wouldn't have mattered, Leona thought now. Mum would eventually have found her niche. Why had Leona always had the feeling that her mother had once loved her father, but had stopped loving him when she realized he didn't love her?

Could love be switched off? Well, not in Leona's case or she wouldn't still be in love with the wrong twin.

She blotted out Henry Moritz's too-charming smile and replaced it with Frank's bespectacled countenance. Was she to be cursed with so wayward a heart to the end of her days?

She emerged from her thoughts and saw her aunt approaching, clickety-clack on the high heels she always wore. When

I'm her age, I'll settle for sensible shoes, Leona thought, noting the puffiness of Ray's ankles.

Ray sat down on the sunbed Rebecca had vacated, lowering herself gingerly and careful not to crease her skirt.

'You missed a lovely party, Leona. And so did your mother on your account, which I perfectly understand, dear. Rebecca wants to make the most of your stay. That nice Mr Pitkin was there and sent his regards to you both.'

Oh yes? 'How long have you lived in Florida, Auntie? I seem to've lost count.'

'I guess it has to be going on ten years, dear. And poor Uncle Murray's been gone for eight of them. If I'd had children and grandchildren, I might not have stayed here. And I can't tell you how much your mother misses you and her granddaughter, whose wedding it broke my heart not to be at.

'If I hadn't gone down with that terrible flu bug Ruby's daughter brought with her from Chicago . . .'

While her aunt went on bewailing her absence from Carla's wedding, Leona was thinking, If my mum really missed me she'd come home.

'My sister is looking a lot better than when she arrived,' Ray said.

Leona glanced across the pool to where Rebecca was laughing at whatever the scrawny woman in the red bikini had just said.

'I'd go so far as to say Rebecca is now a different person,' her aunt added. 'And I'd like her to stay that way.'

'But she's my mother and I want her to come home,' Leona replied.

'Oh my goodness – hasn't she told you yet, dear?'

'Told me what?' But Leona had no need to ask.

Chapter Eleven

ON THE DAY Leona returned from Florida, Howard boarded a plane for Munich. Given their missions, it seemed to Marianne as though two more strands, grey in hue, were now woven into the family tapestry.

Leona had called her immediately, to convey her unhappy news. Marianne had just replaced the receiver when Howard rang up from the airport to ask her to stay in close touch with his mother while he was away.

Howard's conflicting emotions accompanied him on the flight: the filial responsibility he was briefly leaving behind, and the painful pleasure ahead. It was some weeks since he had visited Ben. Could talking to a young child on the phone maintain the bond between them?

Howard doubted it. Like it or not, time and distance could not but diminish his chance of having a real father-son relationship with Ben when he grew up. Love was a vital component of that relationship and Howard's for Ben was guaranteed until the day he died. But the other way round? Well – would Howard now be letting his sick father metaphorically walk all over him if Harry hadn't been a pillar of his childhood and youth? And how was Howard to be that to his son with Ben living in Germany and he in England?

Closing his eyes as weariness overcame him, he allowed himself to re-live the nightmare of his father's changing from the kindly man he really was to the unpleasant person illness had made him.

Harry had by now progressed to the wheelchair included in the consultant's prognosis and had ordered that all the doors in the house be widened. It was no longer possible for Ann to have a moment's peace, since he was able to follow her while she went about her household tasks downstairs, and positioned himself in the hall to shout to and at her when she went upstairs.

It was Howard's daily task to carry his father from his bedroom to his chair, a reminder of how frail in all but spirit Harry now was, and the latter concentrated in his tongue. Frank, who performed that task when Howard went to Munich, had found himself being castigated no less than was Howard.

Only the family would put up with it – and Uncle Nat hadn't – Howard was thinking when the girl seated beside him plucked his sleeve.

'Excuse me, but the stewardess has put on your table your lunch.'

He mustered a smile and thanked her for telling him. 'I was immersed in my thoughts.'

'And I hesitating before disturbing you. I saw that your eyes were closed and thought perhaps that you preferred the nap to the food. Like the man sitting beside me on a flight from Berlin to London, who was not pleased when I wakened him!'

Howard turned to look at her and could not but be charmed by what he saw. Grey-green eyes with a humorous glint in them, a retroussé nose enhancing her pert appearance, milky skin made to seem the more so by her sleek black hair. Nothing wrong with her shape, either, he noted before giving his attention to his meal.

Did the thoughts he'd just had mean he was getting over Christina? No. The ache was still there. At first it had been like a knife cutting into him, but gradually its edge had dulled. His senses too, because this was the first time since Christina left him that he'd looked twice at another woman.

You only looked once, Howard! But that was enough to tell him he was still alive. Emerging from the despondency that had entombed him.

He buttered a bread roll and looked at the girl again. 'Do you live in Munich?'

'I am at present spending some time there,' she replied, 'but my home is in Berlin. You are going to Munich on business?'

'No. I'm visiting my little boy.'

'I see.'

'I married a German girl and – well, things went wrong,' he felt constrained to add.

A pause followed, then she gave him a sympathetic smile. 'When a marriage breaks down and there are children, it is more hard for the man. Usually he is separated from them, too.'

'I didn't try to get my child's custody,' Howard told her. 'Living with his mother is best for him.'

'That was not my ex-husband's attitude,' the girl revealed. 'Once, he kidnapped from me my son and my daughter.'

'That couldn't have been pleasant for them.'

'He does not do that sort of thing any more, and we are now quite civilized with each other and he has remarried.'

'You haven't?'

She shook her head. 'I have time only for my children and my work.'

'Which I gather takes you away from home. Who looks after them when you're away?' Howard inquired.

'I am blessed with a wonderful mother. It is with my parents that I and my children live. Their father he sees them as often as his new wife will allow.'

Howard found himself telling her that his divorce was not yet finalized, and of his father's illness that was making it increasingly difficult for him to visit Ben.

'I am truly sorry for you,' she said when he had finished speaking.

'I'm feeling pretty sorry for myself! But I oughtn't to be boring a total stranger with my problems – '

'I am not in the least bored,' she answered, 'and we must

complete our eating, or the trays will shortly be snatched from us.'

'You're obviously a more experienced traveller than me,' Howard remarked, while they ate.

'Our family business is to manufacture optical lenses and that is worldwide trade. May I ask what you do?'

'The same as you. Work in our family business. It's a retail store.'

'You do not go abroad for the buying?'

Howard's wanting to do so had always been a bone of contention between him and his father. 'No, we buy from the sales reps who come to us.'

'And what are the goods that you sell?'

Was she a Nosey Parker? Or interested in Howard?

She dabbed a blob of chocolate mousse from her lips and gave him a smile that encouraged him to believe the latter.

'Curtains and bedlinen, tablecloths and towels,' he replied. 'That sort of thing has been big business since the British discovered decor and the duvet, though we're still suffering the effects of unemployment, like everyone else. When the recession was at its worst, I recalled my late grandfather telling me when I was a kid that before the war he'd sold men's socks for twopence-ha'penny a pair, and wished we could cut our prices down to the bone. In my granddad's time they sold clothing, as well.'

It was as a cut-price store that the business was established, its profits accrued via turnover. Begun by Ben Klein in the thirties on a shoestring, Howard reflected. And later carried forward by Harry to the substantial concern it now was.

'Our business too was founded by my grandfather,' the girl told him, 'but when Hitler came to power . . .'

She paused while the stewardess poured their coffee and said after sipping hers, 'You are Jewish, like me, are you not?'

But it hadn't occurred to Howard that *she* was.

'So you will understand that for my parents to return to Germany it was not easy,' she went on. 'Their own parents,

97

they had died in the camps. Needless to say, somehow they survived or I would not be here. And how I knew you are Jewish was the Star of David engraved upon your ring.'

'My sister, who lives in Israel, gave it to me.'

'I have my brother living there. He is an army officer and my mother, she worries about him all the time.'

A brief hiatus followed while their trays were whisked away though they were allowed to keep their coffee cups.

Then Howard took advantage of his first encounter with one of Germany's post-war Jewish community to ask a question related to his son.

'What is it like for you and your children, living where you do?'

'Most of the time I don't think about it,' the girl replied, 'but I would not call it a happy situation. The Nazi graffiti has, as perhaps you know, begun appearing here and there, as my parents say it did in their youth. The difference between now and then is that the authorities remove it. And my children, they experience no more anti-Semitism at school than I myself did.'

'I experienced some in my schooldays in England,' Howard told her.

'And I have heard that in your country also are the neo-Nazi groups. But there cannot be for you there the dimension attached to it for Jews in Germany,' she said quietly. 'For my parents what they sometimes see on a wall in Berlin, it must surely freeze their blood. For myself there is an uneasiness that has always been with me.'

'Would you mind telling me why your parents returned?'

She gave him another smile, her expression wry. 'I am aware that to the rest of Jewry our community it is an enigma.'

Howard would have called it a phenomenon.

'I cannot speak for others,' she went on, 'but I would guarantee that all had very personal reasons. As for my parents, they were living first in what was then Palestine, to where they had gone after the camps. It was there that they met and married. Then one night, my father dreamt of his own father and the next morning told my mother of his intention to return to Berlin. In the dream, his father had told him that there being no Jews in Germany was letting Hitler win.'

'That's an amazing story,' said Howard.

'But true nevertheless,' said the girl, 'and it ensured that their children would be born and raised in Germany, for which my brother has not forgiven them. Since returning, my father, he has fulfilled my grandfather's ambition disrupted by the Nazis, that the Schulmann Optics Company continue from generation to generation of our family. My father would have wished it to pass to my brother, but will have to make do with me. My name is Karin Schulmann and I should like to know with whom I am having this conversation!'

Howard introduced himself and they shook hands.

'You know about the Jewish Community Centre in Munich?' Karin asked.

Howard shook his head. 'My wife isn't Jewish.'

'Nor,' said Karin, 'is the man I married. You and I we have much in common, do we not?'

Howard then invited her to dine with him that evening at the Hotel Bayerischer Hof, where he habitually stayed and ate in solitary splendour.

She said when she had accepted, 'If we are to eat in the restaurant, I shall have to dress up!'

'Would I take you to the beer keller place downstairs for *Bratwurst mit Sauerkraut*, on our first date!'

Thus it was that Howard's further entanglement with Germany began.

Chapter Twelve

IN THE WEEKS that followed Ronald's visit, family matters continued to dominate Marianne's life.

Her lecturing Harry on the subject of Ann's devotion and his tyranny had resulted in a shouting match from which Harry had emerged victorious by feigning a pain in his head. Nor was Ann willing or able to accept Marianne's offer to relieve her while she took a break. Harry had informed her that he would be dead when she came back.

The next crisis was Nathan's learning that Ronald, whom he looked upon as a son, was not just leaving the practice but in effect departing from his life. Bridie had called Marianne to ask her, in Leona's absence, to come and comfort her uncle, who had taken to his bed.

Again Marianne had thought, Why me? She had nevertheless driven post haste to Nathan's home, but was not allowed to enter his room.

The news with which Leona had returned from Florida had seemed the final straw. Though his marriage was but a sham, how would Uncle Nat's dignity withstand his wife's deserting him in his old age? He was well known in the community and it would not take too long for the grapevine to do its worst. Added to which the support he might have expected from his daughter had not been forthcoming.

I'm no Sarah Sandberg, nor did I ever pretend to be, Marianne thought, blessed with unlimited patience, the wisdom of Solomon, and a selfless devotion to anyone and everyone in the family.

Sarah would have sorted Harry out in two seconds flat.

Nathan and Leona, too. Somehow she had always found a way of dealing with people.

Marianne's inclination right now was to tell the family to go to hell and let her get on with her work, which between crises she had tried and failed to do.

These were her ruminations on a wet August morning when she had sat staring at the blank paper in her typewriter trying to summon the inspiration that once had come naturally. Had she lost her creative impetus? Would this have gone on for weeks if it were just a bout of writer's block?

Outside the study window the elm tree was tinged with the hue that bespoke an early autumn. The geraniums in the flower bed looked bedraggled from the heavy rain. And the weather matched Marianne's mood.

She dialled her son's number and interrupted *his* work.

'What is it, Mum?' he asked in the crisp tone she herself employed when her concentration was disrupted by a phone call. 'Can I get back to you?'

'No, Martin. I need to talk to you now. The family is coming between me and the book I'm writing, to the point where I've completely dried up. Has that ever happened to you?'

'Frequently! But I'm sure it's a new experience for *you*. I'm not surprised it's happened to you now, though. I saw it coming.'

'Been keeping an eye on me from the distance, have you!'

'And now Dad's gone, I'd much prefer to do so at close quarters.'

It was a moving moment for Marianne. Despite his heavy work schedule and his problems with his wife, her son was concerned for her.

'Which I shall soon be able to do,' he went on. 'There's only one answer to your situation vis-à-vis the family and I intend to see that you put it into practice. You must remove yourself from where most of the action is. Sell the cottage and come back to London.'

PART TWO

1985 . . .

Chapter One

BY THE SPRING OF 1985, the Soviet Union had a new leader whose emergence lent hope to the world, and Marianne had made a trip to Moscow and Leningrad to meet some of her Jewish brethren, for whom oppression remained their lot.

She had returned thinking, There but for the grace of God go I, as she had when she visited the Holocaust Museum in Jerusalem and saw the pictorial evidence of what she had escaped.

Since taking her son's advice she had resumed the travel, which, before Ralph's death, had punctuated her lengthy stints at the typewriter, necessary not just to revitalize her, but to add depth and colour to her novels.

The book she had feared she was unable to write was published the previous year. And in some respects it was for her as if she had never left London.

Her former home in Hampstead was up for sale when she decided to return south and she had bought it without thinking twice, its availability as though Fate had intended her to live out her years alone in the flat in which she and Ralph had spent the bulk of their married life.

In her bleak moments there was the comfort of having Martin – Laura too – a stone's throw away. Also the stimulation of imbibing once again the lively atmosphere of Hampstead Village, where the famous rubbed shoulders with arty young people and a motley of tourists. There was too the pleasure of walking on the Heath, where once she had walked on Sunday afternoons with Ralph.

Now there was only his memory to keep her company. Increasingly Marianne's personal solitude was making itself felt. How had her mother and her grandmother dealt with it? Both had had what they had referred to as 'chances'. Marianne, too. In her working world she encountered interesting men and had dated several. Jake had introduced her to a fellow South African on the lookout for a second wife, which Marianne had not known until Laura whispered the information to her in the restaurant where Jake's matchmaking exercise took place.

His friend had proved to be attractive and personable. But Marianne had yet to meet the man for whom she would renounce the independence she would not have chosen, but valued now that she had it.

With Ralph she had not minded the disadvantages of sharing one's life with another. But they had met and fallen in love when they were young, feeling their way together along a sometimes rocky path, and still friends and lovers when they reached their fifties.

Nowadays, though, Marianne reflected wryly, a relationship did not have to include marriage and the loss of independence that went with it. Even the middle-aged and some of the elderly had accepted for themselves the behaviour patterns that had horrified them when their children and grandchildren began thumbing their noses at convention.

Shirley had had at least two resident boyfriends, no doubt with marriage in mind though it had not come to that. And Uncle Nat had recently found himself a girlfriend two years his senior, with whom he had spent a holiday in Majorca which Leona suspected had included their sharing a room. There would be no shenanigans in his house, though, lest Bridie walk out on him!

Marianne smiled at the thought of two septuagenarians enjoying what would once have been called an illicit love affair. Bend with the wind of change though she had, what would Sarah Sandberg have had to say about that!

She put the cover on her typewriter, at which she was seated musing after completing a difficult chapter, and went to remove a wilted leaf from the Busy Lizzie that lived in the window bay, behind the old leather Chesterfield where she sometimes sat to do her thinking.

Both the plant and the sofa had travelled north with her and back again to this spacious study overlooking the garden. And the bookshelves Ralph had built for her were still there to greet her on her return, albeit painted black by the erstwhile occupiers, to enhance the emerald green they had imposed upon the walls.

A little time and a lot of money had restored the flat to its former ambience, and soon restored too was the rhythm of Marianne's work.

But while I've been pounding my typewriter, family history has gone on writing itself, she reflected while giving her plants a drink of water from the copper can she kept topped-up because Busy Lizzie and African Violet preferred it to be room temperature. She had once lost one of Violet's sisters after thoughtlessly holding her under the tap. Next day, the plant was wilted as if in protest, never to recover.

Begonia and Ivy, though, seemed not to mind about temperature so long as they got their drink. Marianne's habit of humanizing her plants was a family joke. And back with what had gone on in the family since her return to London . . . Well, Marianne Dean was not short of material should she ever try her hand at writing a family saga.

But which author would fictionalize the skeletons in their own cupboard? You took your themes from life overall as you observed it, though an understanding of human nature came in handy when you found your characters behaving on paper as you hadn't planned that they would. When a nasty character suddenly performed an act of kindness, you knew that you had created a true to life person. Nobody was all bad, nor, conversely, all good. And there had to be a reason for the unpleasantness some people habitually displayed, buried deep in their pasts perhaps.

In Harry's case, though, illness accounted for it. His body had let him down, and he was consumed by an inner rage and making others pay for it. Now that Marianne no longer saw him frequently, she was able to put into perspective a situation which had puzzled her when she was on the receiving end.

A situation which time would do nothing to alleviate, as it had for Uncle Nat. Her uncle was now relishing a freedom to be himself formerly denied him. He had not wanted to be a doctor, but obligation imposed upon him by his family had shackled him to that profession. Nor had he wanted the marriage his mother and brother had viewed as a foolproof way of smoothing his path.

Time had proved it the opposite of foolproof, and was there, thought Marianne, any such thing? Even those who set out with goodwill, which her uncle had not, were liable to encounter unforeseen hurdles along the way.

Uncle Nat was a good and respected physician, but his compassion and his clever mind had ensured that, not the vocational calling that had led his friend, Lou, and his nephew Ronald to study medicine. Uncle Nat had hoped to read the classics, and Marianne's mother had told her that his teachers at the Manchester Grammar School had considered him Oxbridge material.

No, my mum wouldn't have put it that way, Marianne thought reminiscently. What did Esther Klein know from that composite word and the dreaming spires it conjured up?

A more prosaic woman than Esther would, even in *her* day, have been hard to find. The conversation Marianne was recalling had taken place in her mother's kitchen and she could still see her mum, immaculate as always, though she had been cooking all morning and was then frying fishballs, carefully turning them in the pan of sizzling oil.

Even when she grew old, Esther had continued taking pride in her appearance. A streak of vanity at odds with her personality, Marianne the author thought objectively. Marianne the daughter found that her eyes had misted with the remembrance.

She left her study and went to take a shower, her mind still engaged by family matters – perhaps because this was the Passover Eve and she had still not accustomed herself to celebrating the festival minus those whose presence had dominated the family Seder tables of the past.

Her Uncle David was notable among them, his glasses slipping down his nose as he read aloud from the Haggadah, and woe betide the child who allowed his or her attention to wander! Time was when Marianne's grandfather, Abraham Sandberg, had conducted the proceedings, his shoulders stooped from his early-immigrant years in a sweatshop, the foul air and the steam from the pressing iron he had wielded responsible for the diseased lungs that had precipitated his end.

In her swish 1980s bathroom, it was hard for Marianne to believe that from such penurious beginnings the comfortably off clan of which she was part had sprung. And with each succeeding generation, it would be the more difficult – if the beneficiaries of their forebears' blood, sweat and tears bothered to think about it, which Marianne doubted. Few had granddads like David, whose taking Laura to see the 'ancestral home' in the old Strangeways ghetto had shaken her rigid and done a lot for her character.

With Abraham Sandberg's death, his mantle had fallen upon David's shoulders, and how strange it had at first seemed to see Uncle David seated in Abraham's chair at the head of the big table in Sarah's dining-room.

Sarah's response to Marianne's communicating that feeling to her was a gentle reproof, and that cameo from the past too now returned to her – herself, a young mother, nursing her baby. And Sarah wearing a grey dress with a white collar to which the little Russian brooch was pinned.

'I'm surprised at you, Marianne,' she had said. 'How can a girl with your intelligence find it strange that a son takes over where his father left off? It's how God arranges things, and what is that child in your arms if not proof of how He arranges the going and coming so a family shouldn't die out? You were pregnant when your grandfather was taken from us, weren't you?'

Not that Sarah had required proof to bolster her faith in God, Marianne thought as the memory receded and another replaced it – of a long gone Seder night when she had seen her Uncle Nat bite back a retort after Aunt Rebecca said something to goad him. Oft were the times, too, when Rebecca had pointedly ignored Nathan at family gatherings. But Marianne, though she had conjectured as to the hell their private life must be, had never seen her uncle less than polite to his wife.

It would be he who conducted the Seder in Manchester tonight, with the old-fashioned courtliness that went with his distinguished appearance. Courtliness, though, was just an acquired veneer, Marianne cogitated while lathering her shoulders in the shower, and not in every case did it live side by side with the integrity that had impelled Nathan to maintain his marital obligations to the last.

Marianne's affection for him had not prohibited her from feeling sorry also for Rebecca. It was not in Nathan's nature ever to have walked out on her. But why had it taken her the major part of her life to put an end to their miserable existence together?

Possibly her long interlude in Florida had served to restore her bruised spirit. The man she had met there could not but have helped rebuild her ego, since she was now Mrs Pitkin. And Nathan now reading English Literature at Manchester University, at the age of seventy-four.

So much for Ronald's asking me not to let Uncle Nat go to seed! thought Marianne, though for a while it had looked as though he might. A further blow, the death of his friend Lou, had followed Ronald's departure to the States. But after his divorce he had miraculously put himself back together. As though that final severing with the past had released the man he had always known himself to be.

While drying her hair Marianne envisaged the other women in the family making themselves presentable for Seder night, as she was. Dressing in your best was part of the tradition, along with the eating of the symbolic bitter herbs and hard-boiled eggs. Ann had probably been cooking all day, with Harry breathing down her neck from his wheelchair, and Marianne hoped there would not be fireworks of the emotional kind when the Mancunian branch of the family gathered at their house for the Seder.

Ann's asking Uncle Nat to bring his girlfriend would not go down well with Leona. Nor would Harry take kindly to Nathan's presence, though he now permitted him the occasional visit.

Marianne could not rid herself of the feeling that her agreement to Laura's suggestion that they stop going north for the festivals was committing family treason. But another feeling went with it. Relief. When the whole clan got together, the atmosphere could be likened to being sealed in a pressure cooker waiting for the lid to blow off, which it frequently did.

Not that the coming together of those of us who live in London can be guaranteed to go smoothly, she thought while pinning Sarah's brooch to her red silk blouse. And Marianne's *bête noire* would be present tonight! Shirley was spending the Passover with her daughter.

Chapter Two

'I THOUGHT, once Hitler was beaten, we could put what he stood for behind us,' Shirley was bemoaning when Marianne entered the living-room.

Laura, beside her by the fireplace, replied, 'But we've learned otherwise. Nor is it just the Fascists we now have to contend with.'

Laura kissed Marianne. 'Sorry about the delay in greeting you. What you came in at the end of was Mum's reaction to hearing that Jake and Martin are on duty outside the synagogue during this evening's service.'

Bessie, resplendent in royal blue velvet, was hovering beside the table, the dish of bitter herbs in her hands. 'I'm not sure where to put this, Mummy.'

'Since Daddy will be conducting the Seder, darling, try to find space for it beside his place.'

'Can I move the salt and pepper pots?'

'If you have to.'

'This reminds me of when we were little and our grand-mother let us lay the Seder table,' Marianne reminisced to Shirley.

'My own recollection of that,' said Shirley, 'is your trying to tell me where everything should be placed.'

'But I wouldn't have got away with it, would I?' Marianne's attempts to chat with Shirley invariably got no further than one sentence.

'If anyone who shouldn't tries to get into the synagogue with Daddy and Martin on duty, I wish them luck!' said Bessie to Laura.

Shirley exclaimed, 'It isn't right for a child of nine to know about such things!'

'Jewish kids in the eighties could hardly not know,' Laura answered, 'since their kindergartens and Hebrew classes now have to be protected. If you read the news in your *Jewish Gazette*, Mum, as well as the personal column, you'd know that there's been no shortage of incidents in the first half of this decade. When someone put a bomb outside the Chief Rabbi of Austria's flat in the summer of '82, I thought back to us discussing the neo-Nazis at Uncle Nat's, the day of the window consecration.'

'Your mother isn't the ignoramus you seem to think!' Shirley flashed. 'I could have told you that day that there'd already been an attack on a Vienna synagogue, and two Jews killed. The paper I read said it was done by Arab terrorists – '

'Why *didn't* you tell us, Granny?' Bessie asked.

'Because I'm not one for political discussions, sweetheart, I never was. It's bad enough that these things are happening. We don't have to talk about them and especially not in front of you.'

'For heaven's sake, Mum!' Laura expostulated. 'One of Bessie's little friends lives in Edgware, where some Jewish kids had bottles thrown at them a few months ago. She also goes to school with a child whose big brother is at Preston Polytechnic, and he didn't keep it a secret from his kid sister when swastikas were daubed on a college Jewish Society poster.

'I can't raise Bessie in a vacuum,' Laura went on. 'She has to live in the real world.'

'And I have to say,' Marianne added, 'that I myself was sickened when I drove past Chalk Farm tube station one day last autumn, and saw painted on a wall: "Hitler is right." '

Bessie was listening with interest. 'But Hitler is dead now, isn't he?'

'Unfortunately,' said her mother, 'his ideas seem to have lived on.'

'There you go again, upsetting the child!' said Shirley.

'Didn't you hear what I said to you, Mum? She has to live in the real world.'

'But there's no need to spell everything out for her.'

'If Jake were here, I'd let him deal with you, Mum!'

'My daughter is no longer her own person,' Shirley said to the air.

'My marriage is a partnership,' Laura informed her. 'Jake has raised two smashing kids and I trust his judgement. Would you say you made a good job of raising me? Ask yourself why I finally ran away from home, which Bessie will never feel impelled to do.'

'Is there nothing you intend keeping from that child!' Shirley marched from the room.

'Before you run after her, Bessie,' said Laura, 'move the herb dish a little closer to where Daddy will sit. He has long arms, but I think you've put it where even he would have a job to reach it without getting up from his chair!'

They watched the little girl do as she was bid and hastily depart.

'Bessie is our family comforter,' Laura said dryly. 'When anyone is upset, or angry, she rushes to kiss and cuddle them.'

'If your mother lived with you,' Marianne responded, 'Bessie would be kept extremely busy! But I do wish you wouldn't have a go at your mum in my presence, Laura.'

'Since when were you easily embarrassed?'

'But she is.'

'That doesn't stop her from embarrassing others. You should hear some of the things she says to Jake. Like how can a man in his fifties keep a woman my age satisfied?'

'She doesn't like him, does she?'

'But I think she finds him attractive and it's causing her problems. One of which is she is probably jealous of her own daughter – '

The conversation ended abruptly when Laura's stepdaughter entered.

114

Janis came to greet Marianne, then eyed the table proudly. 'Laura let Bessie and me lay the festive board without any help.'

'And it looks lovely,' Marianne congratulated her, surveying the gleaming crystal wine glasses and the silver candelabra enhancing the white damask cloth.

'If you're wondering why we moved the table in here from the dining-room, Marianne,' said Janis with a laugh, 'we had to put both of the extra leaves in it, and there was then no room for all the chairs.'

'We're having some last minute and unexpected guests,' Laura told Marianne. 'Lyn is in town to appear with Arnold at a function.'

'She said when I last spoke to her that she'd refused.'

'He managed to persuade her, so I asked them to join us. Matthew is coming, too. When I called him he said he hadn't been to a Seder for years, and it would also be a way of spending an evening with his mum.'

Did Matthew's not mentioning his dad mean he and Arnold were still at daggers drawn? Marianne wondered. Even if they weren't, what could there ever be between them other than a strained truce?

'Matthew asked could he bring Pete,' Laura went on, 'and of course I said yes. Sir Arnold Klein won't be too pleased about that, but it's too bad!'

Marianne's brother had become even more pompous since being knighted in the New Year Honours List. But Laura's remark was twofold. Matthew's bringing along the man he lived with was enough to make the matzo stick in Arnold's throat.

Laura noted Marianne's expression. 'I'll make sure to seat Arnold well away from them.'

'You better had!'

'But I think Matthew and Pete are lovely people,' Janis declared, 'and their private life is their business.'

Marianne watched her leave the room, a tall, slender girl whose tawny hair still had about it a sun-bleached look, though it was now three years since she had lived in South Africa. Her accent, like her father's and her brother's, would continue to denote her country of origin whose politics all three held in contempt. The opposite of Ralph's talking like a New Zealander and being proud of it throughout his life, thought Marianne.

Laura interrupted her musing. 'Janis has turned into a stunner, hasn't she? And if she doesn't get a place at a London college, come the autumn she'll be leaving home.'

'Would that upset you?'

'Well, it's taken us till now to become a real family,' Laura replied, 'and I'd like us to stay together for as long as possible. Jake, too. Edinburgh would be Janis's alternative, and that's a long way away.'

'You'll still have two kids at home.'

'But Jeremy doesn't hit it off too well with Bessie, as you may have noticed! And she absolutely adores him, poor pet.'

Marianne said with a laugh, 'That could be why he's always so rude to her. My grandson too looks pained when Bessie tries to tag along with him and Jeremy.'

'Sending Jeremy to A.P.'s school was a good idea of yours,' said Laura. 'He settled down in this country much more easily than Janis did and it has to be his friendship with A.P. that helped him do so.'

Though Jeremy was now sixteen, and A.P. a year his junior, they were in the same class and had become inseparable companions.

'Janis has lots of friends now though,' said Marianne, 'and, I gather, plenty of outside interests.'

'Which Jake and I are hoping won't result in her getting bad grades in her crucial exams,' said Laura.

'You don't take too many assignments away from home any more, do you?' Marianne said after a pause.

'My family is more important to me,' Laura replied. 'And I bet you didn't think that could happen.'

'Did *you*?'

'No, as a matter of fact. But it has and I'm happy, Marianne.'

Marianne glanced at one of Laura's photographic studies that lent additional charm to the spacious, white-walled room. It was one that had won Laura a photographer-of-the-year award, its setting a harbourside on which some fishermen were untangling their silvery catch from the net.

'I've always liked your black and white pictures best,' Marianne said, 'and the ones you called throwouts and let me have, when you and Jake moved house, have been much admired.'

The town house that David had bought for Laura when Bessie was born could not comfortably accommodate her new family and Jake had found and refurbished their present home, a three-storey Edwardian villa overlooking Hampstead Heath, where property was at a premium, however decaying, and snapped up the moment it came on the market.

'My mum wanted to make the soup and the *knedlach*,' Laura said irrelevantly, 'but I wouldn't let her. This is my home and I wanted to cook the meal for the Seder.'

Before Laura's marriage, chicken broth and matzo balls had not featured in her preoccupations, thought Marianne. It was as if Jake had waved a wand over her and hey presto! The woman she was had metamorphosed into someone Marianne barely recognized.

Marianne too had been a devoted wife, and maternity was the strongest emotion she had known until she also became a grandmother. The inner conflict between home and career had dogged her while Martin was growing up, but she could not have brought herself to waste her other gift from God: her talent.

Laura's past work was exhibited in galleries worldwide. Now, she was limiting herself to accepting only those commissions unlikely to disrupt her family life. Gone too was the time when she had impulsively taken off for wherever with her camera to give free rein to her creativity, jaunts which had resulted in some of her best work, including the picture that had set Marianne's mind on this track, taken on a blustery morning in Cornwall.

On the other side of the room hung a portrait of the man who had changed Laura's life.

'I'm surprised that your husband had time to sit for that,' Marianne remarked, eyeing it.

Laura smiled. 'He wasn't my husband then, and if I hadn't asked him to we'd have gone on treading our separate paths. My work was instrumental in my finding my man.'

But could Laura sustain the sacrifice she had resultantly made? It wasn't for Marianne to dilute the aura of happiness she radiated by warning her that it might not be possible. That sooner or later she could find herself resenting the domestic stricture that was still to her a novelty.

When Jake and Martin arrived with their sons, Marianne watched Laura's burly husband greet her with a bear hug that epitomized his warm personality.

Also, thought Marianne, their relationship. In which affection, not romance, seemed predominant. So much so, Marianne had found herself wondering if Jake was for Laura not just a lover, but the father-figure gone from her life when her dad emigrated to Israel. And the domesticity Laura was now enjoying was perhaps the realization of an ideal-family dream not quite destroyed by her own childhood experience.

Whatever, long may Laura's contentment last, Marianne was thinking when her grandson gave her a wink.

'You're looking very toffed-up tonight,' he remarked.

'Come and give me a kiss, you scamp!'

The kiss delivered, he added with a grin, since it had been necessary for him to stoop, 'Am I growing taller, or are you shrinking, Gran?'

'I haven't reached the shrinking stage yet, and tall though you are, you're still not too old for me to spank you!' Marianne replied.

'First you'd have to catch me.'

'And my legs certainly aren't long enough for that. Another disadvantage of your granny being a titch, A.P., is

I can't reach the top shelves of my kitchen cupboards!'

Bantering with her grandson was one of Marianne's great pleasures. His dry sense of humour matched her own. What had she said to evoke the serious expression now on his face?

'Did Granddad used to reach things down for you?' he asked quietly.

'If he happened to be at home when I needed something from up there. When we lived in the cottage in Cheshire, though, the problem didn't arise.'

'I remember it having low ceilings.'

'So it couldn't have had high cupboards,' said Marianne with a laugh. 'But now I'm back in my lofty flat – well, don't tell your dad, but last week I fell off my ladder while getting down the cast-iron saucepan I use for making carrot and ginger jam for the Passover.'

'I'm surprised you had the strength to lift the pan,' said A.P.

'I'm by no means as fragile as I look,' Marianne assured him, 'and the special jam is the only culinary achievement I'm known for in the family. This is the first year I won't be in Manchester to dole out the jars personally, and yesterday I put a carton of jars on the train and called Leona to ask her to collect it and do the distributing for me. I can't have our relatives up north thinking that my non-appearance at their Seder means I don't care about them any more.'

'What an odd mixture you are!' said her grandson.

And how astute an observation from a boy of his age, since it was Marianne's assessment of herself.

'One day you're the celebrity doing book-signings and the next you're putting jars of jam on the train,' he capped it, 'like your gran sometimes mailed you a tin of strudel.'

'Who told you about that?'

'My dad once said it was the only time he ever got homemade cake.'

One of Sarah's many virtues was her thoughtfulness for others, Marianne recalled. Could Marianne credit herself with having inherited that trait? On balance, yes. And it has to be the bits of Sarah I recognize in myself that account for my incongruities of character.

'I've got a jar of the jam in my car, for you and your dad to take home,' she said to A.P.

'Good, I'll have some for breakfast tomorrow, on the matzos he and I bought in Golders Green. If Mum tries to stop me from having a Passover breakfast, there'll just have to be another row.'

'I don't like the sound of that,' said Marianne.

'But she isn't going to like it,' A.P. went on. 'Believe it or not, I overheard Mum accusing Dad of trying to convert me to his religion. She didn't want me to come here to-night.'

Marianne did believe it. Martin's relationship with his wife was becoming increasingly acrimonious.

'She said he was doing it insidiously,' A.P. relayed, 'and I wasn't sure what she meant.'

'There is such a thing as a dictionary,' Marianne replied lightly. Not for anything would she be the one to tell him what his mother was implying.

Why couldn't Martin's marrying-out have proceeded as smoothly as had his partner's? But Andy and Rhoda had no children. And such was Rhoda's devotion to her husband, if he had wished it she would doubtless have espoused Judaism. A less painful decision for a Protestant perhaps than for a Catholic, since Catholicism, like Judaism, was a way of life.

'In my opinion, Gran, my mum is turning into a religious maniac,' A.P. interjected into Marianne's ruminating.

Marianne's opinion, too. She nevertheless eyed her grandson sternly. 'Now you listen to me, A.P. You are never to speak that way of your mother again.'

'That won't stop me from thinking it.'

'But some thoughts are better kept to ourselves, A.P. That way they don't hurt people we love.'

Marianne could have added that this was a lesson she herself had had to learn. As a teenager she had been too outspoken for her own good.

'How can my telling you what I think hurt my mum?' A.P. countered. 'You're not a blab-mouth.'

'But you want me to take sides with you against your mother,' Marianne answered, 'and that is painful for *me*.'

'Does that mean you'd rather I didn't tell you my troubles?'

Marianne masked her distress with a smile. He was too young to be beset by troubles. But my refusing to listen won't cause them to go away. Instead he would bottle them up.

'When you have things to get off your chest, by all means come to me,' she said kindly. 'But should they concern your parents you must expect me to remain neutral.'

'*I'm* pig-in-the-middle, though, aren't I?'

Marianne remained in the alcove that had allowed them to talk privately, watching A.P. join the youngsters by the hearth.

Shirley and Laura were gone from the room, doubtless to the kitchen, and Martin and Jake checking the table, making sure there was a Haggadah beside each place, a nostalgic reminder for Marianne of every Seder she had attended.

The atmosphere too was the same, born of long tradition, the air redolent of cinnamon and apple pounded with walnuts to a paste, to symbolize the mortar spread by the Children of Israel in their years of enslavement. Marianne could remember a Seder night of her youth when something had gone wrong with her grandmother's matzo balls and jokes were made about Sarah providing not just the mortar, but the bricks.

What right had Moira to deprive A.P. of the warming memories that would accompany his contemporaries in the family through their lives? Stop it! Marianne ordered herself. She could not, however, forget her impression of Moira's family. The stiff-upper-lip Lord Kyverdale, and her ladyship carefully forgetting that she was once a chorus girl.

As if by tacit consent, they did not visit Marianne nor she them. What have we in common other than a grandson? An only grandchild for each. Marianne's recollection of Martin's wedding reception was of a champagne-sipping crowd in one of England's stately homes. Denuded of people it would echo with silence. So formal were the Kyverdales, whenever Marianne envisaged them they were seated at either end of the vast table at which she had only once dined, both resplendent in evening dress.

The memories A.P. would accumulate from his mother's family would be the opposite of warming, Marianne thought, listening to an exchange now taking place between him and Bessie. A.P. plainly wasn't enjoying it, but would look back on it with humour when he grew up.

'If you'll sit beside me at the table, you can share this lovely big Haggadah my daddy has bought for me,' Bessie was pleading.

'No, thanks,' said A.P.

'You don't like me, do you?'

'But I have to put up with you because you're my cousin,' he replied with schoolboy callousness.

'What do I have to do to make you like me, A.P.?'

Marianne was then diverted by Jake's coming to chat with her.

'How's the writer of the family?'

'She's enjoying the hospitality of our entrepreneur,' Marianne answered in kind.

'I'm stuck with that nomenclature, aren't I?' he said with a laugh.

'You must blame your wife for that. It was the reply she gave her mother when Shirley asked what you do. If I hadn't already met you, I'd have expected you to be a portly gent with a big cigar!'

'Hardly Laura's style.'

But nor are you, Marianne silently replied. Laura's taste in men had in the past ranged from the arty to the sophisticated. In her youth, though, she had hung around with pop musicians, including a guitarist who wore pink velvet suits. It had taken Sarah Sandberg a long time to recover from the shock of meeting him.

But unlike the rest of the family elders, Sarah had never given up hope of Laura's eventually settling down with what she had termed 'a nice Jewish husband'. She would surely have approved of Jake Bornstein.

'To tell you the truth, Marianne,' he said, 'I don't know what a gorgeous creature like Laura is doing married to me.'

'Then allow me to tell you,' said Marianne, while surveying his greying, dark hair, and the blue eyes that were probably capable of seeming steely when he did a business deal, 'that Laura considers herself fortunate to be your wife. And I have to add that she has never before seemed to me so content.'

They glanced to where Laura and Shirley were now talking together, the daughter a younger version of the mother. But there, thought Marianne, the resemblance ends.

The peevishness of disappointment was written in the downward cast of Shirley's lips, undisguisable as the lines not quite camouflaged by heavy make-up. Nor could her ageing posture be disguised by the draped silk dress she had on.

As usual, Shirley was wearing black which she seemed to have decided was right for her while still in her twenties. As if, Marianne reflected, she had made up her mind then about the picture she wanted to present throughout her life. But what a pathetically brittle picture it now was.

Laura, though, cared no more now for how the world saw her than she had as a girl. Her concerns had never been those of her mum. Tonight she had donned a green brocade sari that Jake had bought for her on a business trip to India – which some would consider unsuitable for a family Seder – and with that coppery hair, how breathtaking she looked.

Jake cut into Marianne's musing. 'How's the new book going?'

'The one still in my typewriter, or the one in the shops?' she said with a smile. Why was Jake eyeing her tentatively?

'I was wondering if you could spare me a little time, Marianne. There's something I need to discuss with you.'

Need?

'How would it be if I dropped in on you late tomorrow afternoon?'

'Fine. I'll stop work when you arrive.'

Implicit in Jake's request was that Laura was not to know. And such was his tone, Marianne had almost added that she would have the kettle on.

So bleak was Jake's expression, Marianne forced herself to lightly change the subject. 'If the latecomers don't get here soon, we shall find ourselves having a midnight Seder!'

It was a relief in one way, if a prospective ordeal in another, when the four to whom she was referring then arrived and Jake left her side to greet them.

Bessie rapped a spoon on the table and declaimed, 'Pray silence for Sir Arnold and Lady Klein!'

Though Lyn looked as if she would have liked to disappear through the floor, Arnold accepted it as his due and kissed Bessie's plump cheek.

As no doubt he kisses the kids he encounters while electioneering, thought Marianne with distaste. What a smarmy individual her brother had become.

Matthew had entered with Pete, behind his parents, his curled lips reflecting Marianne's feelings, and she saw him glance pityingly at his mother.

If avoiding Arnold was Matthew's policy, Pete's was quite the opposite. Pete has certainly made an effort with his appearance this evening, Marianne noted. The well-pressed suit he had on was a far cry from the baggy trousers and skimpy pullovers that accentuated his girth and were his habitual garb.

'There wasn't time when we met on the doorstep to congratulate you on your knighthood, Sir Arnold,' he said in his booming voice while pumping Arnold's hand.

'Yes, well – that's very good of you,' Arnold mouthed. 'And now if you will excuse me, I haven't yet had a word with our hostess.'

Arnold pointedly detached himself from Pete and Marianne could have hit him! She put a smile on her face and went to lend moral support to Lyn, remarking when Matthew and Pete came to chat to them, 'You two haven't dropped in to see me for ages. What have I done to deserve it?'

'Martin told us you're into a heavy work stint,' said Matthew, 'but when weren't you?' he added with a grin.

Marianne noted the sartorial elegance to which he had bowed as he grew older, his appearance now the public's expectation of well-known actors, the bow tie he was wearing a perfect match with the silk handkerchief in the breast pocket of the maroon velvet jacket skimming his trim waistline.

Pete on the other hand – well, Marianne had marvelled from the first at the alliance between them. Matthew so sensitive and Pete an extrovert whose talent had set him among the outstanding directors of his day, the attention to detail in his work the opposite of the untidiness with which Matthew had to live.

They had met in the sixties, when experimental theatre began revitalizing the British scene, as its off-Broadway counterpart had in the States. Marianne had written a play for their company to perform, and recalled with a smile the panning she and they had received from the critics.

Those days, though, were long gone for all three. Marianne had then been already well on her way, able to take the risk she had and survive the damage. For Matthew and Pete the struggle had been long.

Remarkably, she thought, they were still side by side in every respect, Matthew towering over Pete's avuncular figure, their comfortable rapport no less now than it had always been.

'You must come and eat with us one evening, Marianne,' said Pete. 'We're in town rehearsing our next production. Remember when we had time to drop in on Marianne, Matt?' he added reminiscently. 'And she'd sometimes say she wouldn't be a minute, then disappear to her study and forget we were there?'

'If that's a retrospective rebuke I probably deserve it,' said Marianne.

'It isn't,' said Matthew, 'and if it wouldn't embarrass you for me to say it – I shall anyway – Pete and I haven't forgotten the friend you were to us then.'

'I'd like to think I am still.'

'That goes without saying,' said Pete, 'but the time we're talking about was when gays were ostracized.'

Matthew glanced at his father. 'By some we still are. The last time I had a conversation with my dad – and I can't remember when that was – he said he couldn't believe there was such a thing as a Jewish homosexual. And why did the exception to the rule have to be his son.'

Matthew allowed himself a wry smile. 'Oh well! If he has to suffer me, I also have to suffer him is how I've come to look at it. Cheer up, Mum,' he said to Lyn. 'You and I still have each other and I'm grateful for that.'

'Can I please have your autographs on my new Haggadah, to prove to my friends that you really were at our Seder?' Bessie called to Matthew and Pete.

They laughed and went to join her.

'What Matthew just said – it's how I feel, too,' Lyn told Marianne. 'With my husband living in cloud-cuckoo-land and my daughter shut away in a nunnery, it's as if I have only Matthew left. If anything had come of Margaret's friendship with that young surgeon, instead of her doing what she finally did I might now be a grandmother. And he was a lovely man.'

'But could you imagine Arnold with a Pakistani son-in-law?'

'That could be why Margaret didn't give him one. Not for Arnold's sake, for Ravi's. Arnold had avoided meeting him, when they came to England together for some medical conference. An on-going situation like that, and it would have been, wouldn't be pleasant for Ravi if he and Margaret had married.'

Lyn's face crumpled with distress. 'When I met him, Marianne – well, the way he looked at Margaret, and she at him – isn't it terrible that because of Arnold, their love for

126

each other has gone to waste? And I sometimes think that how Margaret has ended up is her way of paying her father back for being the man he is and its effect upon her and her brother.'

'It would be best,' Marianne replied, 'for you to interpret Margaret's joining the Holy Order she has as her finding comfort in her Faith. How else are you to reconcile yourself to it? And we must hope it is the truth.'

'I shall never reconcile myself to it. If only – '

Marianne cut Lyn short with a remembered saying. 'If only we had some ham, we could have ham and eggs, if we had some eggs.'

'But not at my Seder!' Jake quipped, coming in on the end of their conversation as everyone flocked to the table and the ancient Jewish ritual finally began.

'This is the first time I've sat at a Seder table without my sister,' Harry Klein was declaring in Manchester, 'and how it feels to me is as if our family is cracking up!'

A tear then rolled down his cheek and plopped into his chicken soup. 'The Londoners will, of course, have started their Seder late, without me to organize them. But I bet they'll get a better meal than we're having.'

'How could you say such a thing, when Mum's been slaving over the cooker all day!' Howard exclaimed.

'If insulting me makes him feel better, he is welcome to upset me,' said Ann.

'*Nothing* makes me feel better!' Harry retorted. 'And the truth is I can't wait for God to end it for me.'

'What are we to do with him, Uncle?' Howard said bleakly to Nathan.

'You,' Harry accused him, 'have already done enough! Who was it who brought on my stroke?'

The small gathering fell briefly silent and Leona, seated beside Howard, put a comforting hand on his.

'The only one who could help your father is unfortunately unwilling to do so,' Nathan told Howard. 'Himself.'

Nathan's friend Sybil then intervened. 'Isn't that the case with most people, Nat?'

She received from Harry the first smile seen on his face since he was taken ill.

'At last, someone who understands!' he said. 'All I get from my family is the pity I could do without. If Sybil's going to be my new aunt, Uncle Nat, that's fine with me.'

'But I am in no hurry to acquire a stepmother,' said Leona.

Sybil said sweetly, 'That, you've made more than plain, dear. Unlike my children, who only want their mother to be happy.'

'It isn't their mother I'm concerned about. It's my father,' Leona countered smartly.

Sybil fingered one of her gold earrings and appealed to Nathan. 'Say something, Nat, or I'll ring up for a cab and leave.'

'All I'm going to say to my daughter is she's left it somewhat late to show concern for my happiness. And if anyone leaves, it ought not to be the lady who befriended me when I needed someone.'

'Now we know where we stand, I'll stay,' said Sybil.

'But I,' said Leona, 'don't intend to be driven from a family Seder by a stranger. If everyone has finished their soup, I'll help Ann clear away the plates.'

Sybil, she had noted, seemed to take it for granted that others would wait upon her – and had probably been adored by the two husbands she had outlived.

In many respects she reminded Leona of some of the elderly widows she had met in Florida. Though she lacked their genuine warmth and had not resorted to cosmetic surgery, her preoccupation was to captivate a man.

But how did a woman like her manage to captivate a man like my dad? thought Leona with distaste. There was something kittenish about her, including her small round face, and the hazel-green eyes made feline with the aid of carefully applied eye-liner. Not to mention her cuddly shape, accentuated by an angora dress of a hue that made her look like a *ginger* kitten.

Tonight she had shown her claws. But only Leona and Ann noticed them. Sybil's effect upon men of all ages was plain. They wanted to protect her. The few occasions on which Leona and her husband had been in Sybil's company were enough to display that even sensible Frank had fallen under her spell.

As for my father – there was little doubt that the tiny woman he had met at a Bar Mitzvah made him feel the macho man he most certainly wasn't and that had to be the answer, Leona decided while helping Ann stack the soup plates in the dishwasher.

'What's all that clattering going on in the kitchen?' Harry shouted through the serving hatch.

Only Leona venting her feelings, thought Ann, hoping that it wouldn't result in her Passover china being chipped.

'All we need now is that woman in the family!' she exclaimed to Leona. 'Take a peep through the hatch – '

'If you don't mind, I'd rather not.'

'Sybil is mopping soup off Harry's chin and he's actually letting her! He is able to do it for himself, but he never does.'

'Since he's male, I'm not surprised he's joined her list of conquests.'

'She's welcome to change places with me,' Ann snapped, 'but heaven help your dad if she hooks him and it looks as if she's going to. Bridie will walk out the minute Sybil walks in.'

Ann rested against the sink and said after a pause, 'This takes me back to Sigmund Moritz's big mistake.'

Leona recalled the ageing baby-doll face of the woman Sigmund had married. There was too another parallel. Like Sigmund, Nathan was a clever man – and Sybil as unintelligent as Sigmund's lady-love.

When boredom set in, and it had not taken long, he had bade her farewell and put her from his life and his mind. The large sum of money that came to him when she died intestate was a shock, and he had not spent a penny of it on himself. He had, however, willed it to Frank, in the certain knowledge that money slipped through Henry's fingers and Frank would not see his twin go short.

While they set the dinner plates on the counter, to serve the main course, Ann too was deep in thought. How different this Seder night was from those of times past. Gone was the bustle of activity in the kitchen, the laughter too, all the females in the family getting in each other's way, sharing in the preparations and then in the dishing up of food from huge pots and pans. The pan in which Sarah Sandberg had made soup for Seder nights had resembled a cauldron! Ann recalled with a smile.

But those days were gone, along with what the sociologists called the 'extended family' – which seemed to Ann a clinical term for the caring and sharing she remembered. Future generations would not experience the simple pleasures that Ann and her children had. Instead – well, even marriage itself was now regarded by some as a dying institution.

'I miss Marianne,' she said to Leona.

'Don't you miss Kate?'

'My daughter has lived in Israel for so long, I'm not accustomed to having her with me on Seder nights.'

'But I'm accustomed to having mine with me. When Carla phoned to tell me that Kate had invited her and Alan to spend the Passover with her, I had to stop myself from saying, "Please don't go." '

'And time was,' said Ann, 'when all of us not being together for a festival would've been unthinkable. I've just been asking myself what's happened to Jewish family life – '

'The same as has happened to gentile family life, Ann. It's moved with the century and no longer has time to be what it once was. Which isn't to say that our family doesn't still stick together in a crisis – '

'Since my life is now one big crisis,' said Ann, 'I appreciate how often you and Frank drop in.'

Ann was slicing pickled cucumber when Harry called stridently, 'Are we getting a second course? If not, my nursemaid can put me to bed and Grace can be said without me. I'm not giving thanks to God for a lousy meal I didn't get!'

'Your nursemaid is going on strike!' Ann heard herself retort.

'About time, too,' Leona told her. 'You look dead beat and who could be surprised.'

'Would you mind serving up the dinner, Leona. My legs seem to have turned to jelly.'

'Probably from the shock of what you just said to Harry.'

'I didn't mean to – '

'But Harry hasn't slumped to the carpet, has he? He's still sitting in his wheelchair – and enjoying the sympathetic glances that woman is giving him!' Leona observed through the hatch. 'You should put your foot down with him more often, Ann, and if he has another stroke it'll be his fault, not yours.'

'Could you be that callous with Frank?'

'I would surely have hastened his end long before now! Go back to the table, Ann, and send Frank to help me.'

Frank's first words when he entered the kitchen were, 'Why did you have to embarrass poor Sybil the way you did?'

'You're as gullible as my dad, Frank. And if I don't prise Sybil out of his life, it will be poor Nathan.'

'You're behaving like a jealous daughter, Leona. I wouldn't have expected it of you.'

'If that's how you interpret my concern for my father, then you've lived with me for more years than I care to count without really knowing me,' she replied.

'More years than you care to count, eh?'

'Hand me the oven cloth, will you? And if you're going to look for *double entendre* in everything I say, an experienced lawyer like you won't find it difficult to twist my words.'

131

Frank watched Leona take one of Ann's aprons from a hook and put it on, lest she splash gravy on her dress. A good housekeeper she wasn't, but like all Sarah Sandberg's granddaughters and great-granddaughters, she never dished up food minus an apron. It was a family joke among the men, but incapable now of causing Frank to smile.

'Would you mind telling me what's been going on in here?' he asked while she hastily tied the apron strings in a bow. 'What did you say to Ann to make her suddenly turn on Harry?'

'What did *I* say to her? A better question, Frank, would be why hasn't she blown her top a lot sooner?'

'And the answer is that she loves him. If I may draw a logical conclusion from that, you wouldn't stand for such behaviour from me, no matter how ill I was.'

Had he heard Leona's words to Ann on the subject? No, he couldn't have, with the chit-chat going on around him in the dining-room.

'If that's your oblique way of saying you think I no longer love you, Frank – '

'I've never doubted that you love me,' he cut in. 'But there's more than one kind of love.'

Leona blotted out a mental picture of his twin, wondering why her cheeks were not burning with shame. 'Drain the vegetables, will you, Frank? Or we shall never get this meal on the table.'

He might just as well have said: There's affection and there's passion, and all the difference in the world between the two. But the occasions when their equable relationship was suddenly jarred by Frank were rare. And characterized by the things left unsaid.

One word too many from either of us, Leona thought now, and the life we've built together could collapse like a house of cards, though it was a good deal more solid than that. Since childhood, Frank was to Leona her best friend and that hadn't changed.

She was taking the casseroled chicken from the oven,

assailed by *déjà vu*. How many years had slipped by since she and Frank stood gazing down at the kitchen floor awash with gravy, and swimming in it amid chunks of broken pyrex, the special dinner Leona had cooked because Henry was coming?

Disappointment laced with shame, when Henry called to say he *wasn't* coming, was responsible for Leona's forgetting to use the oven cloth and dropping the hot dish from her burned fingers. And while the mess was being cleared up, the fraught conversation had somehow led to Frank's saying what he had tonight.

When everyone at the Seder table finally had their meal before them, Ann delivered her second shock of the evening.

'I've made up my mind to put Harry in a nursing home. I've had enough.'

'That's what I am to her,' Harry told Sybil. 'A burden that has to be put somewhere.'

Sybil eyed Ann reproachfully. 'How can you do that to your husband?'

'Your two dropped dead, I believe. If you'd had my experience you'd have done what I'm going to without thinking twice.'

Again Sybil appealed to Nathan. 'That's no way for her to speak to the lady who could be her future aunt.'

'Ann is overwrought, my dear,' he replied, patting her hand.

And adding nothing to contradict her estimation of her own status, Leona noted.

'However, I think Ann's intention is a good idea,' Nathan declared.

Harry's response was, 'Living – if you can call my existence that – where I'd get the nursing without the pity would suit me fine!'

Howard, unduly silent throughout the evening, let fly at his father. 'Mum is the one who should be pitied, but I wouldn't expect the man you've become to see it that way!'

He calmed down and smiled at Sybil. 'Please excuse what this Seder night has turned into – '

'If she's hoping to marry into the family, she'll get used to hearing shouting matches,' said Ann.

'What's the betting,' said Leona, 'that there's one going on right now in London?'

'If they're trying to put me off, they won't succeed, Nat,' purred Sybil, 'and I don't think I've mentioned to you that I've always fancied living in Bournemouth.'

Leona envisaged her father sitting on a bench on Bournemouth's East Cliff, whiling away the time with other senior citizens. To what else but that was this crafty creature leading him by the nose? The going to seed that Ronald had feared would surely ensue.

'From what I've seen here tonight, you'll be well out of it, Nat,' Sybil went on.

A remark that brought Nathan up short and caused him to remove his hand from hers. 'I happen to be the only surviving elder of my family, Sybil, and I take that responsibility very seriously.'

'I'm a family person myself,' she mewed.

Nathan surveyed her in silence, his thoughtful expression indicating that he was suddenly seeing her differently.

'You must forgive me for wasting so many months of your time,' he told her courteously.

A show of claws followed. 'Like hell I will!'

If Dad had already given her what she's been after – an engagement ring – a breach of promise courtroom scandal might now be his lot, thought Leona, watching Sybil try to make a dignified exit.

It was Howard who saw her out. When he returned, he said, 'Why did you suddenly break it off with her, Uncle Nat?'

'My son just took the words from my mouth,' said Harry.

'And I have to say that I'm still recovering from the surprise,' said Frank.

Nathan gave them a smile and said brusquely, 'I'm going to leave you to figure it out for yourselves.'

'I already have,' said Leona, 'and I'm proud of you, Dad.'

Once again, Family was responsible for changing the course of her father's life. But this time he had not required coercing, and the outcome was the opposite of the disasters to which family loyalty had led him in the past.

Chapter Three

THE FOLLOWING DAY was one of surprises for Marianne, some better described as shocks.

Ann washing her hands of Harry? And Harry agreeable to entering a nursing home? Uncle Nat suddenly ending his romance seemed but an item of gossip beside those two astonishing developments.

'Your mother doesn't mean it and your father is just playing her along,' Marianne had said when Howard called to tell her.

'Believe it or not, Marianne, Mum is like a new woman since she made the decision. And Dad is now saying he'd have made it himself, but he didn't want to upset her.'

'A likely tale!' said Marianne.

'I agree. But all that matters is it's best for both of them and it's going to happen. It will also ease things for me. I shall be able to go to Germany more often and stay longer. There's something I've been keeping to myself – '

When Marianne rang off her mind was awhirl. Howard's reply to her asking why he was keeping his girlfriend a secret did not bode well: 'There are complications I don't even want to think about.' But sooner or later he would have to, and Marianne hoped that he would not by then be inextricably involved in yet another insoluble situation.

An *unpleasant* surprise was a visit from Shirley, during the afternoon. When the doorbell rang, Marianne thought it might be Jake arriving earlier than he had promised.

'I know you weren't expecting me,' said her cousin, 'but there's no need to grimace! And you still look the mess you always did when there was no special reason for you to look nice,' she added, eyeing Marianne's crumpled jeans and baggy shirt.

'You, on the other hand, look even more sour than usual,' Marianne countered.

'Well, I've never had your capacity for laughing off the rotten tricks life's played on me.'

'Hiding my feelings with a smile, you mean.'

'But you've never spared mine, have you? And why are you keeping me standing in the hall?'

While Shirley followed her into the living-room, Marianne crossed her fingers lest Jake arrive before she left.

Jake had found it impossible to be on easy terms with Shirley – which qualifies him for membership of a big club, thought Marianne. All he needed, Marianne too, was for Shirley to catch him dropping in here!

Shirley glanced around the room disapprovingly, before removing some magazines from the armchair they were occupying and sitting down. 'Nobody would think you were your mother's daughter, Marianne.'

'The same could be said of Laura.'

'Is that some kind of insult?'

'It's just a statement of fact. Unlike you, Shirley, I've never thought that children are obliged to be replicas of their parents. Nor that parents are entitled to harbour expectations. Those who do have themselves to thank if they end up bitterly disappointed.'

'You think you know it all, don't you?'

'On the contrary, Shirley, my philosophy is you're never too old to learn. And I'm still learning.'

'I didn't come here for a lecture, Marianne. Or to be put down!'

'Why *did* you come? We've known each other too long for you to beat about the bush with me.'

'And only once did I fool myself that we were friends as well as cousins.'

Remembrance of herself and Shirley when they were wartime evacuees returned to Marianne. A couple of miserable kids marooned together in the care of a dour Welsh-woman.

'You were always better at doing sums than me – how old were we when we shared that grim experience?' she asked Shirley wryly.

'Thirteen, I think. And grim it certainly was! Whenever I smell carbolic soap, I remember the old dragon washing our hair under that cold water pump in the yard.'

'My most vivid recollection,' said Marianne, 'is of the hours we spent on that little pebbled beach.'

'You scribbling stories and me sketching fashion designs.'

'That was when I decided what I was going to be.'

'Me, too. And we both achieved it, didn't we?' Shirley flicked a speck of fluff from the sleeve of her black suit, crossed her shapely legs and hardened her tone. 'But back to the present – '

Back to us being two women who dislike each other and don't try too hard to hide it, thought Marianne.

'There's something I need you to do for me,' said Shirley.

One of us is nevertheless capable of asking the other for a favour. 'And what might that be?'

Shirley then launched into a tale of how she had overheard Laura and Jake arguing that morning. 'Their bedroom door was closed and I heard them when I passed by on my way downstairs. I had no idea what it was about, but Laura didn't speak to Jake during breakfast and he was skulking behind the *Financial Times*.'

'Come on, Shirley! Jake is hardly the skulking type.'

'You haven't heard the rest of it. When Jake had left for the office, I asked Laura what was wrong and she told me to mind my own business – '

'Good for her,' Marianne cut in, 'and if what you want from me is to find out for you, forget it, Shirley.'

'I haven't finished the story yet. And perhaps you won't think it a coincidence, which I don't, that Laura then went into the living-room, where the au pair was doing the dusting, and fired her.'

'Trust you to put two and two together and make five!' Marianne exclaimed. 'If you can't see that Jake has eyes for nobody but Laura, it's time you got yourself some glasses, Shirley. I'd also suggest that you have your brains tested. Another useful piece of advice, is a woman who messed up her own married life should stay the hell out of her daughter's.'

'What a cruel bitch you are, Marianne! And don't give me that crap about having to be cruel to be kind. You've never shown me a scrap of kindness, so why would I expect you to now?'

Shirley rose from the chair and made the angry exit Marianne had seen her, over the years, make time and again after a confrontation with this relative or that – and most frequently with the man now her ex-husband.

When Marianne first met Peter Kohn he was a bewildered young lad, torn from his family by circumstances neither he, nor his parents, could have envisaged. If they had, they would surely have run for their lives as their more prudent brethren had, long before Hitler marched into Austria.

Marianne had not forgotten Sigmund Moritz's anxiety about his relatives in Vienna. Then an evening came when he received a message from them, and Marianne's father and her Uncle David had taken turns at the wheel to drive him immediately to Dover, to meet a Channel steamer.

Marianne and Ronald, who had persuaded their elders to let them go along for the ride, were fast asleep when they arrived. There were no motorways then, she reflected. Dad and Uncle David must have driven hell-for-leather to get there in time. And seeing the refugees leaving the ship – the expressions on their faces, and the weeping when those meeting them embraced them – was something that would remain with Marianne for the rest of her life.

Also Sigmund Moritz's joy when he espied his great-nephew, Peter, whom he recognized from a photograph though they had not met. And then Sigmund's sorrow when

139

Peter told them that the rest of the family had been taken by the Nazis.

With Peter was a forlorn young girl with whom he had somehow escaped the fate of their two families. Nearly five decades had since passed, but Marianne could still not contemplate that fate without a shudder. It had not taken that long for the evil she had naïvely thought stamped out to prove otherwise.

Catching a glimpse of her workaday appearance in the hall mirror was sufficient to hasten Marianne to freshen up before Jake arrived. Not on your life, though, would she have bothered to brush her hair and put on lipstick had she known Shirley was coming!

While doing so her mind returned to Shirley's ex-husband.

David had taken Peter into his family and had considered him a second son, later welcoming him as a son-in-law. Was it perhaps gratitude for all he had received from his foster-parents, including love, that had kept Peter tied for so long to their daughter?

Little by little, marriage to Shirley had diminished his spirit. Nor could working beside his high-powered wife in the family business have failed to emasculate him. But a trip to Israel had served as Peter's salvation. There he had encountered Hildegard, with whom in their youth he had walked hand-in-hand from the ship at Dover, and he was now married to her.

Peter's was one family story that had ended happily, Marianne thought wryly as the doorbell pealed.

But not for Shirley – whose outrageous conclusion that Jake was having it off with the au pair had surpassed even Marianne's estimation of her cousin's nasty mind.

That isn't to say his wanting to talk to me privately hasn't got me worried. She went to let him in. And this had been the sort of day that drove her from her native north. Family taking precedence. She had barely done a stroke of work.

'Thanks for seeing me, Marianne. I know how busy you are.'

That was what they all said. North and south. As if Marianne's sparing time for her relatives was bestowing a favour. It wasn't like that at all. Simply that publishing was no longer the leisurely ethos many supposed it still to be, but a highly commercial operation that began with the author.

Marianne's not meeting her deadline could be likened to the vital component in a machine going missing. If every author on a publisher's list failed to deliver, the machine would grind to a halt. As for one's creativity – if someone rang up while you were composing a passage not yet down on paper, by the time you'd snarled, 'I can't talk now!' and replaced the receiver the passage you'd been mentally writing had disintegrated never to return.

'I expect you're pretty busy yourself,' she replied to Jake, while he hung his coat on the battered old coat-tree that Ralph had bought in a junk shop, years ago.

'And I'll be off on another of my trips, soon,' he said as they went into the living-room.

Where Shirley's habitual Chanel No. 5 scent still lingered in the air. Would Jake notice it? A thought that brought home to Marianne the two-way deception in which she suddenly found herself enmeshed.

She offered Jake some sherry and said while she was pouring it, 'I have to tell you I've been wondering what you could possibly want to discuss privately with me. Since neither your wedding anniversary, nor Laura's birthday, is looming up, you haven't come to consult me about what to give her!'

'If only it were something like that, Marianne,' he said as she handed him a brimming glass.

'You look as if you need a whisky, but I haven't any. And if you're going to tell me that things have gone wrong between you and Laura, I'm not going to believe it.'

Marianne had not, until today, seen him clad for the office. The business suit he had on, and his dark silk tie, made him look older than he appeared in casual clothes. And an incongruous husband for the woman Laura really was.

Jake sipped some sherry and tried to smile. It had never been easy for him to share his problems, nor was he accustomed to having to do so.

'This morning Laura and I had our first quarrel,' he said eventually. 'There was something she wanted to handle her way and I insisted on it being dealt with my way.'

The au pair had evidently erred in some manner or other, and Marianne could imagine Laura wanting to give the girl the benefit of the doubt. Jake, though, was a man of quick decisions in all his dealings. To achieve what he had he would have to be. And so much for Shirley's supposition!

'Does the quarrel you mentioned concern what you want to discuss with me?' she asked him.

'Directly, no. Indirectly, yes.'

Marianne put down her glass. 'If you're going to talk to me in double-Dutch, Jake, I must tell you I'd much prefer plain English.'

'But this isn't a simple, black and white matter, Marianne. Well, not for me. I'm worried about Laura.' He paused before adding, 'I've also learned that she has a mind of her own.'

'How long did it take you to find that out?'

'I suspected it before I married her – '

'*Suspected it?* You're making a woman's having a mind of her own sound like a criminal trait in her character! In the eighties, there are few women who don't and why the heck shouldn't they have?'

'In principle I agree. But in practice – well, I expect that Laura also had her suspicions about me. That I'm the kind she now knows I am. On the whole, she doesn't seem to be having the trouble coping with me that I'm having coping with her. And frankly – well, I'm dreading the time when Janis tells us she intends living with a boyfriend, and I say, "The hell you do!" and Laura sides with Janis.'

'Has Janis got a steady boyfriend?'

'No, but I can see it coming.'

Jake finished his sherry and Marianne refilled his glass,

trying to make sense of the man he said he was having married a single woman with a child.

'I forgave Laura for stepping off the straight and narrow once,' he said as if he had divined Marianne's thoughts, 'since she did it in order to be a mother. And I adore Bessie.'

Once? As for others of her generation, sleeping with whomever you fancied before settling down had been for Laura the norm, and she would be the opposite of censorious if her and Jake's children did what was *increasingly* the norm. The main preoccupation of many parents of teenage daughters, nowadays, was to make sure they were on the pill.

Jake, though, was as if set in amber. What was Laura doing married to this nice kind man who was in some respects a throwback to the Victorian husband and father? And of course Laura had suspected it! Why else had she kept her randy past to herself?

There was, however, no such thing as starting out with a clean slate, whatever the venture. What you thought you had put behind you was liable to reappear unexpectedly before you, and down you went.

And when the venture was marriage . . .

Jake finally got around to telling Marianne the reason for his visit. 'I want Laura to see a gynaecologist, but she's refused to do so.' He paused before saying, 'You see, we've been trying to have a child – '

'Laura's age could account for her not conceiving,' Marianne replied.

'That's what I keep telling her, and that there could be treatment available. The only answer I get from her, Marianne, is that her not getting pregnant is God's will.'

To Marianne, that sounded like Sarah Sandberg. It certainly wasn't Laura.

'Look – there's something I'd better add,' said Jake. 'If we don't have a child together it won't be the end of the world to me. What would, is if Laura's age *didn't* account for it. The reason I want her to get a check-up is if something is seriously wrong with her, the sooner it's dealt with the better.'

Jake got up to gaze through the window and Marianne sensed that he did not want her to see his expression. There was too in his final words something that bespoke a painful significance for him.

The late afternoon had slipped into twilight, but Marianne could not bring herself to switch on the lamps, such was the atmosphere.

It was she who broke the silence. 'If you want me to talk sense to Laura, Jake, I will. But that would require my telling her that you've confided in me.'

He turned and said, his heart in his voice, 'Marianne, I don't give a damn what you have to tell her. All I'm concerned with is trying to ensure that she doesn't die on me – '

After Jake's departure, Marianne made herself some tea and a cheese sandwich, and took her frugal supper into her study. More frugal than usual, since it was matzo, not bread.

She could not but be troubled by what she had learned and on more than one count. Laura was very dear to her. More like the daughter denied to Marianne than a young cousin.

Nor would she wish on Laura her own experience of trying to have another child. The waiting between one operation and the next. The anxiety. And the final loss of hope.

Though the treatment of infertility nowadays could not be compared to that before new ground was broken, the accompanying tension until you knew, one way or the other, had to be the same. And meanwhile your life revolved around it. Your husband's too, but not twenty-four hours a day. It was your body not his upon which all was centred.

Like birth itself, when even if he was there beside you as modern husbands chose to be, he could not share with you what giving birth meant to a woman.

Marianne's reading of Jake was that he would *not* choose

to be there. But that didn't mean that Laura wasn't precious to him. On the contrary, fear of losing her seemed to be obsessing him. Had another man said what he finally did, Marianne would have told him not to be melodramatic. The emotion Jake had displayed could not be mistaken for melodrama.

She ate some of her sandwich, pondering upon what his relationship with his first wife might have been. Had she perhaps neglected the early symptoms of her illness and Jake been less insistent than he was being with Laura? From what Marianne had learned from Janis and Jeremy, their mother was a bright woman. Whom they had never heard quarrel with their father, Janis had revealed, which could mean she was of that ilk able to manipulate her husband without his realizing it.

Unlike Laura, who shared with Marianne the directness some found unwelcome, a characteristic difficult to restrain. But that wasn't the only reason Laura was having trouble playing the role in which Jake had cast her.

Marianne recalled the dishevelled teenager who years ago had hitch-hiked to London – and presented herself on my doorstep!

As the leopard does not change its spots, nor had the essence of that girl, now a woman, changed. What we are is what we remain, thought Marianne. Only the shell that houses the person is transformable.

'You look as if you need a bath!' Ralph had said to Laura that night. 'When you've had one we'll talk while you have something to eat.'

Or words to that effect and Laura had done as she was bid without argument. So it had continued. In the Deans' easy household the free spirit she was had blossomed. But Marianne feared that her love for Jake had caused her to return the genie to the bottle.

What was her row with Jake this morning if not the cork blowing?

Hard though it was to do so, Marianne switched her mind

to her work. She had intended watching a TV documentary, but with so much time lost today . . .

The interruptions, however, were not yet over. The doorbell rang.

But what a welcome visitor this was. 'A.P. What a lovely surprise!'

'Got any cornflakes, Gran? I've had my meal, but I'm feeling a bit peckish.'

'Cornflakes don't get eaten in my home on the Passover,' she replied with a smile, 'but you're welcome to matzo and jam.'

'Your special ginger jam?'

'None other. You're exactly like your dad was at your age,' Marianne told him en route to the kitchen. 'Cereal was never just breakfast food to him. No matter how big a dinner he'd eaten, half-an-hour later I'd find him scoffing a big bowl of what he used to call "the necessary". When we visited the family up north, though, and there was meat for dinner, he was made to wait the number of hours orthodox Jews are required to before afterwards consuming dairy foods.'

'How very inconvenient,' said A.P. 'Was that why you joined a Reform synagogue, Gran?'

'Well, let's just say the modern form of Judaism removes the necessity for me to feel guilty. Some who are nominally orthodox and show contempt for Reform think nothing of driving on the Sabbath, if they're invited to a Bar Mitzvah at a synagogue not within walking distance. I used to do it myself and park my car where it wouldn't be seen, along with the rest, and it made me feel a hypocrite.'

'I expect I'd feel like you once did if I secretly ate meat on a Friday,' said her grandson, reminding her he was a Catholic. 'And my dad still calls cereal "the necessary". We sometimes sit in the kitchen feeding our faces while Mum's in the living-room immersed in a book. That's when we have our chats.'

Though the closeness between Martin and his son was a

warming thought for Marianne, it was tempered by the knowledge of their alliance against Moira.

Moira's having brought the situation upon herself made matters no easier. She must surely know that A.P.'s increasing involvement with his father's family had not caused his Catholicism to falter. Marianne had come to realize that what Moira feared was the family itself.

And the more A.P. comes towards us, the further Moira retreats from us, she reflected, watching the boy spread butter and jam on yet another piece of matzo. Marianne could not recall the last time she had seen her daughter-in-law. Pressure of work is sometimes a useful excuse, though I've never employed it with Moira.

'May I have an apple, too, Gran?'

Marianne's reply was the one that she and Shirley had years ago received from Sarah Sandberg, when they asked permission to help themselves to fruit from the bowl on her table.

'Have whatever you like. This is your second home.'

'Do you really mean that, Gran?'

'You should know by now, A.P., that I don't say what I don't mean.'

'I was just making double-sure.'

'Is it that important to you?'

Marianne scanned his expression, aware that he was thinking carefully before replying. Keeping her waiting like Ralph used to do when they were discussing something that mattered. An attribute that skipped a generation, since Martin like me is inclined to rush in where angels fear to tread.

Only once had he notably not done so. On the sultry evening that heralded the end of the baking hot summer that took Britain by surprise in 1969.

Marianne had spent the day preparing food for one of the dinner-parties Ralph's new business venture obliged her to give. I was laying the table on the patio when Martin suddenly appeared at my side. She could still see the insects buzzing around the lamps and the rose bushes like spectres in the dusk, their perfume lending sweetness to the humid air. I had to slap Martin's hand to stop him from making short work of the cocktail snacks awaiting the guests on the outdoor bar Ralph had rigged up.

A year had passed since Martin came down from Oxford and met Moira, and Marianne had with mixed feelings watched her son head towards the dilemma with which she herself was faced at his age.

His unexpected arrival that evening was due to his not having been invited to Lord Kyverdale's birthday party and Marianne re-lived the indignation that had gripped her then. But wasn't it like that for Moira with our family? Not for them nor for us was there any chance that the outsider would convert. As things turned out, though, it was necessary for both families to let the outsider in.

For Martin that evening was his moment of decision and he had asked Marianne how she would feel if her grandchildren were baptized. She had known that if she told him it would break her heart, he would not marry the girl he loved. Instead she had said that what she wanted was for him to be happy.

Sixteen years later, all the evidence was to the contrary. She watched her grandson take an apple from the fruit bowl and bite into it, his expression thoughtful.

'About what you asked me, Gran – '

'Would you mind reminding me what it was?'

'I did take rather a long time to answer, didn't I? You wanted to know if it's important to me for this to be my second home. Well, it's like this, Gran. I often feel like coming here, but everyone knows about you and your work. If this is my second home, though, I needn't take that into account.'

'That's excellent reasoning, A.P. I'll let you have a key and then you can come whenever you like, and if I'm working it won't interrupt me. You have my permission to tiptoe into my study to bring me a mug of tea!'

'A sensible arrangement if I may say so, Gran. When can I have the key?'

Marianne did not know whether to laugh, or to cry, but of course she did neither. Had he still been a small child, she would have taken him on her lap for a cuddle. That there were times when the lad needed somewhere and someone to run to was plain. Given the strife in his home, it wasn't surprising.

She fetched her bunch of keys from the Welsh dresser drawer. 'Without my glasses, and I've left them in the study, I can't tell which key is which, A.P. As you can see, they all have tags labelling them.'

'Are your spare burglar alarm keys among them?'

'Where else would I keep them?'

'Where they're not labelled and waiting for burglars to find them. They could then switch off the bell and your neighbours would think it a false alarm. The flat could be emptied before you got back, and your study vandalized, including the manuscript you're working on being torn to shreds. Really, Gran!'

A.P. paused only for breath. 'And at night they'd have time to club you on the head in your bed before leaving, to stop you from phoning the police.'

'What a horrific imagination you have, A.P.'

'Imagination is how I'd like it to stay. I shouldn't think Granddad took the risks you take.'

'He was security mad, love. I have neither time nor patience to be. When I think how people, when I was young, didn't bother locking their doors – well, I ask myself how did we get from that to this.'

'What you just said, Gran, includes that you're not young any more. And it seems to me that you need watching over.'

'I am not yet in my dotage, A.P.!'

'But you don't bother taking care of yourself, do you?'

Perhaps, thought Marianne, because there was always someone who took care of me. Poignancy, though, made this sermon from her grandson none the less amusing.

'That's why I came here tonight,' he went on. 'I decided that the only way to make sure you don't fall off a ladder is to transfer what's on your top shelves to the lower ones. That bunch of keys must be dealt with, too.'

'Go right ahead, I'm sure you don't need me to organize you,' Marianne replied.

Nor did he and tears stung her eyelids as she watched him set to work. He would never bring her the traditional joys of a Jewish grandmother. But his displaying so graphically his concern for her was a compensation she could not have envisaged.

Chapter Four

WHILE MARIANNE WAS TRYING to decide how best to approach the matter Jake had confided to her he rang up, beside himself with anxiety, to tell her it was now out of their hands.

Laura had been rushed by ambulance to the Royal Free Hospital. What had at first seemed just a heavy menstrual period had escalated into a frightening haemorrhage, and it was in a gynaecological ward that Marianne next saw her.

A few days had passed since Jake's visit and when they spoke on the phone, Marianne had detected a note of rebuke in his voice. As if she ought to have done immediately what he had asked of her. Gone at it like a bull at a gate.

More proof that he doesn't know his wife, she thought while threading her way between two patients in wheelchairs in the hospital corridor. Laura's reaction to learning Jake had consulted Marianne would more likely than not have been to lose her temper with both, then stick her head back in the sand.

Unlike me, Laura's never been a realist, Marianne reflected, or she wouldn't have married a man from whom she thought it necessary to hide the life she lived before she met him.

Jake was seated beside Laura when Marianne entered the ward, the scent of the flowers he had brought her overpowering the antiseptic permeating the air.

'I've been telling Laura to let this be a lesson to her,' he said.

'But I am in no mood to be lectured,' said Laura. 'What I'd like, Jake, is to talk woman-talk with Marianne.'

'In that case I'll let the two of you get on with it and take the opportunity to get myself some coffee.'

'They make good coffee at that pastry shop on South End Green,' Laura told him. 'I used to go there with my friends before I knew you.'

Jake turned to Marianne. 'Believe it or not, I've yet to meet any of Laura's old friends. I suggested we give a party for them. For some reason Laura, who loves parties, hasn't got around to it.'

Was that tinged with innuendo? Marianne could not be sure and a moment later Jake was gone.

'Even a man you love can be tiresome in the circumstances I'm now in!' Laura exclaimed. 'Jake's been going on and on at me because I didn't take his advice.'

'About what?' Marianne inquired, po-faced.

She then heard from Laura what she had already learned from Jake, and said when Laura's account was over, 'The way things turned out, though, Jake was right to be concerned.'

'That doesn't mean he had to sit there saying he told me so!' Laura glanced around at the other patients and the nurses flitting hither and thither, and lowered her voice. 'I said to Jake that my not conceiving had to be God's will and I meant it, Marianne.'

Marianne voiced her thoughts in that respect when Jake had repeated it to her.

'Yes, it does sound more like Grandma Sarah than me,' Laura responded, 'but – '

'But nothing,' Marianne cut her short. 'Why would you suddenly come out with something like that?'

'Would it help you to understand if I told you I meant that it was retribution? And in our family – well, who but God would any of us think it was from? I've learned as I've grown older that moulding your life however you please – which I certainly did – doesn't strip you of your conditioning.'

Marianne surveyed Laura's ashen complexion. She had lost a lot of blood and an intravenous drip was attached to her hand. 'Did they tell you yet what caused the haemorrhage?'

Laura nodded. 'But I didn't need telling. And thank heavens Jake hadn't got here yet, when the doctor spelled it out to me. They've advised me to have a hysterectomy. If that isn't retribution, I don't know what would be – '

'Will you stop it with the retribution!' Marianne said firmly. 'The whore of Babylon you weren't.'

'But there's something you don't know, Marianne. When Bessie was two, I had an abortion. You may remember that was the time when my career had just begun to really take off. I was getting a lot of foreign assignments from top magazines and Mum used to come and look after Bessie, so I didn't have to turn them down. It was before the money started rolling in, so I couldn't yet afford live-in help.'

Laura paused to sip some water. 'I sometimes let myself forget how Mum stood by me in every possible way. Once she recovered from the shock of me being a single parent, and from choice, she bent her own life so I could get on with mine. I refused to let her stand the cost of a resident nanny – which Mum being Mum she failed to understand. But it didn't stop her from turning herself into one whenever I needed her.'

'And when she hears you're in hospital – ' said Marianne.

'She'll be zooming down the M1 to be her usual interfering self! – which will of course include trying to have me shifted to a private hospital.'

They shared a smile. What didn't cost money was for Shirley never good enough.

'Jake's already suggested it,' Laura added.

But his reason was that nothing but the best was good enough for his wife.

'I intend to stay put, though,' said Laura. 'I couldn't get better attention than I'm getting here. Also – well, telling the doctor I'd rather my husband didn't know the diagnosis wasn't easy. I have no wish to repeat that request elsewhere.'

'Shall you have the hysterectomy?'

'Since it's necessary, yes.'

'And you're hoping to keep that from Jake?'

'Of course not. Only the bit of the diagnosis which he couldn't handle if he knew about it. All Jake need know is that I have a nice bunch of fibroids,' Laura said whimsically. 'As for the rest – well, the abortion I mentioned was botched. By the guy who made it necessary. He was a medical student. And a real stud.'

A flash of the old Laura, thought Marianne.

'I was desperate enough to let him deal with it,' she went on. 'Where would I have got the money for a proper job? – except by asking Mum. I'd already put her through enough, hadn't I?'

A ward orderly came to take Laura's flowers to put them in water and said, admiring the profusion of red roses, 'Somebody loves you!'

But Jake Bornstein's love, warm and kindly though he was, could be likened to a moral strait jacket. And Laura's situation to that of an idol on a pedestal, albeit in Jake's eyes slightly chipped, but that he had brought himself to overlook. How long would it be before his idol toppled off?

'You could have come to me for the money,' Marianne resumed the conversation when the cheerful black woman had departed the bedside.

'I couldn't have looked you in the face, Marianne, and told you I wanted an abortion for my own selfish reasons. How else could it have seemed to you? Like why I had Bessie, only this time it suited me to get rid of a baby.'

Laura fingered the lace trimming on her eau-de-nil satin nightgown, and Marianne reflected that a wealthy woman's finding herself in a National Health gynaecological ward might serve to bring her down to the basics. All women were equipped with the same plumbing – and the other patients on this ward hadn't got their nighties from Harrods.

'That was when I realized what I'd done to Bessie,' Laura revealed. 'That because I'd wanted a child, but not a man complicating my life, she would never know her father.'

Marianne said after a pause, 'Is it too late to put that right?'

'It sure is and on more counts than one. The guy who

begat her – and he wasn't even a good lay – is an Israeli egghead I selected for the purpose when I did the pictures for a magazine article on him.'

'Did you keep copies of the pictures?'

'Certainly not, since I approached the fathering of my child clinically.'

'You certainly did!'

'How I looked at it was that telling the kid who its father was would lead to its eventually wanting to meet him, with resultant effects on my life. Not to mention on his. He flew back to his wife and kids the next day, taking it for granted that the wild oat he'd sowed the night before wouldn't sprout. How was he to know I'd deliberately taken myself off the pill?'

Laura added with a rueful smile, 'The wild oat, though, doesn't seem to have inherited his intellect. Bessie, bless her heart, remains firmly fixed at the bottom of the class. So much for my private stipulation that the man who got me pregnant must be brainy as well as Jewish. This is some time for me to be telling you all this – with a hysterectomy looming up. When I've reached the end of the road pregnancy-wise. And when I'd have given anything to have a child with the man I love – '

They saw Jake re-enter the ward, carrying a cake box.

'Isn't that typical of him?' said Laura. 'Nobody could say Bessie didn't finally get a wonderful dad.'

Chapter Five

ON THE DAY Laura underwent a hysterectomy Leona's daughter, Carla, gave birth to her first child.

Marianne and Shirley were drinking tea together in Marianne's kitchen when Leona telephoned her good news.

'Some more of our grandmother's almonds and raisins,' Shirley said when the receiver was replaced, 'and I felt like saying that to Leona. That she's got the raisins and I'm sitting here chewing the almonds.'

'I'm glad you didn't.'

'But you wouldn't put it past me to've diluted her joy, would you?'

Marianne let that pass. 'Knowing Leona, I'd say her concern for Laura already has.'

'Well, we're that kind of family, aren't we?' Shirley replied. 'When you went through what you did, trying to have another baby, I kept my fingers crossed for you.'

Marianne was astonished to hear it, and had the good grace to say, 'I appreciate that, Shirley. How long are you thinking of staying in London?'

'A loaded question if ever I heard one. I'd intended staying only a couple of days. As you know, I'm very involved with the Manchester 35 group, and – '

Marianne interrupted her to say, 'I have a lot of admiration for the way you and your friends in that group campaign for Soviet Jewry, year in, year out.'

Shirley's altruism in that respect was for Marianne her sole redeeming feature.

'But you've always looked down on me, haven't you?' Shirley went on. 'From your ivory tower.'

If that's how Shirley sees me, so be it, Marianne thought with a mental shrug.

Shirley was thinking, What does Marianne really know about me? While she was off doing her own thing and the heck with her parents, I was helping my dad achieve what he did. And does she think because it's nearly twenty years since I lost my son I've recovered? Forgotten I once had one? All I have now is a daughter who keeps me at arm's length and money I'd be daft if I didn't try to enjoy.

Since people are not privy to each other's thoughts and we do not see ourselves as others see us, there was no likelihood of Marianne's and Shirley's relationship ever being other than it had always been.

The mutual understanding necessary to friendship had eluded them all their lives and, but for the blood tie, Marianne would not have offered Shirley her company while Laura was in the operating theatre, an impulsive gesture she now regretted.

Shirley returned to the question Marianne had initially asked. 'Leona said on the phone she hoped I'd stay on in London for Carla's baby's Brith.'

The newborn member of the clan was a boy and his ritual circumcision a major event.

'It would be letting Leona down if I didn't stay on,' said Shirley.

Family loyalty again, thought Marianne wryly.

The event fell on a Sunday, which enabled all the Mancunians but Harry to be present.

Notably absent were Leona's mother and Frank's twin.

Henry Moritz's not putting in an appearance did not surprise Leona, though he was currently living no farther away than Rome. As for her mum's saying on the phone that Mr Pitkin didn't feel up to flying the Atlantic – how could a brand new husband come before a great-grandson's Brith?

Leona sat holding her daughter's hand, while the baby was

being circumcised in the next room. Waiting for the cry of *Mazeltov!* from the assembled men to tell them that the deed was done.

'I can't bear to think of my baby being hurt,' Carla said.

'I imagine all mothers feel that way at this moment,' said the attractive girl seated on the other side of her, like Carla the wife of a rabbinical student. 'Well, I certainly did, though I knew like you do that the baby is given something soaked in wine, to suck, so he feels nothing – '

'And I've seen some drunken babies in my time!' said Ann, whose newly-relaxed demeanour had amazed those who had not seen her since Harry entered the nursing home.

The circumcision ceremony was taking place in the bedroom of the small flat Carla and Alan were renting for the duration of his studies.

'It's a good thing women are excluded from the actual Brith,' Ann remarked, 'or Alan would've had to take down the bed to make space for us.'

'I'd get claustrophobia if I had to live in this place,' said Shirley.

Marianne could not resist replying, 'Where you live doesn't matter, Shirley, what does is who you live with. If living alone hasn't taught you that, it has me.'

'You though,' Shirley retorted, 'were lucky enough to have a happy marriage!'

If Shirley thought luck was responsible for that, small wonder that hers had failed.

'Doesn't the spread on the table look lovely?' was Ann's way of interceding. 'But when didn't it at a Brith in our family?' she added reminiscently.

Marianne recognized one of Ann's fruit cakes, and a fancy gateau that had to have been made by Shirley. The Victoria sponge was Lyn's speciality. And the Viennese *Sachertorte* Leona's, from a recipe handed down by Frank's aunts.

The dish of chopped herring was Marianne's contribution – nobody would be surprised to know it wasn't homemade!

Laura, not yet out of hospital, had asked Jake to supply some smoked salmon on her behalf.

My grandmother used to say that food is Jewish comfort, Marianne recalled with a smile. In times of sadness Sarah Sandberg had put a meal on the table and instructed her family to eat.

Today's occasion, though, was joyous, and the baby's paternal grandparents, Ronald and Diane, had flown from New York to be present, both looking as if the change they had wrought in their lives agreed with them.

On the table, too, was a platter of the little sesame seed cakes that featured in the Sephardi cuisine to which Diane had introduced her Ashkenazi in-laws in the days when it was an uncommon occurrence among Manchester Jewry for those of the two very different cultures to intermarry.

Marianne's mind travelled back to Ronald and Diane's engagement party, held in the near-mansion her father's wealth had acquired when the Sandbergs were still struggling their way upward. In the main, Jews of Spanish and Portuguese descent had arrived in Britain with money to help them on their way – and those of us, like me, she thought, whose family background included early-immigrant privation, used to look on them as snobs. Their settling on the leafy, south side of the city, and us on the north, had lent credence to that impression, and their calling the place where they met to play bridge and tennis 'The Country Club' hadn't helped! The club was still there.

How many years did it take for what was once in effect two communities to become one? Marianne was musing when Diane said with a laugh that she had almost left the sesame seed cakes baked in New York on the plane, such was her excitement at the prospect of seeing her baby grandson.

'It was lovely of you to think of making them for the Brith,' Carla told her.

Diane, whose suit looked as if it came from Fifth Avenue, said quietly, 'The credit, though it was I who made them, must go to your father-in-law. It was Ronald who reminded me of the family custom, that the women each contribute something to the spread.'

A moment of silence followed and Carla's friend, though not a member of the family, could not have sensed something unspoken having evoked it. Diane's long seclusion, and the reason for it, was such that she might not have made the transition back into the world without Ronald's help.

'I'm so sorry Moira wasn't free to come today,' Carla said to Marianne. 'Martin told me she's just been promoted to editorial director. I'm really pleased for her.'

And would that Marianne's daughter-in-law were the friendly, uncomplicated young woman that Carla was, reading no more into Moira's sending her regrets than the face value.

'It would have been nice, if things hadn't gone wrong for Howard, to have had Christina here, too,' Carla added. 'I liked her.'

'Well,' said Ann, 'you'll soon be a *rebbetzen*, won't you? – a rabbi's wife must be charitable to everyone.'

The cry of *Mazeltov* then issued through the wall and Carla said tremulously, 'Thank God the surgery is over.'

While they listened to the men praying in unison, Marianne's thoughts remained with Moira and Christina, to whom the family came to seem a threat: I can see how en masse they would find us overpowering, but we can't help being how we are, it's bred in us. For Jews family is as important as our religious rituals. Why else would I stand by Shirley when necessary, and she by me? I seem to remember, the night Ralph died, her appearing as if from nowhere and sitting holding my hand. And me letting her! Nor could Marianne doubt that Shirley's sympathy was on that occasion genuine. Family loyalty was a deepening enigma to Marianne.

It was Nathan who returned the infant to Carla and with mixed feelings placed her firstborn in her arms. The irony of his granddaughter and David's grandson marrying had not escaped him. How ironic too that their love was responsible for another David Sandberg entering the family. The baby had been given David's name, and would henceforth be a reminder to Nathan that love was more productive than hate.

The elder David, though, had anglicized his surname. While Nathan sipped the wine someone had handed him, listening with half an ear to the genial *mohel* relaying a tale to Alan and the fellow rabbinical students helping him celebrate, he allowed himself to journey backward in time.

To one of the most heated family rows he could remember, and many there had been. That one had taken place in the kitchen of his parents' home and he was sure his mother was present. But for some reason she was not part of this memory. Only his father, seated in the rocking chair by the fire.

For once, Nathan reflected with a smile, my father stole the scene. Abraham Sandberg had long since let his wife, the indomitable Sarah, take the reins – and what a runaway horse her extended family must eventually have come to seem to her.

Nathan's middle brother was there, too. But when did mild and gentle Sammy ever make his presence felt? The opposite of David, whose announcing his intention of changing his name to Sanderton had evoked in his father an unprecedented wrath.

Abraham had sprung from his chair to confront David eyeball to eyeball, hurling at him words to the effect that the family name was no longer good enough for his big-businessman son.

It was the one and only time Nathan had ever seen his confident brother quail. But David had nevertheless gone ahead with what he said he was doing for business reasons, lending strength to Abraham's words.

Thus his son Ronald was Dr Sanderton. But *his* son would be Rabbi Sandberg. Alan's decision to study for the rabbinate was coupled with his reverting to the family name.

As though, Nathan thought now, Alan's dedicating his life to Judaism had made him the more aware of his immigrant forebears and he saw himself as their standard bearer.

A gale of male laughter prodded Nathan from his musing.

'Mind you,' the *mohel* was saying, 'that was just one of the occasions when I've seen a father turn green and faint at his baby's Brith. Alan, though, bore up remarkably well, he only turned grey! – but it will be some time before his son causes that to happen to his hair. May I please have another slice of that scrumptious gateau?'

'Thank you for the compliment,' said Shirley.

'You actually made it?'

Marianne hoped he would not inquire who made the chopped herring.

The women were grouped around Carla, plates of food in their hands. 'Another redhead in the clan,' Shirley remarked, admiring the baby.

'But his features aren't Carla's, they're Alan's,' said Ann.

'Isn't it remarkable,' said Carla's friend, Tricia, 'how a baby in the room acts like a magnet, for women?'

'Apart from his having hair my colour, I don't think he resembles either of us at present,' said Carla eyeing him raptly. 'When my maternity leave ends, I'll have trouble prising myself away from him to return to work.'

Shirley looked horrified. 'You're going to hand over that sweet little thing to a baby minder? Your daughter reminds me of mine, Leona.'

'I have to work, too, Mrs Kohn,' Tricia told her. 'How else would Carla and I get by, married to men who aren't yet earners? It's necessary for us to subsidize their grants – '

'And a fortune they'll *never* earn,' said Shirley, which did not surprise her relatives.

Lyn, who had so far said little, remarked to Carla and Tricia that she had often wondered how clergymen's wives found time to raise their children.

'It's a daunting thought!' Tricia replied. 'But somehow we'll cope. Right, Carla?'

'You bet!'

Leona surveyed her daughter. Where had the pert little girl gone to? In her place was a calm and contented young woman. Nor did Leona doubt that Carla was capable of sharing with Alan the responsibilities of his calling.

Tricia's appearance was of a blonde fragility, emphasized by her pretty, pink dress. But the way she had responded to Lyn's remark implied her strength of character. Her husband, a bearded young Berliner, was now conversing earnestly with Howard. What were they discussing?

Marianne too had noticed. Also Howard's strained demeanour, though he had done his best to join in the celebrating. His little boy, no longer the youngest of the clan, was now six. And no one was under the illusion that Howard had learned to live with the separation.

Howard's rarely mentioning Ben was but his method of dealing with his inner feelings. Nor had he yet brought the boy to England, a further disappointment for his parents. When Marianne tackled him about it, all he was prepared to say was that Christina would rather he didn't. Why hadn't he asserted his paternal right? – a question Marianne had stopped herself from asking. What went on between her nephew and his ex-wife wasn't her business.

The welfare of her great-nephew, though, was, and each time a neo-Nazi incident in Germany was reported in the press her skin prickled with apprehension.

Christina was now remarried, and Ben the half-brother of twin toddlers, a boy and a girl. Marianne was happy that he would now grow up with the sibling companionship she'd had from Harry and Arnold. But what was the twins' father like? There was too the doubt that Ben could fit into that German gentile family. A child whose looks would not for a moment allow those raising him to forget he was fathered by a Jew.

Did Christina want to forget it? Given that she had finally fled, Marianne thought the answer had to be yes. Christina had suffered the ongoing effects of past events in which she herself had played no part. And when would a Jew stop being for a German a reminder of what he or she preferred not to think about?

Christina, though, was a kindly girl and would surely not have refused Howard's request that their son be allowed to visit his British grandparents.

She was also, Marianne reflected, of that ilk of markedly feminine women who allow their men to make the decisions. Before her remarriage her father would have done so for her. And now – well, it had to be her new husband exerting his influence.

Meanwhile, but a single ray of brightness had lit Howard's life since Ben was whisked from him: the girlfriend he saw on his trips to Germany. Why he had not brought her to meet the family remained a mystery.

Chapter Six

❧

BEFORE 1985 DREW TO A CLOSE, a young Viennese relative whom the clan had not known existed presented himself on Laura's doorstep.

'You are Laura Kohn the photographer?' he inquired politely.

'What can I do for you?' she replied warily.

Even a caller as presentable as this lad could be up to no good nowadays, and she had as always left the chain on the door.

'I am not wishing for you to do anything,' he said with a smile. 'Only to introduce myself to you. My name is Kurt Kohn, and I say to you, how do you do?'

'Kurt Kohn was my paternal grandfather's name,' Laura said when she found her voice, 'and if I seem astonished, I am!'

She undid the door chain and ushered him inside. 'My father isn't going to believe this,' she told him on the way to the living-room. 'He thought all his relatives died in the Holocaust.'

'Except for your father and mine, it is true that they did,' the boy confirmed, 'and Father will be so happy to learn that his cousin, Peter, survived. He too thinks himself the only one of his family who did. I shall telephone tonight to Vienna to tell to him this *wunderbare* news. I am unable to reach him in the daytime.'

Laura could barely control her excitement. 'Sit down and make yourself comfortable, Kurt. You and I have a lot of catching up to do. My father lives in Tel Aviv. He and his second wife – my parents divorced – have a restaurant there.

My stepmother does the cooking. What does *your* father do?'

'He is a surgeon. My mother also. And it is not guaranteed that I shall reach him on the telephone tonight. It is not unknown for them both to be called in the evenings and from their beds to operate.'

'And his name is Leopold, isn't it? It would have to be, since my dad told me he had only one male cousin.'

'What mine told to me,' said Kurt with a laugh, 'is that he and Peter, when they were young, found it necessary to ally themselves in a family full of girl cousins who enjoyed to make fun of them.'

A shadow flitted across Laura's pleasure in meeting Kurt. The girls he had just mentioned were her family too. She would not let herself dwell upon how their short lives had ended.

She forced herself to smile when Kurt said in his pedantic English, 'It is now definitely established that we are relatives.'

But Laura had not required confirmation. There was about Kurt something that reminded her of her father. The snapshots she'd seen of Peter as a boy, and he had retained the same slim stature and finely modelled features she was surveying now. Like Laura's dad, Kurt would look youthful even when his mid-brown hair turned grey.

'How did you find me, Kurt?'

'It was not too difficult. I have since arriving in London to study seen your name in magazines – and have looked for your telephone number and your address in the directory – '

'Lucky for you, *and* for me,' said Laura, 'that unlike my author cousin, I'm not ex-directory. But once you'd looked me up, what took you so long?'

'It is not for me simple to explain that to you – '

'Before you do, tell me what you're studying and how long you've been here.'

'I have enrolled in October for a psychology course.'

'Why not in Vienna where the great pioneers in the field made their mark?'

'There I shall afterwards study further,' he replied. 'My parents have advised me that it would be good to spend some time not in my own country.'

A lad who listened to his parents! Laura told him that Janis too had enrolled in October. 'She's reading English Literature, and is an active member of the University Jewish Society. Have you joined it, Kurt?'

He shook his head. 'The friends I have made at college are not Jewish.'

'Janis has gentile friends as well and they support the activities I mentioned. If they didn't, they wouldn't be her friends and she'd tell you it's time you joined in them, Kurt.'

Jewish students were increasingly finding it necessary to unite against anti-Semitism on some of Britain's college campuses. We can no longer fool ourselves that the bits and pieces we heard about before Janis was a student are isolated incidents, thought Laura. Monitoring of what was happening up and down the country provided a disquieting picture.

'Is it at me you are now frowning?' Kurt asked hesitantly.

'Certainly not.' But even on the joyous occasion having him here was for Laura, the menacing outside influences Jews in the eighties had found themselves having to live with were liable to impinge from afar.

Even a bride arriving at a synagogue on her wedding day was not spared the sight of those guarding the premises, often with walkie-talkies in their hands, and she would surely recall that along with her happier memories.

'And let me say to you what I haven't yet said, Kurt,' Laura went on, giving him a warm smile. 'You are welcome to come here whenever you feel like a home-cooked meal, or the company of your cousin and her family.'

'I much appreciate the kindness that you are offering to me. And why I did not to contact you more soon – you are a well-known person, are you not? Who might perhaps have thought – ' Kurt brushed a recalcitrant lock of hair from his brow. 'I am sure that you must understand what I am meaning.'

167

'Since you put it that way, I suppose I do. Help yourself to something from the fruit bowl, Kurt.'

'I have been thinking that the grapes look extremely tempting,' he said, doing so. 'They are not South African grapes, I hope?'

'The only products of that country allowed in this house are human beings,' Laura answered, 'and there are some who wouldn't be. It's where my husband and his children come from, and you're unlikely to meet people more against apartheid than they are.'

'I am pleased to learn that we have in common more than our blood relationship.'

They exchanged a smile.

'But I have not yet finished explaining why I had hesitated to telephone or to call on you – '

Kurt deposited some grape pips in an ashtray on the coffee table, his expression rueful. 'One evening when my parents were not at home, I telephoned an American industrialist whose name is Kohn. He was visiting Vienna and there was about him an item in the newspaper. He was staying of course at the Hotel Imperial –

'My mother, she is the sole survivor of her family, as my father thought that he was,' he added after a pensive pause, 'and for me to have only my parents – it was not a good feeling. Since I have not mentioned brothers or sisters, you will have correctly assumed that I have none,' he said, collecting himself.

Laura, who took being one of the clan for granted, thought of all the times in her youth when she'd felt like telling them all where to go. Kurt, though, yearned for what he'd never had.

'I was connected to Mr Kohn's suite, but it was his gentleman secretary who spoke with me,' Kurt went on. 'After I had told to him that I am possibly a relative, he promised to pass on the message and that Mr Kohn, he would call me back. He did not do so.'

'And if that Mr Kohn *is* perchance one of us, which I doubt, it strikes me we're better off without him,' Laura said.

'It was my impression also. But I trembled to press your doorbell, after I had obeyed the impulse to open the gate and had walked up the drive. Today I am to lunch at the home of a girl who lives in Hampstead, and have found myself in the avenue where Laura Kohn lives.'

Janis entered the room clad in her bathrobe and towelling her hair. 'Why didn't you tell me we had company, Laura!' she said, stopping short.

Kurt rose from his chair, displaying the good manners apparently still prevalent in Vienna, Laura registered. If Jeremy were here he would grin at Kurt's being so polite to his sister.

While introducing them Laura thought humorously that something in the air did not bode well for the girl who had invited Kurt to lunch. Even attired as she was, Janis remained stunning. The two seemed unable to take their eyes off each other.

It would be some time before Laura realized that what she had witnessed that morning was love at first sight.

Chapter Seven

HOWARD'S FIRST MEETING with Karin had not rendered him momentarily dazed, nor caused his heart to thud, as was the case for Janis and Kurt. His relationship with the beautiful German girl had nevertheless deepened into something a good deal more than he might have wished, though he was still not sure if he loved her, or she him.

When he was with her the painful burden he carried was briefly eased. But how few those interludes had been, he reflected on yet another flight to Munich. And on this trip as on some of those preceding it, there was no certainty that when he arrived Karin would be there.

He had never failed to let her know when he was planning to visit Ben, but, even so, her involvement in her father's business meant she might be required at the head office in Berlin, or to deal with a company crisis elsewhere.

They did not waste time discussing their work when they were together, but Howard's impression was that much of Karin's was that of a trouble-shooter, a function requiring the steeliness he found hard to relate to the warm femininity she displayed to him.

Since she had yet to suggest that he go with her to Berlin to meet her parents, he had not asked her to visit him in England. Are we biding our time, he asked himself, while a stewardess refilled his coffee cup. Or playing safe? Thankful for the little we have and scared to make a move forward from which there would be no going back?

What we're doing, Howard mused, is living for the present with no thought for the future, lest it lead us to the conclusion that together we don't have one. Meanwhile, three years have slipped by, during which, though Karin's work doubtless took her to England frequently, she hasn't bothered calling me because she had to fly back to Germany the same day. And the one time she did call from London where she was staying overnight, Howard was stocktaking at the store and unable to get away. Ours is that kind of affair and there's nothing to be done about it, was Howard's final thought as the announcement he sometimes heard echoing in his head resounded: 'Ladies and gentlemen, we shall shortly be arriving at Munich Airport.'

Karin had given him a key to her pied-à-terre. But how often, by now, had he stayed there alone?

While the aircraft made its gradual descent, he re-lived a conversation he had had with Christina a year ago.

'I'd like Ben to stay the night with me, if you don't mind.'

'I do mind. Where would he stay with you but in your girlfriend's apartment? Where Ben he has told me he sometimes eats lunch when he is with you. I do not think it suitable he should see his father in bed with a woman to whom he is not married.'

'Then I'll take a room for him and me at the Bayerischer Hof.'

'I could not ask you to make such a sacrifice. The answer to your request is still no.'

How and when did Christina become so smug and sanctimonious? Howard thought. Well, she's the one who's got Ben, isn't she? And is now married to a man from her own strait-laced background – if you don't count the beer swilling. But she was as mad for me as I was for her when we met at that ski resort. Would marriage have been the outcome, though, if I hadn't got her pregnant?

With the benefit of hindsight, Howard doubted it.

He was shocked when he discovered he had deflowered a virgin, a rare species at the après-ski parties that featured in the winter sports scene. Howard remembered Christina tearing herself from his arms at the crack of dawn, to be back in her bed before her room mates awakened. Also his having a comical vision of one of them doing what she was and their bumping into each other on their way back to the room. In retrospect, though, it struck him as part of the hypocrisy imposed by some parents upon their children.

Ben's being born in Manchester had enabled Christina to fool hers that he had arrived prematurely. And Howard had let his family think whatever it suited them to think – which probably varied from person to person.

One thing was sure, though. Respectability had once more enveloped Christina! Which wasn't to say there hadn't been an element of sourness detectable in her references to his sleeping with another woman. Does that perhaps denote that the hefty guy who replaced me doesn't come up to the standards I set for her in bed? he conjectured as the plane touched down.

If so, it might teach Christina that she can't have everything – and who's being sour now!

Karin was waiting in the arrivals hall and blew a kiss when she saw him.

The one they shared when Howard reached her, for which it was necessary for her to stand on tiptoe, implied how much they had missed each other.

'It's been too long,' Howard said gruffly when they were walking, hands entwined, to where she had risked getting a parking ticket, 'and I don't think I can go on this way.'

Karin's reply was an eloquent glance, her fingers tightening on his.

It was then that Howard allowed himself to accept that Germany now had a double hold on him. It was not any more just to see his son that he boarded a plane for Munich. The hope that Karin would be there was equally emotive and no less important to him.

When Howard went to collect Ben it was Lisl Schmidt who opened the door.

'Please to come in, Howard,' she said, pleasant as always.

He wiped his feet on the doormat and followed her to the living-room of the substantial house Christina's father had bought for her when she remarried. This was the first time that Howard had been invited any further inside it than the hall.

Mr Schmidt didn't offer a penny, though, towards buying the house we lived in in Manchester, he reflected. And I'll never let what I do for my children be conditional on their pleasing me. Meanwhile I have only one child and he isn't even living with me.

'Where's Ben?' he asked, sounding more curt than he had intended. Christina's mother was a nice woman and didn't deserve to take the flak. It was too late now, though, for Howard to do what he should have – say to her, 'How are you?'

Her husband had died last year and she was now living with Christina, an arrangement Howard knew was not uncommon in Germany. People here didn't just leave their widowed parents to get by as best they may. The family outings he had observed in Munich's squares and parks on Sundays were invariably complete with the elderly, leaving the onlooker in no doubt that Germans had more time, *and* respect, for their senior citizens than could be said of the British.

'Please to sit down, Howard,' said Lisl, 'there is something I must to tell to you.'

Howard remained standing, his stomach performing a somersault – or so it felt. 'Is Ben ill?'

Lisl shook her head. 'He is in the playroom.'

'Then what is all this about? I only have the rest of today and some of tomorrow to spend with him and the time we're together is very precious to me.'

'You think I do not know that? Christina, she knows it also.'

'Is Christina at home?'

She gave him a weary smile. 'No, and if my guest does

not sit down I cannot. I am having trouble with my varicose veins.'

Howard put himself into a club chair, his bulky overcoat which he had not unbuttoned wedging him, and his muffler suddenly feeling as if it was choking him. Perspiration had broken out on his forehead and it wasn't just due to this overheated room. Something was terribly wrong.

Lisl sat down opposite him, her fingers pleating the embroidered apron she was wearing and her plump face creased with distress. 'Ben, he does not wish to see you, Howard.'

A silence followed during which Howard's tongue seemed glued to the roof of his mouth and the part of him that wasn't numbed took an inventory of the setting in which the indictment was pronounced.

Gleaming white paintwork and a wood block floor. A coffee table, with magazines neatly piled upon it. A sofa, blue like the chairs and the rug. A vase of yellow chrysanthemums on the broad window ledge, and a bust that could be Beethoven, on a corner pedestal. The gloomy oil paintings in ornate gilt frames, that had hung in the Schmidts' hall. A photograph of Christina's father atop an upright piano, on which some sheet music was propped.

'Who's the musician?' he asked as detachedly as he had surveyed the room.

'Your son.'

My son who doesn't want to see me.

'Ben, he is having lessons. Did he not tell that to you on the telephone?'

Why would he bother telling *me*?

'He did not put away the music after he has this morning practised,' Lisl went on, adding with a smile, 'but for once he has remembered to close the piano.'

The smile did not remain long on her face and a sigh accompanied her next words. 'Today he did not just to close it, with a crash he did it. It was fortunate that Christina and Hans they had already left to go to Uncle Ernst's and Aunt Elsa's diamond wedding celebration.'

Uncle Ernst the one-time SS officer, Howard registered with the once-removed feeling that was helping him get through this.

'It is a luncheon at their house,' Lisl told him. 'All Christina's cousins have come from other cities, together with their children. There has been much excitement in the family, and Ben's little brother and sister they have for the occasion new clothing. Ben also, and when you telephoned to tell to Christina that today you were coming – Ben, he has been beside himself with the disappointment.'

Howard said stiffly, 'If Christina had mentioned it, I'd have put off my visit until next week.'

'I know that, Howard. Christina also. But it is not for her, she says, to put for you the obstacles to seeing Ben. We had the trouble with him when you came for the visit in December. Then too Ben he was looking forward to a party, when all the children play games together and eat special sweetmeats. It was Hans who gave to him the talking to that his father would be lonely without him at Christmas.'

Chanukah, actually, Howard silently replied. He had brought with him gifts for Ben from all the family. Also a *menorah* and some little coloured candles.

While Lisl gazed pensively into space Howard's mind returned to the day he and Ben had spent together in Karin's flat and lonely described it despite his having his son with him. Ben had played listlessly with the toys sent by his British relatives. In the light of what Howard now knew, 'dutifully' was probably a better word.

When evening came Howard had lit the candles in the *menorah* and had sung for his son the Chanukah songs Jewish kids everywhere sang with their parents on that festival. Ben mustn't be allowed to forget the traditions from which his mother had removed him, Howard had thought. How else was he to grow up feeling himself part of his father's family?

What an empty exercise that was in the context of a child's life, he realized now. And what I've become for Ben is the person who disrupts his. Who turns up once in a blue moon and sometimes stops him from doing what he was looking forward to. If we lived in the same town, or even in the same country, and he saw a lot of me . . . A futile thought.

'I appreciate Christina's husband giving Ben that talking to,' he said in the same stiff tone that was all he seemed capable of right now.

Lisl replied, 'Did you perhaps suppose that Hans, he was poisoning against you Ben's mind? That has never been the case. Hans will not allow Ben to address him as "Father". He would not think it fair to you.'

A snippet of information that implied Ben wanted to and another stab for Howard, though again it was as if he were anaesthetized.

'Hans is the good father to your son,' Lisl declared.

He could be a paragon of all the virtues and Howard would resent him none the less. Hans not Howard would share the ups and downs of Ben's childhood, the good times and the bad. Kicking a ball around the garden with him on summer evenings and helping him build a snowman in winter, like the one Ben mentioned to me the last time I came to Munich. Cheering him on, on his school sports day. And ticking him off when he required it.

Howard cleared his throat and rose. 'While I understand why Ben doesn't want to see me today, I can't just leave it at that.'

'I did not expect it that you would. It was however necessary to prepare you.'

But there was no such thing. Even if Howard had seen this final blow coming its effects could have been no less devastating.

'The playroom is at the head of the stairs,' Lisl told him, 'and I shall let you go alone.'

Howard slowly made his way there, his heart heavy. He could hear on the other side of the door, to which was pinned a cardboard bunny that seemed to be leering at him, the sound of a tin drum being bashed. And who but Ben was doing the bashing?

He forced himself to open the door. What was he afraid of? Rejection had already been dealt him. The drum, together with a stream of German, was hurled at him. A toy truck and more abuse in the language now his son's followed and Howard simply could not handle it.

He groped his way down the stairs and out of the house, pain replacing the merciful numbness, his eyes blinded by tears and with him the picture of an angry little boy venting his feelings upon the person he held responsible for his unhappiness.

Had Karin not been in Munich that weekend, Howard would surely have headed for the nearest beer cellar and got himself drunk.

When he walked into the flat, which in some respects resembled an office, she was at her desk compiling a report and switched off the word processor when she saw his face.

'Why is Ben not with you? What has happened?'

'The answer to both questions, Karin, is my son has sent me packing.'

'A six-year-old boy cannot do that to his father.'

'I wouldn't have thought so myself.'

'And if he does, the father does not have to accept it. Take off your coat, Howard. It is soaked from the rain.'

'I didn't notice the rain.'

'In Munich it rains often.'

'But I wouldn't know that, would I?' Howard answered, divesting himself of the soggy garment.

'Your hair is dripping water on to your collar!' Karin went to fetch a towel.

Howard usually took a bus from the leafy suburb in which Christina lived, or hailed a passing cab. Today he had plodded his way to Karin's downtown flat on foot, seeing and hearing nothing. Like a zombie, he thought now, that deadened feeling with him again.

Karin handed him the towel and draped his coat and muffler on a chair near the radiator, to dry them off.

How could she be so practical when he'd just told her something so shattering? But Karin, he had learned, always kept her feet on the ground. Her life despite her divorce and its repercussions was not in the mess Howard's was. She was a highly organized person in every respect. One who managed to fit in a lover and two children with the demands of her work.

Why had he put it that way? Well, she certainly fits *me* into her schedule. But Howard had no grounds for supposing that her kids didn't come first for her.

She poured him a *Schnaps* and insisted he drink it at one gulp. But the brandy did not revive his spirits. Nothing could.

'Would you like to eat something, Howard?'

He shook his head. 'I ate breakfast on the plane.'

'And you intend it should also suffice for lunch? I have in the refrigerator some cheese and also some sausage – '

'You're behaving like my great-grandmother used to!'

'Sensibly, you mean.'

'That isn't what I'd call it.'

Karin sat down beside him on the sofa and took his hand. 'If sympathy is what you wish for, I assure you that you have mine. But I would call how *you* are behaving unrealistic. The situation you have told me of, with Ben, it is not going to change overnight, and possibly it will not do so in the immediate future. I myself would not accept it. Whether you do, or do not, if you want to go on living you will have to eat.'

'All right, Karin! If it'll make you happy I'll have a bloody sandwich!'

'And I shall attribute that outburst to your red hair,' she said before departing to the kitchen.

Not only practical, but unflappable, thought Howard.

It took but a trice for Karin to reappear with the sandwich.

Hyper-efficient, too. 'Thanks for looking after me,' he said ungraciously. 'That's not what an affair is supposed to be about, though, is it?'

'There is one kind of affair and there is also another kind,' she replied.

'What does that mean?'

'That I have had affairs before you came into my life. But I did not feel for the men what I feel for you.'

Howard put down the sandwich and took her in his arms. 'Since I didn't have so much as a one-night stand between my marriage breaking up and meeting you, I'm not in a position to say the same. But what I can say, Karin, is the feeling I have for you could be love.'

He paused and stroked her hair. 'When I said I wouldn't know if it rained often in Munich – well, what I was really saying was, how often have I been here? My visits to Ben haven't amounted to more than about four a year. And I sometimes ask myself how I've come to care for you the way I do, when the times we've been together don't even add up to the number of trips I've made here – '

Karin broke away from him and went to lean against the desk. 'Trips you have made to see Ben. Not to see me. And please, Howard, do not construe what I have just said as jealousy of your child. It is not that at all.'

'Then what, exactly, are you saying?'

'What I am saying concerns why I have not bent my life always to be in Munich when you come here.'

'My impression of you isn't that you're the sort of woman who plays hard to get.'

'I nevertheless have my pride.'

'And that's what we're talking about?'

'Partly, yes. But there is more to it than that. I have known from the start that you have no respect for German Jewry and have found myself being defensive on that account. I made clear on the day we met that I do not find it easy to live here. The attitude of those Jews who would not has turned those of us who do into a community of apologists.

179

Why else would I have told a stranger on a plane my father's personal reason for returning?'

'I'm finding this difficult to relate to what we're discussing.'

'Very much related is that if it were possible for you to take Ben to England, you would turn your back on Germany.'

'But not on you.'

A pause followed while traffic sounds drifted upward from the street and a clock on one of Munich's baroque buildings chimed three. Howard had intended taking Ben tomorrow morning to see the *Glockenspiel*. The clockwork figures adorning the town hall danced twice daily and were a delight to children. Well, that was now out. And momentarily it was for Howard as if he had no sense of time or place, but was isolated with Karin at the point of no return.

'What would your answer be, Karin, if I asked you to marry me?'

She replied unhesitatingly, 'That I love you, but I cannot think just of myself. My parents – they are growing old, and my father could not run the business without me. I must also consider my children, whose education would suffer if they were uprooted from their schools and to a country where their basic knowledge of the language would be for them a setback.'

'You have it all worked out, haven't you?' said Howard.

'To think ahead has always been my way, and this discussion had to take place between us eventually.'

'But there's only one aspect of what you said that I'm interested in right now.'

'Which aspect was that?'

'That you love me, and for the moment the rest can go hang. I want you to come to England and meet my family.'

'Only if you will reciprocate and come to Berlin. Ben also, if it can be arranged. It is time our children got to know each other, Howard.'

Though he had not meant to mention marriage, uttering the words had confirmed for Howard that he wanted to share the rest of his life with Karin. And knowing she loved him was as balm to his soul, after Ben's rejecting him.

He would not, of course, give up on his son. Nor was he prepared to accept that the hurdles Karin had listed were insurmountable.

Chapter Eight

ARNOLD'S CALLING HER was a rare occurrence for Marianne. When on a blustery spring morning he did so, her reaction was as always somewhat wary.

Listening to his lengthy reasons for not having been in touch, doodling on her notepad and wishing Arnold would get to the point of his call, regret that such was their relationship had its depressing effect upon her. Once, she'd felt close to both her brothers, and still did to Harry despite the change in him.

The change in Arnold, though, was as if he had erected a wall of pomp between himself and the family. 'Cut the excuses, will you!' Marianne interrupted him. 'I haven't been in touch with you, either.'

'Just so long as you understand I haven't stopped caring about you, Marianne.'

'Nor I about you.'

But Arnold's caring had its limits. In some respects he and Jake Bornstein were two of a kind. Except that Jake's narrowness seemed only to apply to his nearest and dearest. Jake would have a fit if his son were gay, thought Marianne, but his attitude to Matthew and Pete was that their private lives were their own. Arnold, on the other hand, applied his personal standards across the board and would, were it in his power, turn back the clock so far as homosexual freedom was concerned.

Matthew remains the skeleton in Sir Arnold Klein's cupboard, Marianne was reflecting when he said, 'So will you do it for me?'

Her wariness returned. 'Will I do what?'

'You're no different now from when you were a kid!' he exclaimed. 'Thinking your own thoughts instead of listening to what I'm saying to you. It used to drive me mad.'

'Would you like to hear some of the things about you that drove me mad? I could also put that into the present tense.'

'Let's not get into a row, Marianne. Blood remains thicker than water. And I want a favour from you.'

'Oh yes?'

'Why must you sound so hostile?'

'Get on with it, Arnold!'

'Repeat myself, you mean, because you didn't hear a word I said. Were you working when I rang?'

'On the synopsis for my next book.'

'And no doubt you went on doing so in your head. All right, I'll forgive you.'

He wouldn't, though, if he knew what Marianne's thoughts had been, since he took himself and his views so seriously discussion with him was impossible.

'I'm giving a dinner-party at the Inn On The Park,' he informed her, 'and I need you to hostess it for me. Lyn has refused point blank. But her lack of co-operation is nothing new, I regret to say. My rise from small beginnings to where I now am owes nothing to my wife.'

'I'm surprised that you actually remember whence you came,' Marianne replied. 'And has it never occurred to you that your wife also has a point of view? No, Arnold. I will not play hostess at your bloody dinner-party! Ask your secretary to do it.'

'That wouldn't be suitable. And you might find it an enjoyable evening.'

'I doubt it.'

'Look – I don't recall ever before asking you to do anything for me. And believe it or not there's nothing I wouldn't do for *you*.'

'In that case, Arnold, I'll make a bargain with you. I'll play hostess if you'll include Matthew and Pete in your guest-list.' As good a get-out as any.

183

'Are you out of your mind, Marianne? Some of my parliamentary colleagues will be there. Also a couple of important industrialists. And I'm thinking of inviting an American I'm told is the best in the game when it comes to ghosting memoirs. I'd like your opinion of him, for when the time comes.'

'I'm relieved you're not thinking of commissioning me! Why are you giving this dinner-party?' Marianne inquired.

'It's one of the things that from time to time it's necessary for me to do.'

'But the bargain I'm prepared to make with you remains the only way you'll get me in on the act.'

Arnold said after a pause, 'Since it's more than likely that my son and his friend will be touring a play, I think I can safely take the risk.'

Marianne had lost her gamble, and if her brother lost his . . . Matthew was unlikely to turn down an invitation from the father whose respect he longed for but had never won. If he let himself view it as the hand of friendship, what a disappointment he'd be in for.

What have I done? Marianne was chiding herself when Arnold asked her to get her diary to check some possible dates.

Neither could have known that the date they set would be recorded in twentieth-century history under the heading 'Chernobyl'. And for Marianne that date was to prove doubly memorable.

Meanwhile the busy pattern of her days continued. The synopsis on which she had been working when Arnold called was approved by her editor, and once again she gave herself to the gestation that preceded the birth of a book.

Her grandson had made good use of the latchkey she had given him. There were times when Marianne was so immersed in her work she did not hear A.P. enter the flat, and would later find him eating a snack in the kitchen, or doing his homework in the living-room.

Eventually the frequency of his visits began to worry her.

Visits they're not, she finally accepted. A refuge was what her home had become for him.

Nor was there any longer the pretence that Marianne had even a non-relationship with her daughter-in-law. They never saw each other, and if Marianne rang up and Moira answered the phone the few words she uttered were cursory indeed.

When Martin dropped in, he would talk about his work and Marianne about hers, as they always had. They chatted about A.P. too, but when had Martin last mentioned Moira? When had Marianne last mentioned her? It was as if by tacit consent they avoided a subject painful to both.

On an evening when A.P. had sought refuge yet again, Marianne asked herself how her grandmother might have handled the situation. Marianne, though, had never been the manipulator that Sarah was.

'My mum's at church and I don't know why she doesn't take her bed there,' A.P. had said when he arrived. 'And Dad of course is at Uncle Andy's, working as usual.'

It was now an empty house that the lad was escaping from. She watched him make short work of his third helping of cornflakes. Well, at least it wasn't affecting his appetite.

'I wouldn't mind moving in with you, Gran,' he said.

That did it! Someone must give Moira a talking to and it would have to be Marianne. Martin could use one, too. The way things were looking, what was there to lose?

Moira awaited with some trepidation her mother-in-law's arrival at the restaurant, wishing that she herself had not arrived too early. But the days when she would calculatedly have kept Marianne waiting were long gone.

She could remember discussing with Rhoda Frolich, when they were newly-weds, how best to handle their mothers-in-law. But where had tactics and trying to assert themselves got them?

Umpteen years later, though Andy's mother was now dead

and buried, Rhoda said a day never passed without Andy saying he wished he had treated her better. Reminding Moira of a thought she had once had in that respect, that the invisible cord that bound Jewish sons to their mothers was not severed even when the mother went to her grave.

Nor was it just the mother. It was the intangible that Jews called Family. An example of which, Moira recollected, was Andy's once having spent the little he and Rhoda had in the bank, in order to fly to the funeral of an Israeli relative he had never met.

So much for Moira's trying to ensure that her son would not fall prey to that intangible. And who could blame her for withdrawing from the fray to the sole comfort she had?

She saw Marianne enter the restaurant – greeted by the owner like the celebrity she was. How could that tiny woman exert the influence she did? It was she, not Moira, to whom Moira's husband and son took their troubles. If it weren't for her – what she represents – how different my life might have been.

Marianne would not have been so hypocritical as to kiss Moira's cheek, nor did she offer a platitudinous greeting. All she felt able to say was, 'I'm pleased you weren't too tied up to lunch with me.'

She had called Moira's office and finding her unavailable had left a message. A secretary had called back to accept the invitation.

'I presumed you had something to discuss with me and cancelled another date,' Moira replied.

'Thank you for showing me that respect,' said Marianne. Was this cold formality all that was left to them?

She noted Moira's pallor – which currently matched Martin's. How nice it would be if she could just pack the two of them off on holiday and all would come right.

Regrettably it would not, since they would return to the same state of affairs they had left behind. Nor would Moira have taken kindly to the suggestion if it came from Marianne.

Somehow, though, Marianne must try to dispel the chilly

atmosphere. 'Remember when you came up to London to stay with Ralph and me? And I took you to lunch and then to buy a pram?'

Moira had a picture of that day engraved upon her mind, along with others like it. Herself heavily pregnant, and Marianne ushering her into John Lewis' babywear department where they had first bought the washable nappies now largely replaced by disposable ones.

'Didn't we lunch at Genaro's?'

'I believe we did.'

'I recall us both gorging ourselves on that wonderful cannelloni with the spinach filling and the creamy sauce,' said Marianne.

'What a remarkable memory you have.'

'Only for some things.'

And Moira's remembrance included her own resentment of Marianne's behaving as if the unborn babe was hers too.

'I seem to be seeing rather a lot of that pram's occupant now he's a teenager,' Marianne said carefully.

'You're that sort of grandmother,' Moira replied.

The thinly veiled innuendo did not escape Marianne. But Moira's failing to see her own contribution to the situation was an all too human frailty, she thought while scanning the menu.

'One thing I do remember, Moira, is your fondness for fish. That was why I chose Wheeler's.'

'But if you don't mind, today I'd prefer steak.'

Nothing more was said until the waiter had taken the order, after which Marianne saw no alternative but to take a deep breath and plunge in.

'Shall we agree to speak our minds, Moira? I seem to recall us doing so that time you stayed with Ralph and me. And my afterwards believing that it had cleared the air. But I was wrong about that, wasn't I? Now, here we are, years later, with no more understanding between us than there was then.

'I have tried my best to be the opposite of what I believe we then discussed. *Jokingly* discussed. The archetypal Jewish mother. But you weren't joking, were you, Moira? I knew that at the time and took a good look at myself.'

'In the caricature sense you're not one,' Moira replied.

'Thank you for that.'

'But there is nevertheless something about you I spent years of my marriage to your son struggling against.'

Marianne went on buttering a roll. 'Has it never occurred to you that the "something" you mentioned might be all in your mind?'

'A preconception, you mean? I admit that I did have one. But it didn't take too long for it to be confirmed. That's your grandmother's brooch you're wearing, isn't it?' she remarked. But it wasn't just jewellery that Sarah Sandberg had passed down. 'Why, exactly, did you ask me to lunch with you, Marianne?'

Despite the sudden hostility in Moira's tone Marianne kept her own even. 'Well, let me put it this way. There has to be a reason for A.P.'s preferring my home to his own and it isn't my chicken soup.'

'I wouldn't call your providing him with a latchkey discouragement. On the contrary – '

The waiter's arrival with their first course cut short the conversation.

'You would like the black pepper on the smoked salmon?'

'No, thank you,' said Marianne.

Moira made no reply.

A moment of silence followed his departure and they went through the motions of squeezing lemon juice on the luscious-looking delicacy.

Marianne forked some into her mouth. It was delicious, but the food wasn't what they were here for.

'I am not the one to deny a child his need when it is made graphically clear to me,' she responded to what had sounded like an accusation. 'But that is neither here nor there, Moira. What I'd like is for my grandson no longer to have that need.'

'Then I'm afraid,' said Moira, 'that you're crying for the moon. For once, Marianne, you're not being realistic. The real picture, and I may as well give it to you, is that the closer my son draws to his father's family, the farther he grows away from me.'

'But that could have been avoided, couldn't it? And it isn't too late to right matters now.'

'Which matters are you referring to, Marianne? The situation between my son and me? The travesty my marriage now is, perhaps? Or the situation that no doubt causes you to lose a lot of sleep? Your daughter-in-law's keeping her distance from the clan.'

'All three, Moira, and you're welcome to know that I lose sleep about this entire, unhappy state of affairs. But it's what you said finally that's at the root of it.'

'Please believe that I tried.'

'I do.'

'But after a while I had to retreat.'

'Our family isn't your enemy, Moira. I must now ask *you* to believe something. We care about you.'

'The caring is part of it, Marianne. Since your memory is so good, you might recall that at several family gatherings I went outside to get some air. On one occasion you followed me and asked if I was feeling ill — I think it was at your grandmother's ninety-ninth birthday party. Every single member of the family was there and we were all crowded into your mother's flat. But it wasn't that. I'd had the same claustrophobic feeling at the last few family gatherings and panic went with it — '

'Has that happened to you under any other circumstances?' Moira shook her head.

It was then that Marianne realized that her daughter-in-law required psychiatric help.

But who is going to tell her? Not me.

Martin was that day lunching with his old friend Bill Dryden in the Oxford pub that was the setting for Bill's introducing him to Moira.

'When you called me, I almost said Martin who?' Bill quipped with the dry smile that Martin recalled from their youth.

'I should've reacted similarly if you had called me.' Martin surveyed Bill's well-bred face with affection. 'When we do get together, though, however long the interim it's as if I'd seen you yesterday.'

'On this occasion I wouldn't say that applies visually,' Bill countered. 'I've had time to acquire a bald patch and I don't recall your demeanour being the one it is.'

Martin gave his attention to his soup, then put down his spoon. 'I never could fool you, could I?'

'And I seem to recall, back in our commune days, that our friendship almost came a cropper when I stopped you from fooling yourself.'

'Me, too,' Martin said with chagrin. 'And I never did bring myself to thank you. Instead, I wasted time licking my wounds when you read my brain-child and told me I wasn't a novelist.'

'Your finally accepting my judgement was thanks enough. And our lunching here is certainly an exercise in nostalgia,' Bill remarked while refilling their glasses with Burgundy.

'In our undergrad days we couldn't afford to lunch here,' Martin reminisced, 'though at table in our seat of learning we were somewhat splendidly wined and dined.'

'My father,' said Bill, 'has been known to joke to his friends that Oxford metamorphosed me into a connoisseur of vintages if not into a professor.'

'When mine said that sort of thing he wasn't joking!'

'They might both have changed their tune had they tasted that dreadful plonk we were constrained to imbibe at the commune.'

'And I sometimes wish myself back with what Omar Khayyam conjured up in a couple of lines.'

' "Here with a Loaf of Bread beneath the Bough, a Flask of Wine, A Book of Verse – and Thou – " ' Bill quietly quoted.

'I shan't bother asking how you knew.'

'That all is not well with you and Moira? If I may dip into *The Rubaiyat of Omar Khayyam* again,' said Bill, 'she wasn't, figuratively speaking, beside you singing in the Wilderness in the days you're now yearning for. The Wilderness wasn't quite Paradise for you then, though I have to say it was for me.'

The onlooker sees more of the game than the participants, Martin reflected. Or was it that there was much I didn't let myself see?

They fell silent while their soup plates were removed and roast beef with Yorkshire pudding put before them. Visible from the dining alcove was the bar beside which Martin had first set eyes on Moira, its polished oak patina seeming timeless as did the pewter tankards hanging above it, and the hunting prints on the wall that were there when Martin was a student.

Time, though, had moved on and with it his hope of happiness had crumbled to dust.

Bill was helping himself to roast potatoes and cauliflower, his appetite as ever belied by his bony appearance.

'Is your life with Sukey still paradise, Bill?'

'Good Lord no! I should like to meet the fellow who a decade and a half on could honestly say his marriage is.' Bill spooned horseradish sauce on to his plate and poured a small pyramid of salt beside it.

'When I first saw you do that,' Martin said with a smile, 'you and all the others who did it at table, it seemed to me symbolic of the difference between you lot and a grammar-school lad like me. In our house the salt was conveniently shaken on the food – a habit I've never lost,' he added while doing so.

'I'd agree it's more sensible,' said Bill, 'but one's conditioning will out and is apt to remain in matters of more importance than how one deals with condiments.'

'My son deals with condiments his mother's way,' said Martin, 'but I've never minded.'

'Why on earth would you mind something so trivial?'

'One thing leads to another, Bill.'

'A cliché that could mean anything.'

'But in this case it means that the things I do mind have finally led to the impasse that impelled me to call you. When you said you were shooting a documentary in Oxford this week, it seemed destined that I tell you in the place where I fell in love with my wife that my marriage is as good as over.'

Bill stopped eating and dabbed his lips with his napkin. 'Steady on, old chap, or you'll be lapsing into some of the purple prose in that manuscript I implored you to burn.'

'What you actually said was that the novel was lifeless. That was Moira's opinion too, though she'd refrained from saying so lest it hurt me. I have to tell you, though, she doesn't give a damn about hurting me now.'

'It isn't my advice you want, is it?' Bill said after a pause. 'Not that I feel equipped to dispense it. A marriage isn't a book.'

'To whom but you can I get how I feel off my chest, Bill? The situation is long past the stage when anyone's advice would help.'

While Bill went on eating, Martin unburdened himself at length, his meal forgotten.

'I find it remarkable that your son hasn't banged your heads together,' Bill declared when Martin finished speaking. 'Our daughter once did that to Sukey and me. Her usual method of effecting a truce between her parents is to threaten to leave home.'

'The difference,' said Martin, 'is that Mary Lou isn't the sole reason for you and Sukey staying married.'

'Then I better had offer you some advice. Though I've seen him but seldom since he was baptized, your boy is my godson and oft have I chided myself for allowing that relationship to dissipate into no more than Christmas and birthday gifts.

'I shouldn't think you want any pudding, Martin. Nor me.

While we're waiting for coffee, if you wouldn't mind I'll light my pipe.'

Bill fumbled in his jacket pocket for his ancient briar and a worn leather pouch. Waiting for him to fill the pipe and light it, which required numerous matches, reminded Martin of his own impatience years ago when their conversations were frequently interrupted while Bill lit and relit his pipe.

When eventually he resumed speaking his tone was stern. 'I shudder to contemplate the damage already done, Martin, by your son's living in the atmosphere he doubtless does. A couple remaining together for the sake of their child, or children, is a situation more harmful than protective. To which I might add that you and Moira could end up in the loony bin, if this state of affairs continues.'

'Just so long as we have separate rooms, Moira would say to that, since it's already our *modus vivendi*. And if that's where they put religious maniacs she is certainly headed there,' Martin declared.

'You didn't include the latter in what you told me.'

'You're Catholic like she is. The last thing I want is to offend you – '

'Something of a lapsed Catholic nowadays, Martin, Sukey too, and we haven't allowed Mary Lou to grow up with the fear of eternal damnation instilled in us. When we were sharing unwedded bliss in the sexual revolution the sixties was, Sukey went on calling it "living in sin" and had to steel herself to go to confession.'

Bill paused to fidget with his pipe. 'Lapsed I may be, Martin, but I haven't forgotten the hold my religion is liable to exert on those who allow it to – '

'The same could be said for Jews and Muslims, Bill. As on a less personal scale the militant settlers on the West Bank, and the Ayatollah's followers are currently demonstrating!'

'But returning to the *highly* personal – '

'I was about to. If Moira and I split up, there's no chance of me getting my lad without standing up in court and revealing his mother is going off her head. I couldn't do that

193

to Moira, Bill, and voluntarily she wouldn't let me have our son. Church and work, in that order, are what her life revolves around. There's nothing I can do to change things, but nor can I allow A.P. to be raised by her without me there. That's the impasse I mentioned, as you'll now gather.'

'But were you going over the top when you called her a religious maniac?'

'There are statues of Jesus and Mary all over the house, Bill, and that's the least of it. I've thought of having a word with her priest, and I almost did when she put one in the bathroom.'

'What stopped you?'

'I'm a Jew, aren't I? And nowadays Moira isn't beyond calling me one, though she hasn't yet included an adjective. I sometimes feel that what she'd like to do is crucify me – '

'As was once done to another Jew,' Bill said wryly.

'And the rest of us are still paying for it. It must be hard for you to relate all this to the Moira you knew.'

'And I would like to hear her side of this story. It seems to me that another lunch shared by old friends is called for, Martin. I'll give her a ring.'

Thus it was that Marianne's dilemma was fortuitously solved. Bill decided to invite Moira to dine at home with him and Sukey. By the end of the evening both he and his wife had arrived at the conclusion Marianne had.

It was Sukey who accompanied Moira on her first visit to the eminent psychoanalyst in whom Martin, though it was necessary for him to pretend ignorance of what his friends had engineered, allowed himself to put his hope.

Chapter Nine

ARNOLD LOST HIS GAMBLE as Marianne had feared he
might. Matthew and Pete were rehearsing a play in London
and accepted his invitation with alacrity.

'I ought not to have agreed to your cunning bargain!' he
fumed to her as they stood together in a cocktail lounge at
the Inn On The Park awaiting his assorted guests.

'If you hadn't, I wouldn't be here, done up to the nines,
when I'd much prefer not to be,' she countered, 'and I'm
about to make another bargain with you, Arnold. I shall
perform my role with good grace and you must show the
same to Matthew and Pete. If you don't I shall disgrace you
by getting drunk, which I only did once in my life and Ralph
told me, after I'd passed out and he'd brought me round, that
I'd taken off my shoes and danced on the table.'

'I can only hope that wasn't at one of his dinner-parties!'

'It was at one of mine.'

'You gave separate parties, did you?'

'One might just as well try mixing oil and water,' Marianne
replied, 'as people from the arts with those who have cash
registers where their hearts should be. The time I got drunk
some of my pals were helping me celebrate the aspect of
getting one's first novel published that none but writers and
the like would understand.'

'Do you still see those people now you're successful?'

'Did you drop your old friends after you were knighted?'
Marianne responded.

'I haven't had time to acquire many.'

'Me neither, but somehow I have. And I have to tell you
you've missed a lot, Arnold. To reach the peak of ambition

'with nothing but that in view has to be a lonely climb and I imagine you're feeling the chill now you're there.'

Marianne paused pensively while watching a lady mount the ornate staircase and head for the powder-room – did she know she had a ladder in her wispy black tights?

'The pals I got drunk with now have a lot of demands on their time, as I do,' she told Arnold, 'and one or two are very big names. We still keep in touch though and manage to meet occasionally. After my return to London I wasn't short of invitations to dinner or whatever, but I didn't expect it to be maintained. I know what their working lives are like and so is mine.'

'I am neither feeling a chill, nor have I yet reached the peak of my ambition,' Arnold harked back.

Which has to be a baronetcy, thought Marianne. And why not for a man to whom the influential people he entertained were nothing more to him than stepping stones?

She glanced at her wristwatch and said impatiently, 'Your guests seem to have decided en masse to make a late entrance!'

'Including the two I was coerced into inviting! If Pete puts his arm around Matthew's shoulders this evening, as I saw him do at Laura's, I shall die of shame – '

'There was once a time,' said Marianne, 'when even you would've thought nothing of it. Unfortunately we're now living in an era when interpreting something so casual is influenced by the eye of the beholder, and that coloured by the anti-gay propaganda I'm sure you approve of.'

'It's the eye of the beholders I'm worried about! Including the chap I'm considering to ghost my memoirs. If he rumbles those two – '

Marianne cut short her brother's distasteful words. 'One more remark like that, Arnold, and I shall leave you high and dry, wait for Matthew and Pete in the lobby, and take them out for an evening all three of us would enjoy.'

The woman Marianne had watched head for the powder-room emerged wearing tights of a different shade and entered the bar to join a group of couples standing with champagne glasses in their hands and animated smiles on their faces. Had she rushed in to a late-night pharmacy and grabbed some replacement tights from the stand those places all seemed to have for such emergencies?

Such are the observations and conjectures of my trade, Marianne reflected dryly. Even on a night out – and what an experience this one might prove to be – a novelist doesn't stop working. Was the woman widowed, or divorced? Feeling somewhat out of things, as I've been known to when with a party of couples –

Arnold prodded her from her musing. 'Would you believe it, the first thing Matthew asked me after accepting the invitation was would his mother be there.'

'I certainly would, Arnold, and it should tell you something, shouldn't it? Lyn loves him warts and all. Being gay is in that respect no different from an assortment of other things parents might view as shortcomings in their children. You, on the other hand – well, is it too late for you to realize what you've done to your son? For you to let fatherly love take precedence to your prejudice?'

'Lower your voice, will you?'

People had begun streaming from the bar in to the restaurant.

'If you knew the disappointment that boy is to me, Marianne,' Arnold hissed. 'I could kick myself for taking him to the Manchester Opera House when he was a school kid to see whichever Shakespearean play it was that we saw. It was after that he told me he wanted to be an actor. I laughed and said at his age I'd wanted to be a professional cricketer – '

'You were no good at cricket, though, were you? The same can't be said of Matthew's acting. Aren't you proud of what he's achieved?'

'I would rather he were a street-sweeper than what, thanks to you-know-who, he became.'

Trying to get through to Arnold was like butting your head on a brick wall! Marianne eyed their reflections in a mirror beside the lift. Was that portly gent really the lad she'd grown up with? The woman clad in black and red, her hair streaked with silver, the kid who'd minded the shop with him and Harry while their parents ate a hasty meal?

All that remained of that Arnold was the dimple in his chin. And of that Marianne, naught but the simple hairstyle she had not let the dictates of fashion change. As for Harry . . . just thinking of him was a source of distress. Her envisaging his running his business from a wheelchair had not taken into account the self-pity consuming him though he rejected compassion displayed by his family. Marianne's daring to voice her expectation had resulted in one of his tirades, including that the sight of him in the store would frighten the customers away.

'If my guests kept me waiting this long, I'd be in the bar knocking one back!' she exclaimed to Arnold. 'Why don't you and I do that?'

'It isn't the done thing.'

And according to the 'done thing' was how Arnold had lived his life, except for his marrying out. An exception that had since proved the rule!

Matthew and Pete were the first arrivals, Matthew sartorially elegant as always and Pete looking as if he had tried his best.

'We got here too early,' said Matthew after they had kissed Marianne, 'so we hung around downstairs.'

'Too early?' said Arnold. 'You are half an hour late!'

Pete bathed him with a smile. 'Eight for eight-thirty, your secretary said, Sir Arnold. It was I who spoke with her when she called to confirm the time.'

'That accounts for it,' Arnold said with relief to Marianne. 'I had begun to think the cabinet minister I've invited had decided to snub me at the eleventh hour. He is known to be somewhat mercurial and has done that to others. As for the young woman who called you,' he said to Pete, 'thankfully she is not my secretary but a stand-in while that reliable person is on leave.'

When Arnold went to have a word with the head waiter

about the delay, Matthew said to Marianne, 'I shall probably spend the evening pinching myself to believe I'm here! How did my father talk you into hostessing the occasion?'

'Can't a woman do her brother a favour?'

'I'd say that depends on the brother. Have you any idea why he invited *us*?'

'Since you're no longer starving theatricals, it couldn't have been that,' she said lightly.

'When we were, I only recall eating a meal in a restaurant with him once and it was at my suggestion,' said Matthew. 'I was daft enough to think, since I'm his son, he might like to be one of those prepared to help us get the company started.'

Matthew had a mental picture of himself striding out of the place, heads turning to watch his stormy exit, and his father left stranded with his sole meunière at the table. The flat refusal to contribute a penny hadn't come as a shock, nor was it the reason for this remembrance remaining so painful. Matthew had cut short Arnold's expressing his opinion of homosexuals by revealing the truth about his own son.

On the tube train back to the dump he and Pete had then called home, he had found himself seated beside one of the young actresses he encountered at auditions. What was her name? No matter, it was what she said on the train that had heightened his feeling of having let his father down: 'If only you were straight, Matt – it's a real waste.'

Matthew was left in no doubt that she fancied him and she was by no means the first girl to be disappointed in that respect. But it was another kind of waste that had from then on dogged his father. Despite Arnold's noxious attitudes, the effect of Matthew's being gay upon his parents' natural expectations continued to haunt him. He could no longer let himself hope that his sister would one day give them grandchildren.

Arnold returned from the restaurant, consulted his watch, and tried to look interested while Matthew and Pete spoke of their plans to tour Europe with their new play.

'What's the theme?' he had the good grace to inquire.

'The rise of neo-Nazism,' Matthew replied.

'Then you'd better take care,' Arnold cautioned him, 'or you and the rest of your company could find yourselves getting beaten up by some of the thugs whose activities your play is about.'

'Does that mean you actually care what happens to me?' Matthew asked jocularly.

Arnold gave him an agonized glance. 'Don't ask bloody stupid questions! And if I may say so, you've lost weight since I saw you last. Are you working him too hard, Pete?'

'We have been going at quite a pace.'

'The flesh doesn't seem to drop off you, though.'

'I don't use up the nervous energy actors do each time they give a performance, Sir Arnold.'

And Matthew is giving one this evening, thought Marianne – of a son at ease with his father. When she saw the two of them together, what with Arnold's antics and Matthew's putting on a brave show, it was sometimes like watching comedy and pathos side by side. Arnold had just let his mask slip though and fatherly feeling was briefly visible.

'Directing,' Pete went on, 'doesn't knock the hell out of you in the same way and expending your energy is just for the duration of rehearsals.'

'After which *you* no doubt sit in the wings noshing chocolate while Matthew knocks the hell out of himself on stage,' Arnold said rudely.

'Bananas, as a matter of fact,' Pete replied with a bland smile. 'Chocolate doesn't agree with me.'

Only for Matthew would Pete put up with what he has from Arnold over the years, thought Marianne.

The arrival of several of Arnold's guests together could not but be a relief to all four. Introductions were made and drinks served. Arnold was constrained to hide his dismay when Matthew and Pete were engaged in conversation by the cabinet minister, who proclaimed himself a theatre buff.

Marianne had not known until Arnold primed her for her

duties that she was to be the sole female. A situation which would have sent Lyn into a panic – and on past occasions probably had, she was thinking, when the final guest made his appearance.

Marianne's first impression of Simon Newman was of a bearded man of medium height whose smile was somewhat quizzical.

Arnold added after introducing them, 'Marianne is a novelist, Simon, but you must have heard of her.'

'I have to confess I haven't. Am I going to be forgiven?'

His style matches his expression, thought Marianne. 'Certainly by me, though possibly not by my brother,' she said. 'I understand that you are a ghost writer, Mr Newman, so there's no likelihood of my having heard of *you*.'

The glance he gave her was as if he had said, '*Touché*'. Or ought she to interpret it as: 'We're quits in the first round'? A sparring bout was what their brief exchange had felt like and when the party went to the table, Marianne was none too pleased to find Simon Newman seated beside her.

It wasn't just her ruffled ego, or his bad manners in not pretending he *had* heard of her. There was something about him she found disturbing and so it continued. A consciousness of his presence even while her attention was engaged by others.

As course followed course, and the wine and the talk flowed, Marianne played the role required of her, dispensing charm to the industrialists, discussing Tory concerns with Arnold's colleagues, promising the cabinet minister a signed copy of her next novel, and winking surreptitiously at Matthew and Pete when she received from them tongue-in-cheek glances.

Only with the cultured American on her right did she make no effort whatsoever, replying when he addressed her and immediately turning away.

Not until late that night, when she was finally alone and forced herself to examine her behaviour, did Marianne let herself recognize the reason for it. She had not expected ever to encounter a man capable of resurrecting in her the feelings she had thought buried alongside her husband, nor would she have wished it.

Simon Newman was that man.

Chapter Ten

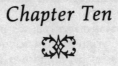

BESSIE AWOKE ON HER BIRTHDAY and tiptoed downstairs to see if the mail had arrived. Her relatives never forgot to send her a card. And now she was ten, perhaps they would stop calling her 'little Bessie'!

She also got cards from her friends, but they didn't come through the letter-box. If her birthday was on a weekday they were given to her at school. This year, though, it was on a Saturday and she wouldn't receive them until her party, this afternoon.

There was no sign of the postman when she peeped through the living-room window and she went to the kitchen to get herself some bread and jam.

Why was I born with a sweet tooth? But Janis was, too, and she's slim. Not tubby like me! And why do Jeremy and A.P. have to tease me about it? It isn't fair!

These were the thoughts of the none too happy child Bessie had become, though her mother was blissfully unaware of it. Having supplied her child with a father, and the added bonus of a sister and a brother, it had not occurred to Laura that all might not be well.

The little girl, however, had, after her initial euphoria, found the change wrought in her life not in every way to her liking.

Once the centre of her mother's world, she was now but one of the family. Though not exactly jealous of Janis, who was never less than kind to her, it was not easy for Bessie to come to terms with Laura's closeness to Janis.

A more temperamental child would have communicated that all was *not* well by giving vent as Ben so graphically had to Howard. Bessie, though, communicated her private feelings only to her diary, which she kept hidden as little girls are wont to do.

Though she called it her diary, it was an exercise book and on the cover she had printed in red crayon: 'My Secrets'.

She would never break her promise to her mummy to keep certain things just to themselves, she thought when reading and rereading her account of 'the lovely time when it was just Mummy and me.'

Except for Mummy's boyfriends, but they had come and gone, like the housekeepers had, she remembered while eating her bread and jam. Nothing was like it is now.

The thud of the mail landing in the hall sent her rushing to fetch it.

'Look, Mummy! Grandpa and Hildegard have sent me a great big card from Israel,' she said brandishing the envelope as Laura came downstairs and gave her a hug.

'Happy birthday, my darling. And I think I espy an even bigger card! That one will be from Grandma Shirley,' Laura added dryly.

'It is.'

Laura watched Bessie open the pile of envelopes, recalling how in her childhood and youth the family had never failed to remember her birthday. There were some who still did.

It was on my thirtieth that I stopped short and took stock of my life. Never a dull moment, my career looking promising, but something lacking. And to whom but Marianne would I have gone for comfort?

Laura would not forget spending that day mooning at Marianne's flat. How Marianne had eventually pronounced that the lack she felt was stability, which required a permanent relationship.

My reply was along the lines of, 'No fear! I'm not bending my life to include a husband, like you have. But that needn't mean I can't be a mother.'

It was then that Laura had made the decision that culminated in Bessie's birth. And the look Marianne gave me when she walked me to my car was as if she thought she was seeing me off to get myself pregnant immediately! My reputation was that things are no sooner said than done and hang the consequences.

'What are you smiling about, Mummy?' the consequence of that decision inquired.

'It's my daughter's birthday and I love her very much.'

'Even though I'm not pretty?'

'You will be when you lose your puppy fat.'

'When will that be?'

'I didn't lose mine till I was sixteen.'

'Six more years of Jeremy calling me "Pudge"!'

They had taken the cards to the kitchen and Jeremy entered as if on cue.

'Happy birthday, Pudge!'

'See what I mean, Mummy?'

'It's just his fond nickname for you,' said Laura.

Bessie's face lit with hope. 'Does that mean he loves me?'

'Yuk!' said Jeremy. 'And yuk to my other sister behaving as if Kurt is Romeo and she's Juliet.'

'This house doesn't have a balcony,' Laura said with a laugh.

'The balcony is all that's missing!' Jeremy opined. 'Would you like me to cook you a special birthday breakfast, Pudge?'

'That's very nice of you, Jeremy, but I'm dieting.'

'Since when?'

'Since I found out that if I don't, my puppy fat could stay on me till I'm sixteen. And when you make the sandwiches for my party, Mummy, please put some of the fillings on crackers, for me. I've made up my mind.'

Laura managed not to smile. One look at the desserts and gone would be Bessie's resolve. 'You can do that yourself, darling. With twenty little girls coming to tea, the whole family is going to be busy. You can start blowing up the balloons after breakfast, Jeremy. Kurt will help you when he gets here.'

'That'll be a change from him sitting looking in Janis's

eyes,' said Jeremy with the disgust of a lad whom Cupid's arrow had yet to pierce.

Janis then entered wearing the dreamy expression to which the family had become accustomed, poured herself some orange juice and went to gaze through the window.

Laura's humorous thought on the day Janis and Kurt met had proved to be good judgement. After lunching with the girl he had mentioned, he had returned with flowers for Janis and the two had gone for a walk on the Heath. Laura could not have foreseen then what she now thought more than possible. That her young Viennese cousin might one day also be her son-in-law.

Their youthful affair – if such it could be called – had about it an aura at odds with the earthiness that characterized most such relationships nowadays. Why else had Jeremy – not known for his lyrical imagination – equated them with Romeo and Juliet? Perhaps because there was no other way to describe them.

The balcony isn't the only thing that's missing, Laura thought. Unlike the Montagues and the Capulets, there's no family enmity to stand in their way. Laura and Jake had met Kurt's parents when they had visited their son in London and had found them charming.

Jake joined his family singing, 'Happy birthday, dear Bessie,' and lifted the little girl high in the air, to whirl her around rumbustiously.

'Careful, Dad, you'll break your arms,' said Jeremy.

'But next year I'll be a feather-weight, Daddy,' Bessie said when he put her down. 'There won't be so much of me to love.'

'Yuk, yuk, yuk!'

'Just you wait and see. And my big sister hasn't remembered it's my birthday – '

Janis emerged from her daydream and came to set that right.

'Falling in love makes people forgetful, doesn't it, Mummy?'

'And if Jeremy says "yuk" again I shall bop him on the head. Let's get on with our breakfast.'

Jeremy dished up the eggs he was scrambling while Laura replenished the toaster and Janis fetched the marmalade to the table.

Laura wished she had her camera handy to snap Bessie's comical expression as she watched everyone else tuck in and restricted herself to an apple. But the time would come when she would remember her daughter's tenth birthday as when the nightmare began.

Chapter Eleven

THE OVERT ANTI-SEMITISM in Austria, revealed to the world during the run-up to that country's Presidential election, was made the more personal for the clan by Kurt's presence among them.

By then he had met not just the Londoners but the Mancunians too. His being Sigmund Moritz's relative was sufficient to ensure him a welcome from those to whom Sigmund was a pillar of their own past.

'I can't believe the Austrian people will choose a man with Waldheim's background to be their President,' Jake said to Kurt one evening after the family had watched the *Nine O'Clock News*.

'Have a banana, Bessie,' said Laura.

'No, thanks.'

'A plum then – '

'Will you stop it, Laura!' Jake exclaimed. 'If she wants to diet, let her.' He turned to Kurt. 'What those people we just saw interviewed in the street said – well, didn't it come as a shock to you?'

'Not exactly. But then, I live in Austria. You do not. Did your father not tell you,' he asked Laura, 'how when Hitler marched into Vienna he received a rapturous reception?'

Laura shook her head. 'But I always had the feeling that there was a good deal my dad had blotted out. It couldn't have been a pleasant memory for him, could it? That the people he had grown up among – he'd have been about fifteen at the time – cheered their heads off at what for him and his family was like the knell of doom.'

Laura paused pensively. 'He never told me, either, about

the night his parents were taken by the Nazis – which was probably the equivalent of Germany's *Kristallnacht*, when the sound of breaking glass while all the Jews were rounded up was part of the horrific scenario,' she said with a shudder.

'From such details my parents also have spared me,' said Kurt, 'but each time there was an anti-Semitic incident in Vienna – and I find it significant that there are many more now that Waldheim is standing to be our President – my father would recall the *Anschluss*, how he watched from a window of his family's apartment the rejoicing that greeted Hitler's arrival.'

'Isn't it possible,' said Laura, 'that the people thought if they behaved otherwise they might go the way of Jewish citizens?'

A sardonic smile curled Kurt's lips. 'That has always been the excuse and it has suited Jews who returned there, my parents included, to accept it. But I ask you now did the French toss flowers at those who occupied France, as the tanks rumbled by on the Champs-Elysées?

'France is but one example. And those who did would have been labelled collaborators and made to pay for it after the war. Austria, on the other hand, was by some means recorded as a victim despite the joyful acquiescence we are discussing. And for the people now to say they will not have Waldheim besmirched – '

'They're not all taking that attitude,' Janis corrected Kurt.

'But should they elect him President, it would be for me an admission of their own guilt as a nation.'

'That was quite an impassioned speech, Kurt,' said Jake.

'Perhaps because it is a matter about which I, other young Austrians also and not all of them Jewish, am greatly concerned.'

'Can you spare some of Kurt's passion, Janis?' Jeremy said with a grin.

She hurled a cushion at him. 'It will be heaven help the girl *you* fall in love with!'

'Janis and I,' said Kurt, 'shall warn her not to fall in love with you.'

They were seated contentedly hand in hand on the sofa and exchanged a radiant glance.

But when, thought Laura, would romance not be enough for them and sex become an urgency? Jake would not countenance Janis's marrying while still a student, fond though he had grown of Kurt. If and when they decided to live together – well, Jake's reaction to that was something Laura preferred not to contemplate.

There was too the uneasy prospect of Janis's living in Vienna if she married Kurt. Among people like those who had told the TV interviewer that they supported Waldheim.

Laura would not let herself envisage there ever again being a Hitlerite manifestation of anti-Semitism. But if I were Austrian, I might now think it wise to up and run. If for no other reason than I wouldn't want to live my life uncertain if my next-door-neighbours were privately Jew-haters.

Laura was then forcibly reminded of what was manifesting itself in her own country.

'Kurt and I haven't told you yet,' said Janis, 'about something utterly disgusting we learned at the meeting we were at last night. A boy at one of the northern polytechnics had dog dirt put through his letter-box – as if the swastika painted on his flat door wasn't enough!'

'I'm glad you didn't tell us while we were eating dinner,' said Jeremy.

Then the telephone shrilled in the hall and he went to answer it.

'If it's for me, I'm not in,' Jake called to him.

'Engaged in one of your tactical deals, are you?' Laura said with a smile.

'No, I'd just like an uninterrupted evening at home.'

It was not to be.

'It's Marianne, for you Laura,' Jeremy said when he returned, 'and she didn't chat to me like she usually does. She said there's been a death in the family.'

Chapter Twelve

ONCE AGAIN the clan gathered for a funeral in Manchester. Since Judaic law decrees burial of the dead without delay, not all of Harry Klein's relatives were able to be present.

His daughter, Kate, had by chance been visiting her parents when Harry suffered his second and fatal seizure and it was she who supported her mother at the graveside.

Howard, beside the rabbi, had in his eyes an expression that caused Marianne to wonder if he was tracing his father's end backward to the night he and she returned from Germany without Ben.

What, though, had the time between then and his drawing his last breath been for Harry but a *living* death? There are those able to come to terms with severe disablement, but Marianne's brother had not been one of them. Instead he had tortured himself and those who loved him.

But what a good man the real Harry was. He did not deserve to be going to his grave without having seen his only grandson again, Marianne reflected with sorrow as the simple coffin customary in her religion was lowered to its resting place.

Her Uncle Nat's face looked paper white. But this was the cemetery in which all the elders of the family were buried, where he too would one day lie. She had not seen him for some time and was affected by his increased frailty.

The woman who had briefly revitalized him had not been replaced by another, and he had since achieved the English Literature degree to which he had aspired. What did he do with his time now? Alone in that echoing house with Bridie, who would surely have retired to her native Ireland were it not for her loyalty to him.

My grandmother, thought Marianne, would have suggested to Leona that she take her father to live with her and Frank. Sarah wouldn't have paused to consider if that arrangement would work and would doubtless have succeeded in contriving it.

While Howard recited the solemn *Kaddish* prayer for his father, it struck Marianne that since Sarah's death she had come to truly know her. How often have I asked myself what my grandmother would have done and been led to examine the consequences of some of her manipulating?

Who but she had influenced David and Nathan, each in their turn, to put practical matters before love in their choice of a wife? That David and Miriam had not married was in its way tragic. And Nathan's life with Rebecca equally so.

Am I being disloyal to my revered grandmother's memory? No. There'll never be another like her. The fabled matriarch had not ruled her family with the proverbial rod of iron, but with an influence capable of moulding lives. She had always left the final decision to you. And all her intentions were unarguably good. Not all of her remembered wisdoms, though, had in the long run proved wise.

Marianne eyed Sarah's nearby tombstone and silently told her, You weren't quite so perfect as I thought, and it makes you easier to live up to.

After the funeral, while the next of kin were partaking of the ritual mourners' meal in Ann's living-room, Kate stopped trying to swallow down hard-boiled egg and salt herring, and turned to her brother.

'I've asked Mum to come and live with me in Israel, Howard, and I hope you won't mind.'

'Have you discussed it with your husband?'

'Aryeh told Mum on the phone that he hoped she would now come and get some pleasure from her granddaughters.'

Howard put down the bagel he was trying to eat and managed to smile at his mother. 'I agree with Aryeh that it's

212

time you had some pleasure, and if that's what you want to do, go ahead.'

'Thank God,' said Ann, 'that I'm blessed with wonderful children and the same kind of son-in-law.'

'You still think I'm wonderful, after what I did to you?' Howard said wryly. 'And by the way, Karin sent you her love when I called her.'

'When you brought her to meet us,' said Ann, 'your dad said, "That's the right girl for our son." '

'For once I'm in complete agreement with him.'

Arnold then astonished them all by bursting into tears.

'Today, I don't feel in the least like Sir Arnold Klein,' he said to their further amazement. 'I'm just a man who's lost his brother.' He glanced at a photograph of Harry that stood on the china cabinet. 'Nobody could have had a better one,' he told Howard. 'I wish I'd had the chance to say that to your dad.'

He dried his eyes and added gruffly, 'If you'd like me to, I'll stand in for him when you get married.'

'I'll hold you to that, Uncle.' Howard turned to Ann. 'Have you given Kate your answer, Mum?'

'Not until I'd made sure you wouldn't mind. But how better could I spend the years I have left?'

A sentimental interlude followed while Ann and Kate hugged each other and more tears were shed.

Howard too had done his share of weeping today. Only Marianne had remained dry-eyed. The brother she knew had died a long time ago.

Lyn entered with a coffee-pot, Laura and Shirley behind her carrying cups and saucers, sugar bowl and milk jug.

'Couldn't you find a tray?' Ann said to them.

'What does it matter?' said Shirley.

It doesn't, thought Marianne, but it illustrates that with some folk the niceties prevail whatever the circumstances. Grief or no grief. When she arrived here this morning she had found Ann dusting the furniture, making sure her home was spick and span in readiness for the housewifely eyes of the women who would sit with her in the living-room prior to the departure of the cortège.

My mum made me clean the bathroom before my dad's funeral, Marianne recalled, in case anyone went in there to use the loo – not that it had required cleaning, any more than Ann's house is ever other than immaculate. I remember thinking, How can my mother spare a thought for that, when she's just lost her husband? I felt like ticking her off.

The longer you lived, the better you came to understand the quirks of human nature, and the keeping up of appearances essential to some if they themselves were not to fall apart. On the day Shirley's son was buried, I was as shocked as everyone else to see her dressed like a fashion plate. I had a lot to learn and I still have.

She saw Howard glance at Ann and Kate, and put down his cup.

Howard cleared his throat. 'There's something I have to tell you and there's no time like the present.'

A moment of silence preceded his saying that his father's death, coupled with his mother's decision to emigrate to Israel, had resolved a personal dilemma with which he had lived for some time. He then relayed the events of the morning in Munich he would prefer to forget.

'It was like being told straight that there was no way of me being a father to my kid. As if someone had drawn me a picture of his future and I wasn't in it. On that same day, Karin made it clear that there was no chance of her coming to live with me in England – '

'So you're now going to live with her in Germany,' Kate cut in, 'that's what you're telling us, isn't it?'

'My way of putting it would be that I'm going to where my son and the woman I love are.'

'Which happens to be the country responsible for six million Jews being consigned to their deaths. How could you, Howard!' Kate flashed. 'And what about the business Dad devoted most of his life to and left to you?'

Howard gave her a poignant smile. 'There was a time when

I took the business as seriously as Dad did. But when Ben was taken from me – well, I wouldn't wish it on anyone to get their priorities straight in the way I was made to. As for how I can bring myself to live in Germany, allow me to tell you that principles and repugnance get set aside when personal happiness is at stake. If you'd rather not visit me, Kate, I'll come to Israel to see you – '

'Don't bother,' she replied, rising to stand behind her mother's chair, her hands on Ann's shoulders as if forging an alliance with her that bespoke the future.

'You seem to have forgotten that Aryeh's grandparents were among the six million I mentioned. He wouldn't have you in the house and nor would I. It was bad enough your marrying a German, but what you intend doing now puts you beyond the pale.'

The colour had drained from Ann's face as she listened to the makings of a rift between her children. And the pleasure of living with Kate and her family will be side by side with her private distress, Marianne reflected. As Howard's long overdue happiness would be marred by estrangement from the sister he adored.

Marianne exchanged a glance with Shirley, who had to be thinking, as she was, of their grandmother's legendary words. Nor was it surprising that Sarah's long experience of life's vicissitudes had led her to call them what she had.

PART THREE

1987 . . .

Chapter One

THE FAMILY WAS REPRESENTED at Howard's wedding by Marianne, Laura, and Jake.

'Not much of a show of loyalty, is it?' said Laura as they journeyed by taxi from Tegel Airport.

It damn well isn't, thought Marianne. 'One just has to accept that for some of us principle won the day,' she said, 'and I have to admit it was necessary for me to steel myself to go with Howard to Munich five years ago.'

'If it weren't that they're swotting for exams, Jake and I would have brought Janis and Jeremy along to swell the numbers,' said Laura. 'What I regret most, though, is that Martin isn't here to be Howard's best man.'

'No more so than Martin does.'

'But you don't say no when you get an out of the blue summons to LA from the producer who sent one to Martin and Andy,' said Jake. 'Writing the lyrics and music for a Hollywood spectacular could put them where the West End show Laura and I saw didn't.'

'That wasn't because of their contribution to it,' Laura put in. 'When the critics predicted the show's early demise they said with one voice that it was miscast.'

'Given the casting couch legend,' Jake said with a chuckle, 'we must hope that whoever the Hollywood producer is currently sleeping with knows how to put a number over.'

'You're leaping ahead somewhat, Jake!' Marianne said edgily. 'There's a long way to go between Martin and Andy being invited to LA for discussions and their being offered a contract.'

Should the contract be forthcoming, they would then be

expected to write the music and lyrics on site, a suite provided for them and the producer breathing down their necks. Martin's domestic situation was stressful enough without that further strain. Marianne hadn't expected ever to wish that a step forward in her son's career would not happen.

If this one did, he would be unable to take A.P. with him to the States. She knew that were it not for Andy, he would not be half-way across the Atlantic now, his lad left with a mother whom therapy had so far failed to help. How, though, could Martin let down the partner who had shared his struggle at the moment when the top seemed attainable?

Marianne had no doubt that by now his priorities had undergone the same painful adjustment that Howard's had.

'Meanwhile,' said Jake, 'a feature of Howard's wedding will be the last minute stand-ins. He'll probably ask Karin's brother to be his best man. And I'll be honoured to play the part in the ceremony Arnold promised that he would.'

The absence of Arnold and Lyn was due to Matthew's falling ill. He had complained of dizziness after giving a performance and Pete had insisted on his seeing a doctor. A hospital appointment had followed and he was now an in-patient undergoing tests.

Nathan too was at present unwell. Which elderly person would recover easily from being mugged in broad daylight outside their own front door, Marianne thought with a surge of anger. Would this be the end of Uncle Nat? Though his bruises had faded he had not yet shaken off the psychological effects, demonstrated by his not since having left the house. Too many senior citizens in this age of violence had similarly retreated with their memories of a world that was for them a safe place.

The taxi-driver interrupted Marianne's distressing thoughts. 'Here is Kurfürstendamm,' he announced, halting at some traffic lights, 'where is the beautiful stores and cafés of Berlin.'

'I'd have liked to see the Unter den Linden,' Marianne remarked as the driver turned left into the broad avenue, its pavements thronged, and the buildings at first glance as lacking in character as Prince Charles had pronounced some of their London counterparts to be.

'Unter den Linden,' said the driver regretfully, 'is on the East Berlin side of the Wall. My children and my grand-children, they have never known it otherwise,' he added with a sigh. 'But I remember when it was not required to have a visa to drive beneath the Brandenberg Gate. When I and my wife – she was then not yet my wife – would stroll on a Sunday along Unter den Linden, the lime trees all about us, and mingle with the rich in the pavement cafés.'

Such was his nostalgia, his listeners could not but be moved. Not just nostalgia, yearning, Marianne registered.

Resentment replaced it. 'Now, we must think ourselves fortunate persons that we are allowed a day pass into East Berlin!' he exclaimed while turning the car into Fasanen-strasse. 'My wife she has living there a cousin with whom she has grown up. But her cousin's children and grandchildren – to them we are the corrupt capitalists . . .'

The stocky Berliner shook his grizzled head. 'Here is Hotel Bristol Kempinski,' he said collecting himself.

He pulled up outside the elegant entrance where a porter had hastened to the kerbside to open the taxi door. Another was sweeping invisible litter from the broad steps, a task that seemed to Marianne out of key with the top hat that was part of their livery.

Laura exchanged a smile with her. 'I didn't stay in such style when I came to Berlin to take pictures. It must have been considered too expensive by the magazine I was taking them for.'

Jake paid the taxi-driver and remarked as they entered the hotel, 'I'm still not comfortable about Karin's parents paying our hotel bill.'

'Since they insisted we must be their guests, you must accept it with good grace,' Laura replied. 'Howard mentioned that the Kempinski has a pool and a gym. The latter could do wonders for your spare tyre, Jake!'

'Would you mind, Laura, if while we're away from home we took a rest from the subject of losing weight?'

Laura's smile faded. 'I had briefly let myself forget and now you've reminded me. We still can't get Bessie to stop dieting,' she told Marianne while they waited at the reception desk.

Laura's anxiety on that account was no secret to Marianne, but she kept her tone light. 'Bessie is probably afraid of putting the pounds back on, and you must admit she doesn't qualify to be called Pudge any more!'

'Jeremy still calls her that, though, and I think he always will. That could be why – '

'If I may just have the last word on the matter,' Jake cut in, 'after which I don't want it raising on this trip again, it isn't for a kid of Bessie's age to make her own decisions. You ought not to have allowed it, Laura.'

'I seem to remember your saying to me repeatedly, "If she wants to diet, let her!" And with some force,' Laura retorted.

'By then it was too late. The reason I didn't interfere at the start was that it could have caused trouble between you and me. Your habit of indulging Bessie's every whim isn't how I dealt with Janis and Jeremy.'

'I see.'

Trouble there none the less was, nor had they left it at home, Marianne registered. Had she doubted it, Jake's tight-lipped expression while he signed the book, and Laura's hurt silence, would have told her so.

Gliding upward in the sleek lift that epitomized the hotel's glossy décor, Marianne recalled the afternoon when first Shirley and then Jake had visited her.

Laura's marriage had since appeared no more prone to ups and downs than any woman might expect. It was plain that she and Jake were still in love – but what did Marianne know of the separate and private feelings of either? Or, indeed, of what went on within their own four walls in their everyday life with their children?

Marianne would not have thought Laura capable of bending

her life to accommodate her marriage as she had. A reliable daily housekeeper had replaced the long line of au pairs, and she was continuing to refuse work that would take her out of the country.

She's now more of a family woman than I ever was or could have been, Marianne reflected. On the surface, that is. The inner Laura, that independent spirit, had to be still there. And there must be times when that person strains at the leash that's the price of her marrying Jake – whom Shirley had thought was secretly bedding the current au pair.

Anything more out of character would be hard to conceive, and the mystery of Laura's suddenly firing Ingrid was eventually solved for Marianne by Janis, in a conversation on the theme of justice.

Janis had cited Ingrid's fate as an example of *in*justice. 'My dad caught her bringing her boyfriend into the house when she thought we were all asleep. Letting him in, actually. But if Dad weren't such a killjoy, she could've done it openly, like her friend was allowed to. Dad's making Laura fire her wasn't fair.'

Since Jake wasn't what Janis called a 'killjoy' towards the world at large, his reason was clear. He would not have that example set to his daughter in his own home, thought Marianne, eyeing him as they stepped out of the lift. And it was fortunate for Janis that she herself apparently qualified for the description 'an old-fashioned girl'.

The porter led them along a thickly carpeted corridor to the two lavish and interconnecting suites reserved for them by Karin's parents.

Alone in hers, Marianne could not but be aware of her solitary state. Nor that she hadn't forgotten the man she encountered at her brother's dinner-party. A brief encounter was all it had been – and she would rather not think of the impression of her he had doubtless carried away with him.

She had unpacked and was combing her hair when Laura knocked on the door and entered, eating a peach from the fruit basket provided with the compliments of the hotel management.

'Did your outfit for the wedding get crushed, Marianne? Mine would have if it hadn't been Jake who did the packing! I've never shed the habit acquired in my roving days of just stuffing whatever into a bag ten minutes before taking off.'

Some small talk followed, then Laura said after a pause, 'You didn't do much travelling without Ralph, did you? I expect you're missing him right now.'

'I still haven't got used to being alone, if that's what you mean,' Marianne replied. 'I doubt that a woman widowed after many years ever does. But if you want the truth, I don't miss marriage.'

'You wouldn't consider marrying again?'

Marianne laughed. 'Like my mother used to say – though not in that context – it's manners to wait till you're asked.'

'But should you meet the right man – '

'Another of my mum's favourite sayings was that well-known cliché about crossing a bridge when you come to it. And still another, which could be more to the point, is not to meet trouble half-way!'

'I didn't imagine that your marital relationship was trouble-free,' said Laura, 'whose is? But essentially you and Ralph were happy together, weren't you?'

'That doesn't mean that at my age and stage I would lightly let myself in for sharing my life with a man again.'

'There's something familiar about this conversation.'

'It's more or less a repeat of one we had years ago,' Marianne told her dryly, 'but then it was me talking to you like a Dutch auntie. We've switched places, Laura, and I must say I find it amusing. You'd like me to settle down. But I'm not exactly having a rave-up!'

Jake then came to suggest that they go for a stroll on the Kurfürstendamm.

'I called Karin and Howard to let them know we've arrived,' he added, 'and Karin's parents have invited us for dinner this evening. She mentioned that the Café Kranzler is where the

smart Berliners go for coffee and pastries in the afternoon –
and you know me for pastries, Laura!'

'If only Bessie was still saying that.'

'Stop it, will you?'

Again the note of strife Marianne had detected earlier was
briefly in the air.

Laura dispelled it with a self-deprecatory laugh. 'Who'd
have thought I would turn into a mother hen?'

'Not me,' said Marianne, 'but I'd say that most women
have that potential. I've never considered myself one, but I
have to bite my tongue when I see Martin out without a coat
in winter! Remind myself that a grown man would take even
less kindly to maternal supervision than he did as a child.'

She donned her red leather jacket and slung her bag on
her shoulder. 'Shall we go and mingle with the Berliners, as
Jake suggested?'

Avid observer though she was, Marianne could find no
pleasure in this trip. Nor was the reason solely repugnance
attached to the past, she reflected while Laura and Jake went
to put on their coats. There was no shortage in the present
of reminders of that past, and not just in Germany.

In Britain the National Front had a new and well-educated
young leadership said to have initiated a long-term plan to
infiltrate every walk of life. It was no longer just a matter of
mindless thugs marching and doing their worst in the streets.

Marianne switched her mind to matters less disturbing and
went to join Laura and Jake in their suite.

When they had been bowed from the hotel – such was
the handsome young porter's deference – Marianne recalled
Howard's mentioning that the Berlin Jewish Community
Centre was also situated on Fasanenstrasse, and suggested
that they take a look at it before going to gorge themselves
on pastries.

Where the Centre now stood was once a synagogue burned
down by the Nazis in 1938. In the forecourt were some
surviving fragments, left as a reminder.

Jake pointed silently to a grey concrete wall, on which was

a memorial tablet bearing the Star of David. Momentarily none of them was capable of speech, nor were they when they entered the building and saw in the columned hall inscribed in bronze the names of the concentration camps.

Marianne could see from where she stood a library in which several young people were seated at tables as if studying. Some small children passed by in a group escorted by a girl who was possibly their teacher – which meant there was perhaps a kindergarten in the building.

When they left and were heading towards Kurfürstendamm, she suddenly registered the absence of guards and remarked upon it.

'It's possible they're placed out of sight,' Jake opined, 'since I can't imagine them not being required here.'

'What I can't imagine,' said Laura, 'is having to see that inscription in the hall each time I went there – if I lived in Berlin, I mean.'

'Those who do, though, will long ago have stopped noticing it,' said Jake. 'They couldn't live with that in the forefront of their minds all the time.'

Before they had reached the street corner, a reedy-looking youth drew abreast of them and was about to stride on when Marianne addressed him.

'Excuse me – didn't I see you in the library at the Centre?'

He slowed his pace and smiled politely. 'I also saw you. It is not unusual for the Jewish tourists who keep kosher to make use of the restaurant upstairs.'

'We just dropped in to have a look at the place,' she told him.

'And what, if I may ask, was your impression?'

'As Jewish community centres go, I found it somewhat posh,' she answered with a laugh.

'Posh?'

'Well, let me put it to you this way,' said Jake. 'I'm from South Africa, though I now live in England. I also do a lot of travelling and few of the centres I've seen could be called show-pieces.'

'Perhaps,' said the lad, 'that is what, in addition to its functions, the Berlin Centre is. A testament to a new beginning I wish that my parents had not made!'

'You speak very good English,' Marianne remarked while he simmered down.

An untoward warmth then lit his expression. 'But it is Hebrew that I wish for my language and before too long I hope never again to speak what is unfortunately my mother tongue. I have been accepted to study the Torah at a seminary in Israel and there I shall remain.'

They had paused on the corner before parting and Marianne noted the boy's uncovered head. 'In the Centre you were wearing a *yamulke* –'

'And you are wondering perhaps why now I am not? I could not be more orthodox. I am also forgetful. Today I was late to see my dentist and in the hurry I forgot to put on my hat –'

'Please don't bother explaining to us,' Marianne said with a smile, 'I ought not to have passed the remark I did.'

He went on nevertheless, his horn-rimmed glasses enhancing his earnest expression. 'I am never without a *yamulke* in my pocket, but to walk in the streets of Berlin wearing a skull cap I could not bring myself to do.'

'What do you suppose would happen to you if you did?' Laura asked.

'I am not afraid, please do not think that. In some districts it is not impossible that I might be abused, with words or fists, but it is not that.' He paused as if carefully considering. 'It is just that in Germany we do not draw attention to ourselves.'

He shook hands with them and departed.

'I wouldn't like to live with the implication of that,' said Jake as they joined the throng enjoying the spring sunshine on Kurfürstendamm.

'It could be all in his mind,' said Laura.

'Exactly,' said Marianne, 'but what we live with in our minds is liable to be damaging. And if that lad is an example of his generation of German Jews I'm sorry for the lot of them and not surprised he's escaping to where he can be himself.'

A contemplative silence followed and Marianne was briefly assailed by a sense of isolation amid the bustle. Aware of the pedestrians, young and old, going about their daily business, the traffic and its accompanying sounds, all about her the vibrance she had expected of Berlin and a brashness she had not expected. She was here for just a few days. Did the Jewish Berliners and those elsewhere in Germany live day in, day out, with the feeling the boy had put into words? Keeping it locked inside themselves?

'What's the betting,' said Jake, 'that there's no middle ground in the younger generation's attitude? That they either decide to make their escape, like that youngster has, or try to forget they're Jewish and live accordingly.'

'That last bit would be history repeating itself,' Laura replied, 'and if that was how Karin came to marry out, I'd say there's a lesson in it.'

'But what I suggest we do now, girls,' said Jake, 'is stop looking for significances and try to enjoy ourselves. It isn't like my wife to walk by store windows without pausing,' he joked to Marianne.

'I was about to do so, love.' Laura steered Marianne towards a display of elegant fashions. 'Could this be where Karin gets her marvellous suits from?'

Marianne glanced towards a section of the Kurfürsten-damm reminiscent of Oxford Street. 'Well, she doesn't get them from off those rails!'

'Nor will Howard, now he's in her father's business,' said Jake.

'You may not have noticed it, but Howard's suits are tailor-made,' Laura rebuked him.

'I was speaking figuratively, my sweet. Howard's lifestyle has changed in more ways than one.'

Laura said as they strolled on, 'He told me he got a shock the first time he came to Berlin and realized quite what a wealthy family he was marrying into, that Karin is what the tabloids would call an heiress. Do you think she deliberately kept that from him, Marianne?'

'I shouldn't think money entered either of their heads.'

'And Karin,' said Jake, 'doesn't wear her bank balance on her sleeve.'

'Any more than you do, love,' said Laura. 'I too got a shock when I learned what yours was!' she added with a smile. 'But it isn't just money we're talking about. Like you said about Howard, it's lifestyle and we don't live like the landed gentry, some of whom you could buy and sell. I understand that Karin's family do.'

They halted at the Café Kranzler, situated on a busy corner, the pastries they coveted well in evidence on the plates of those seated at the outside tables.

While casting his eye in search of an unoccupied one, Jake said, 'If I were Howard, the day after I became a family man again I'd apply for Ben's custody. I can't wait to meet that kid, by now he's like an off-stage character to me.'

'And as every playwright knows,' said Marianne dryly, 'a character never seen on stage is often responsible for much of the action.'

'Lest that was too subtle for my husband,' said Laura, 'what Marianne means is that were it not for Ben, none of us, including Howard, would now be in Germany. Howard wouldn't have met Karin, would he? But don't you go suggesting to him what you just mentioned, Jake. It has to be his and Karin's decision.'

Marianne laughed. 'If she'd lived long enough, it might have been Sarah Sandberg's carefully contrived decision! And I doubt that she'd have seen fit to take a child from its mother. Shall we see if there's a free table inside, instead of standing watching others guzzle?'

'Inside there won't be the same atmosphere,' Jake opined, leading the way.

He could not have been more right.

After mounting a spiralling wrought iron stairway, its

appearance a freshly painted white, it was as though they had been transported backward in time to the thirties. The waitresses, deferential and clad in brown, their organdie aprons and caps a discreet beige, seemed as if preserved from that era, as did the aged clientele.

After they had ordered coffee and chosen their pastries, Laura voiced their mutual impression. 'I wish I had my camera with me. This has to be a slice of pre-war Berlin set in amber.'

'And there's something about it that's giving me the creeps,' said Marianne.

'Since you mention it, me too.'

'But we mustn't let it put us off our nosh,' said Jake.

There was in the genteel atmosphere, enhanced by the women without exception wearing hats and the equally formal attire of the men, a sense of time for them having stood still, though they themselves had grown old, thought Marianne.

Since one thought leads to another, she found herself thinking, This is the generation that let Hitler do what he did, who got on with their own lives while people like Karin's parents were dragged from their homes and dispatched in freight trains like animals to the slaughter, to the camps where death was the fate of the majority.

Fifty years later, here this lot were, smiling and chatting as if their consciences were clear. Did they ever let themselves remember that what was once a sizeable Jewish population was largely gone to dust at their nation's hand?

The coffee and pastries were brought to the table, but Marianne continued musing. Laura and Jake too had fallen silent. Matters more pressing than the past would not fail to make their mark upon Howard, she thought, watching Jake heap sugar into his cup and recalling her own horror when she had read in *The Times* – or was it in the *Guardian*? – about a board game called Dachau being on sale here. That the heinous history of that concentration camp was serving as a cosy family entertainment in some German homes.

Eventually, it was withdrawn from the market, and no doubt on government orders. Successive German governments had since the war fallen over backwards to ensure that their country was seen to be trying to make amends for the unmendable.

But there are times, thought Marianne, when that seems no more than a cosmetic exercise. How could it not when the pus kept seeping from a still festering boil?

An analogy not conducive to enjoying the custard in the *mille-feuille* on her plate. Nor was it just her unfortunate choice of imagery that caused her to put down her fork. She had had her fill of what the senior citizens blithely feeding their faces represented for her.

'Whenever you two are ready, I'll be happy to leave,' she said to Laura and Jake.

'And there's no need to say why,' Laura replied.

That evening the three were transported in style to Karin's home. Her father had sent his Rolls to fetch them, the chauffeur's uniform a matching shade of grey.

The house and grounds too lived up to their expectations. What the estate agents back home could genuinely describe as designed for gracious living, thought Marianne as the car glided along a broad, curving drive bordered by tall trees and halted outside a mansion reminiscent of the country hotels in which she and Ralph had sometimes spent weekends.

The white-haired couple who greeted them did not have the aura of *nouveau riche*, which Marianne had half expected. There was something about Walter and Lili Schulmann that told you the lifestyle they enjoyed now was that from which events had horrendously removed them.

Though both were survivors of the camps, the experiences neither would forget had left no outward mark upon them, Marianne observed while sipping a glass of excellent dry sherry and participating in the pre-dinner conversation in a tastefully furnished drawing-room, its colour scheme muted gold and pastel blue, and a vast Chinese carpet underfoot.

She was conjecturing how many years it must have taken to weave the carpet when she heard Ben say doubtfully to Howard, 'Is the lady in the red dress *really* my great-aunt, Daddy? I didn't know I had an English one.' Ben then glanced at Laura and Jake. 'And are that lady and gentleman *really* my cousins?'

Howard laughed. 'You can take my word for it, Ben. Though Jake is not your blood relative, he became related to you when he married Laura.'

A qualification that rendered the little boy the more bemused his expression denoted.

'You haven't forgotten how to speak English like we do,' Marianne said to him with a smile. 'I expected you to have a foreign accent.'

'Now I see more of my daddy I get more practice,' he replied, smiling up at Howard.

Marianne exchanged a glance with Laura. What more than that did Howard require to make his own uprooting from England worthwhile, and Karin was a bonus any man would value. She and Laura had hugged Ben when they arrived, such was their emotion.

For us it was a reunion with the kid we remember, Marianne thought. For him, though, we were strangers and he was entitled to back away from us.

Five years was a long time in a child's life. But Ben was still the image of the great-grandfather dead before he was born. Marianne's dad. On that account alone she would always feel drawn to him, but given his set-up could not expect it to be reciprocal. He would never, like Bessie sometimes did, pop in to say hallo to Marianne on his way home from school.

Nor, though Howard and Karin were to set up home in Munich, would he live with them, Marianne wagered. Howard would not go back on his decision not to try to part him from his mother.

She watched Ben join Karin's children on a sofa beside the hearth, where they were seated playing what looked like the German version of Scrabble. The mellow afternoon had preceded a chilly April evening and a log fire lent cheer to the room, casting its glow upon the three small faces bent over the board game.

Tomorrow, Ben would become a stepbrother to Magda and Rudy. Would the time come when he would resent their living with his father, while he did not? If so, it would be one more heartache for a child for whom life had never gone smoothly.

'Why not draw a family tree for Ben?' she suggested to Howard. 'Then he'll know where he is with our lot!'

All three children glanced up at her, their expressions puzzled.

'I should like please to know what type of tree is that,' said Rudy.

'Does our family in England have an orchard?' Ben asked Howard.

Magda, two years her brother's elder and as fair as he was dark, then wanted to know if it was perhaps an apple orchard, or did the trees bear pears like the one in her grandparents' kitchen garden.

The adults were unable to hide their amusement.

'They are laughing at my English,' Magda said to Rudy, 'and it is unfair. I am only nine and do not speak it often.'

'But from now on you will,' said Howard, 'and you're doing very well. So is Rudy. It was what you and Ben said about the family tree that made us laugh.'

Karin smiled at the guests. 'If you will please for a moment excuse me, I shall explain to the children in German what is a family tree.'

So intrigued were they, the board game was abandoned and a questioning session began.

'When was our tree planted?' Ben asked Howard.

'Shall I begin with Sarah and Abraham stepping off the herring boat, Marianne?'

'Given all that's happened since, I'd say that was far back enough.'

But not for Ben. 'Who were Sarah and Abraham and where did they come from?'

'It was they who put down new roots,' Howard told him. 'They were your great-great-grandparents, Ben, who left Russia in 1905.'

'But why did they travel on a smelly herring boat?'

'When people have to run for their lives, they're not choosey about how they travel, son.'

'Why did they have to run for their lives?'

Howard's brief resumé of how the Sandbergs had fled the pogroms, and his explanation of that word, had a sobering effect upon the children and a moment of silence followed.

'But our name is not Sandberg,' said Ben. 'Did what you told us also happen to the Klein family?'

Howard shook his head. 'They came from Vienna.'

'Because of Hitler?' Rudy inquired.

'Long before anyone knew there'd one day be a Hitler,' Howard replied, 'when the worst that was then happening to Viennese Jews was getting their windows broken, that sort of thing.'

'Jewish people have too often had to run for their lives and it is unfair,' said Magda.

Her grandfather, on his face a reminiscent expression, emitted a long sigh. 'We have learned not to expect what is fair, *Liebchen*.'

'But the time when we had to accept that was our lot is over,' said Marianne.

'A sentiment now being forcibly expressed by the black South Africans,' Jake put in. 'I'd prefer the force not to be necessary, but more strength to their elbow is how I feel.'

'How could you not?' said Laura, toying with the jade necklace that matched her pleated silk dress. 'You're one of the other scapegoat race, aren't you? But the worst of it for us is now, we hope, in the past.'

'Hope isn't enough,' Marianne declared, 'and certainly not

with what has again begun happening. Austria is an alarming example, and I'm reminded by what Howard told Ben about our Viennese forebears that they were wise to make their exit while the going was good.'

'What are forebears?' Ben wanted to know.

'The people from whom we're descended,' she explained, adding to the adults, 'It seems an impersonal way to describe one's grandparents, but they died years before I was born.'

'I remember my English grandparents a little,' Ben said, 'and I was sorry to hear that my grandfather had gone to heaven, even though my mother told me he will now have no pain.'

A moving moment for Howard and about to be the more so.

'He and my English grandmother were very kind,' Ben went on. 'I once picked most of the flowers from a border in their garden to give to my mother. After I'd done it, I wished I could put them back and expected to be scolded.'

'They would certainly have scolded me,' said Howard.

'But they weren't even angry and I still got the sweets they'd promised I could take home. When will you draw me the family tree?'

'You'll have it before Karin and I leave on our honeymoon.'

'You must now explain to us in German what is a honeymoon,' Magda said to Karin.

When the adult laughter had again subsided Karin replied, 'I shall leave the three of you to learn what it means in due time.'

The butler then appeared with a second tray of canapés and Laura slapped Jake's hand when he helped himself to four.

'I don't get caviar and pâté de fois at home!' he said, giving Marianne a wink. 'Do Sainsbury's stock such delicacies?'

'If I thought Bessie would eat them, I'd find out.'

Laura's expression had shadowed. Jake's too. Your kids can cast a blight on your pleasure in their absence no less than they were liable to when you were with them, thought

235

Marianne. Lucky for me in some ways that I only have one!

The private exchange between Laura and Jake had taken place while the sherry glasses were being refilled and a lightheartedness in keeping with this being the eve of a wedding replaced the sober conversation that had predominated, engendered by Frau Schulmann recounting an amusing incident when she last visited her Israeli grandchildren.

'It would be nice for me to have my brother and his family here,' Karin said when her mother had finished speaking, 'but he was unable to get leave. His unit it is being kept increasingly busy on the West Bank.'

Karin was standing beside the fire and gazed unhappily at the leaping flames, her small figure in a flimsy cream dress seeming suddenly pathetic.

'My sister-in-law, she will not come to Germany,' she went on, 'nor allow her children to do so. And Howard, he now has a problem with his sister – '

He went to put his arms around her. 'We mustn't let any of this spoil our wedding day, Karin.'

How could it fail to? thought Marianne, listening to another eloquent sigh from Herr Schulmann, a man of few words. The lightheartedness hadn't lasted long, but such was Howard and Karin's situation – Howard paying the price of his decision and Karin no doubt blaming herself for the rift between him and Kate. Whether or not he would have come to live in Germany solely on Ben's account was now purely academic. The die was cast.

The English butler, a dying breed in his own country, entered to announce that dinner would be served and Marianne allowed herself just one more thought on the distressing aspect of tomorrow's joyous occasion: There was no such thing as undiluted happiness and all too often it was Family that watered down the cup.

Chapter Two

LAURA AND JAKE arrived home from Berlin refreshed by the few days together without their children, and found Jeremy alone before the television set eating chocolates.

'Janis and Kurt are at one of their meetings tonight,' he said without removing his gaze from the gyrating pop group on the screen.

'Where's Bessie?' Laura inquired.

'Where she always is when she's been on a bender. And I'm trying to watch *Top Of The Pops*.'

Laura switched off the set.

'What did you do that for!'

'Because I want an explanation from you, Jeremy. "A bender," you said. What does that mean?' Surely not drink at Bessie's age? But the things kids got up to nowadays, you never know. And Laura's knees felt weak.

Jeremy's response to his entertainment being cut short was to rise and stand, hands thrust in his jeans pockets, and glare at Laura. 'You didn't have to do what you did.'

Though it was not Jake's policy to insert himself into Laura's dealing with the children, he did so now. 'Don't be so damn rude, Jeremy. And I too want an answer to what Laura asked you.'

Jeremy cocked his head towards the near-empty chocolate box on the table. '*There's* your answer. Bessie ate most of them and she's now throwing up.'

Laura's relief was such that she had to sit down.

'It isn't surprising that Bessie is sick after gorging herself on chocolates,' Jake said to her, 'since she never eats anything sweet.'

'That's what *you* think,' said Jeremy. 'It isn't me who scoffs all the cake and biscuits that are gone from the tins in double-quick time. And where they end up is down the loo but not by accident.'

While Laura and Jake were trying to make sense of that, Jeremy went on with his revelations.

'I don't know where Bessie got the bright idea from, but for ages she's been pigging everything she feels like and afterwards sticking her finger down her throat to get rid of it.'

'Oh, dear God,' Laura said to Jake before turning on Jeremy. 'If you knew, why didn't you tell us?'

He avoided her eye. 'Perhaps I should have – '

'You're damn right you should have!' Jake thundered. 'Does Janis know?'

'If she does she hasn't mentioned it to me.'

'What sort of family is this?' Jake said incredulously to Laura.

'Not the sort I thought it was,' she said heavily. 'It seems that you and I haven't done as good a job as we let ourselves think.'

What a shock it was to find that under this roof were three children concerned only with their individual needs. Two of them, though, were no longer children in the real sense. There were times when Bessie was left in their care if only for an evening – and this was the outcome!

'Look – ' began Jeremy.

'No, *you* look!' said his father. 'I want to know why we were left to find out about this the way we did.'

'All I can say, Dad, is – well, I didn't think it was for me to be the sneak I once accused Bessie of being. And I found it funny, to tell you the truth, that a kid who once scoffed everything within sight couldn't any more without chucking up – '

'Funny?' Laura shouted.

'I stopped thinking that when I found out about her finger-down-the-throat trick.'

'Did Bessie tell you she does that? And allow me to inform you that none of this is funny!'

'No, I caught her at it. You two were out and after pigging it on ice-cream she went upstairs. A minute or two later I went to get something from my room and I heard Bessie retching. She hadn't locked the bathroom door and I went in to try to be helpful. I didn't get further than the doorway though, I stopped in my tracks.'

'Are you sure that's what you saw her doing?' Laura asked hopefully.

'I'd rather not conjure up what I saw, but you can take my word for it. And something's just come back to me, Laura – I once watched a TV documentary about girls who ate what they liked and kept slim by doing that. Bessie watched it with me. That has to be where she got the idea from. Can I switch the set on again now?'

'No, you damn well can't!' said Jake. 'And the next time I hear some clever pundit spouting that there's no statistical evidence that kids get their ideas from TV – '

Jeremy declared before departing that it was their responsibility, not his, to monitor Bessie's viewing but to do so they would have to spend more evenings at home than they did.

Laura sat mentally wringing her hands, a new experience for her. 'What are we going to do, Jake?'

'Number one, take Bessie to a doctor.'

'You don't think a good talking to would suffice?'

'I'm afraid not, Laura, and you must forgive me for not taking Bessie's dieting as seriously as you did. I'm now kicking myself both for that and how testy I've been with you about it.'

Laura managed a shaky laugh. 'No need to kick yourself, love, Jeremy has just succeeded in bruising the pair of us. I feel as if I've been through a mangle wearing rose-coloured spectacles and had them smashed.'

Jake went to sit beside her on the sofa and took her hand. 'We're in this together, Laura. Whatever it takes to get Bessie right you can count on me, as I know I could on you if it were Janis or Jeremy.'

Whatever it takes to get Bessie right. Warming though Jake's words of reassurance were to Laura, there was to them too a chilling ring.

Chapter Three

HALF-WAY THROUGH a lunchtime signing session at Hat-chards, Marianne looked up to greet the next person at the table and did a double-take. Simon Newman lining up to get my signature? This had to be a hallucination.

'I got off on the wrong foot with you,' he said, 'and since then I've been in New York. This seemed as good a way as any of my going out the door and coming in again.'

On his face was that quizzical smile. Had this not been a public appearance Marianne, though her heart was thudding, would surely have burst out laughing.

'May I call you this evening?'

'Since I can't talk now, please do. But my number is ex-directory – '

'Or I'd have called you before I left for the States.'

Marianne turned to the young man standing beside her and received from him a wink. He was one of the promotions people whom her publishers employed and escorting authors to signings was part of his job. He had in the past accompanied Marianne on some of her whirlwind tours, necessitating their spending the evenings together, and had told her it was a relief to be with an author who preferred to retire early and in some respects reminded him of his mother.

Marianne Dean, though, was now behaving like some of the younger novelists of Paul's acquaintance. I am never going to live this down! 'Would you mind scribbling my home phone number on a scrap of paper, Paul, while I sign the book for Mr Newman?'

'Why not write the number under your signature?' said Simon.

'Wouldn't that be defacing the book?'

'On the contrary,' he answered, holding her gaze.

Blushing like a schoolgirl and aware of Paul carefully not looking at her, Marianne did as she was bid.

That evening, seated opposite Simon in the intimate atmosphere of a French restaurant, Marianne, despite having acknowledged his effect upon her, was prey to confusion.

Why had she said yes to his dinner invitation without thinking twice? As if whatever was going to happen between them was inevitable and there was no point in stalling. It had been that way with Ralph. But she was then just a girl. Not a mature woman in control of her own life.

'I couldn't get you out of my mind,' Simon said.

No, stalling would not feature in this relationship. Nor had one of the flippant replies other men who had crossed her path received from her sprung to her tongue.

Instead she remained silent, studying his face in the candle light, noting its lived in look, the fine lines beside his grey eyes, and the vertical creases above the bridge of his nose, denoting as those on her own face did that concentrating was how he spent his days.

'You believed what I just said, didn't you, Marianne.'

A statement, not a question, as if he too had no doubts.

'I had that trouble about you.'

'Have you been to New York?'

'Several times, to see my American publishers. And I now have cousins living there.'

'It's a city that has to be seen through a New Yorker's eyes and you must do that with me.'

'You might find me too objective to see things through your eyes,' she warned him with a smile.

'And you have plenty to learn about *me*, I guess! Like why and how I became a ghost writer, though I'd set out to be what you are — a story that would figure large in my autobiography if I thought it worth writing, which I don't.'

Was that quizzical expression born of an inner self-deprecation? If so, the second love of Marianne's life was in that respect a replica of her first. And how often had she guiltily attributed to her success Ralph's finally giving up on his own hopes?

But she had met Simon at a later stage in *his* life. When the damage, in whatever form it had taken, was long since done, she reflected while hors d'oeuvres were served to them from a trolley and the wine poured.

By now, according to Arnold, Simon had made a name for himself though his name didn't appear on his books. Success of a kind, and he probably made a lot of money ghosting memoirs in an age when politicians and pop stars alike saw themselves as worthy subjects for public consumption. In Arnold's case he doubtless had posterity in mind!

Success of a kind because it had to taste bitter, given Simon's failure to achieve what he had set out to be.

'Your brother mentioned that you're widowed,' he said while they ate.

'Did he also tell you I have a son and a grandson?'

'No, and it hadn't occurred to me that you might be a family woman. You don't look like one.'

Marianne laughed. 'What does a family woman look like?'

Simon surveyed her smooth, olive complexion upon which a few lines were there to tell the tale. The dark eyes that right now seemed opaque and unfathomable. And the silvering hair that was at odds with her youthful shape. Did she work out in a gym every day to stay that way? Somehow he doubted it. She wasn't the sort to spare time for her looks, nor need she. It was the woman herself though, not her looks, who'd got to him. And without trying to.

'My idea of a family woman,' he replied, 'has a somewhat careworn appearance you don't have. My sister has two daughters, both divorced, and never stops worrying about them and their teenage kids. I myself haven't experienced the pleasures and otherwise of parenthood. Only a marriage that ended in my forties and put me off getting involved again,' he added after a pause, 'which I guess I'm now doing.'

'And with a female you seem to have incorrectly assessed,' said Marianne. 'Not that you're alone in making the mistake you did. I've often been told I come over as a dedicated career woman. I admit that I am, if that's what a compulsive writer who's never been in it just for the money can be called.'

She ate a sliver of marinated mushroom and put down her fork. 'But that isn't the whole of me, Simon. I'm also a family woman in more senses than just the parental. One of a big clan and there's rarely a dull moment – for want of a better way of putting it.'

'Does that mean your family sometimes get in the way of your work?'

'And how! For some reason I'm the one they come to with their problems. My hostessing my brother's dinner-party was how he solved his when his wife opted out and I can't say I looked forward to that evening.'

'But looking back?'

'I'd say it was a milestone in my life.'

'In mine, too.' Simon raised his glass. 'You and I still have far to go before we know each other, Marianne. Here's to our step into the unknown!'

Simon's introduction to Marianne's involvement with her family was not long in coming.

She had invited him in for a brandy when he took her home, neither sure if what they felt for each other would be physically consummated on their first date, the only certainty that they did not want to say goodnight.

They were seated together on the living-room sofa when the telephone rang.

'In my family, at this hour that could be an emergency,' Marianne said, rising to answer it.

It was past midnight and an emergency it proved to be.

'Can you come, Marianne?'

'I can barely hear you, Lyn, this must be a bad line – '

'It isn't the line, it's me. We've had terrible news and I can't deal with myself, let alone with Arnold. We're at the flat.'

'I'll be with you as soon as I can get there.'

Simon had seen Marianne pale. 'What on earth is the matter?'

She had replaced the receiver and was staring down at it.

'Take a sip of this,' he said bringing her glass of brandy.

'I can and must pull myself together without it,' she said, managing to do so. 'I've had a lot of wine tonight and I'm going to need a clear head. My nephew is ill, Simon. I didn't let myself believe he might be a victim of Aids. That was his mother on the phone and her voice was enough to tell me that Matthew has it.'

She mustered a wan smile. 'What an end to a memorable evening. And I must now go where I'm needed – '

Simon's response was neither the awkwardness nor the repugnance with which many would have greeted Marianne's revelation that the late-twentieth-century plague had touched her family.

'Come on. I'll drive you there,' he said.

Though not taking her own car would mean having to call a cab for the return journey, she accepted Simon's offer, which seemed to her a display of moral support boding well for their relationship.

'I met Matthew at the dinner-party,' he reminded her when they were driving down Haverstock Hill, 'and I liked him.'

'You also met Pete, with whom he's lived for years. And the idea of infidelity on the part of either of them – ' Marianne voiced her thoughts. 'Well, I'm finding it hard to believe.'

'But gay couples are no less human than the hetero equivalent,' said Simon. 'One of the few faithful marriages I know of, back home, was recently hit by Aids. The wife imbibed more than usual at one of the out of town sales conference shindigs her job lets her in for and woke up in bed with some guy.'

'Did she tell her husband?'

'I doubt it. But he sure found out when she passed on to him what was passed on to her.'

'It would have to be something of the kind that got Matthew or Pete in bed with a stranger.'

'And Pete will be a lucky guy if the tests he'll now have to have don't prove positive.'

When Marianne arrived at the Westminster flat, Arnold opened the door and Lyn, red-eyed with weeping, stumbled into her arms.

'Much good it will do for you to come to me with your sympathy,' said her brother.

Marianne, her arm around Lyn, followed him into the claustrophobic room in which he had spent more of his life than in the house in Manchester he still called home.

'It's Matthew whom my heart breaks for,' she replied crisply, 'in which I include his having you for a father.'

Arnold turned on her like a raging bull. 'So speaks the aunt my son has always looked up to! But instead of taking the stand *I* did about his aberration, what did *you* do? Supported it, that's what!'

He glared at Lyn. 'Like his loving mother did. And I sometimes had to laugh about me ending up the outcast. I'm not laughing now, though, and I hold you two as much to blame for the retribution that's finally come to prove me right as I do that bastard Pete!'

'If you want to follow in the footsteps of our late father and brother, Arnold, you're going the right way about it,' Marianne said quietly.

'That would suit me fine.'

Arnold glanced at a framed photograph of his daughter, composed and smiling. Who would have dreamed, when that picture was taken, that Margaret would one day enter a convent and the door clang shut on her contact with the world outside for all time.

'What have I left to live for?' he said.

'Certainly not me. That's been plain for years,' said Lyn.

Arnold added as though he had not heard her, 'I shan't be able to hold up my head in public when the news gets out.'

Lyn's nerves finally snapped. 'Even though his son has a fatal disease, Sir Arnold Klein doesn't stop thinking of himself! Nothing has changed and I hate you, Arnold!'

Such was her hysteria she began pummelling him with her fists. 'I could kill you! Not for what you've done to me, for ruining both our children's lives!'

Marianne dragged her away from him and led her to the sofa. Never had she seen her brother look so shocked. But people rarely knew their effect upon others and especially not those as self-righteous as Arnold had become.

'Did you hear what my wife said to me, Marianne?'

'I would rather not have heard any of what you've said to each other.' Marianne stroked Lyn's awry hair. 'What I now want to say to both of you is enough with the histrionics. Apportioning blame might be an emotional release for you two, but it won't help Matthew. He needs you now where he's never really had you – side by side supporting him together.'

Arnold said after a silence, 'They discharged him from hospital this afternoon, and you-know-who had the *chutzpah* to ask us to leave them alone together this evening.'

Marianne forced herself to be patient. 'What you're calling *chutzpah*, Arnold, was a very understandable request. If you don't want your son to depart this life believing that how he lived it was more important to you than he himself, you are going to have to show him the understanding he's yearned for and never received from you.'

Marianne went to the kitchen to make them some tea and returned to find them sobbing in each other's arms.

Why was it that shared sorrow united the estranged as nothing else could? She put down the tray and made her exit, the happy evening that had preceded this family tragedy far from her mind.

When she emerged from the building Simon Newman's Honda was still there.

He got out to open the door for her. 'I thought I'd hang on, Marianne.'

'That was thoughtful of you, Simon. I'd intended ringing up the hire car firm my brother uses, but the circumstances were such that it went from my head.'

'Just as well I did hang on, then. Or you'd now be trudging to the main road in the dark and I can't have that!'

A proprietary remark that for Marianne rang a warning bell.

Chapter Four

MATTHEW'S HAVING AIDS was as if a bombshell had hit the family.

'I can't believe this has happened to us,' Shirley said on the phone to Laura.

'If that's what you rang up to tell me, Mum, you said it the last time you called me.'

'You're not going near him, are you?'

'I beg your pardon?'

'If, God forbid, you got it you could pass it on to the children.'

'Mum! You don't get Aids the way you get measles.'

'Does that mean you *are* visiting him? And does Pete know yet if he's got it, too?'

Laura went on mixing the pudding she was making to try to tempt Bessie, the telephone receiver wedged between her ear and her shoulder.

'The reply to your second question, Mum, is Pete's tests were positive but the virus hasn't attacked him and if he's lucky it won't. To answer your first query, of course we're visiting Matthew. It cheers him up to see us. And Jeremy and A.P. often go round there to play him some of their tapes.'

'Jeremy and A.P.? You're joking, I hope.'

'You hope in vain, Mum.' Laura was enjoying telling her mother what people like her needed to be told. That an Aids victim wasn't the modern equivalent of a leper. 'Janis and Kurt visit Matthew regularly,' she went on, 'and Carla and Alan sometimes take little David with them. Matthew says Alan is the sort of rabbi who might have helped him find religion.'

'It's a pity he didn't.'

'Well, it might perhaps have helped him now,' Laura replied. 'But given the number of gay clergymen there are nowadays, religion wouldn't have stopped Matthew from being gay and I'm sure that's what you meant.'

Shirley's response was, 'You don't take Bessie to that den of iniquity, do you?'

Laura hung up on her.

How did a woman like that produce *me*! But what have I done to my own daughter?

The family now had two of its members undergoing psychoanalysis – though Moira barely qualified as a member. Bessie's analyst had made a pronouncement shattering to Laura: Her little girl's real problem wasn't a fattie's desire to be a sylph, but a deep-seated insecurity.

How has my adored child got that way? thought Laura. Did it begin when I was often working away from home? But I've made up for that since I married Jake. Is it due to my taking care not to show Bessie the favouritism she doubtless expected? And do Jake and I know any of our children better now than we did before Jeremy let the cat out of the bag?

Laura now watched over Bessie obsessively and such was the tension at home, it was not surprising that Janis and Jeremy spent as little time there as possible. Bessie's teachers had displayed sympathy and support; seemingly she was not the first anorexia case they had encountered among their pupils though the others were older girls. And their reason for starving themselves less complicated than my daughter's, Laura thought with distress, given the willowy shapes of the young models in TV commercials, even those advertising chocolate, a succulent bar dominating the ad – and what a conflict that sets up for a girl with a sweet tooth.

What was anorexia but another side effect of the consumer society in which the setting up of role models was part of the hard sell and had a lot to answer for?

Laura, though, now knew she could not blame her child's condition entirely upon that, but was in some way answerable herself. Meanwhile Bessie was on the downhill path and seemed not to care that she now resembled a currant-eyed scarecrow. Indeed, there were times when Laura sensed that she was relishing being the source of anxiety she had become to her parents.

Laura transferred the pudding mixture to a baking tin and found she had not switched on the oven. The hell with it! Bessie wouldn't eat it and Janis and Jeremy were invited for dinner at Matthew's tonight. This was the housekeeper's day off, and Laura felt like a caged lion alone with its frustration and fruitlessly lashing its tail.

A moment later she was dialling a Manchester telephone number.

'Uncle Nat?'

'That's Laura, isn't it?'

'None other.'

'I sometimes confuse your voice with Marianne's.'

'How're you doing?'

'As well you didn't ask *what* am I doing. The answer would be I've turned into an idle old man. I used to wish I had time to spare for dipping into my library, but when you have the time – '

'I seem to remember, though,' said Laura, 'on one of my visits north finding you doing a bit of gardening.'

'What long memories you and Leona have. That's the sort of thing my daughter keeps saying to me. A younger person's way of getting an oldster out of his rocking chair! But I intend getting out of mine for a few days. I'm coming to London to see Matthew.'

'He'll be thrilled to hear it – the rest of the family here, too, and I in particular am more than pleased.' Laura was unable to maintain her cheerful tone. 'Relieved would be a better word, Uncle Nat. I rang up to ask if you'd come and stay with me for a while. The truth is – well, I'm in the heck of a mess and it's something even Marianne can't help me sort out. My granddad once told me that you sometimes helped your patients in more ways than the physical.'

'I never denied them a listening ear, if that's what you mean, but tranquillizers have largely and regrettably taken over from that.'

'Grandpa said you'd got to the bottom of why a little boy was stuttering and after you'd ticked off the parents he soon stopped it.'

Was Laura due for an eventual ticking-off from Uncle Nat? If so, she thought, I no doubt deserve it. She gave him a resumé of the nightmare situation in which she now found herself.

'And you kept that from *me*?'

'You haven't been too well, have you?'

'I'm much improved and even if I weren't, would I let you down?'

Chapter Five

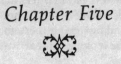

HOWARD WAS WRITING his weekly letter to Matthew, to whom though they were raised in the same town he had not felt close when they were children. Nor did he now, but that made it none the less distressing that his cousin was slowly wasting away, that Matthew might no longer be alive when the hydrangea Howard could see through the window bloomed again.

A picture misted by time rose before him. Sabbath afternoon at his great-grandmother's house, the highlight of the week for the family. Cakes and sandwiches on the tea-table. The adults all talking at once. His sister and Matthew's together with their dolls. And Matthew watching Howard and Mark play cards behind the sofa, where Sarah Sandberg for whom the Sabbath was sacrosanct would not cast her eye upon the schoolboy sinners.

Mark and I, the twosome we were, never thought of asking Matthew to join in. Kids didn't realize that exclusion could hurt and Matthew wasn't the assertive sort. He had known too, as the adults did, that Howard and Mark felt more like brothers than second cousins.

Closer than some brothers, Howard thought now, given that my dad and Uncle Arnold had only the blood tie in common. But as if with a single mind, Howard and Mark had volunteered together to lend their strength to Israel's fight for survival in the '67 war.

Kate too, and Howard could remember Mark's granddad aiding and abetting them against their parents' wishes. David had driven them to London, paid for their tickets, and put them on a plane with other youngsters who had dropped everything to do what they knew had to be done.

Planeloads of kids like us arrived from all over the world, Howard recalled, and our going there to take over essential jobs vacated by those mobilized for active service helped keep the wheels turning.

Only Howard and Kate, though, had come back, and she to tell the family she wanted to make her life in Israel with Aryeh, whom she had met and fallen in love with there.

Howard had not forgotten his parents' reaction to their seventeen-year-old daughter's decisiveness. Nor Sarah Sandberg's saying it was God's will that a new branch of the family take root in hallowed land. Well, words to that effect. When gripped by emotion Sarah had tended to wax lyrical. Like her legendary almonds and raisins, which Howard had thought amusing until he found himself tasting them.

What would Mark have said about my living in Germany? Would he too have been censorious? The lad I remember would not. But who could know, had Mark lived, that events wouldn't have changed him as they had others in the family? You started out with only your genes dictating your personality, but life could turn you into someone you yourself barely recognized.

There was no guarantee that Howard and Mark, born on the same day, would still be thinking alike at the age of forty – a landmark Howard had passed last week, and as always on his birthday he had thought of Mark.

Did Kate ever think of Margaret, once her closest friend? Or had she firmly put from her mind the cousin whose adult path was so different from her own? The path perhaps, but in effect not the destination, Howard reflected – Margaret in a closed-order nunnery, and Kate living in one of Israel's ultra-orthodox enclaves.

What Matthew and I now have in common is, for each of us it's as if we no longer have a sister. Do my letters cheer him up? Or serve to remind him of how, when we were all kids, Mark and I had no time for him? But that didn't stop him from writing to me when Mark died. By then, Matthew was a drama student in London.

Karin popped her head around the study door. 'Supper will soon be ready, Howard. And we have an unexpected visitor.'

'Be with you in a minute, darling – '

'The visitor is Ben.'

Howard put down his pen and rose. 'What is he doing here on a weekday? Is something wrong?'

'From his expression I would say so. But he did not and I would advise you not to question him.'

There remained, and perhaps always would, no-go areas in Howard's relationship with his son. But the same went for Karin and her kids. When Magda and Rudy returned from spending time in Berlin with their father and one or the other seemed tetchy, or subdued, she held her tongue.

Howard sometimes marvelled at her being the down-to-earth person she was; that despite her background her priorities were the same as his; that she didn't want servants to wait on her, or a chauffeur to drive her around, but was content with the life they now shared.

He followed her into the live-in kitchen that epitomized their lifestyle. Though this house was a wedding gift from her parents, its atmosphere was of the real world, poles apart from the home in which she had grown up.

Somehow Karin managed to cope with the twin demands of domesticity and her career. She had not wanted resident help and like Laura employed a daily housekeeper. But she was now carrying Howard's child. This evening her ankles looked puffy. And he had not yet voiced his anxiety about the frequent commuting between here and Berlin that their living in Munich necessitated. Though she had cut down on her business trips elsewhere, delegating some of them to her personal assistant, there were still times when she flew to wherever at a minute's notice.

Howard, on the other hand, was anchored to a desk in Munich and marvelled too at how easily he had adapted to dealing with the paperwork for transactions involving goods he never saw.

'Where there's a will there's a way,' had proved true for Howard in all respects. He had got himself back into his son's life and Ben was here on a weekday, to prove it, an event that despite the lad's troubled demeanour could not but gladden Howard's heart. *I'm no longer just the father who brings him here on a Sunday morning and takes him home in the evening. He's come to* me.

'Something smells good!' he said to Karin with a surge of exuberance. 'What's Rudy missing by eating at his friend's house tonight?'

She was adding salt to a pan of soup, and Magda laying cutlery on the red and white checked tablecloth that lent colour to the dining alcove – one of Karin's homely touches that Howard still found surprising.

'If I tell to you what is for supper it will not then be a surprise,' Karin said with a smile, 'and it is I who have cooked it, since I arrived home early. What Frau Schwartz has made for us I have put into the deep freeze.'

Karin paused to taste the soup. 'Ben, he has had his supper, but I am hoping he will join us for dessert.'

'If we're having ice-cream, I'm sure he will,' said Howard.

'How did you guess?' said Karin.

And how inane this conversation is, thought Howard. *But she's helping me deal with whatever's troubling Ben and I couldn't have a better wife.* Howard had never known his son so silent.

'There is also some of Frau Schwartz's *Apfelkuchen* in the refrigerator,' Karin went on with the charade. 'On Sunday, Ben, he asked for a second helping.'

'If he does not want it, I would like to have it with my ice-cream,' said Magda.

Howard thought it time to prod his lad into saying something. 'Why don't you and Magda share the *Apfelkuchen*, Ben?'

'I don't feel like eating dessert this evening and when I

256

told my mother she made a fuss and asked if I was feeling ill.'

'I would worry that Magda and Rudy were ill if they had said they did not want dessert,' said Karin. 'That is how we mothers are.'

'But I'm not ill!' Ben replied with feeling. 'And my mother said I was making it up, when I told her what has upset me.'

He was standing beside the window, his expression now mutinous.

'How about telling your dad what's upset you?' said Howard.

'While he is doing so,' said Karin, 'Magda and I shall go upstairs to her room and decide what she shall wear for her friend's birthday party.'

'We have already decided I shall wear my new skirt and blouse – '

Karin took her by the hand. 'Come along, Magda.'

Ben waited for the door to close behind them before saying perceptively, 'Karin knows that this evening it's only you I've come to see, Daddy – '

'And I'm always here for you. I want you to know that. Let me add, though, that angry as you seem to be with your mother she loves you as much as I do and –'

'But I wasn't making up what I told her!' Ben interrupted. 'And she didn't give me time to tell her everything!'

Howard put a hand on his shoulder. 'Calm down, lad. Let's make ourselves comfortable, shall we?'

They sat down on the padded window-seat, Ben's favourite place to curl up with a book when he came on Sundays and the family stayed at home.

Did he feel part of this family? Howard hoped so. 'Come on, then. Out with it, I'm listening.'

'There are things I don't understand, Daddy, and they stop me from being happy.'

'Would you like to tell me what sort of things?'

'Once, at Uncle Ernst's house, he said to me that the Jews are lying. That there wasn't a Holocaust. I didn't know what that word meant and when I asked him, he said it wasn't necessary for me to know. Only to believe him, like all the children in his family do.'

Good old Uncle Ernst! The one-time SS officer. 'Was your mother there when he said that to you?'

Ben shook his head. 'If she had been, I'm sure she would have told him what I did. That you're a Jew and you don't tell lies.'

Would Christina have risked a confrontation with her family's venerable elder?

'When I told her, she said I must excuse Uncle Ernst because he's very old.'

But still spouting the poison of his younger years and getting away with it, thought Howard.

'It isn't just Uncle Ernst,' Ben went on. 'There's a new boy at my school who's moved to Munich from Dusseldorf. Today he said to me and some other boys the same as Uncle Ernst said to me. About the Jews lying.'

'Did you give him the same answer you gave the old man?'

Ben nodded. 'And afterwards all the boys, not just him, made jokes about my nose!'

'Is that what your mother accused you of making up?'

'Not exactly. But she didn't believe me when I told her the boy from Dusseldorf made himself a moustache with a pencil, raised his hand and said, "Heil Hitler! Juden araus!" '

How many budding neo-Nazis were there in West Germany's schools? The incident Ben had described wasn't something Christina would easily bring herself to believe possible in the eighties.

Nor did Howard want to believe it, but his son hadn't dreamed it up and a chill had settled in the pit of his stomach. There was little doubt that Ben was suffering the effects of the computer games Howard had heard about. Lodged by their programmers in easily accessible 'mail boxes' which kids who had home computers could call up.

How more insidious could the implanting be? And where

it would do the most damage. What were the children but the nation's future?

The games had caused a public outcry heartening to Howard, but the authorities had failed to find out who the programmers were. As for the content – a 'Hitler lives' theme summed it up, with all that implied, calculated to turn the erstwhile Führer from the monster he was into a national hero and the Jews again into scapegoats.

'Like me to have a word with your headmaster?' he asked Ben.

'No thanks, Daddy. That wouldn't do me any good with the other boys.'

'Whatever you think best. But remember that you're not fighting your battles alone. I'm supporting you.'

'Now I've told you, I feel better. Can I change my mind and have some *Apfelkuchen* and ice-cream?'

Howard got him a large helping of both.

'I used to like Uncle Ernst, but I don't any more,' Ben said while eating his dessert.

But it would be some years before he saw the old man and others of his ilk for the truth twisting self-deceivers they were. By then most would have gone to their graves and still saying, *'Heil Hitler!'*

Meanwhile it was more than possible that some were putting their money where their mouths were, financing those 'Hitler lives' computer games. Who was it who said that the evil men do lives on? Probably Shakespeare. And there were those in Germany, as elsewhere, trying to ensure that it did.

When a few days later Hess's death in Spandau prison was revealed to have been suicide, Howard could have had no more chilling a confirmation of his fears. Neo-Nazis from far and wide, young and old, had begun crawling out of the woodwork to pay homage alongside their German counterparts to the 'martyr' of their creed.

Chapter Six

NATHAN HAD NOT BEEN TO LONDON since his great-grandson's Brith, and Carla had asked Laura to let her meet his train, a rare opportunity for her to have her grandfather to herself.

She watched him slowly make his way up the steep incline to the ticket barrier at Euston Station, where she was waiting with David, now a toddler, in her arms.

'That lad is some weight for you to carry!' Nathan joked after they had greeted each other and were walking to where Carla had parked her car.

'Talking of weight, why don't you carry David and I'll take your suitcase, Grandpa – '

'That would be no hardship for me,' he said. 'How often do I get to hold him?'

When they had swapped loads, Carla said lightly, 'Do doctors ever get themselves checked up?'

'When this one last did he was told he had angina, which he already knew. But nobody needs to worry about him. His little pills for an emergency are always in his pocket. So what's new with you, Carla? Is Alan still set on going where Reform rabbis aren't recognized? Why, after all his years of studying, would he want to go and bang his head on a brick wall?'

'I'll let him tell you himself.'

'He doesn't have to, it was a rhetorical question. A challenge was always what that boy relished.'

'There's more to it than that, Grandpa. Many Israelis now want to live the Reform Judaism way. What I'm saying is that Alan feels called to go where he is needed. Some Reform rabbis already there have more than one congregation apiece to cope with, though they don't yet have synagogue buildings. One day they will be recognized – '

'I hope you're right. But with the ultra-orthodox ruling the roost in Israel, it will take a lot more people standing up for their rights than seem to be doing so now.'

Carla gave him a smile. 'You were the Reform pioneer in our family, weren't you?'

'And oh, the wrath it brought on my head! Marianne was the first to follow in my footsteps and we were made to feel like partners in crime, I recall.'

'Some of the things I've heard about Marianne when she was young imply that she was what you might call before her time.'

Nathan laughed. 'Independent was always the word for her.'

But it's my uncomplicated granddaughter who's ended up a Reform rebbetzin, he reflected, eyeing Carla affectionately as she put David into his car seat and buckled the belt.

Nathan had heard she was making a good job of her congregational duties. She was the sort to whom it came naturally to lend herself to what her choice of husband requires of her.

An old-fashioned girl and there weren't too many of them around. Sensible too, and this was Nathan's opportunity to get her impression of what was going on at Laura's.

'When did what's happened to Bessie begin?' he asked her.

'The dieting? Or what Alan and I think it's all about?'

'You've discussed it between you, have you?'

'Everything concerning everyone gets discussed in our family, Grandpa.'

'It always did,' he said dryly, 'and often behind the person concerned's back! Whenever my ears burned I knew why, and now it's Laura's turn again, which it hasn't been since her marriage. It once occurred to me that a family is a web of intrigue.' And at the time Nathan had viewed Sarah as the mother spider enmeshing those over whom she ruled.

When had he had that thought? On a train. On the way back from London after lending himself to Marianne's marrying out — *secretly* marrying out and he the sole family representative at her wedding. What was that, he reflected in retrospect, but my showing them I wouldn't let them do to her what they'd done to me? Something I didn't then have the guts to express in words.

'But in addition to yours, Marianne's is the opinion we all value,' Carla went on.

And given the past, what a joke that was.

'Marianne doesn't know if she's coming or going at the moment,' Carla told him, 'what with one thing and another I don't know when she finds time to work. Or to see the boyfriend none of us has met.'

Once the family met him, Marianne's private life would be private no more and Nathan didn't blame her for keeping it so as long as she could.

'You still haven't answered my question about Bessie,' he said to Carla.

'I can't tell you anything definite, Grandpa. But Alan and I do have our theories.'

Carla halted in a line of vehicles held up at the traffic lights on Golders Green Road. 'Sorry to bring you this round-about route to Laura's, but she asked me to pick up some pickled brisket from Bloom's.'

'Remembered I like it, has she?' A moving moment for a man growing too sentimental with age! Surprised to find himself taking the pride in his family he did.

Nathan watched Carla toy with a lock of her hair, as she had as a child when immersed in thought. Around her neck was the silver watchchain that had once adorned the portly frontage of her paternal great-grandfather, Sigmund Moritz. She had worn it at her son's Brith, as Marianne habitually wore Sarah's brooch.

Such were the mementoes people passed to their descendants, bric-à-brac of one kind or another meaningful to them in their own lifetime. Also the bits of themselves that Nature passed down. Abraham Sandberg's colouring was still going strong in the family. And Nathan's great-grandchild – well, nobody could say that David isn't the image of me.

'The London traffic is terrible!' said Carla after crawling to the lights in time for them to change to red yet again.

'That I can see for myself, love, but it doesn't help me to get a preview from you about Bessie. Your telling me whatever you know could help with the detective work I'm here to do – '

'It isn't what I know, Grandpa, it's how things seem to me – that Laura just got married to Jake and took it for granted that they and their kids would then live happily ever after. But family life isn't like that, is it? Everyone under the roof is an individual with their own needs and their own thoughts. And I'm sorry for Laura now her bubble has burst.'

Bessie's first words to Nathan after greeting him were, 'If you've come to stop me from dieting, I'm not going to.'

Nathan began as he intended to continue. 'I didn't know you were on a diet, love. When your mum and I chat on the phone we have more important things to discuss.'

'Well it's all anyone ever talks about around here.'

Something would have to be done about that. Nathan changed the subject and followed Laura to the kitchen. 'Taken any interesting photographs lately?'

It was Bessie who replied. 'My mummy is too busy worrying about me to take photographs, and making cakes I won't eat.'

About that too.

'We haven't been away for a holiday this year,' Bessie told him while he and Laura were drinking the coffee percolated and awaiting his arrival.

'It isn't quite freshly made, Uncle,' Laura apologized. 'I forgot about the detour I asked Carla to make.'

'My mummy gets absent-minded because of me,' said Bessie.

Did Laura know what a shrewd little monkey Bessie was? No, anxiety had blinded her.

'And we didn't go on holiday, Uncle Nat, because I have to keep seeing my analyst.'

We're living in times when the vocabulary once associated with Hollywood films issues naturally from the mouths of babes and sucklings, Nathan registered. And oh, the desperate lengths this child had gone to to prove her own importance. Why was it necessary for her to prove it? Not just to those around her, but to herself. Bessie's emaciated appearance wasn't the only pitiful aspect of her plight.

Laura offered Nathan the biscuit barrel. 'I know you like shortbread. Don't be shy!'

'Don't bother asking me to have one, Mummy.'

'I wasn't going to.'

Bessie looked taken aback and left the room.

A silence followed her departure, then Laura mustered a smile. 'It's good to have you here, Uncle Nat.'

'But you are going to have to change your tactics.'

'I got the message! Didn't you notice? But it's going to take more than that, I'm afraid.'

Laura then relayed to Nathan the psychoanalyst's shattering pronouncement.

His response was delivered with asperity. 'How much did it cost you to find out that insecurity is responsible? This isn't the first time I've had cause to think myself in the wrong field of medicine!'

'If you get Bessie right, I shall think you a miracle worker, and Jake that you're a witch doctor,' said Laura.

Chapter Seven

THOUGH FOR SOME AIDS VICTIMS the disease is slow in tightening its grip, Matthew was less fortunate. He had, too, turned a blind eye to the symptoms and was now paying the extra price of his own procrastination.

The truth was that Pete's infidelity, not his, was responsible. But that knowledge was theirs alone. Matthew would not have it added to his father's hatred of Pete, who would gladly have swapped places to make amends.

Meanwhile Matthew's worsening condition continued to hover over the family like an ominous cloud. He had several times been hospitalized, and Pete had abandoned his own career to be with him when such crises arose and take care of him when he was discharged.

Driving home after visiting Matthew, Marianne reflected that love had many faces. Pete was now displaying one of them. But perhaps the only all-enduring and selfless love was that of a mother for her child. Lyn rarely left Matthew's side.

Arnold, though, had picked himself up and gone on being Sir Arnold Klein, MP, saved from the disgrace he had feared by the press not having done their worst. Given that Matthew was a well-known actor, and the ferrets employed by the tabloids, Arnold must somehow have managed to pull the right strings.

If my brother hadn't had his public life, he would now be in pieces, thought Marianne. What but his parliamentary obligations had helped him put himself back together, and that wasn't just due to his being the man he was. It was the difference between a mother and a father. Lyn's impetus was solely her son's need.

But unless he was out of London, a day never passed without Arnold's dropping in to see Matthew. They were playing a hand of gin rummy together when Marianne left that evening, and Arnold had accepted Pete's invitation to stay for dinner, evidently no longer scared of catching Aids from the crockery and cutlery, and that was something!

Marianne negotiated a bend in the road and instructed herself to stop being unkind to her brother. People couldn't help being how they were. And Arnold, like Lyn, had to be putting up a brave front, silently screaming with pain behind the smiling façade, watching Matthew slip away and powerless to halt the slide.

One day there might be a cure for the deadly disease, but it would come too late for Matthew. This bleak, English summer, if summer it could be called, matched Marianne's feelings as she slowed her car in yet another deluge of rain, in the traffic jam on Hampstead High Street.

She had lost count of time since the night she learned that her nephew was doomed, and Simon's proprietary words, even though lightly spoken, had rung that warning bell in her mind. It hadn't stopped their affair from blossoming, though, for such in the full sense of the word it now was.

And my life the more complicated because of it, she thought. There are now three compartments instead of two. Work, family, and Simon.

Compartments? Well, I'm certainly keeping Simon in one. Trying to avoid his meeting even Laura. Perhaps because he's something I've never had: a haven I can escape to, she let herself accept while garaging the car.

She had put the kettle on to boil and was in her bedroom changing into a comfortable housecoat when the doorbell rang.

That couldn't be Simon; he was in New York. And A.P. had a key.

'Martin! What a lovely surprise.'

'You might not think so when you hear what I've come to tell you.'

More trouble. Marianne watched him hang up his raincoat. 'I know you only live round the corner, but in weather like this I would've expected you to drive here – '

'I felt like a walk and the hell with getting wet. A.P. isn't here, is he?'

'He doesn't drop in as often as he used to.'

'Well, he's reached the age of discretion, if only in some respects. That has to account for it.'

'And what is that supposed to mean?'

'Come off it, Mum! He knows his gran's got a boyfriend and far be it from him to play gooseberry.'

Marianne led the way to the kitchen, so Martin would not see her blushing.

'In case you think I mind, I don't,' he told her.

'That's very big of you!'

'Isn't it time I met the guy?'

'You're my son, not my father!'

'You think I do mind, don't you?'

Martin watched Marianne get a couple of mugs from the dresser and pop a teabag into each of them. 'Look, Mum – '

'Yes?'

'I didn't come here to talk about this, but since we're on the subject, let me tell you what you once told me. All I want is for you to be happy. Having said that, well, your life is your own.'

Marianne was lifting the kettle and put it down again. 'Since when, Martin?'

He eyed her silently while she resumed making the tea. 'You're right. In many ways it never has been. And I suppose that makes what you've nevertheless achieved the more remarkable.'

'But I, Martin, have never seen myself in that light. I just do what I have to do and somehow get through it. How I do sometimes see myself is as an expert juggler!'

'And about your boyfriend, I'd be lying if I said the idea of my mother having one didn't amuse me in one way and sadden me in another.'

Marianne brought the tea to the table. 'Believe it or not I am able to understand that. If my mother had remarried, I'm sure I should have had mixed feelings. As for your amusement, at your age I also thought people of my parents' age were over the hill – '

'You, Mum, are never going to be over the hill. You can still run circles around the lot of us.'

'But I sometimes wish I didn't have to. And when I said over the hill, I was referring to the relationships young people think their elders are no longer interested in, or capable of.'

Martin surveyed his mother, still an attractive woman, her dark eyes glowing – and not just her eyes. There was about her a new radiance. He'd been too immersed in his own misery to notice that the air of resignation she had worn with a smile since his father's death, as if the aspect of life she had just described was over for her, was gone.

'You're in love with Simon Newman, aren't you? It isn't just an affair.'

'We care a great deal for each other, Martin.'

'Matthew told me he's a nice guy.' Martin gave her a cheeky grin. 'So when's the wedding? And who's going to give you away? Me? Andy wouldn't expect me to welch on *that* commitment, to fly to LA for a meeting that comes to nothing.'

'You're letting your imagination carry you away! Marriage hasn't been mentioned and if it were I don't know what my answer would be. Drink your tea and tell me why you're here.'

'To let you know that *my* marriage is over.'

Martin's tone was as final as his words and Marianne, distressed though she was, knew she must accept the inevitable.

'Psychoanalysis is helping Moira sort herself out,' Martin revealed, 'and I hope for her sake she'll end up a normal person again – if there is such a thing! She's now able to talk to me about her obsession. The root of it, Mum, is a guilt problem about marrying out.'

'Did her analyst say so?'

'They never do, you're not better until you see for yourself what's wrong with you.'

'Bessie's analyst told Laura his findings – '

'And I heard on the family grapevine what they are. In the case of a child he'd require the parents' co-operation in the healing process, wouldn't he? But he wouldn't have told Bessie even if she were old enough to understand.'

Martin paused reflectively and drank some tea. 'I find it remarkable that my lad seems unaffected by the insecurity he's lived with for most of his life. It doesn't make sense, does it? There's Bessie, one of a happy family. A.P. on the other hand – '

'May we get back to Moira?'

'She now attends *group* therapy sessions, though it goes against the grain for a private person like her. I can't imagine Moira loosening up and discussing her deepest feelings with others.'

'Perhaps her psychoanalyst thinks that's what she needs,' said Marianne. 'Is she still seeing him?'

'He sits in on the group. Moira says everyone – including her – screams and shouts at each other when someone says something that riles them. It seems she was rattling on about her marriage being ruined by her Jewish in-laws – '

'She didn't put it quite that way when I took her to lunch.'

'Pulling strings behind my back, were you?' Martin said with a weary smile. 'Thanks for trying, Mum.'

'If Moira was able to tell you what you've just told me, I'd have thought that boded well for your relationship, that it indicated the possibility of a new understanding,' Marianne said, allowing herself some hope.

Martin dashed it to the ground. 'All Moira tells me is bits and bobs and they're never about her own contribution to the action. I got that information from Bill Dryden, who keeps me posted. Moira sees a lot of him and Sukey, and I'm immensely grateful to both of them.

'As you may remember, I had no option but to pretend ignorance of Moira's undergoing therapy. It wasn't until she switched to the group kind that she herself put me in the picture. It was then necessary for me to feign surprise. There've been times, Mum, when I've had cause to think I'd have made a good actor.'

And how hard it must have been for Marianne's open and honest son to live the lengthy lie he had. The older he grew the more he looked like his father, but Ralph's hair hadn't turned grey before he was forty.

'To complete the information Bill gave me,' he went on, 'after Moira said what she did about our family, one of the others accused her of having a guilt complex because she'd married out of her religion, and of blaming us for what she'd done.'

Marianne said wryly, 'It strikes me that participating in group therapy could turn one into an amateur psycho-analyst.'

'I don't doubt it,' said Martin, 'since learning to understand what ails yourself must surely lead to your delving into the behaviour of others. I imagine that's what the participants are encouraged to do, that it helps to put their personal problems into perspective.'

'Did Bill say that Moira accepts the accusation hurled at her as the truth?'

'It's still early days for that, Mum. But looking back, I'd say she's lived with guilt on that account since our wedding day. If we'd married in church, things might have been different for her, but that she didn't ask of me. It seems to me now that her excessive devoutness is her way of trying to make amends for her marriage not being sanctified.'

Marianne said after a pause, 'But *you* haven't lived with guilt because you married out, have you?'

'Perhaps because you relieved me of it, by giving me your blessing. Moira never got that from her father and he's the one who counts in that family. Nor, needless to say, did she get it from her great-uncle now a cardinal and not the first of the Kyverdales to wield that power. He wasn't at our wedding, of course, and that could've been when what she had done first hit Moira.'

'And you think how she feels towards our family is all tied up with her guilt?'

'It has to be.'

'Not necessarily. From what she said when we lunched together, it was plain that she finds us overwhelming and pathologically so. She didn't put it in the words I'm using, but my impression then was that Moira had to retreat lest we soak her up. It made me re-think the tragedy of Howard's first marriage – '

'Are you saying the family had that effect on Christina, too?'

'Well, I do think that we over-simplified that situation. Christina too was an outsider, and too much in love with Howard to have considered the built-in hazards to her marrying a Jew. Confronted with his family – well, she said it all in the note she left Howard when she'd had enough, didn't she? That she couldn't go on feeling herself the enemy in the camp.'

'That's the direct opposite of your soaking up theory,' said Martin.

'It's nevertheless something we did to her en masse,' Marianne replied. 'One way or another I wouldn't say that marrying into a clan like ours was something anyone of a different persuasion would find immediately comfortable. Your dad didn't know what had hit him!'

'But he got used to it, didn't he? I would say it depends upon the person. How long did it take Lyn to feel herself one of us?'

'I wouldn't know. I used to think her something of a chameleon, before she proved herself incapable of playing Lady Klein. Not only does she feel she's one of us, we feel that way about her. But in the light of more recent experience – Moira is a graphic example – I have to conclude that neither having a family of their own contributed to Lyn and your dad each finding their place in ours.'

'May we add to that,' said Martin, 'the religious factor I

still hold responsible, despite what you've been saying? Unlike Lyn and Dad, Moira's background has the strong pull that ours exerts upon us. I was never more conscious of the grip it has on me than on the night I asked you if you'd mind your grandchildren not being Jewish. In a lesser way I am still occasionally prey to it when consuming a ham sandwich. It will be with me till the day I die.

'The difference between Moira and me, though – between Moira and most people – is that I'm capable of shrugging off my sins and she isn't. I'd go so far as to say that she'll never rid herself of her guilt without ridding herself of me. That, however, she is about to do, and with my full compliance.'

Martin reached for an apple and bit into it, as his son had at Marianne's table so often, while his parents' marriage dragged on in the private hell it had to have been for both of them.

'Does A.P. know yet that his mum and dad are splitting up?'

'It was he who told us that we should.'

'Adding, no doubt, that he'd had his fill of the pair of you!'

'If he'd said that, I wouldn't blame him,' Martin replied, 'and could be what's helped him to survive in one piece is his having you to come to. All he said, though, was that when he goes off to college, in October, there'd be no reason for his parents to stay married. Moira told him she agreed and I said it was a sensible suggestion.'

'Fortunately for that lad,' said Marianne, 'he is not only sensible, but also philosophical.'

But what a way to end a marriage! Clinical was the word for it, and their child the instigator of what he knew was best for them.

'Well, he's your grandson, isn't he?' Martin answered dryly. 'He wanted to be the one to tell you, but I drew the line at that.'

'When are he and Jeremy leaving on their travels?'

'Europe on a shoestring, you mean! What I wouldn't give to re-live that time in my own life. Someone once remarked to me that youth goes unappreciated by the young. With the benefit of hindsight I had to agree. And before you know it, you're looking back on it,' Martin added.

Marianne sensed the motley emotion churning within him. How wouldn't it, now he and Moira had finally called it quits? And gone forever was the breathless quality of dreams as yet unrealized with which he had hand in hand set forth with her.

Never was there a truer example of someone little by little having the stars knocked from their eyes than Marianne's son. Like his father, Martin was a romantic. It was there in the lyrics he wrote and had helped, together with Andy's music, to achieve the popular success their partnership had accrued.

'I haven't yet heard that new song of yours that's doing so well in the charts,' she said to him.

'It isn't one of our usual boy-meets-girl ballads, Mum. I sat down one night and wrote some lyrics about a guy getting screwed by life – and felt like calling the song "Poor Martin"! Andy was reluctant to set them to music. Now, he thinks like I do that this could be a turning point for us. Since it hit the charts, our producer's been seeing it that way, too. Cynicism, it seems, is a highly marketable product. Given my own experience, I ought not to be surprised.'

'On a personal level, though, it can be highly erosive,' Marianne answered. 'Do your mother a favour, love, try not to let your experience erode your future – '

'On a personal level I don't seem to have one.'

Marianne put her hand on his.

'Please don't get sentimental on me,' he said with a shaky laugh. 'Right now, it wouldn't take much to reduce me to sobs! On the way round here, I was thinking of you and Dad. How you had your tiffs, but went on loving each other. But for Moira and me – well, it was as if we both just watched what we'd once had slowly disintegrate and knew there was nothing we could do about it.

'Even with the will to do so, we couldn't put our marriage back together. There is literally nothing left.'

'But something good came of it for both of you,' said Marianne, 'for me, too. Your son. Please tell him that his being discreet about his gran having a boyfriend needn't include not dropping in here to be given some extra pocket-money for his trip to Europe.'

Marianne's jocularity helped revive Martin's spirits. 'I'll suggest that he phones you to fix a suitable time,' he replied in similar vein. 'The last thing he'd want would be to interrupt a tête-à-tête breakfast – '

Marianne tried not to blush but again found herself doing so.

'I was joking, Mum!'

'My love affair isn't a joke to me.'

'Then why not let the guy make an honest woman of you?'

'If and when a proposal is put to me, the honest woman I am and have always been will have to deal with her own uncertainty on the subject.'

Marianne reverted to the one from which they had digressed. 'Howard told me on the phone that A.P. and Jeremy will be spending some time with him and Karin, in Munich.'

'They've also been offered hospitality by Karin's parents when they get to Berlin. And Henry Moritz told Frank to let them know they'd be welcome to sleep on his living-room floor, in Paris.'

'Given Henry's couldn't-care-less approach to all but political causes, they will probably have to sweep the floor, first!'

'You've never approved of Henry, have you?'

Marianne got up to make them each another mug of tea. 'It isn't for me to approve, or disapprove. Like you said to me about mine, his life is his own – and in Henry's case that couldn't be more true. For me, Henry epitomizes the proverbial rolling stone gathering no moss, and I find that rather sad. I don't doubt that he's accumulated some of the scars nobody can hope to escape, but for most of us living also provides the simple human pleasures Henry hasn't known since he put the mundane behind him and set forth on his endless banner carrying.'

'If by the mundane you mean his hometown,' said Martin, 'Henry's in Manchester at the moment. A.P. called Leona to get his Paris phone number, and it was Henry who picked up the receiver.'

'Let me remind you,' said Marianne, 'that Manchester is also my hometown, and I have never thought it mundane. The place I grew up in isn't there any more, changed out of recognition by what passes nowadays for architecture and planning. Prince Charles is giving some of those responsible the rebuke they deserve, in my opinion, for what's been done to some of Britain's cities, Manchester included!'

'Calm down and make the tea, Mum!'

'Why I'm het up is part of what I had started telling you. Despite the many years I've lived in London, at heart I've remained a Mancunian. And there's still the throb of life in Manchester that there always was, Martin. Mundane indeed! It's people who make the atmosphere of a city, and those like you, who've never lived up north, don't know what they've missed.'

'I think what you're talking about, Mum, is how everyone feels about the place they were raised in.'

'Probably. If the family hadn't driven me to it, I'd never have left the north again.'

'Nor would you have met Simon Newman.'

Marianne let that pass.

'Did you know that Frank's been suffering from work stress?'

'No, but I know now! Who passed that titbit on to you?'

'I think it was Laura, when I last spoke to her.'

'Did it ever strike you, Martin, that absolutely nothing happens in our family without the lot of us getting to know about it?'

'You do seem to have a down on the family tonight!'

Marianne added milk to the tea and returned with the mugs to the table. 'What I'm coming to have a down on,

Martin, is the institution a family is. Look what it did to Howard's first marriage. Not to mention its effect upon yours. I may as well tell you now that I've been protecting my love affair from the family. And in a way I envy Henry. What but the family did he turn his back on, to live his own life?'

'Since I'm part of what you're protecting your affair from, forgive me for feeling hurt,' said her son. 'Why don't you and Simon Newman pack up your typewriters and go and live on a desert island?'

'Nature didn't equip me with Henry's self-absorption,' Marianne replied. 'And what's the betting he's in Manchester to collect yet another handout from his twin?'

'Frank isn't there, Leona told A.P. after he'd spoken to Henry. He's taking a break in the Lake District.'

'If Henry had known that, he wouldn't have wasted money on flying to Manchester,' said Marianne. 'Leona probably added to his disappointment by telling him it served him right for never letting them know he's coming. And he won't get a penny out of her. She hates his guts.'

'Well, he was the one she wanted, but he didn't want her, did he?'

Marianne put down her mug. 'How did you know that?'

'How did you know Henry gets handouts from Frank? Like you said, there are seemingly no secrets in our family and that includes family history. I thought you were telling me one when you revealed to me nearly twenty years ago that you and my father had to get married – '

'I didn't put it that way.'

'How you put it doesn't matter. It wasn't the disgrace in my day that it was in yours. And I knew you loved each other. What does matter is it's something private that my mother told me and I've never repeated it to a soul – not even to Moira. It strikes me now, though, that all this time the whole bloody family has to have known, but carefully kept their knowledge from *me*!'

Martin got up and kissed Marianne's cheek. 'I was hurt by

what you said about protecting your love affair, Mum. But I owe you an apology. I'm beginning to see what you mean.'

'But let's not forget the other side of the coin. When your dad died – well, the first few weeks were the worst, needless to say, and I wasn't left to grieve on my own twenty-four hours a day. You know how I feel about Shirley, but she would sometimes turn up out of the blue – never without one of her fancy gateaux! – and I was glad to see her.

'It was the same with Ann and Leona. I'd hear a car pull up outside the cottage and a minute later one or the other of them was walking up the path. And I was never without visitors in the evenings. Everyone rallied round me, like we're all doing with Matthew now.'

Martin watched the driving rain lashing the window and smiled sourly. 'If there were no redeeming features to the institution we're discussing, it would have capsized long ago.'

'In some families, be they Jewish or gentile, that has begun happening,' Marianne replied, 'given the times we're living in. And despite all I've said on the subject, I'm thankful that ours hasn't changed, that the blood tie still means something to us and has kept us from going our separate ways.'

Chapter Eight

BESSIE'S CHILDISH SECRETS too were destined to remain private no longer. Jake came upon her improvised diary while searching in her room for a magazine she had borrowed from Laura.

By then Nathan had proved himself to be the miracle worker Laura had wryly mentioned.

Bessie's wanting to borrow the magazine, indicative of her renewed interest in anything other than herself, had together with other signs of her progress seemed nothing short of miraculous to her parents.

Nathan had stayed with the family for two weeks, during which he had succeeded in establishing a close rapport with Bessie, asking her to be kind enough to show an old gentleman the local sights, and in her parents' presence exchanging winks with her, as if the two of them shared in-jokes.

On the day Nathan left, Laura was the recipient of a lecture, if not of the ticking off she had anticipated.

'There is more than one kind of insecurity,' he had informed her. 'Some folk, kids included, have a greater need than others to feel loved. Unlike Janis and Jeremy, Bessie is unable to take for granted that being one of a family guarantees affection from one to another.

'Let me give you an example, Laura. There were ways in which I felt myself put through the mill by your grandfather, my brother, David. But I never doubted that he loved me –'

'Nobody in this house has ever put Bessie through the mill,' Laura had interrupted.

'But all families indulge in everyday squabbles, afterwards forgotten. Not by Bessie, though. Instead she questions if whoever said the sharp word really loves her. I'm not suggesting that you all begin handling Bessie with kid gloves. There's been too much of that already since she did what she did to capture the special attention she craves.

'There are other ways of giving that to her, and she needs it from you especially. When did you last spend time alone with her? Take her out for an evening, or an afternoon, just the two of you? Let her know that she's still your little girl, like always, despite your now having two other children? The way a sensible mother would with her elder child after giving birth to a second?

'I don't doubt you'd have done that, Laura, if your family had been increased in the usual way.'

'It wasn't though, was it? If I'd done what you think I should have – '

'I understand – don't think I've failed to. It might have occurred to you nevertheless, had you thought about it, that Janis and Jeremy had each other. What you couldn't have known, but events have proved it, is that Bessie is less resilient than they are. She has felt it necessary to live up to them in her mother's estimation, to Janis in particular.'

'Did she say so?'

'Not in so many words, but those are my findings for what they're worth. I've made a bargain with her, and there's nothing left for me to do. The rest is up to you.'

'What was the bargain?'

'If you follow the advice implicit in what I've said to you, and your having a word about it with Jake and his kids wouldn't come amiss, you'll find out.'

Laura had begun by inviting Bessie to lunch with her at the restaurant in Regent's Park Zoo, expecting her daughter's reply to be a reminder that she was dieting. Instead, the invitation was accepted and the child had done her best to eat something.

Afterwards they had fed buns to the animals, a somewhat poignant exercise for Laura given the circumstances.

It would be some time before Bessie was able to enjoy

and digest a normal diet, but she was receiving affectionate encouragement from her family, a more positive form of attention than her self-inflicted starvation had commanded, and at her own request was no longer seeing the psycho-analyst.

The summer vacation period over, she had now returned to school, but Laura had continued to set aside time for her. On Saturday mornings they shopped for this, or that, in Hampstead High Street together and lunched at one of the cafés where other little girls were to be seen with their mothers.

Bessie was now taking an interest in clothes too, and today Laura had bought her a new outfit from the children's boutique on Heath Street. Her weight was not yet such to fill out the garments her height required, but it was still early days and Laura was right now a far happier mum, she reflected gratefully on the evening her peace was due for a battering again.

Nathan had kept in touch by telephone and had said that displaying trust in Bessie was now essential to ensure there would not be a setback. If the child thought that gorging and afterwards making herself vomit was still what her parents expected she might do, it would damage the self-confidence she was gradually building.

She had recently been allowed to resume outings without supervision and was now, wearing her new outfit, at her friend Val's birthday party. Though some of the little girls she knew had eschewed the company of an unsightly anorexic, Val's had remained steadfast and theirs seemed to Laura a friendship likely to endure throughout their lives.

Like mine with Peggy Morris, she thought. Peggy alone of all my old pals in Manchester didn't cut me off when I became an unmarried mum. Some of the others though, Laura had heard, were later not averse to letting drop that they went to school with me, when I became famous as well as infamous!

Peggy now lived in Melbourne and they saw each other

only when she came to England to see her folks. True friends, Laura had learned, were the few you still had when life had weeded the others out. It was as well that people had families to rely on.

These were her musings while she sat in the living-room with her feet up, waiting for Jake to return with the magazine he had offered to fetch for her from Bessie's room. A more considerate husband than he would be hard to find. During the anxious period now behind them he had cut down on his business travels, rather than leave Laura to cope alone.

Tomorrow though, he was off to Hong Kong and they were enjoying a quiet hour or two with the house to themselves. Jeremy was away with A.P. on the broadening trip that would precede their sheltered interlude at Oxford, and Janis at the theatre with Kurt – a change from the University Jewish Society activities necessary to combat increasing anti-Semitism on too many college campuses.

'Would you mind coming upstairs, Laura?' she heard her husband call.

She was half-way there when he added crisply, 'There's something in your daughter's room I'd like you to see.'

Laura stopped short and gripped the banister. The way Jake had put it was as if he had slapped her face, and even more hurtful. To me, Janis and Jeremy and Bessie are *our* children. Well, she'd just learned it wasn't like that for Jake.

'What's all the fuss about?' she said coldly when she joined him beside the spilled mound of childish junk on the floor.

Jake brandished a dog-eared exercise book. 'This,' he replied. '"My Secrets" your daughter has called her scribblings. Would you care to take a look at them?'

'No, thanks. And you ought not to've invaded Bessie's privacy.'

Jake laughed brusquely. 'It's her mother's privacy I seem to've invaded.' He opened the exercise book. 'Allow me to refresh your memory, Laura, by reading something aloud to you: "My mummy had lots of boyfriends, but I only liked the ones who didn't mind me coming in bed with them for a cuddle." '

Laura felt the blood ebb from her face, but stood her ground. 'All right. You didn't marry an angel and now you know it.'

'But I didn't know it before I married her, did I? She made sure of that.'

'Perhaps because she knew in her bones that you are in some respects a "Mr Barrett of Wimpole Street".'

'And what does that make her?'

'A bloody fool, for thinking that didn't matter.'

'That isn't how I see it.' Jake flicked over a page in the exercise book, his expression grim. 'And what I find equally appalling is what I'm about to read to you: "When I grow up I want to be exactly like my mummy." '

Laura's response was, 'I'm no angel and you're respectability personified, but I doubt that Jeremy has any desire to become a replica of his father. And I repeat that you had no right to open and read that book.'

'Shall I tell you why I did? It was hidden under all that stuff now on the floor. While searching for the magazine – which I still haven't found – I accidentally knocked that lot off the table with my elbow. If we hadn't had the trouble with Bessie we've had, I should just have smiled and returned it to its hiding place. But with a kid like her – well who knows what's going on in her mind and what it could later lead to?'

A silence followed and it was as though a wall had risen between them. Not a wall, my past, thought Laura. And how incongruous was the setting, the ambience of innocence all around me, she registered eyeing the little-girl décor, frilly curtains at the windows, the flounced dressing-table, the teddy bear Bessie still slept with propped up on the pretty pink duvet.

'I'm the woman I am, Jake,' Laura said quietly, 'and it's come as a shock to you. If you don't love me enough to live with what you now know, I'm better off without you. Would you mind putting Bessie's exercise book back exactly where you found it? I don't want her damaged by this. I'll help you gather up the stuff you knocked on the floor.'

But while they shared the task, they remained worlds apart. 'Worlds' is the right word, thought Laura. It isn't the age difference. It's how we lived before we met and how we tick. It would be a relief not to have to pretend any more. For Laura not to have to watch her tongue.

For two pins she'd call it a day, here and now. Pack her things and Bessie's and ask Marianne to put them up till she found a flat.

'Let's get a move on with this,' she said. 'Or Bessie will soon be home from Val's party – '

'But Janis, no doubt, will go somewhere after the theatre and stay out half the night! And Jeremy hasn't kept in touch since he left England.'

'It's time you stopped expecting him to,' Laura replied.

'In your opinion.'

If Laura called it a day, she'd be walking out on Janis and Jeremy, too. 'I also have an opinion about your expectations of Janis. Let me put it to you this way. What young people can't do with their parents' approval, they are just as likely to do without it. You might consider attaching that to Jeremy also, since he's about to leave home.'

Laura paused briefly. 'But since I may not be their mum for much longer, I should perhaps keep my opinions to myself.'

Jake stopped restoring some books of fairy tales to their disorder on the table. 'Why does Bessie keep so much junk? All those beads and bangles and dolls' clothes she used to play with but doesn't any more? And what the hell are you talking about, Laura?'

'The answer to your first question is Bessie is a hoarder, like her namesake was. My gran never threw anything out. She also had a passion for cut glass and the family used to call her house the crystal palace – '

'How did cut glass get into this conversation?'

'I don't really know, but since it did, I'll mention too that

I had it in mind to give half of my gran's collection, left to me and still stored in Manchester, to Janis when she marries. The other half will be kept for Bessie. Plain though she is, goodness shines out of her and the right man will recognize it and value her.'

Another silence followed, then Laura again spoke her mind. 'To me, Jake, *both* are my daughters, and Jeremy is *my* son. Janis and Jeremy have become to me a precious legacy acquired by my marrying you and I'd have liked to have known the woman whose blood children they are. She has to have been someone very special. It was you I fell in love with, but the children you brought with you to our marriage are a bonus any second wife would be thankful for.

'When you summoned me upstairs and referred to Bessie as *my* daughter – it was as if what I believed to be a real family was no more than self-delusion.'

'How like a woman to twist a man's words! The way I felt when I read what I did, it's remarkable that I remember what I said, but my words weren't meant for the interpretation you gave them. A family is built on more solid ground than mere words, Laura.'

'But however solid, the ground shook for you, didn't it? How is "Mr Barrett" feeling now?'

'Is that going to be your name for me from now on?'

'I'm still not sure there's to be a "from now on".'

'My dearest girl, it never entered my head for a second that there wouldn't be – '

'In that case I can now tell you that "Mr Barrett" has long been my private nickname for you.'

Jake managed to smile.

'If you could make that a laugh,' said Laura, 'we're on our way.'

'Give me time,' he said, and took her in his arms.

Chapter Nine

HAVING HER BROTHER-IN-LAW to stay, and in Frank's absence, could not but be a strain for Leona.

She was relieved when he bade her farewell and astonished, ten days later, when he again appeared unannounced. Henry had said he was going to London to see Matthew and Leona had assumed he would fly back to Paris from there. Instead, she learned, he had afterwards gone to visit friends in Edinburgh.

'Where don't you have friends prepared to put up with you and to put you up?' she asked him. 'And you'd better be back in Paris before the two lads you promised can stay with you get there.'

They had just eaten dinner together and Henry was watching her stack the dishwasher.

'If you hadn't refused to tell me where Frank is staying, I'd be back in Paris now,' he replied.

'Without visiting Matthew, no doubt.'

'You do have a dreadful opinion of me, don't you?' he said dryly. 'Believe it or not, I'd intended visiting Matthew.'

'But I have things to do this weekend, Henry. We're not all like you, with endless time to fritter away. Since I told you Frank was away for two weeks, you can't expect me to entertain you between now and Sunday.'

'Heaven forbid! On the other hand, you can't expect me to have refused the lift to Manchester I was offered by a chap I met in Edinburgh. Train fares grow more astronomical by the minute.'

Leona scraped some leavings from a plate to the pedal bin. Frank giving Henry handouts and I can't afford to have a waste disposal unit fitted to my sink!

'Anything I can do to help you?'

Yes. Stop popping up in my life to remind me how much I still want you. 'No, thanks.'

'Why wouldn't you let me take you to a restaurant to eat? You didn't have to cook after your day's work, which has to be heavier with Frank away and you holding the fort.'

An uncharacteristically thoughtful remark. 'What do you suppose I do every evening, Henry? Your brother, too. While you're living your carefree life, Frank and I come home from the law centre, put a meal together between us, discuss the cases we don't have time to during the day, watch some TV on the odd occasions we don't bring work home with us, and that's it.'

'My carefree life? Well – I suppose that is how it seems to you.'

'How could it not? You're still on the roller coaster you boarded when you were young, aren't you? With the accompanying thrills that analogy implies. I'm not saying your political activities aren't sincere – '

'What exactly are you saying?' Henry cut in.

Leona put some detergent into the dishwasher, shut the door and pressed the switch.

'I suppose that you've made a mess of your life – though that wasn't what I started out to say.'

She took off her apron and Henry followed her to the living-room.

'Remember when Frank and I came to Paris in the sixties?' she went on. 'To get you out of gaol, during the student revolt?'

'For which I've remained immensely grateful to you.'

'Cut it out, Henry! Nobody in our family demands gratitude and even you should know that. My mind sometimes returns to the girl you were living with at the time – '

'Julekha was one of the good things that I've encountered on my rovings.'

'But that's what she's remained for you. Just an encounter and it helps prove my point. I recall your once bringing her to Manchester. Though the family would've preferred her to've been Jewish, needless to say, I'm sure that our late lamented elders let themselves hope that at last Henry was about to settle down, have a homelife instead of wandering the world taking some of the risks that in your time you have.'

The September evening had grown chilly and Leona paused to ignite the gasfire, gazing reflectively into the flames. 'You had a stove of some sort in your flat in Paris, didn't you?'

'It had several amenities my current place of abode doesn't have. Julekha, not I, paid the rent for that place.'

'Well, Frank and I didn't think you could have afforded it! Since money as well as time you're known to fritter away. How could you have let her, though, Henry? Your brother certainly wouldn't have. My father had to persuade Frank to let him buy us a house when we got married. Dad would have paid for one twice this size, but Frank isn't the man to've ignored, even when he was young, that the upkeep would be his responsibility.'

'It seems to've been yours as well.'

'That was my choice,' Leona replied. 'If I hadn't wanted to work, he would gladly have supported me. Since I did, our careers – if such they may be called! – have been as much side by side as our personal life.'

'And has it yet occurred to either of you that I'm not the only crusader in the family? What the hell else have you two been doing since you set up practice where you did?'

'The difference, Henry, is that isn't how we see ourselves. You do.' Leona sat down on the sofa and said pensively, 'That time we came to Paris, and Julekha cooked a curry, was a memorable evening for me. It was as if I'd seen a new side of you, Henry. The last thing I'd expected was to find framed photos of your relatives in your home. I hadn't expected it to be a home, just a temporary accommodation. But that wasn't its atmosphere.'

'For that you must blame Julekha! The woman's touch – '

'I'm not accusing you of anything, Henry, just telling you

how surprised I was. About the photographs especially. I seem to remember seeing on display too a brass pestle and mortar Rachel Moritz had brought with her from Vienna.'

Henry glanced at the candlesticks on the mantelpiece. 'Those wouldn't have been much use in my life. Frank's the one with the Sabbath candles set up, so they were passed to him and I got the heirloom you noticed. Like the photographs it goes with me everywhere. Make what you will of that.'

'I have.'

'You're not just observant, Leona, you're also perceptive. Got a shock though, didn't you, to discover a sentimental streak in me?' Henry added as though it was necessary to provide an excuse, 'Everyone seeks warmth in bleak moments and memories stirred by reminders of times past are known to serve that purpose – even for a reprobate like me!'

'Nobody, to my knowledge, has ever called you quite that.'

' "Quite" being the operative word. The stove you mentioned was a bit of an eyesore,' Henry harked back, 'not that I minded.' He smiled reminiscently. 'Sometimes, on Julekha's day off from the hospital, we'd drive out to the country and collect some of the pine logs I liked to burn. What a magnificent scent there'd be from the stove that evening – '

'And you evidently have sentimental memories of Julekha.'

'I wouldn't say that. I'm still in touch with her, by the way. She eventually used some of her wealth to set up a children's clinic. Paediatrics you may remember was her speciality.'

'Is she now married?'

'No, as a matter of fact. Margaret once ran into her when she was nursing in India. The clinic is in Bombay.'

'Another city where there'll always be a bed for Henry Moritz!' Leona exclaimed. 'And please don't interpret that as well you might. Julekha plainly thought the world of you. Why didn't you marry her?'

Henry went to gaze through the window at the night-time suburban scene: the leaves of a laburnum, soon to be shed, lit by a street-lamp; a mellow glow suggesting cosiness within, behind the drawn curtains of the houses opposite; a couple strolling past, arm in arm.

'Why didn't you marry Julekha, Henry?'

'Do I have to answer that question?'

'Let me do so for you. Settling down is the last thing you want, isn't it? The responsibilities that are the price of marriage. The aggro that children dole out along with the pleasure they bring.'

He turned to look at her and Leona saw that his fresh complexion had paled. But it was time that someone gave it to him straight.

'There's only ever been one woman for me,' he said, 'but by the time I realized I loved her she was my brother's wife. I've spent my life staying away from you, Leona, lecturing for a pittance, in this country or that, burying myself in the political scene wherever – Heaven help the world, there is still no shortage of evils to fight – filling my time in the only way I know how. And kidding myself that I'd got over you.'

Leona was thankful that she was sitting down. Oh dear God . . .

'When Frank got that virus on the eve of Carla's wedding, and I let him down after promising I would give Carla away,' Henry went on, 'you no doubt thought me a callous bastard – '

She had.

'I got as far as the airport, but I couldn't bring myself to fly to Manchester and stand beside you under the *chupah* during the wedding ceremony. Stand in Frank's place, when it's where I yearned to be and still do. I had no intention of ever telling you this, Leona – '

'And oh, how I wish you hadn't,' she replied. 'You see, Henry, life has played on you and me one of its little jokes. And somehow that makes how I've spent so many years despising you – and myself for wanting you – now the more painful to bear.'

They looked at each other with the length of the room

289

between them, in a silence fraught with a danger both recognized.

It was Henry who broke it. 'We are going to have to forget that this conversation took place.'

'But we never shall,' Leona replied, 'and in a way, what each of us now knows is comfort, if of the cold kind.'

'If you were married to anyone but Frank – '

'But we can't do the dirty on your brother, can we? Nor on the loving husband Frank has been to me.'

Chapter Ten

HENRY'S YOUNG GUESTS were not due in Paris until later in the month and were meanwhile shedding some of their preconceptions of Germany.

Both A.P. and Jeremy had expected to experience the wariness and repugnance expressed by their elders. Instead, it was for them no different from arriving in any of the foreign countries they had visited on family holidays in the past.

'There must be something wrong with me,' said A.P. as they stood beside a carousel at Munich Airport, their eyes glued to the luggage whizzing towards them. 'According to my gran, my skin should have prickled when I stepped off the plane on to German soil.'

'It wasn't soil, it was tarmac, and you can shake hands with *me*,' said Jeremy.

'I'm relieved to hear it. I thought it might be because I'm only half Jewish. I see my rucksack coming – ' He grabbed it. 'And there's yours, Jeremy – '

They walked from the luggage hall in thoughtful silence, overtaking a well-dressed woman with two bulging Harrods bags atop the suitcases on the trolley she was pushing. Ahead was a mother who had seated a small boy on her trolley, walking beside her an older boy carrying her duty-free goods.

While absently observing those around him, A.P. was trying to make sense of Marianne's personal reaction to arriving where he now was. His gran was a highly intelligent woman, not a hysteric like her cousin Shirley, who let off steam about everything and had said that nothing would persuade her to go to Berlin for Howard's wedding.

A.P. and Jeremy were present when Shirley had a row with Laura about her and Jake going. Laura had said she had overcome her feelings a few years ago when offered an assignment to take pictures in Berlin, and would do so again for Howard's sake.

While they waited in the queue to show their passports, Jeremy said with a grin, 'Didn't you even get half of a skin-prickle?'

'You were entitled to a whole one!'

'And I'm asking myself now, what's the big deal?'

'I have to conclude,' said A.P., who at times displayed a ponderousness of speech Marianne attributed to his Kyverdale connection, 'that it's pointless to apply logic to how the older people in the family tick in this respect.'

'Well,' said Jeremy, 'feelings don't spring from the mind, do they? But in this case they do have some factual basis. Could be that the difference between us and them is we weren't around when the Nazis did what they did – '

'Nor was Laura. She wasn't born till after the war – well, not unless she's older than she looks – '

'She's forty-two.'

'As old as that? She looks about thirty,' A.P. opined.

'I'll tell her you said so! But I've met Jews no older than thirty who feel like Laura and my dad do about Germany.'

'So did I, until today. You said that feelings don't spring from the mind, Jeremy, but that isn't necessarily so. There are some that can be all in the mind and we're here to prove it.'

'An important factor in what we're discussing,' Jeremy replied with the assurance of his generation, 'is that people of our age group are more open-minded than our elders ever were.'

'Indubitably,' said A.P. 'Another factor, if I may say so, is that our lot is farther removed from the events that made our elders' blood run cold. In my view they'll never get it out of their systems. In that I include Laura though she'd have been a babe in arms then, and the thirty-year-olds you mentioned are similarly afflicted. They'd still have been imbibing hatred of Germany and Germans with their mother's milk, wouldn't they?

'And it isn't only Jews who find all things German repulsive,' A.P. added. 'My Grandma Kyverdale lost her brother in the war. Grandfather wanted to buy her a Mercedes for her sixtieth birthday, but she refused to have a German car.'

Jeremy absently watched the little boy carrying a duty-free bag transfer it from one hand to the other, as they shuffled their way towards the officials in the booths.

'What you just told me, A.P., sounds more like a matter of principle than of revulsion,' he said.

'Whichever. I thought it was only our people that sort of thing went on with.'

Jeremy said after a pause, 'You feel Jewish though technically you're not, don't you?'

'But believe it or not that doesn't give me any problems.'

'How could it not?'

'That's a question I used to ask myself, but I think I now know the answer.'

Jeremy had to wait to hear it until they had shown their passports and proceeded through the barrier.

'Once again we're talking about feelings,' A.P. went on, 'and my feeling Jewish has to have come from sharing in the traditions, and all that, of my dad's family. My mum doesn't have a big family. Christmas and Easter at the Kyverdales' is a different experience from the noisy Chanukah parties and Seder nights I don't have to describe to you.'

A.P. smiled reminiscently. 'To call the Kyverdale get-togethers sparse and formal would be an understatement. When we sit down for Christmas dinner – well, Grandfather would have to slide the condiments several metres to my grandmother at the other end of the table, if there weren't also a salt and pepper set beside her place! Get the picture, Jeremy?'

'But it doesn't quite clarify what you're saying.'

'What I'm saying is that my Catholicism, though I'm a

293

true believer, doesn't permeate the whole of my life. Judaism, on the other hand, though it isn't my religion, seems to have done so. I've tried to explain to you how that's happened, since it can't, scientifically, be a case of one half of my blood – the ethnic half – being stronger than the other. Conditioning has to enter into it.'

'It might have been a different story, though,' said Jeremy, 'if your mother had come from an ordinary Catholic family.'

'I'm absolutely sure it would have been,' A.P. replied. 'I want to be a journalist, as you know, and lose no opportunity to gain experience. All grist to a writer's mill, is what my Grandma Marianne calls it. Once, when she mentioned she was going to a wake when the father of a Catholic friend of hers had died, I persuaded her to take me along. Except for the whisky swigging, the atmosphere – all those aunts and uncles and cousins together in one big room, not to mention the friends – reminded me of some of our family gatherings. As you said, Jeremy, if my mum's background had been ordinary, I'd probably be subjected to what you might call an inner tug-o'war that began in my childhood and wouldn't let me alone for the rest of my life.'

They had proceeded through customs, rucksacks on their backs, though some other young people were halted for theirs to be inspected.

Howard was awaiting them, his face alight with pleasure, Ben by his side.

'Talking of inner conflict,' said Jeremy, 'there's a kid unlikely to be as lucky as you in that respect.'

Before coming to Germany, the two lads had stayed for a few days in Cornwall, where Jeremy's gentile girlfriend was working in a hotel during the summer holidays. It was for this reason that he was unable to phone home, since hitch-hiking to St Ives for the purpose he had was not with his parents' knowledge. A.P. too was thus constrained to lie to Martin and Moira, rather than let down his friend.

Though one lie is known to lead to another, Jeremy had been unable to bring himself to call London and pretend he was in Munich. Why does my dad have to put me in the position he has? he thought, as they walked with Howard and Ben to the car park. He and Laura don't refuse invitations to mixed marriage wedding receptions. Why is Dad's inflexibility about marrying out only applied to his own children?

He would not have that problem with Janis; there'd never be anyone but Kurt for her. Jeremy wouldn't be thinking of marriage for years. Lindsey was just a girl he'd met at a party. All right, so he was highly attracted to her. Next month, though, Jeremy would be off to Oxford and she to Leicester University. Attraction was all it was. Had Jake Bornstein never been young! How on earth did a woman like Laura live with him?

Since Jeremy knew nothing of the confrontation that had taken place between Jake and Laura, the stand he then determined to take, that he be allowed to live his own life, would prove less difficult than he imagined, though Jake would not metamorphose into the opposite of 'Mr Barrett of Wimpole Street' overnight.

Meanwhile, he managed to ignore the aftertaste of the deception imposed upon him and listened, en route to Howard's home, to the plans his hosts had made for him and Jeremy to meet some young people.

'We have a very active Centre here,' Howard told them.

'Magda and Rudy – they're my stepsister and stepbrother – go there,' said Ben.

'There's no need to tell them who Magda and Rudy are, they know,' Howard said with a smile.

'Do they also know I have other brothers and sisters, Daddy?'

'Since you now have so many, Ben, there must be times when you yourself have to count them on your fingers!' Howard lightly exaggerated.

'I'm not that bad at arithmetic.'

Christina now had a baby son in addition to the twins.

And Karin had recently given birth to a girl whose red hair pinpointed her as a descendant of Abraham Sandberg.

'I'd like to go with Magda and Rudy to the Centre sometimes, but my mother prefers me not to,' said Ben.

Reminding A.P. of his own childhood, and how thankful he was that that part of his life was over. This kid, though, was still living through it. 'Don't let that get you down,' he said ruffling Ben's shock of dark curls.

'Please don't do that,' said Ben, 'it's what my mother is always doing and I don't like it.'

Because it was she who did it? A.P. conjectured. Though I've never felt subjected to a religious conflict, always felt certain about that part of me, there was a time when Mum wouldn't let Dad take me with him up north and I resented my mother so much I couldn't bear her to touch me. Dad eventually won that battle though, and I've ended up feeling sorry for Mum because she didn't have the sense to see what she was doing.

He glanced at Ben, seated beside Howard in the front of the car. Looking back you saw things differently and were able to find compassion. While you were little and it was happening to you, though . . . 'Like you, I'm only half Jewish,' he told Ben, 'and I too found that in some respects difficult.'

The little boy turned to look at him. 'How do you find it now you're a grown up?'

'If you like, you and I can have a chat about it while I'm in Munich.'

'Could we have one today? I'm only at my dad's house on Sundays, but I could come on my way home from school tomorrow if that would suit you better – '

'Don't worry, Ben,' said Howard, 'the chat will be fitted in.'

'It's nice for me to have some of my English family here. I've been looking forward to it,' Ben said to A.P. and Jeremy. 'Daddy said you're both going to Oxford University when you get home. I'd like to go there, too – '

296

And maybe he will, thought Howard. Who could foretell the future – well, certainly not me! Meanwhile, the rapport established in a trice between Martin's son and mine is something good to be going on with. Ben could have no better role model than A.P. who had come through his own traumatic childhood more intact than Martin could have hoped for.

That evening, A.P. and Jeremy found themselves in an ambience their preconceptions could not have allowed them to imagine might exist in Germany.

The Munich Jewish Centre was a hive of activity that reminded Jeremy of the venues in which he had sat at meetings with Janiş and Kurt in London. Posters on the walls, announcing communal functions, and people folding and putting into envelopes mimeographed information, enhanced the atmosphere.

They were introduced by Howard to a group of boys and girls of around their own age, and invited to join them at the table where they were drinking coffee.

'Is British Jewry as concerned as we are about what is now happening in Israel?' a sloe-eyed girl of buxom build inquired. 'It is what we have been discussing.'

Howard had told them he had yet to meet a young person at the Centre who did not speak good English and so it was to prove.

'I should think it's worrying to Jews everywhere,' Jeremy replied.

'You would like coffee or a Coke?' one of the boys asked.

'We'll have what you're having,' said A.P., 'and by the way, I'm not technically Jewish.'

'Technically?' said the pretty blonde seated opposite him.

'My mother is Catholic.'

'Oh,' she replied with a smile, 'the wrong half! I also have had that problem, but I have converted. My sister, though, she does not wish to know of the blood we have inherited from our father!'

'Isn't she as entitled to her choice as you to yours?' A.P. answered.

The boy getting A.P. and Jeremy their coffee from a nearby counter returned with it to the table, and said crisply, 'It is not just those like Helga, children of mixed marriages, who when they reach our age make the choice that Helga's sister has. Many who are fully Jewish, like myself, have chosen to go the way of much of Germany's pre-war Jewish community. Hitler, of course, eventually reminded them that a Jew, no matter how he denies it, remains a Jew.'

'Even,' said Helga, 'if they have only a drop of Jewish blood in their veins, that may one day be used against them. How is the neo-Nazi situation in your country?'

A.P. left it to Jeremy to put her in the picture.

'The repercussions of Hess's suicide were alarming for us,' she said when he finished speaking.

'For us, too.'

'But for German Jewry there is of course an added dimension,' said the boy who had brought the coffee. 'My name, in case you did not catch it when Howard introduced us, is Karl. Howard is my boss, did he tell you? I work for the Schulmann Optics Company at their Munich office. My father also and he has made friends with Howard.

'Our community is not as large as those in Frankfurt and Berlin – '

'But you seem to keep active,' Jeremy cut in.

'If I did not have this place to come to, until I emigrate to Israel, I do not know how I could go on living in Germany,' said the sloe-eyed girl. 'That is how many of us feel. And for me it is even worse. Since my parents, they are not of German origin, their family was Turkish, they are not among those who returned, as Karl's family did.'

'My grandmother could not take the climate or the insects in Israel,' Karl said apologetically to Jeremy and A.P. 'It was where she and my grandfather intended to stay, when they settled there after the camps. Both had survived Dachau – '

'And how they can bear living now so close to it I fail to understand,' said Helga.

'Would you expect when they returned to Germany they would not choose the city where they grew up?' Karl flashed, his tone now defensive rather than apologetic.

Do they have this sort of contretemps all the time? Jeremy wondered. If so, he was sorry for his German Jewish counterparts. What a complex situation theirs was.

He listened to the ensuing list of reasons which accounted for those at the table with him and A.P. having been born where they would rather not have been born. The latter was more than plain, though some seemed to feel constrained to defend their families and others to bitterly blame them.

The girl who had said she was of Turkish origin was among those who held no brief for their parents being here.

'I said that for me it is worse and I shall tell you why,' she capped the conversation for the visitors' benefit, her mature bosom heaving with emotion under a white sweater that made it the more eye-catching. 'My parents came to Germany only for business reasons. Money is all that my father is concerned with. Karl, like some others at this table, comes here often with his family. My family does not wish to be part of the Jewish community and I am ashamed of them. My brother is no different from Helga's sister. They are as it happens dating each other and would make a fine couple!

'But should they later marry,' she continued her diatribe, 'what is to become of their children? They will not be brought to this Centre, and more strength will be lost to us.'

Though Jeremy rather fancied her, he changed his mind about asking could he see her again, such was her intensity – and all of it political, it seemed! 'That's what the rabbis in England are saying about what intermarriage is doing to British Jewry,' he said.

'It is not intermarriage that we are discussing,' she flashed, 'it is the special responsibility that German Jewry must honour.'

'If that's how you feel, why do you intend deserting German Jewry and emigrating to Israel?' A.P. inquired.

She flared at him as she had to Jeremy. 'In your opinion does that make of me a traitor? I am going where I shall not be undervalued.'

The conversation then turned to the build up of tension on the West Bank.

'The Arab unrest, and how Israel is dealing with it, is having its effect on British campuses,' Jeremy put in. 'Well, certainly on some of them.'

'When,' said Karl, 'did what happens in Israel not affect Jews everywhere?' His accompanying sigh seemed that of a weary old man.

'Any excuse will do, for those with a mind to, to have a go at us,' Jeremy declared.

Later, when he and A.P. emerged to the main road where Howard had told them they could catch a bus, he found himself drawing a breath of relief.

'Do you think the people we met tonight ever think or talk to each other about anything else, A.P.?'

'Well, they certainly seem what one might call obsessed with their situation.'

Jeremy paused to consider. 'It isn't a happy situation, is it? The feeling I got about some of them was that they feel trapped in Germany by circumstances – '

'And that girl in the white sweater came over as a caged tiger!'

'Leaving the cage out of it, she would sure be a tiger in bed!'

'And I was aware that you wouldn't mind bedding her. Lindsey's that sort, too, isn't she?'

'Since you couldn't have failed to hear through the wall, from your virgin couch in that dump in St Ives that passes for a flat, you doubtless have grounds for making that remark,' Jeremy replied with a grin.

'Not many would make the sacrifice you did for a pal,' he added as they walked past a darkened florist's shop and crossed the street.

'It was no sacrifice, Jeremy, which isn't to say the duplicity it entailed didn't go against the grain.'

'I'm hoping you'll return from this trip initiated into the rites of passion. Doesn't it bother you that you're the only male virgin either of us knows? And that probably goes for all the females of our acquaintance, too – '

'Yes, but I shan't let that be a reason for my joining the club,' said A.P. 'I'd prefer my initiation ceremony to be conducted by the right girl.'

Had Marianne been privy to her grandson's words, she would have recognized him as the romantic his father and grandfather were, and perhaps have found herself fearing for him since along with romanticism went the capacity for disillusion.

A suitable candidate for A.P.'s initiation presented herself to him and Jeremy immediately they arrived, three days later, in Berlin. She was also to prove the direct opposite of the young people they had met at the Centre in Munich.

They were standing amid the bustling throng outside Tegel Airport, waiting to be collected by Herr Schulmann's chauffeur, whom Karin had said would be there to transport them to her parents' home.

'Imagine us getting into a Rolls, dressed in our grubby jeans!' said Jeremy. 'Not to mention our rucksacks. We ought to've been firmer with Karin about making our own way there – '

'Since they know we're students, how else would they expect us to look?' said A.P. 'Grandfather Kyverdale no longer bats an eyelid when I show up at the stately home looking like this. Did you pack a jacket and tie, to wear for dinner, though, like I told you to?'

'Laura made me bring a suit, but it'll look like hell after how it's travelled – '

'There'll be someone only too pleased to press it for you – '

'And I wish now we hadn't accepted the Schulmanns' hospitality! It would've been more fun to stay at a hostel, there'd be girls staying there, too – '

'That would have been unkind to Karin,' A.P. countered. 'We couldn't have done it.'

'Why,' said Jeremy, 'did my dad have to marry into a family where there's practically no escaping relatives anywhere in the world!'

'And I sometimes find it difficult to believe,' said A.P., 'that it all began with the Sandbergs and Moritzes settling in a ghetto in Manchester at the turn of the century.'

'Please don't go all historical on me,' Jeremy snapped, 'and why is that stunning girl eyeing us? Handsome we may be, but not that handsome – '

'Well, my fly isn't undone, is yours?' A.P. laughed when Jeremy glanced down to make sure.

The girl then hesitantly approached them, her long hair gleaming like ripe corn in the afternoon sunlight and tossed by the wind.

'If it's you she fancies, I'll consider it one I owe you,' Jeremy had time to say before she reached them.

'If you are not whom I am here to meet, this will perhaps seem to you a joke,' was her preamble. 'Are you waiting to be taken to where you are going in a Rolls-Royce?'

'I'm afraid so,' said Jeremy.

The girl managed not to laugh. 'Then I shall instead take you there. My godfather, Herr Schulmann, apologizes that he himself had need of his car this afternoon and he has asked me to deputize. I am Rachel Greenbaum, how do you do?'

They introduced themselves and shook hands with her, Jeremy doing the talking while they walked to where she had parked her car, and A.P. trying to recover from the impact of her gaze and the musky scent she was wearing. Both had gone to his head.

Jeremy registered A.P.'s expression, gave him a wink, and allowed him to sit beside her in the blue Audi that matched her eyes and her clingy sweater. She too was wearing jeans, the kind that hugged her narrow hips. And probably had a designer label stitched inside the waistband, he wagered. Nor would it be Jeremy's fault if A.P. didn't get the chance to confirm that. Berlin was where the action was and Jeremy wasn't going to spend the few days they had here on cerebral pursuits.

'I'm pleased that Herr Schulmann needed the Rolls today, and I'm sure my cousin agrees,' he helped A.P. along.

'Well, it's nice that we got to meet you, Rachel,' A.P. ventured.

Jeremy would then have added, 'What're you doing this evening?' What was the matter with A.P.?

'You would in any case have met me,' she replied. 'My godfather he has asked me to show to you Berlin, if of course you would like that I should – '

'I accept the offer with alacrity,' said Jeremy.

'And I with double alacrity,' said A.P.

Rachel laughed, a mellow peal that went with the vibrancy of her voice. 'I could not wish for a more charming response.'

But A.P. is going to have to do a lot better than that, thought Jeremy. Though he didn't see all that much of the Kyverdales, their formality had sure rubbed off on him when it came to girls.

'I am invited to dine tonight at the Schulmanns',' Rachel told them, 'my parents also. Afterwards the four will settle down to play bridge and you shall see Berlin by night. I promise you I shall be a good guide.'

But for A.P.'s sake, not a good girl, hoped Jeremy. 'In case there's a disco or two included in our nocturnal itinerary,' he said, 'it would be useful perhaps if we could meet up after dinner with one of your girlfriends.'

'That is already tentatively arranged. Paula, who was with me at school in Switzerland, has made herself available.'

Well, that sounded encouraging, thought Jeremy as Rachel began pointing out to them buildings that had become the landmarks of West Berlin.

'I wouldn't mind visiting East Berlin,' said A.P. recovering from his reverie. 'Jeremy and I had intended to, but we can go there by train. From the Zoo station, Karin told us – '

'That will not be necessary, we shall make it part of our programme.'

'This is really terribly good of you,' said A.P. 'We really appreciate the time you're giving us and the trouble you're taking.'

They had halted at a traffic light and Rachel turned to smile at him. 'It is no trouble, I am looking forward to spending time with you. And Paula will be delighted to meet your cousin.'

Jeremy hadn't any idea what Paula would be like, but for A.P.'s sake was pleased that the allocating of partners had indicated Rachel's choice.

After giving them tea, Frau Schulmann went with Rachel to the door, leaving the butler to show A.P. and Jeremy to their adjoining bedrooms.

'If the young gentlemen would care for their unpacking to be done for them?' he said trying to avoid looking at the shabby rucksacks they had not allowed him to carry.

'Thanks, Parker, but you would have a job unravelling the contents of our luggage,' A.P. said with a smile. 'A pressing iron wouldn't come amiss, though.'

'I was about to suggest it, sir. If you would leave the garments in your rooms while you take a bath, you will find them as you would wish them on your return.'

'That's jolly nice of you, Parker.'

'My pleasure, sir.'

'We can draw our baths ourselves.'

'As you wish, sir.'

The stilted exchange was conducted on the galleried landing while the butler opened with a flourish first one bedroom door and then the other.

'Will there be anything else, Mr Dean?'

'If we require something we'll ring for the maid,' A.P. replied.

'Very good, sir.'

Parker waited for them to enter their rooms before departing.

A moment later they met again in the doorway allowing access from one spacious chamber to the other.

'This is like a French farce!' said Jeremy.

'Not a French farce, a British one,' A.P. said with a grin, 'and the more farcical for its German setting. It's always been my belief that an English butler can turn whatever setting into a bit of old England and this proves it – '

'If you say so, Mr Dean. The manner born isn't in it! If you hadn't been with me, I'd have wished the floor would open up and swallow me, not that I didn't anyway. And a bit of *old* England is right. Shall you employ a butler when you become Lord Kyverdale?'

'I doubt it and my grandfather probably suspects that he is the last of the line to perpetuate the class distinction he inherited with the title. The new England is a different dish of tea, though Grandfather, if he thinks about it, wouldn't let himself accept it.'

'You intend to go on drawing your own bath, do you? I never heard that expression before. It has to be as archaic as the crumbling class system you mentioned. Shall I let drop to Rachel that you're destined to be a lordship?'

'Not unless you want it revealed that your father is a millionaire.'

'I've never needed to use that to land a girl.'

'If you had to, she wouldn't be worth landing, would she? Shall we now draw our baths?'

After dinner, Rachel retired briefly to change from her frilly white dress into more casual clothing.

'You have my permission to put on again your uniform,' she said with a laugh before departing.

They returned wearing unwrinkled jeans and tee shirts. While they ate, the garments left heaped on their beds had been meticulously pressed.

Paula proved to be a bubbly brunette, as Semitic in appearance as Rachel was not.

'There's a big Jewish community centre here, isn't there?' A.P. remarked as the four headed in Rachel's car for the first of the several clubs and discos they were to visit.

'If you wish to go there, you must do so without me,' said Rachel, 'and Paula will say to you the same, as would all our friends. If the Jewish activities are what you have come to Germany to observe, you must find those interested in them to show them to you.'

'Frankly,' said Jeremy, 'we had a basinful of that in Munich and I'd welcome a change.'

'In that case,' said Rachel, 'I shall keep my promise to escort you. Had you not said that, I would have introduced to you my elder sister, who lives, eats, and thinks Jewish.'

'Some of our generation at home are like that,' Jeremy told her. 'Most, though, are what I'd call the happy medium, like me.'

'With German Jewry there is no such thing,' Paula informed him.

'Why is that?'

'According to my parents, who side with my sister against me,' said Rachel, 'the community here is in a special position.'

'I agree,' said Jeremy, recalling the intensity with which the girl in Munich had spoken of it.

'I had not yet finished. We have to be seen to be standing together, my father says, not only by our host country, but by Jews elsewhere who have contempt for our living here. I did not ask to be born here and shall not allow the past to spoil for me the present,' Rachel declared.

The kind of silence Jeremy had not expected to feature in this outing briefly followed.

It was Paula who broke it. 'What Rachel has said cannot be easy for those who do not live here to understand. We and our friends do not want the responsibility laid upon us by our families' return. Those prepared to shoulder it are welcome to it.

'Speaking for myself, as for every person I have only one life and shall make the most of it in my own way. If you encounter sufficient German Jews, young or old, you will find that there are two kinds and must draw from that your own conclusions.'

Rachel turned the car into a parking space and pulled up. 'From here we shall continue our night out on foot.'

Though Berlin by night, the cosmopolitan atmosphere throbbing with life, could not but be exciting to the sheltered youngsters A.P. and Jeremy were, there were moments in this noisy venue, or that, when they found themselves exchanging an uneasy glance.

The four were consuming nothing stronger than Pepsi, but there was about the girls a false intoxication. Something that didn't ring true, as if they were determined to enjoy themselves.

Like those people Jeremy and I saw sitting in deck-chairs wearing raincoats and sou'westers, on the beach at St Ives, thought A.P., as if they weren't going to let a wet day ruin their holiday. But what sort of pleasure was that?

Rachel and Paula too had resolved not to let something get the better of them and it wasn't the weather. It had to be connected to the choice both had made. To the feelings they had expressed in the car.

After a while, even Rachel's engaging laughter began to sound to A.P. artificial, and suddenly the girl he had thought might initiate him to the rites of physical love seemed to him pathetic, if none the less attractive.

When at the end of the hectic round she parked the car on the tree-lined avenue leading to the Schulmanns' mansion and wound her arms around his neck, her proximity and her perfume again overwhelmed him.

'My godparents have a summer-house,' she whispered. 'Shall you and I go there and leave the car to our friends?'

Why was A.P. having last minute scruples, with her breasts thrusting against him and her hand wandering to his thigh?

They weren't scruples, they were second thoughts. A girl who'd let you lay her when you were little more than strangers wasn't the one he wanted to remember as his first lay.

It was she who broke away from their embrace.

Since her hand had reached its destination, A.P. wasn't surprised. His erection was no more, as if dismissed by those second thoughts.

'Our visitors have had an exhausting day,' she said to Paula, breaking up the action on the back seat. 'I suggest that we now allow them to retire to their solitary beds and rest.'

'We'll see you tomorrow,' said Jeremy, sounding dazed as well he might.

'I am not too sure about that,' Rachel replied.

A moment later the car was zooming down the drive.

Jeremy stopped wiping lipstick off his face. 'What the hell did you do to her, A.P.?'

'I'm afraid it's a question of what I didn't do to her.' A.P. felt in his pocket for the key the butler had reluctantly provided and let them into the house.

'Are you going to stay a virgin for the rest of your life?'

'Just until I find the right girl. I imagine we shall now be left to explore West and East Berlin unescorted and I have to say I'd prefer that. If we're distracted by girls, it's bound to dilute our impressions and I might one day need to dip into mine for something I'm writing.'

'One way and another I'm beginning to see myself as the wrong companion for you on this trip,' Jeremy said scathingly as they tiptoed upstairs. 'It ought to have been your grand-mother!'

Chapter Eleven

❦

OCTOBER 1987 WAS a month that Marianne was unlikely to forget, she thought while gazing through her study window to where once had been her beautiful garden.

It was now November 5th, the mist of approaching winter hovering, and there would be no shortage of fallen branches for the children to burn on their Guy Fawkes bonfires tonight.

The hurricane that had wreaked havoc in the south of England, changing the landscape as it felled the sturdiest of ancient trees, tearing tiles from rooftops and mowing down fences, had done its worst to the ornamental bushes Marianne and Ralph had planted together years ago.

Were that not depressing enough, a stock market crash had followed, reminding Marianne that it was some time since she had met with her stockbroker, that being a widow put you in control of matters you'd been pleased to leave in your husband's hands.

Marianne's disinterest in how her earnings were invested had been a source of amusement to Ralph. 'Yet you think of yourself as an independent woman,' he had once said. She still did. Why else was she keeping Simon waiting for an answer to his asking her to marry him? He had finally got around to it last week – another reason for October being memorable.

Etched upon her memory too was the day she had driven her grandson to Oxford to enter the next phase of his life. Amid the dreaming spires where intellect was for a brief while nurtured before the real business of living began.

His parents had offered to take him together to New College, where Martin had once been a student. What a kick my son would have got out of that, thought Marianne. Which father wouldn't? He had, however, hidden his disappointment when A.P. said he would like to be ferried with his belongings by Marianne.

If Moira too had felt rebuffed, it was for her as for Martin just one more disappointment. Eventually they would surely come to see it as Marianne had. How could the lad have borne for them to take him to college together, when he knew they would not be under the same roof when he returned?

Moira was still living in the house and Martin had moved into a service flat until he found a place suitable to accommodate A.P.

Marianne recalled her conversation with A.P. when he had clutched as at a straw at her telling him to consider her place his second home. He would now have three to choose from, but given the circumstances would not know a real home again until eventually he himself set up home.

A telephone call from Laura interrupted Marianne's musing.

'Bessie's having a bonfire party tonight. Fancy coming along?'

'I have a date with Simon.'

'He's welcome to come, too.'

'I'm not sure that fireworks are his scene – '

'Come off it, Marianne! He's an American. Lighting fireworks on every possible national holiday is their popular pastime. But any excuse for his not meeting the family, and for none of us meeting him, will do! This is beginning to get a bit hurtful, Marianne.'

With that Laura rang off, leaving Marianne angry both with her and with herself.

Briefly she paced the room she sometimes thought of as her cell. The place in which she was imprisoned with her work, hour after hour, day after day.

Self-imprisonment, but that's my privilege. If I marry Simon, he'll make demands on my time when he isn't working, or suffers an attack of writer's block. Ralph had left for work early in the morning and returned in the evening when Marianne was ready to put the cover on her typewriter. *Life with Simon will be unpredictable and gone will be my régime.*

Will be? Or would be? Indecisiveness was still with her. Could she live without him? Did they love each other enough to make the concessions necessary for two writers to share a life and continue to meet their deadlines?

Nor, for Marianne, was a deadline her sole incentive. There was and always had been within her a creative dynamo that drove her without respite until a novel was complete. How would Simon live with that – the part of her he didn't yet know? With a woman who sometimes got up in the middle of the night to set on paper ideas that would not let her sleep.

Marianne plumped up the cushions on the Chesterfield. *I could have done without this dilemma at my time of life! But Simon has brought to this time of your life something you'd thought gone forever.*

'You can't have the ha'penny and the bun, Marianne,' Sarah Sandberg's voice echoed in her head from the past. 'Nobody can.'

Nor were the best things in life necessarily free. In Marianne's experience there was a price to pay for everything. Was she prepared to pay the price of marrying a man she loved?

That evening she found that Laura had taken the matter of his introduction to the family into her own hands.

'I got a call from your cousin – the one who's a photographer,' Simon said when he dropped in for a drink earlier than Marianne had expected him. 'She said we're invited to her kid's bonfire party. But you already know, no doubt. I guess she called me too to be polite, since I haven't yet been to her home.'

'I haven't encouraged my family to clasp you to its bosom, Simon.'

'Or me to clasp it to mine. If you think I didn't know that, you must take me for a fool, Marianne. I seem to recall suggesting more than once that we invite your relatives for Sunday brunch to my place, or yours. You never did anything about it, though, and I was aware that wasn't because you couldn't be bothered scrambling eggs for a crowd and dishing out bagels with cream cheese and lox.'

Simon smiled dryly. 'Who are you ashamed of? Me, or them?'

'Neither! And if you're going to be snide about this, you can go to the bloody bonfire on your own.'

'I don't mind missing out on the bonfire. What I do mind is that I haven't yet met your son and his wife.'

'They're no longer together.'

'Since when? Don't bother telling me. I'm not curious, Marianne. Just shocked that a relationship I thought the closest I'd known could exclude your letting me in on something as distressing for you as what I've just – by chance – learned. Maybe I am the fool you think me.'

Marianne watched him drink the Scotch she had poured for him and get himself another.

'Is this to be the first time I see you get drunk?'

Simon eyed her contemplatively and made no reply.

She sipped some of her sherry and put down the glass. 'The truth is, Simon, that I wanted to keep you to myself. Once you become part of my family scene – '

'The honeymoon we haven't yet had would be over – is that what you mean?' he cut in.

'Sort of, though I have to say that was a cock-eyed way of putting it.'

'Then let me put it differently,' he answered. 'You're reluctant to let me into the full context of your life is how I see it.' He paused to share a long glance with her. 'The love I have for you, though, has changed my life. To give it to you straight, you now *are* my life.'

'But you are neither a parent, nor a grandparent. My being both ensures that I can't say to you what you've just said to me. On our first date I told you I'm a family woman – remember? And in the fullest sense.'

'Apart from your midnight dash to your brother's though, I have yet to see you in action.'

Marianne mustered a smile. 'If you'd seen me in action between then and now, you might wish you hadn't popped the question you did last week! Would you care to withdraw it?'

'You're not getting off the hook that easily!'

'I'm not yet on it, am I?'

'But I was hoping to put a ring on your finger and take you with me to New York next month. My agent has something special lined up for me.'

Marianne made a quick decision. Call it a step forward in the decision-making process. 'I need a break after finishing a first draft. Could you manage a week in Bermuda?'

'With you? You bet.'

'I'm told it's idyllic and not a long flight from New York. Why don't we do that, Simon? But without the ring on my finger.'

'You're a slippery fish to catch, Marianne!' he said with a laugh. 'But I'm still hoping to land you and okay, we'll do it your way. Drink up your sherry and we'll go watch that effigy Britishers burn on bonfire night go up in smoke.'

They left the flat and walked to Laura's home hand in hand, fireworks lighting the night sky. Like a couple of kids, Marianne thought. Next time she counted her blessings she would add Simon.

Chapter Twelve

❧❧❧

ON THE DAY they were to leave for New York, Marianne
called Simon early in the morning.

'Hi, hon! If this is to remind me to pack the special tea
you're taking for your cousin, I already did so. If the customs
guys open our baggage they'll think we intend setting up a
tea shop!'

'Did I waken you?'

'I've had juice and coffee and was about to go take my
shower. Did you get a good night's sleep?'

'I haven't been to bed.'

'Don't tell me! You got some new ideas about the first
draft you thought was finished and spent the night making
revisions. What am I going to do with you! You'll have to
get some shut-eye on the plane.'

How light-hearted he sounded. But not for long. 'I can't
go with you, Simon.'

'Say that again?'

'After you left last night I got a call from my sister-in-
law – '

'The one you said lives with her daughter in Israel? The
press are now calling what's happening in Gaza and the West
Bank an uprising. But you told me your relatives live in Tel
Aviv. It wouldn't affect them. Why in the hell can't you go
with me?' And why did I, before asking you, waste time
mentioning something irrelevant to *us*? Because I'm still
trying to take in this last minute let down by the woman I
love.

'The call was from Lyn, Matthew's mother,' Marianne
said. 'There's been another crisis, his worst yet and it's still

314

going on. He couldn't breathe and was rushed to hospital by ambulance. They say it's pneumonia and the outlook is grim.'

'I'm sorry to hear that.'

'As if that weren't enough for Lyn to take, after the doctors had spoken to them Arnold let Pete have it. He's been bottling it up for years, holding Pete responsible for Matthew's being gay. Pete is now in pieces.'

'All concerned have my sympathy,' said Simon, 'but why does this have to mean you can't go with me?'

'If you have to ask that, you're not the man for me, Simon.'

'Damn right I'm not! Nor you the woman for me.'

A moment later each had replaced the receiver and stood staring down at the telephone. Marianne in Hampstead and Simon in Highgate, a ten-minute drive from each other, but for both it was as if a yawning cavern now stretched between them.

What is it with her? thought Simon. Is she some kind of masochist? She'd looked forward to this trip as much as he had, even gone out and bought herself new outfits to wear in Bermuda. Okay, so her sister-in-law needs some support, but Laura's around, and also that young rabbi and his wife I met at the bonfire party. Well, Simon had sure seen Marianne in action now! But why did it have to be her, and why did she stand for it?

He could not have known how often Marianne had asked herself that question, or that she was again doing so. If ever there were a reluctant and unsuitable unofficial matriarch, it's me!

The answer to why she stood for the demands made on her, though, lay in what she had finally said to Martin on the night they discussed pros and cons of the institution responsible for her present plight.

Come what may, she was thankful that hers was a family that continued to stand by each other.

Simon took his shower, tidied his kitchen, checked his briefcase, dressed and left for the airport like a robot going through the motions of getting where it was programmed to go. Robots didn't feel pain and he would hold his at bay for as long as he could.

Marianne allowed herself the luxury of soaking in the bath, threw on fresh clothing, drank some strong tea, got into her car and returned to where she was needed.

Neither had yet come to grips with how their brief telephone conversation had ended. That the words they had said could not be unsaid and implicit in them was the end of their affair.

Chapter Thirteen

❦

SIMON HAD ANTICIPATED a wait of up to two hours after arriving at Kennedy Airport, before Marianne joined him after proceeding through immigration. The line for foreigners entering the country could stretch, four abreast, like a mile-long snake curving itself to fit into the overheated space, any time of year. And this was the week before Christmas.

Making his way past those who had no option but to put up with inconvenience of that sort after flying the Atlantic, he thought it time something was done about it. Foreigners came to New York on business, but he couldn't imagine them doing so if they could find an alternative market.

He was still not letting himself think of Marianne. The Scotch he had consumed on the flight, the movie too, had helped blot her out. When the thought of her inserted itself he would go on making himself dwell upon something else, like the seemingly arrogant attitude of New York's immigration authority, as he had just now.

He had also anticipated sharing with her the suite he'd reserved at the Plaza! Put that thought away, too, he ordered himself as a cab carried him there.

'You bin to the UK for woik or for pleasure?' the cabbie inquired.

'What makes you think I've flown in from there?'

'I've seen the tag on your baggage. What am I, blind? Believe you me, a guy in my lina woik gotta keep his eyes skinned, or packa pistol, wid what goes on in this city! You a New Yorker?'

'Born and bred.'

'So I shouldn't have to tell you. You ain't one of them

limeys who wants to know why I got a cast iron screen between me an' who I'm drivin'. I took a look at you, though, an' slid it back, like I do when I pick up limeys at Kennedy. I got family in the UK. My mom was a GI bride. Came from a city called Manchester. You ever bin there?'

'No.' I thought I might soon be marrying into a Manchester family, Simon wanted to tell him, but you didn't unburden yourself to a cab-driver, friendly though New York cabbies could be if they hadn't got out of bed the wrong side that morning.

'My mom took me to see her folks when I was a kid, but I never bin back. Always meant to, but never made it. Things get in the way, you know how it is.'

Simon did. And the hell with Marianne's family!

'You don't have a home in New York, you're askin' me to take you to the Plaza?'

'I live in London.'

'They say that's some city, still civilized.'

'Depending on what you compare it with.'

'Me, I live in Queens and it has to be better than where I was raised. The Bronx ain't fit for human habitation no more!'

Simon rested his head against the seedy upholstery, his gaze on the skyline that was for him like no other; the pure symmetry and soaring strength of it never failed to take his breath away. He was home again.

In London, to where he had escaped for a change of scene, he felt the lonesome exile he was. After the three years he had spent there he'd been thinking of up'n running again when he met Marianne. Up'n running was right! A writer without ties could live anywhere, all he needed was an agent wherever to find him work, and a typewriter.

So it had been for Simon since his marriage broke up. Kids would have kept him in New York, provided too the stability of a sort even a divorced guy got out of being a father. He'd have had them to stay on the weekends and on their school vacations.

Minus that incentive to stay put, he had lived for a while in Madrid, lured there by his admiration for the author he had in his youth hoped to emulate, Ernest Hemingway. Me and all the other aspiring male novelists of my day, he thought now.

Marianne, though, had revealed that she had hoped to emulate nobody, just to be herself. In spite of that, her books had been compared in some reviews with the work of Howard Spring. There was about them, Simon had thought after getting one of Spring's novels from the library, the same rich texture, and a social content that didn't stop them from being a good read.

Again he ordered himself not to think about her and tried to give his attention to the cabbie's continuing monologue about the changes time had wrought to their home town.

When eventually he was unpacking his bag in the splendour he had hoped to share with her, he found that one of the numerous packets of tea she had asked him to put into it had split. Had she been with him they would now be laughing together. The white shorts he had brought to wear in Bermuda looked as if a swarm of black flies had settled on them.

Simon glanced around the bedroom. Opulent described it. The richness of the fabrics and the carpet. The ornate furniture. The perfume drifting from a vase of flowers. He had not stayed here before, but had chosen it as a setting for Marianne. She, though, would probably have giggled when she saw it.

He recalled saying to her on their first date that he wanted to show her New York through the eyes of a New Yorker. Since then he had found himself seeing through her eyes much that he had not really looked at before. She took nothing at its face value. And they shared a lot of laughs, though Simon wouldn't have called himself, before he met her, the kind who saw the funny side.

He had reserved a suite for them in Bermuda at the Elbow Beach Hotel, a setting that would charm Marianne. But Bermuda was now out. At the bottom of his bag was the lightweight clothing he wouldn't require. Such was his inertia after Marianne called, he had not bothered repacking. And what in the hell was he to do with eleven packs of Lyon's Red Label tea?

The shortbread intended for her cousins was in her own bag. There was no reason, though, for them not to get the tea.

Though Simon had neither their telephone number nor their address, the switchboard operator was patient and helpful. At these prices she should be!

A woman whose voice implied she was the gentle sort, its north of England accent reminiscent of Marianne's and Laura's, answered.

'Is this Mrs Diane Sanderton?'

'Who's speaking?'

'My name is Newman – '

'Marianne's friend! Please excuse me for sounding wary – '

'No need to tell me why. When I lived here I also had my share of crank calls. I have something for you from Marianne.'

'She always was a thoughtful person. We were thrilled to hear she was coming. And needless to say upset when she phoned today to tell us why she had to cancel her trip. Ronald will be home from the clinic soon and we're in this evening, if you'd care to visit us – '

'This evening I have to eat dinner with my agent, jet-lagged though I am. I'm here on business. If Marianne had come along you'd have seen a lot of her this week. All she had scheduled was a lunch with someone from her US publishers.'

'It's time Marianne had a real break. She works too hard,' Diane declared.

And that isn't all, thought Simon. 'I'm not yet sure what my own schedule will be,' he said. 'If I don't manage to drop by your home, I'll get the tea to you somehow. It would be useful to have the clinic phone number, in case when I call again you're not at home – '

For the next few days Simon's time was fully occupied,

the ageing rock star whose autobiography he was commissioned to ghost write expecting the attention that went with fame and wealth.

Had Marianne been present she would have noted Simon's quizzical expression, while night after night over dinner and the brandies that followed he listened attentively to a still handsome man, whose youthful face implied he had had it lifted, talk on and on about himself.

There was big money in this one for Simon, his agent kept reminding him when they met for lunch, or in one of the pep talks he delivered to reluctant clients before meetings with lawyers to discuss the bartering that drawing up a contract usually entailed, a process that Simon preferred to leave to his agent. But on this occasion the guy who handled his affairs had wanted him in on it – possibly he thought it was time Simon saw how hard he worked! Having seen it for himself, Simon wouldn't swap places with him.

Money, though, had never been Simon's incentive any more than it was Marianne's. At first he had envied her the creative rewards she had achieved that he hadn't, but you didn't go on envying the woman you loved. Admiration had fast replaced it.

All thoughts led him back to Marianne. And he couldn't bring himself to go spend a cosy evening at home with her relatives. Nor had he time to.

Eventually he called Ronald at the clinic and invited him for a drink at the Plaza.

'I was leaning on the bar, waiting to be paged,' he said after Ronald had introduced himself and they had shaken hands.

'But you didn't know I'd seen a photo of you! Laura took some at Bessie's bonfire party. On the one she sent us, you and Marianne were both clutching sparklers.'

That evening had seemed to Simon a turning point for him and Marianne. The welcome he had received, the glow from the leaping flames lighting her face and the rockets zooming skyward along with his hopes.

'Having a photographer in the family helps keep my wife and me in touch,' said Ronald. 'As Marianne may have told you, we're a very close clan.'

'If that weren't so she'd be here with me.' Did Simon's tone sound as bitter to Ronald as it had to him? 'What can I get you to drink?'

'A cola will be fine, I'm a soft drink guy.'

They sat down on a couple of stools just vacated.

'Like you, I can't stay long,' Ronald said. 'There's a patient at the clinic I must keep an eye on tonight.'

'Don't let me forget to hand over the tea.'

'Is that what the something you mentioned on the phone to Diane is? What a treat! When we're offered a cup of tea over here, we say no thanks.'

'In case I do forget, there's enough of your favourite brand, in the bag I've dumped beside my stool, to keep you going for quite a while.'

'Are you that absent-minded?' Ronald said with a laugh.

'Not as a rule. But right now your cousin has me so distracted I barely know what I'm doing!' Simon added though he had not intended to. 'There's a strong resemblance between you and Marianne, by the way.'

'So we've always been told. But her hair isn't yet pure silver!'

'Mine was getting there when I met her and she's sure as hell now speeding it on its way,' Simon declared after gulping down his Scotch. 'Why am I telling you this?'

'Could be you need to tell someone and I happen to be her cousin and handy. Marianne, bless her heart, isn't a woman many guys would find easy to live with.'

'We're not living together. I've asked her to marry me.'

'And she's struggling to hang on to her independence?'

'How did you guess?'

'I've known her all my life, haven't I? Too much independence has always been her trouble, though I reckon the guy she married in her youth learned to live with it. Ralph was a terrific person. An artist who never made it but didn't let that sour him.'

Simon's first intimation of the similarity between himself and the man whose replacement he wanted to be. If you didn't count that Ralph hadn't let disappointment sour him!

He glanced around at the happy-hour throng in the bar. 'Yuppie' described most of them. Young executives, male and female, and some not so young, uniformed in the slick suits that went with their workaday scene. A sprinkling too of those for whom cocktails at the Plaza or wherever was a nightly ritual of their sophisticated world. They would afterwards dine here in the lavish surroundings that matched their own image, or go on to some smart restaurant, not just to eat but to see and be seen, while the large chunk of citizens on welfare, some without roofs over their heads, continued on a route known only by those at the bottom of the heap.

Simon was beginning to think like Marianne! Reminded again in her absence, as so often in her presence, that knowing her had changed how he saw things.

'Are you as loyal to your family as Marianne is?' he asked Ronald.

'It's an affliction all of us suffer from!'

'Why did you put it that way?'

'Perhaps because that's how it sometimes used to feel to me,' Ronald said reflectively. 'I'd find myself doing something inconvenient and think to myself, "Damn the family!" The sort of thing I'm talking about is all behind me now, though.'

'It isn't for Marianne and I have to tell you her family involvement is damaging our relationship.'

Ronald drank some Pepsi and rattled the ice in his glass. 'My answer to that is that it's up to you not to let it.'

'If I knew how!'

'The only advice I can give you is to accept Marianne the way she is. Let me add, though, that if she marries you, you'll be getting a rare gem.'

For the remainder of the half-hour they spent together they chatted, like the strangers they were, about the ghost still stalking Wall Street after the crash, Mr Gorbachev's 'glasnost', and the implications of the Holocaust Memorial in London having been defaced.

It was the personal topic they had briefly discussed that remained with Simon after Ronald's departure and allowed him no sleep that night. He had not needed telling that Marianne was a rare gem. But how was he now to prove how highly he valued her? And that there was more to the man he was than she supposed. That, though, he must first prove to himself.

Chapter Fourteen

❋

THOUGH RONALD HAD CALLED MARIANNE to thank her for the tea, she had not heard from Simon. Christmas, which they had anticipated spending together in idyllic surroundings, came and went without a word from him.

New Year's Eve too, for which Marianne had refused all invitations in order to remain by the telephone, hoping that Simon might see the beginning of another year as a good time to set things right between them.

After two more weeks had slipped by without his contacting her, her own hope of setting things right began to fade. Why had she let love put her at the mercy of a man! She was old enough to know better.

Marianne could not have known that Simon had not called her lest she hang up on him and had gone to spend some time at his sister's home in New England, hoping that the quietude of surroundings less frenetic than New York and London would settle his nerves and help him think things out.

Meanwhile Matthew had survived to return home, and Janis and Kurt had announced their engagement. They had not done so until Matthew was pronounced out of danger and on the day he was discharged from hospital had gone immediately to let him congratulate them. Marianne was present when that moving scene took place. Janis and Kurt as radiant as young lovers were known to be, their presence lighting up Matthew's sickroom. And he with a smile on his face like the splendid actor he still was.

The almonds together with the raisins once again, Marianne had thought. And she herself not going short of the former right now.

At such moments memories of her grandmother returned to her and she would recall their private chats in Sarah's kitchen, the heart of her home. Women like Sarah Sandberg, though, weren't bred any more. Few nowadays displayed the single-minded devotion to what nature was said to have intended our purpose on earth to be. Instead we've sought and many of us achieved the equality with men for which we're neither biologically nor emotionally equipped. The price is the conflicting priorities career women have to live with.

On the last day of February, Marianne finally heard from Simon. A typed message and without a signature in an envelope postmarked 'Wellesley'. 'Just to let you know I haven't forgotten you.'

He had gone to ground at his sister's but who cared? She had better begin forgetting *him*. The nerve of the man!

Marianne resorted immediately to her personal therapy, burying herself in her work as she had after losing Ralph. She began editing the first draft of her new novel and by March was immersed in writing the manuscript she would deliver to her publisher.

As always her strict régime was interspersed with family crises. Matthew was briefly hospitalized yet again. Martin and Andy had a difference of opinion that seemed to herald the end of their long partnership and Marianne's son spent two days at her flat discussing it with her. She was relieved when the matter was amicably settled and she able to resume work. No sooner had she done so than Ann called from Israel with a problem.

The Palestinian uprising, now said to be in the control of PLO agitators, had impelled Kate and her husband to throw in their lot with the militant West Bank settlers, with whose biblical views of Judaea and Samaria they agreed.

'How can they take their kids where the violence is?' Ann had said with feeling. 'I've tried to dissuade them till I'm blue in the face. All Kate says is it's up to me if I return to England or go with them.'

326

Ann had not returned to England to live alone. She could not have brought herself to live in Germany had Howard suggested it. In many ways, Marianne had reflected, Ann was a throwback to those previous generations. Without a husband and children, what would they have had to live for?

Having family on the West Bank was a disquieting thought, another anxiety at the back of Marianne's mind, though her work remained at the forefront and she would have no trouble meeting her deadline.

She had told herself she could live without Simon. But not without a garden and had expended money, and time on Sundays, on replacing the bushes injured beyond hope by the freak hurricane, splurging too on a flowering cherry and a quick-growing Russian vine for the patio wall.

She had paused at her typewriter before beginning a new chapter, noticing the first touch of pink, a sign of approaching summer, on the cherry tree, when Janis appeared outside the window.

'Why didn't you ring the doorbell?' Marianne said with a smile.

'I know your study is at the back and thought it'd be less bother for you to let me in through the patio door, like you have.'

'I could use some tea. You've come at the right time, Janis.'

'No time's the right time for you when you're working, Marianne, and we all know it. But I need to talk to you.'

Janis said as they went to the kitchen, 'This is something I can't discuss with Laura.'

Marianne put the kettle on to boil. How often had she done so in similar circumstances? When she'd lived up north, too, and this was the same kettle. What a tale it could tell.

'I'm pregnant, Marianne.'

Old-fashioned girls were the kind who still got pregnant by accident. 'Why can't you tell that to Laura? And leave dealing with your dad to her – '

'I'm thinking of having an abortion and she's dead against it.'

For highly personal reasons, thought Marianne.

'I couldn't tell her even if she weren't,' Janis went on. 'She wanted another child so much and it didn't happen. How can I say to her that I want to get rid of one?'

Janis burst into tears and Marianne gave her a paper tissue, and put a comforting hand on her shoulder.

'I *don't* want to get rid of my baby, Marianne – '

'Are you absolutely certain you're pregnant?'

'The result of my test was positive. I got it today.'

'Why can't you and Kurt bring forward the date of your wedding? You wouldn't be the first couple to marry while you're still students and you finish your courses this year – '

'Kurt knows nothing about this and you must promise me that you'll never tell him.'

Marianne's reaction was, 'I'd advise you, love, not to start out on your married life by trying to hide from him what you've told me.'

'I'm not going to marry Kurt. He doesn't know that yet, either.'

Marianne made the tea and brought it to the window alcove where Janis had seated herself.

'If ever there were a love match it's you and Kurt,' she declared. 'What on earth's gone wrong?'

Janis blew her nose and said after a pause, 'I couldn't live in Vienna, Marianne, that's what's gone wrong. When Jeremy and A.P. got back from their trip, they told me that being in Germany didn't have the effect upon them they'd expected it to. It probably wouldn't on me, either. But it's a different matter to live somewhere than just to visit, isn't it? Uncertain of the people around you.'

Had Janis but known it she was voicing Laura's private fears for her in that respect, when it became plain that Janis might one day marry Kurt.

'Uncertainty breeds apprehension, doesn't it?' Janis went on. 'As you know, Kurt and I were staying with his parents in the spring, when the fiftieth anniversary of the *Anschluss* was commemorated. There was Nazi graffiti everywhere, though the official commemoration was designed to display quite the opposite. And slogans we used to think long dead were shouted amid some of the scuffles resulting from police intervention.'

Janis drank some tea and paused again. 'Kurt has since heard from his parents that an exhibition chronicling the history of the Viennese Jewish community, mounted with the co-operation of the city authorities, was patrolled by armed guards and everyone had to deposit bags if they were carrying them, coats too, I think, with the attendant before entering.'

'Security has to be maintained all over the world, nowadays, Janis. I had to deposit my briefcase when I once spent an hour at the Museum of Modern Art in New York, between appointments.'

'But anti-Semitism wasn't involved in that. The attendant at the exhibition I mentioned apologized to Kurt's mother for her having to leave her bag with him. She was reluctant to do so, some notes concerning one of her patients were in it. He said that it was just for that particular exhibition the precautions were considered necessary.

'Kurt was as sickened as I was by it. But I knew long before then that I couldn't live in Vienna, when on a previous visit Kurt's parents weren't able to meet our plane and we took a taxi. The driver spoke English. I was my usual talkative self, making conversation about what a beautiful city Vienna is.

'The route to Kurt's home took us past the Hotel Imperial and the driver pointed to it and told me proudly that Adolf Hitler had slept there. He must have seen my reaction to that through his mirror, and hastily added a list of royalty and the like who had slept there too. I think it was that that finally did it, Marianne. An ordinary middle-aged man driving a taxi saying what he had to me in the adulatory tone impossible to mistake.'

'Okay, Janis. I now know how you feel and why. What I don't understand is why you afterwards got engaged to Kurt.'

'I was still fighting it, it's as simple as that,' Janis replied.

'What it took to finally decide me was getting pregnant. I hadn't looked as far ahead as bringing up the children I didn't yet have, in Austria. With a foetus now inside me, I have to think of that. It made me think of Howard, who had no choice, his child was already in Germany and of course he now has another. To inflict the tensions I couldn't live with myself on my kids is something I just can't do.'

'Kurt loves you, I'm sure he'd do anything rather than lose you,' Marianne said quietly, 'including making his life in England.'

'No need to tell me that. But supposing things don't go right for him here, Marianne? He has a place waiting for him in Vienna, after doing his post-grad course, that will assure him a consultancy eventually. Given the state of the National Health Service, shortage of money for research and all that, he could be old and grey by the time he makes it and there's no guarantee that he'll have done so, even then.'

'What you're saying is that his brains and his parents' contacts combine to ensure his future.'

'In a nutshell, yes. Why should someone of Kurt's ability go to waste because of me? He means too much to me for me to let him make that sacrifice.'

'But the choice should be his.'

'I've already made it for him.'

Marianne surveyed the girl's fragile beauty, seeming the more so when tragedy had overtaken her. Tragedy of her own making. How more selfless could love be than hers for Kurt?

'What shall you give as a reason for breaking your engagement, Janis?'

'One lie is as good as another, and only you will know it is one.' Janis got up and kissed Marianne. 'Thank you for listening. I had to tell someone.'

'In return I want you to promise me that the abortion necessary for this deception will be done competently.'

'I shall make use of some of the money left to me by my mother.'

Who would turn in her grave if she knew that, thought Marianne. Another secret in the family and one that will go with me to my own grave.

Chapter Fifteen

JANIS WASTED NO TIME in putting her plan into operation. Her little sister, much recovered but still easily distressed, had today gone home from school with her friend Val and was spending the night there. Jeremy was safely out of the way in Oxford. Only her parents and Kurt were seated with her at the dinner-table when she aimed her verbal dagger at her lover. But there is no way to do this kindly, she thought in the silence that followed.

Jake was the first to find his voice. 'Left it a bit late to change your mind, haven't you? Your wedding date is fixed for October. I've already reserved a suite at the Savoy for the reception, and Kurt's parents have spent time looking for a flat for you – '

'All that,' Laura cut in, 'is the least of it!'

Jake stared down at the lamb chop on his plate. 'You're right, dear. It is. What I'm doing is letting the practical inconveniences stop me from thinking of my daughter's suddenly – '

'It isn't sudden, Dad.'

'Is that a fact? Well, you could've fooled me!'

'Me also,' said Kurt, his complexion a deathly white. 'And I do not believe that Janis means what she has told us.'

'She had no right to do this the way she has!' said Laura angrily. 'You are entitled to have been told first, Kurt, and privately.'

Circumstances Janis had chosen to avoid, lest Kurt take her in his arms and her resolve fail her. 'This seemed a good opportunity to get it over,' she said.

'Get it over?' Kurt's expression was as if she had slapped his face. 'How can you be so cruel, Janis?'

'I'm beginning to think I didn't know my own daughter,' said Jake.

'That isn't surprising, Dad, since I've found out I didn't really know myself. But I'm still only twenty-one. That's too young to settle down for life. Well, it is for me. I know that now. After I get my degree I want to see a bit of the world.'

'I would gladly do that with you,' Kurt told her.

'You're missing the point,' Janis replied. 'Freedom to be my own person, to find out what I really want, is what it's all about.'

'Another Henry Moritz in the family!' Laura exclaimed.

'I like Henry and I'm sure he'd put me up at his place if I happened to be passing through where he's living at the time,' Janis rattled on. 'Howard and Karin would, too, if I decided to spend some time in Munich. And I wouldn't mind seeing for myself what's going on on the West Bank. I might do that first. I think I'll give Kate a ring –'

'That girl,' Jake said to Laura, eyeing Janis anxiously, 'has gone clean out of her mind –'

'On the contrary, Dad, I've just come to my senses. And by the way, I've decided to spend a week or two in Switzerland. I shall leave at the weekend and do some of the required reading for my finals there.'

'Who the hell do you know in Switzerland?' Jake thundered.

'Not a soul. That's what I'm looking forward to. If nobody minds, I shall now leave you all to recover in my absence.'

Janis got up and left the room. Those remaining stunned at the table could not have known that she was unable to maintain her cruel charade for a moment longer. Or what it had cost her to lie as she had with Kurt's hurt gaze riveted to her.

Jake poured himself some water and drank it. Suddenly his throat felt parched. This is just like the time we found out what was going on with Bessie, and that Jeremy knew and he hadn't told us, he wanted to say to Laura.

They exchanged a glance and he knew that she too was recalling that traumatic occasion. Did anyone know their own kids? What went on inside their heads? Nathan had somehow set Bessie on the road to recovery. Janis though – well where would she go from here? Hers wasn't a sickness, it was a newly-discovered thirst for life.

Meanwhile the casualty of that discovery looked as if he might break down if one more word were said to him. It would have to be a careful word.

Jake cleared his throat. 'All Laura and I can do, Kurt, is apologize to you for our daughter's behaviour. On the good side, and it will be some time before you're able to believe there is one, there's an old saying with a lot of commonsense to it: Better before than after.'

'We don't want you disappearing from our lives,' Laura added kindly. 'We were looking forward to your being our son-in-law, and girls have been known to change their minds. Whatever comes or goes, though, you and I are cousins. The day you appeared out of the blue was a happy one for me.'

'For me also, Laura. But if we are to see each other after I have graduated, you must come to Vienna. I shall never return to London. Janis will not change her mind. And if she were to say that she had, how could I ever again believe in her?'

Kurt rose and managed to smile politely. 'If you would now to excuse me, I have not the appetite for finishing my dinner and shall take myself for a walk on the Heath.'

Laura and Jake went with him to the front door. On the hall table was the aquamarine engagement ring he had given Janis.

Kurt paused for a moment gazing down at it. 'When I put that ring on Janis's finger, I told her that I had chosen it because it matched her eyes. But who is to know what truly lies *behind* the eyes of their beloved? Nor, as poets would have us believe, are the eyes the mirror of the soul. That I now *do* know.'

He departed with the ring in his pocket, leaving behind him a couple again confronted with the unseen hazards of parenthood.

'He'll get over it,' Jake said heavily.

'But will we?'

'All I can say to that, Laura, is one expressive word. Kids!'

Laura added an adjective. 'Bloody kids! Even when they grow up they're not out of your hair – '

Jake strode towards the stairs.

'Where do you think you're going?'

'To give Janis what she deserves. How dare she destroy Kurt and leave us to pick up the pieces like she did!'

Laura took his hand and led him back to the kitchen. 'Pour me a brandy, would you? And have one yourself. The bottle's on the counter; I used a drop in the sauce for the chops.'

Jake stemmed his anger and did as he was bid.

'I shall never make that special sauce again,' said Laura, removing the unfinished meal from the table. 'It will always remind me of this. Like I haven't been able to look at chocolate truffles since the terrible night we both remember. They were what Jeremy was noshing and Bessie in the bathroom throwing up when we got back from Berlin.'

'Jeremy is now the only one of the three who hasn't put us through the mill,' said Jake.

'But his day will no doubt come. Nor is there any guarantee that what Bessie's put us through in her childhood will be her one-off contribution to what we're discussing.

'I'm coming to think, Jake, that picking up the pieces is one of the things parents are for. Janis, though, has staked her claim to freedom, to put it mildly. She must be allowed to get on with it, learn from her own mistakes like I had to. You of course, darling, never made any!'

'I certainly didn't make one when I married *you*.'

They took their drinks into the living-room and sat together in shared and silent contemplation, unaware that their daughter lay on her bed consumed by sorrow, the familiar objects of her girlhood all around her and the future seeming a vacuum stretching endlessly ahead.

Chapter Sixteen

IN THE AFTERMATH of Janis's charade, Marianne thought her own thoughts and maintained a philosophical veneer that belied her apprehension as to what would now become of the girl who had wrought sudden and drastic change to her own life as well as to Kurt's.

The news of the broken engagement had reverberated on the family grapevine in person and by telephone, the manner of Janis's ending a romance that had seemed written in the stars as incredible to all as her having done so.

Weeks later the family was still trying to fathom what would always remain for them a mystery – how had the girl they knew changed out of recognition as if overnight? By then, both Janis and Kurt had written their final examinations, he afterwards departing immediately for Vienna, and she to Paris where Henry Moritz was still based and had, of course, offered her the makeshift accommodation to which all his young relatives and friends were welcome.

She had remained in Switzerland for ten days and on her return had come immediately to tell Marianne that the deed was done and she felt fine. Physically, perhaps. But for how long would she wear the air of bravado which only Marianne knew was a mask? Time was a faster healer for some than for others.

A breezily worded postcard from the girl who had confided in her arrived with Marianne's mail on one of the wet August mornings that characterized the summer of 1988 as it had last year.

Rain, rain, rain! And no further word from Simon Newman since he sent that one-sentence reminder of his existence.

Unfortunately for Marianne, she needed no reminding.

An hour later, while she was reading the proofs of a novel to be published later in the year – and cursing the printer for playing games with her prose – the doorbell rang and she included in the cursing whoever was interrupting the most tedious and exasperating task required of an author.

When she opened the door sarcasm leapt to her tongue. 'The ghost writer again appears in the flesh. Well, well!' A gust of anger impelled her to add, 'Where the hell have you been and what have you been doing?'

'Thinking of you from afar. The rest is a long story and I'd rather not tell it standing on your doorstep.'

'Then you had better come in and while you're here you can listen to a few things I have to say to *you*.'

'How is Matthew?' Simon inquired following her to the living-room.

'He's been in and out of hospital several times since the crisis that brought about *our* crisis. Right now he's home again. Thank you for asking,' Marianne replied tersely.

They sat down opposite each other, Marianne on the sofa and Simon in the armchair that once was Ralph's. Marianne felt like telling him to get up and sit somewhere else. He had almost succeeded in inserting himself into the place Ralph had occupied in her life – but not quite! And assumed that all he need now do was make excuses for his lengthy absence and she would accept them like the gullible female he evidently thought her.

'Kindly get on with it,' she said to him. 'I have to finish proof-reading my new novel.'

'With a bit of luck, this time next year I might be reading the proofs of my first,' Simon replied. 'You asked what I've been doing since we last saw each other and now you know.'

Marianne was astounded.

Simon smiled at her expression. 'If you thought me holed up with a broad, I have to tell you it was with a typewriter, working on a first draft I've since sent to my agent that he thinks is promising.'

She could not but congratulate him. Nor was it false, she really was pleased for him.

'But I've told you the end of the long story before the beginning and the middle,' he went on.

'I'm still listening.'

'Something happened to me in New York, Marianne, and it set me thinking along with feeling sorry for myself. I began seeing everything differently from how I had before. Looking beneath the surface is one way of putting it, and that includes my own surface, the veneer I'd worn for years though I didn't know it.'

Part of which was the mocking smile Marianne had quickly realized was self-deprecation, and not the one on his face now.

She said frostily, 'So you decided to take yourself off and have another go at writing a novel? Leave our affair hanging in limbo except for the brief communication I received from you.'

She added when Simon got up to gaze through the window, 'I hope you're noticing the roses in the garden opposite. It was winter when you left for New York – '

'And mild for the time of year, I recall.'

'I was referring to how long you've been away and taken for granted I'd still want you when you returned.'

'Do you?'

'Unfortunately, yes. But I'm old and wise enough to know that what I want isn't always what's best for me. There's going to have to be a good reason for your behaving towards me the way you have.'

Simon turned from the window to look at her. 'I took nothing for granted. On the contrary. I stayed away until I'd proved something to myself, or I wouldn't be worthy of you. You'd told me on the phone I wasn't the man for you – '

'What I said wasn't attached to how you earn your bread.'

'But it seems to've served as shock treatment in more ways than one. I'd given up on myself, hadn't I? Done what some would call prostituting my art, though I knew it was in me to be what I'd set out to be. Taken the easy way out.

'Once I began work, though, it was as if I was driven,' Simon went on reflectively. 'There was no way I'd have given up and come back to you empty-handed, so to speak. My not calling, or writing you, was part of the state of suspended animation I was in – '

A state familiar to Marianne. A harsh word from someone you cared about and bang went the creative high you were on.

'If you'd hung up on me – ' said Simon.

'I understand. But you could have explained by letter.'

'I didn't want to let you in on it until it was all done,' he replied, 'it's as simple as that. Your being the incentive for the whole thing makes that kind of weird, I guess, but it was how I felt. If the book doesn't get published and you still don't marry me, I'll have the satisfaction of knowing I tried. Will you, or won't you, Marianne?'

'I'd be a fool if I didn't. Come and sit beside me – '

Tears were stinging Marianne's eyes. Simon not worthy of me? Few men would have bared their soul to a woman as he had, nor found the grit at his age to try again. Minutes slipped by while they held each other close, passion firing the kiss that followed but the thankfulness for each other in that first embrace still there.

'My sister's loft was where I spent the whole time,' Simon afterwards resumed his story. 'Norma, like you, is a sucker for her family – but let's not get into that again! The loft was her daughters' playroom when they were young kids and later Norma had it adapted as their private apartment.

'Each of them had her own telephone up there,' he added dryly, 'one between them wasn't enough! Also there's a house line to the kitchen. If the girls felt hungry, they'd ring down and Norma would load up the dumb waiter that was part of their American dream set up.'

'Was their father still alive then?'

'If he had been his daughters might not have grown up

340

thinking the world owes them a living, an idea they got from how their mother has always been with them.'

Simon paused reflectively. 'Norma's husband was a bit like Jake Bornstein. The sort who doesn't see his children go short, but makes sure their feet are kept on the ground.'

'That's an accurate assessment of Jake, but you hardly know him, how did you sum him up so well?'

'Evidently my vision had begun to undergo a change before I went to New York. How could it not with you at my side, though you weren't when I realized it?'

Simon straightened Marianne's hair, awry from their lengthy embrace. 'Remember me telling you you'd changed my life? What I'm now saying has to be included in that. My perceptions have heightened, it seems, along with the rest of your effect upon me! Where was I?'

'Discussing your sister and what you evidently consider her folly.'

'Which in a nutshell is that Norma inherited her husband's business, put in a high-powered manager, and is still spending the dollars that continue to roll in on her daughters, not to mention on their kids. Our parents sure didn't spoil Norma and me, nor would they have if they'd been well off,' Simon added.

'That could account for your sister's spoiling her own children.'

'But back with my story, I went to Wellesley for Christmas, got the idea for my novel, mentioned it to Norma and she offered me the loft to work in. I sometimes worked evenings as well as days, but she never made me feel I was just making use of her.'

'I'm looking forward to having her for a sister-in-law,' said Marianne.

'But first we have to get married. How about a quick elopement? I only flew in to Heathrow this morning, my bag is still packed.'

'I couldn't do that to the family.'

Simon laughed. 'No, hon, of course you couldn't.'

Chapter Seventeen

❈

THE THIRD LOVE AFFAIR of Marianne's life was with the island of Bermuda, where she and Simon spent a delayed honeymoon.

Sweet-scented blossom dripping from trees forming natural canopies overhead, frangipani mingling with honeysuckle in tall hedges lining the narrow lanes, the plethora of flowers of delicate hue and of a shimmering brilliance upon which to feast the eye, combined with the overall air of repose to enthrall her.

'Bermuda truly is paradise,' she said to Simon when they had returned from a morning stroll to the balcony of their suite, which afforded a view beyond the hotel's terraced garden of an ocean too blue to believe it was the Atlantic lapping the creamy pink shore.

'So you keep saying, hon,' he replied with a smile.

'And if I lived in New York, I'd take time off to spend some long weekends here.'

'Given it's such a short flight, a lot of folk who live on the East Coast do that. Only a cancellation could have got us this suite at such short notice at this time of year.'

'Short notice is right,' said Marianne, 'and I remain uneasy about nobody knowing where we are. Not even your agent and I told the family if they needed to get in touch with me they could do so via him – '

'We made a bargain, didn't we, hon? –' Simon reminded her '– when we decided to come here instead of returning to London immediately my business in New York was done. That we'd have one week entirely to ourselves, let nothing impinge upon it. I don't see your family grudging you that.'

They had married in September and on their wedding eve Simon's agent had called with good news. A publisher was interested in his novel, but had suggested changes for Simon to consider and make if he agreed.

This had seemed more important to both than the holiday in Antibes that was to have been their honeymoon. Simon had already moved into Marianne's flat, a more spacious home for a couple than his Highgate pad, and it was there that he settled down to work, Marianne finding that her reservations about sharing her life with another writer could be set aside.

Simon's adherence to a strict routine was similar to her own. If things were not going well, he stayed at the typewriter trying to work it out, not so of all authors. Some found it best to take a break. For others it proved unproductive to work for more than a few hours each day.

It bodes well for our marriage, she had thought, that in this respect too we tick the same way. That we're not going to irritate each other with inconvenient requests to be kept company.

Included in the sharing was Marianne's mentally biting her nails along with Simon after the revisions were mailed to his agent, and the champagne toast to his novel when in December a deal was done and Simon summoned to New York to meet the man who would be his editor.

Marianne had accompanied him and they had afterwards agreed that it seemed fated for them to fly from there to Bermuda a year late, but husband and wife.

Tonight they would board the British Airways direct flight to London, and spent their last afternoon in Marianne's paradise shopping for gifts in the quaint harbour town of Hamilton, where the store frontages had, apart from a few, retained the appearance of a bygone era, gloss conspicuous by its absence, and on the main street the waterfront was unimpeded by buildings, enhancing the pleasant atmosphere as did the friendly faces of Bermudians going about their daily business.

Marianne watched some uniformed schoolgirls, panama hats atop their heads, turn the corner of a steep incline leading to the bus station, and remarked, 'How very English Hamilton seems. I could live here and feel welcome.'

She gave her attention to some paperweights in a shop window. 'I wouldn't mind one of those for my desk.'

'Let me buy it for you, hon.'

'A useful souvenir of Bermuda,' she said with a smile.

Marianne chose an ovoid of solid glass in which was embedded spiky leaves of red and green. They turned it upside down to examine the base and burst out laughing. The useful souvenir of Bermuda bore a label: 'Made in Scotland'.

'Please excuse us,' Simon apologized to the confused lady behind the counter, 'my wife and I share a strange sense of humour.'

They left the shop with the paperweight which would ever after be for them a memento of a week of love and laughter.

The opposite of laughter greeted them on their return to London. A note informing them that Matthew was dead and buried had been slipped through their letter-box.

Marianne immediately called Laura and received from her a dressing down. 'Only you could have dealt with Arnold at the funeral. He tried to keep Pete away from the graveside and ended up scuffling with him. Needless to say, Lyn was in a state of collapse without that. How could you just have gone off, Marianne, without letting anyone know where you were!'

'Isn't that what you did when you eloped with Jake?' Marianne retorted.

'I've never been the one in the family whom everyone relies on – '

'And from now on, that person isn't going to be me!' Marianne slammed down the receiver and found that she was trembling.

Further telephone calls to her relatives almost reduced her to tears. Though not all rebuked her as Laura had, she was in every case the recipient of reproach. When finally she steeled herself to call Arnold and Lyn, it was he who answered the telephone.

'Thanks for the expression of sympathy,' he said to her. 'But when it came to it, you weren't there when I needed you. If we'd known where you were . . . but you made sure we didn't.'

Martin arrived to find his mother drinking brandy and her husband looking on silently.

'Laura let me know you're back.'

'There was no reply when I called you.'

'I popped out to buy my Sunday morning bagels.'

'And have you come here to say I've let the family down, Martin? Which is how I've been made to feel.'

Martin eyed the bottle at Marianne's elbow. 'Something had to account for your early morning tipple and now I know what. So you weren't here for poor Matthew's funeral, a lot of good it would have done him if you had been.'

'But others were deprived of my moral support, for want of a better way of putting it! The one time I'm not where I'm needed everyone, in their own way, lets me have it. Even Alan seemed shocked that I'd gone away without leaving a phone number. What right has the family to take me for granted, Martin?'

'If you want the truth, Mum, I have to say it's your fault. When did my mother not bend over backward to be where she feels she is needed? I've sometimes thought you'd elected yourself to fill your grandmother's shoes.'

'If that's how it appears, allow me to inform you that I was dragooned into it. First by Uncle Nat, and then by – '

'The person you are,' Martin cut in. 'Learned your lesson now?'

'Too true I have and I'm thinking of doing what you once suggested Simon and I should do – pack our typewriters and go to live on a desert island.'

'No need to ask me twice, hon, only Bermuda isn't a *desert* island.'

Chapter Eighteen

❧

MARIANNE'S DECISION to make her home in Bermuda was as if she had finally put her first marriage behind her. The flat in which she had, on her return there, expected to live out her years alone, redolent of her life with Ralph, was sold along with the furniture they had chosen together. Closing the door upon it for the last time had seemed to her a symbolic gesture.

When she boarded the plane which would transport her to her paradise island, it was without regrets. Gone were the shackles she had one way and another worn since her twenties, the more so since her grandmother's death. Though it had always been within her power to detach herself, it had not seriously entered her head to do so until events impelled her to take the step she had.

Impossible to detach, though, was her emotional tie with the family. Her departure from their midst had stunned her relatives and it was not without an occasional pang of guilt that she settled down to her blissful new life. From time to time she would wonder how those who had for so long relied upon her were coping in her absence, and find it necessary to brush that thought aside.

Initially, she and Simon lived in a rented apartment. By the spring of 1989 they were installed in a rambling villa overlooking Elbow Beach, its verandah festooned with greenery and spacious enough for them to work at either end of a long table, their preference though the accommodation allowed a study for each of them.

'Want me to get it, hon?' Simon asked one morning when the telephone shrilled persistently inside the house.

Marianne rose and stepped over the extended lead from her electric typewriter. 'I will, your deadline is sooner than mine. We must get some sockets fixed out here for our typewriter plugs, Simon, before we trip headlong on the way into the house.'

'How about having a phone out here?'

'Not likely!' Marianne replied. 'One of us would snatch up the receiver the minute it rang, like I used to in England when someone interrupted my work. This way, I manage to shut it out and people don't usually hang on too long.'

Marianne hastened to the hall to end the shrilling and was due for a surprise.

'How nice to hear your voice, Laura,' she said warmly, though assailed by apprehension. The days when she had received panic calls from the family were over and her contact with them maintained by letter. 'Is something wrong?'

'Well, it's ages since we heard from Janis, but I didn't ring up to tell you that. I'd like the recipe for your Passover jam.'

The airy, flag-stoned hall was not yet furnished, work had come first for both Simon and Marianne. She carried the telephone from a window ledge to the foot of the stairs and sat down, her expression amused.

'Only a millionaire's wife would call Bermuda from England to get a recipe!' she said to Laura after supplying it.

'Probably. But why should the family be deprived of the jam you used to make for them, just because you're not here any more? We shall miss you at the Seder, Marianne.'

'And I shall miss all of you.'

'Remember the time Jake and Martin were on guard duty at the synagogue on Seder night?'

Marianne saw herself and Laura standing by the hearth. Laura a radiant and seemingly contented woman. And I doubting that she could sustain the role she was playing. A pudgy Bessie clad in blue velvet was hovering beside the table, the dish of bitter herbs in her hands. There, too, the happy teenager Janis was.

347

Oh the traumas the family has since lived through, privately and together, Marianne reflected. 'How long ago that seems,' she said.

'But Jake is down for the same duty this Passover,' said Laura. 'Nothing has changed in that respect.'

'It's nice to be where I don't see the anti-Semitic graffiti I sometimes saw in England,' Marianne remarked.

'Removed yourself from a lot of things, haven't you?' Laura said lightly.

Marianne was nevertheless aware of an implied reproof. 'Physically, yes. Mentally and emotionally, no,' she replied. 'There's no escaping from oneself, Laura, as events in your own life must have proved to you.'

'That makes it no easier for me to understand your doing what you've done, Marianne. There's never an ill wind, though!' Laura went on with a laugh. 'Now you're out of the picture, my mum has come into her own. Lyn says she doesn't know how she'd get by without her. She's taken to keeping an eye on Uncle Nat, which he won't let Leona do. And the Manchester Seder will be at her place this year.'

'It was never at my place, too much work,' said Marianne recovering from her astonishment.

'Could be my mum is trying to outdo you!'

Or that Shirley was the sort who blossomed when made to feel needed. Whatever, Marianne was pleased that her cousin was at last tasting the rewards of putting others before herself.

'Mum has also persuaded Arnold to take Lyn on a world cruise,' said Laura, 'to help them put time and distance between themselves and their tragedy. She says she wishes she and my dad had done something like that after my brother died.'

'Let's hope that going off on their own will do something for their marriage,' said Marianne.

'Mum has that in mind too,' Laura answered. 'She's told Arnold that Lyn isn't to know it wasn't his idea.'

A behind-the-scenes string-puller in Sarah Sandberg's class, thought Marianne, which I never was, though in character for Shirley. Possibly Sarah's matriarchal qualities were dispersed between her three granddaughters, though Leona had yet to prove that she had inherited any of them other than Sarah's shrewd mind.

'Tell your mother I wish her well, Laura. And good luck with the jam-making.'

'Want me to send you a pot?'

'Why not? I'm still one of the family.'

Marianne returned to the verandah, but not to her typewriter. Instead she stood feasting her eyes on the view, the lush vegetation, palm trees gently swaying and beyond, the ocean seeming as smooth as azure glass.

'Why the rueful expression?' Simon inquired after hearing the gist of her conversation with Laura.

'I had to come and live in Bermuda to find out I'm not indispensable!'

'And as my agent would say, every author should have such a punishment. It isn't like you not to see the funny side, hon.'

'I do.'

'But you expected the clan to fall apart without you. When it comes to the crunch, family-wise and otherwise, our people have a history of doing the opposite. It's what we're renowned for and why we've survived to tell the tale.'

Simon came to stand beside her. 'You've done your bit, Marianne. Time to rest on your laurels.'

Though Marianne would not have put it that way, the parallel Simon had drawn was as balm to her soul. Since the Sandbergs and Moritzes put down roots in England, eight decades ago, their seed had scattered. But the unity bred in us in the home, generation after generation, is still going strong and so it was for Jewry itself. The two were inextricable and there could be no stronger weapon against the renewed attempts, overt or insidious, to complete the task Hitler had begun.

Marianne switched her mind to matters more mundane. 'I made us some tuna sandwiches for lunch.'

'Why don't you go get 'em, while I cover our typewriters? Those little yellow birds that waken us in the mornings are liable to gunge up the works again when we're taking our lunchtime stroll!'

Such was the peaceful pattern of their days – the shared interest their work was to them, the loving companionship of their marriage. Minutes later they were walking, hands entwined, beside the surf.

What more, thought Marianne, could a woman in her autumn years ask? For herself, nothing.

'When the guest room's fixed up, I'd like to invite Howard and Karin to stay,' she said, halting to pick up a cowrie shell. 'They could use a break, and without the socializing that goes on in hotels. My sister-in-law who lives on the West Bank too.'

'You'll never change, Marianne.'

'If I did, I wouldn't be the person you married. Any regrets?'

They sat down on the sand to eat their lunch and Simon eyed the filling oozing from the bread roll Marianne handed him. 'Only when she forgets to go easy with the mayonnaise on my sandwich, like she did today.'

Fontana Paperbacks: Fiction

Fontana is a leading paperback publisher of fiction.
Below are some recent titles.

- ☐ SHINING THROUGH Susan Isaacs £3.99
- ☐ KINDRED PASSIONS Rosamund Smith £2.99
- ☐ BETWEEN FRIENDS Audrey Howard £3.99
- ☐ THE CHARMED CIRCLE Catherine Gaskin £4.50
- ☐ THE INDIA FAN Victoria Holt £3.99
- ☐ THE LAWLESS John Jakes £2.99
- ☐ THE AMERICANS John Jakes £2.99
- ☐ A KIND OF WAR Pamela Haines £3.50
- ☐ THE HERON'S CATCH Susan Curran £4.50

You can buy Fontana paperbacks at your local bookshop or
newsagent. Or you can order them from Fontana Paperbacks,
Cash Sales Department, Box 29, Douglas, Isle of Man. Please
send a cheque, postal or money order (not currency) worth the
purchase price plus 22p per book for postage (maximum postage
required is £3.00 for orders within the UK).

NAME (Block letters)_____

ADDRESS_____

_____